THE
SAXON
MIGHT

The Song of Ash
Book Three

JAMES CALBRAITH

FLYING
SQUID

Published May 2020 by Flying Squid

Visit James Calbraith's official website at
jamescalbraith.wordpress.com
for the latest news, book details, and other information

BRITANNIA SUPERIOR, c. 450 AD

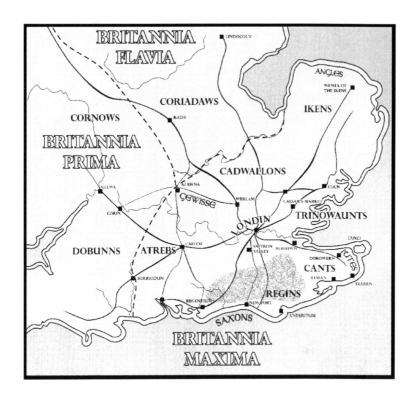

BRITANNIA MAXIMA, c. 430 AD

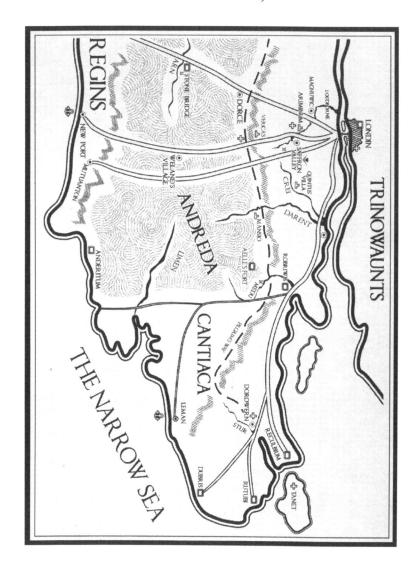

LONDINIUM, c. 450 AD

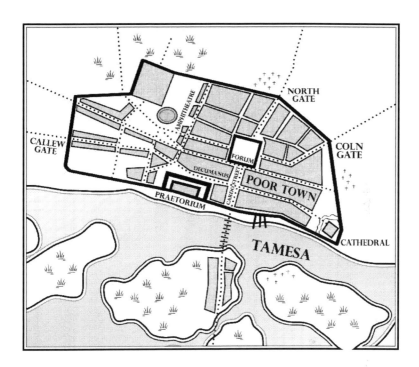

ISLE OF WECTA AND SOLU, c. 450 AD

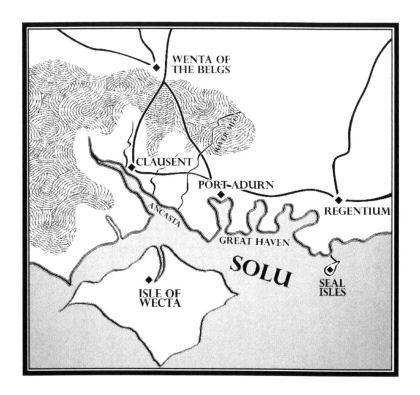

CAST OF CHARACTERS

Londin

Ambrosius: *Dux* of Britannia Prima Maxima
Brutus: Commander of Londin Garrison
Deneus: Oyster merchant
Fastidius: Vicar General of Londin, Ash's Brother
Wortigern: Former *Dux* of Britannia Maxima
Wortimer: Wortigern's son, current *Dux* of Britannia

Iutes of Londin:

Beormund: chief of the Iutes of Poor Town
Birch/Betula: a warrior of Poor Town
Eadgith: bladesmith from Poor Town
Raven: a warrior of Poor Town
Rhedwyn: Iutish princess, niece of Hengist

Britannia Maxima

Elasio: *Comes* of the Cadwallons
Catuar: *Comes* of the Regins
Masuna: *Comes* of the Atrebs
Odo: *Decurion* of the Gaulish cavalry in Cantiaca
Peredur: *Comes* of Trinowaunts
Worangon: *Comes* of Cantiaca

Saxons:

Pefen: chief of the Saxons, unifier of tribes
Aelle: Pefen's son, chief of the Saxon warbands in Andreda
Hilla: a warrior from Andreda
Bucge: chief of a Saxon tribe
Weorth: chief of a Saxon tribe, commander of Port Adurn

Iutes:

Hengist: chief of the Iutes of Tanet
Haesta: Hengist's cousin
Haegel: elder of the Meon Village
Croha: child of farmers from Meon Village

Britons:

Alatuc: chief of Briton village on Wecta
Muconius: Chief Councillor in Clausent
Solinus: rich merchant from New Port

GLOSSARY

Aesc: Saxon spear

Ceol: Narrow, ocean-going Saxon ship

Centuria: Troop of (about) hundred infantry

Centurion: Officer in Roman infantry

Comes, pl. Comites: Administrator of a *pagus,* subordinate to the *Dux*

Decurion: Officer in Roman cavalry

Domus: The main structure of a *villa*

Drihten: War chief of a Saxon tribe

Dux: Overall commander in war times, in peace time — administrator of a province

Fulcum: Roman shield wall formation

Hiréd: Band of elite warriors of *Drihten's* household

Gesith: Companion of the *Drihten,* chief of the *Hiréd*

Liburna: Roman war ship

Mansio: Staging post

Pagus: Administrative unit, smaller than a province

Praetor: high administrative or military official

Pugio: small Roman dagger

Seax: Saxon short sword

Solid: large gold coin

Spatha: Roman long sword

Villa: Roman agricultural property

Wealh, pl. wealas: "the others", Britons in Saxon tongue

Witan: the gathering of elders

PLACE NAMES

Andreda: Weald Forest
Anderitum: Pevensey, East Sussex
Ariminum: Wallington, Surrey
Callew: Silchester, Hampshire
Cantiaca: Kent
Caesar's Market: Caesaromagus, Chelmsford, Essex
Clausent: Bitterne, Southampton
Coln: Colchester, Essex
Dorowern: Dorovernum, Canterbury, Kent
Dubris: Dover, Kent
Beaddingatun: Beddington, Surrey
Britannia Maxima: a province of Britannia, capital in Londin
Britannia Prima: a province of Britannia, capital in Corin
Ebrauc: York
Eobbasfleot: Ebbsfleet, Kent
Leman: Lympne, Kent
Londin: Londinium, London
Medu: River Medway
New Port: Novus Portus, Portslade, Sussex
Port Adurn: Portchester
Regentium: Chichester, Sussex
Robriwis: Dorobrivis, Rochester, Kent
Rutubi: Rutupiae, Richborough, Kent
Saffron Valley: Croydon, London
Solu: Solent
Tamesa: River Thames
Tanet: Isle of Thanet, Kent
Wecta: Isle of Wight
Wenta of the Belgs: Winchester
Werlam: St Albans, Hertfordshire

PART 1: 450-452 AD

CHAPTER I
THE LAY OF BEORMUND

The world is a black void.

The only light I ever get to see is that of the torch carried by the slave who brings me the bowl of gruel and a bucket of slop water. I estimate it happens twice a day, but I have no way of knowing for sure. The torch gives just enough light to allow me to make out the shadows of the place of my captivity: the contours of the red brick arches, the simple, utilitarian stone columns at the back, the pipe orifice half-buried in sediment, the cold damp rising up the steam-worn walls. I know enough of these kinds of places to guess where I am — in the vaults of an old, disused bath house. The room where I'm kept must be the *frigidarium*, but with the bricks of the cold pool removed and most of the stonework dismantled and turned into dividing walls. I think I've been here before… Not as a captive, but as captor.

I don't know how long I've been kept here. My first days in the cell are hidden behind an impenetrable bank of fog. I was thrown onto the cracked *caementicium* floor, my legs chained to the wall. My hands free, I would lash out at the slaves and they'd beat me back with reed canes or wooden sticks, depending on their mood.

Sometimes, a young man would appear, roughly my age, with black, curly hair and cunning eyes, in rich robes of a nobleman. He'd watch as the slaves beat and tortured me, and he'd laugh. Then he'd grab my hair and raise my head up and tell me I'd be dead if it wasn't for…

If it wasn't for…

I can't remember.

Then he'd spit in my face and kick me in the gut, and leave, laughing again.

At length, even the young man stopped coming. I succumbed to the wounds, the cold, the hunger, and came down with a rabid fever. I'd cross death's door and then return, to find myself drenched in a pool of my own vomit, faeces and blood. Worms grew in my wounds and pain spawned madness in my head. I wailed and thrashed on the floor like a dying beast, scorched by the flames of fever, frozen by the chills. And when, by some miracle, I pulled through, I could remember nothing, not even who I was, or why I was put in this wet, dark place. If I was a prisoner, then of what court? Was there a trial, a verdict? Who put me here, and on what grounds — was it the young nobleman? How long was I to be imprisoned? Why was I still kept alive? The slaves who brought me food would not answer any of my questions. They weren't mutes — I heard them curse when they stubbed their toe on a brick. My captor must have ordered them to stay silent in my presence. What secrets were they keeping from me?

It took me days before I started recalling the first hazy details. It was like being born again and having to learn everything from the start, except this time I was locked up in the darkness, all alone, for eternity.

I am Aeric, son of Eobba, war chief of the Iutes. My countrymen and I have crossed the whale-road and landed on a mud patch in the land of the Britons, refugees from a distant war. I have a sister, Rhedwyn. I sinned with her, and for that crime I am imprisoned in this dungeon for life…

No, that didn't sound quite right.

I am Ash, a slaveling, found on a beach in Cantiaca. A foster child of an Old Man and an Old Woman, who were attendants of the baths at Ariminum *villa*, south of Londin. I have watched my foster father die in the bowels of a bath, and refused to help him because I wanted to be free. For that crime, I am imprisoned in this dungeon…

But this, too, is not the full story.

I am Fraxinus, son of Pascent, brother of Fastidius. I was a Councillor at the court of *Dux* Wortigern in Londin, ruler of all Britannia. I have joined his rebellion against Rome and the Church, I have blasphemed against God, and for that crime, I am imprisoned…

All of it sounded true, and yet none of it *felt* accurate. Have I really committed all those transgressions? If so, then undoubtedly I deserve to rot in this hellhole. Some of my memories seem more akin to dreams than reality. The women in my life all blur into one, sometimes red-haired, sometimes fair-haired, green-eyed, blue-eyed; I take their bodies on the cliffs, in the forests, under the stars, in cold, ruined bath houses like the one I'm in now… I remember fighting, a lot of it, swords slashing, spears thrusting and axes flying, duels, roaring charges and stalwart defences, great battles on the beaches and small skirmishes on the river crossings. My memories are soaked in the blood of warmongering and the sweat of passion.

And there's still more. Books in ancient language, chronicles and poems, history and geography of distant lands; prayers and rituals, lofty churches and underground temples; gods of the Iutes, gods of the Britons, gods of the Romans; beasts slaughtered in sacrifice, cold waters of a baptismal font, all jumbled together until I can no longer tell which is which.

I glance at my body in the light of the slave's torch, my thin hands and famished stomach. Though ravaged by illness and starvation, it's a body of someone still young. Could all of this have happened to me in such a short lifetime? It almost feels like the memories of several people are struggling inside my head. The Iute prince, the Briton slaveling, the Roman courtier... I can't possibly be all three of these at once. Which one am I, really? I sense the answer to this mystery lies in figuring out who is keeping me prisoner, and why.

I am no longer alone.

Two other prisoners have been brought to the bath house, and thrown into the remaining cells of the *frigidarium* chamber. I can hear their agonising wailing through the thin brick walls. Soon, one of them falls silent. I hear the slaves grunt as they carry out the body. The other captive falls quiet, too, and I fear him dead also, but after the slaves bring me porridge and slop, he speaks.

"Is anyone there?"

The voice speaks in the Imperial Tongue and sounds somehow familiar, even distorted through pain.

"I'm here," I reply in the same manner. "Who are you?"

"Thank God! I'm Deneus of Caesar's Market. I own salt flats and oyster beds off the eastern coast — or at least I used to... What about yourself?"

Caesar's Market... I remember this place. Something happened there. And that name, Deneus. I know that name.

"Hey, are you still there?"

"Yes," I reply hastily. I remember now. Dene of Caesar's Market, the salt tycoon, who helped me and my brother... *Fastidius...* with... something.

"I'm..." I hesitate to remember which name he would have known me by. "Fraxinus of Ariminum. I don't know how long I have been here. Or why." One memory triggers another. "I was with *Dux* Wortigern at Sorbiodun, and then..."

"Fraxinus! The Roman Iute? They told us you were dead!"

Roman Iute. Is this who I am? These words hurt like a thousand wasp stings.

"You know me?"

"*Do* I? Do you not remember me?"

"I don't remember many things..."

"Do you at least remember how you got here? This whole mess started when you and the *Dux* disappeared after that fight with Wortimer."

Wortimer. The name rings a bell.

"What *mess?*"

Dene's reply is cut short by one of the guards barging into his cell and beating him into silence. "No talking!" the guard shouts before going back to his post.

We're only able to talk further in the brief intervals when the guards change or get bored with looking after us and disappear somewhere upstairs to play with dice and whores. It's amazing how patient you become after months of solitude. I await Dene's every word as if it was a lover's whisper. It takes days before I can compose the entire picture of the situation in Londin from his snippets of information.

It's been over half a year since Wortimer returned from the Council of Sorbiodun, alone, but armed with a powerful story that he proceeded to sell to the people of Londin. It was a story of perfidy and betrayal — but not his own. The heralds who recited the tale on the corners of the city called it *the Massacre of the Long Knives.*

"They said the Iutes attacked the Council and slew Wortigern, you, and most of the courtiers. Only with Ambrosius's help did Wortimer and a handful of his men survive to tell the tale."

[18]

"That's preposterous. And nobody asked why would the Iutes even do that? They are our allies."

"*Were*, boy. Wortimer made up some story about his father wanting to marry the Iutish Princess against her will, which angered the Iutes. The people of Londin didn't need much persuading to turn against the pagans — they never liked them in the first place, as you may remember."

The Iutish Princess... *Rhedwyn!* I remember her — I remember her vividly... Something happened between us — but the memory is confused.

"This girl Wortigern wanted to marry... What happened to her?"

"I have no idea. I don't know much about what's going on in the city — I was minding my own business in Caesar's Market until they came for me."

"You never told me *why* they came for you."

This is days — weeks, maybe — into our intermittent conversation. Dene has grown weaker over time, his voice quieter. Coughing fits interrupt our brief exchanges more and more often. It feels like speaking to me is the only thing that's keeping him sane — or even alive.

"Wortimer needs money. He's been spending his father's treasury left and right, funding his mercenary army, building churches and monuments to himself, and buying the support of the plebs. He needs me to sign my properties over to him."

"Can't he just take it by force?"

"He still needs the Council's backing, and for this, he needs to keep up the pretence of acting lawfully... He's made up fake charges against everyone even remotely supportive of his father. Most of my friends are either dead or exiled, their businesses confiscated."

"Exile sounds better than this. I would choose it without hesitation."

"I wouldn't give him the satisfaction. This can't last long. Sooner or later, the people will see Wortimer is just a puppet of Ambrosius and Aetius, preparing Britannia for Rome's return."

But it does last. A month passes, by my estimate, then another. Sometimes, another prisoner joins us in the third cell — another wealthy Roman, or a captive Iute, but never for long. At least Dene knows the purpose of his suffering, knows he can end it, one way or another; neither of us can guess for what reason Wortimer is keeping me alive.

"Maybe he's forgotten about me. I almost died here once, nobody came to help me."

"Wortimer does not forget grudges. It's more likely that Ambrosius told him not to kill you. They must have some plans for you. Something to do with the surviving Iutes, I wager."

But Dene never finds out what Wortimer's plans are. One day, the guards take him away. When he returns, he's too weak to speak in anything but a weak whisper.

"He's grown smarter," he musters a warning. "And stronger. Whatever he wants from you, you'll be wise to heed him."

"What about you? Have you chosen the exile?"

"It's too late for me. I'm afraid I... no longer have a choice."

These are his last words. At next mealtime, I hear the slaves grunt as they drag out his body from the cell.

I have a new conversation partner now. Not a prisoner — a slave. By some miscalculation, one of the guards who brings me the daily slop turns out to be one of my own people.

"A Iute!" he exclaims in delight after I speak to him in his own tongue. "Where did they get you?"

"At Callew, a long time ago. You?"

"*Callew?* I don't know that village."

"It's... in the West."

"Was it near Beaddingatun? I think they were the first to fall. I was captured at the Siege of Robriwis. I'm Beormund. I'm... I *was* the *Gesith* there."

I now have enough of my memory restored to remember Robriwis well. Rhedwyn and I met there briefly before the Battle of Crei. Her naked body, sweaty from the bath, blazes before me in a spasm of ecstasy. I scratch at my face to let the pain clear my mind.

Robriwis, the great, impregnable fortress guarding the crossing of the River Medu… If it's under siege, that means the Iutes have been forced out of the lands given them by Wortigern outside the land of Cants. Beaddingatun, Orpeddingatun, Waerlahame… Once the main force of the *Hiréd*, the Iute chieftain's household guard, perished in the massacre at Callew, these villages were an easy prey. How many people lived there when Wortimer's forces descended upon the defenceless farmsteads? How many women and children were slain…?

"We beat them once before," I say. "We'll beat them again."

"You were at Crei? A glorious battle… Donar was with us that day. But this is different. There's a new army in Londin, new warriors, coming from Wodan knows where. Good fighters, not brute roughs like the last time."

"What do they look like?"

"They wear scale or mail, metal helmets, many carry swords and long shields, some even ride horses."

"Do they bear any marks?"

"Eagle on the helmets and a diagonal cross on the red shields."

These must be Ambrosius's Legionnaires in Wortimer's service. Or maybe even true Roman soldiers, trickling from across the sea. Not the full might of Aetius's army — that must be occupied elsewhere — but even a few hundred regulars would make a difference in the war against Iutes.

I try to piece together the complete story of Wortimer's conquest of the Iutish villages from Beormund's tales, and from what memories I manage to regain of the land around Londin. I trace the movement of armies in the brick dust on the floor, in the darkness, mapping it in my mind. It's a good exercise; I feel both my sanity and my mental abilities growing back, as if a wound somewhere in my head was slowly sealing. I fear the recovery is too slow, that Beormund will disappear like so many slaves before him before I gain the full view of the situation outside.

There is a gap in the map I'm building. It's not obvious at first — after all, I can only see the map with my mind's eyes. When I spot it at last, it strikes me like a flash.

"What of the Saxons and the Regins?"

This baffles him for a moment. "You mean those bastards from Andreda? They never came to our help. The wood, and all the roads but the main highway south, are sealed off. Not even the Eagle helmets dare to venture there."

Then Aelle and his father are safe, at least. And their predictions came true. All the preparations, all the traps, the ramparts, the restored hillforts were now proving their worth. I realised this made me feel relieved. Aelle was a murderer and a thief, a cause of untold woe to me and my family... But as long as he was roaming free in Andreda, there was still hope for the Saxons and the Iutes in Britannia...

"I don't suppose you have any news from the Angles in the North," I ask. "Or the *Gewisse*."

"These are *witan* matters. I was just a warrior." He puts his torch to my face and studies me. "You ask strange questions. You look younger than me, yet you speak like an elder at a *witan*. Who are you, really?"

"I…" I don't know how much I can trust him. Is he really who he says he is? Though I faintly remember fighting alongside a warrior called Beormund at one time, I can't recall his face. Or it could be another Beormund altogether. It sounds almost too much of a coincidence to have a Iute guarding another Iute, and one as important as myself.

"I worked at *Dux* Wortigern's court. It was my job to know and record matters of Saxons, Angles and Iutes."

Beormund's eyes narrow. "I knew I'd seen you somewhere before. You must be the one they called Ash. We fought the Pict raiders together, once. They say all this is your fault."

It takes all my power not to shout out in protest. "How — how so?"

"They say you tried to steal the heart and body of Princess Rhedwyn, who was already promised to God and Wortimer. It was this betrayal that angered him so much he decided to destroy all the Iutes."

"It's not true. It was Wortimer who stole her from *me*."

I sense that this isn't strictly true, either; something else happened between us, I'm sure of it — but I'm also certain it had nothing to do with Wortimer.

He stares at me in silence, until the other guard's clunking steps sound in the hallway.

"If Wortimer stole her, then where is she now? Nobody has seen her since she and the *Hiréd* went West," he asks.

I feel as if he's just punched me in the gut.

"How would I know? But I'm telling you the truth."

"Maybe you are, maybe you aren't." He sighs. "It doesn't matter. Once Robriwis falls, we're lost... The Iutes will have to take to sea again — or perish."

Another month passes. The slave who replaced Beormund has a pox-ridden rat's face. He slobbers and spits at me when serving the gruel and slop. He doesn't bring enough food to sustain me — I suspect he eats it himself.

Nothing is happening again. I sense my sanity slipping away as the hunger and boredom return. Darkness tightens around me with every passing day. The air in the bath house grows cooler — winter must be coming. I don't know how much colder it can get here before I submit to exposure.

And then, *he* comes back.

Wortimer sits down on a stool and looks around the cell in disgust, covering his nose with a piece of wet cloth.

"You seem healthier," he says with a sneer. "The diet and exercise serves you well?"

"Why are you here? Now? I thought you forgot about me."

He coughs before answering. I imagine the stench here must be unbearable, though I've long grown used to it.

"She begged me to keep you alive," he says. "Said she'll do anything... And she did." He bears his teeth in a lewd grin. "But that's not why I didn't kill you. Ambrosius — remember him? Wanted to spare you in case the Iutes were more difficult to deal with. He thought we could use you in some way — as hostage, or a puppet ruler... But now, you're no longer necessary."

She's alive...? At least, she was for some time after Callew... Unless he's just boasting about what he did to her to further break my spirit.

"The war..."

"Couldn't be going better. We finally convinced old Worangon to join us. Robriwis is now besieged on both sides. It will fall soon, and when it does, the Iutes are finished."

"And you came here to gloat? What do you want me to do?"

"Nothing. Except to die in an entertaining manner. Which is exactly what you will be doing in a few days, along with the rest of the prisoners."

I shrug. "If you think death will scare me, you're a few months too late."

"We'll see about that. I've been putting the old amphitheatre to good use these past weeks. A bit like what the Romans did in the times of the martyrs, but this time, it's the pagans who suffer. And believe me, none of your people went to hell *quietly*."

I don't give him the satisfaction of an answer. He waits a bit in silence, until the door screeches open. A slave enters with the new bucket and a bowl of gruel. I haven't seen him before.

Wortimer stands up, furious. He throws the stool at the slave. "I said I wasn't to be disturbed!" he growls. Seething, he stares at the slave, then points his finger at him. "You'll be joining the others at the amphitheatre tomorrow!" he exclaims and storms out.

The slave puts the bucket and the gruel bowl beside me. As he does so, he drops something clanking on the *caementicium* floor.

"Beormund sends his regards," he grunts.

I pick the small bundle up. Wrapped in a piece of dirty rag is a thin, tapering piece of steel. I smell some rust on it, though when I rub it off, the metal underneath is solid and sturdy. It's weapons-grade steel, a shard of sword or spear-head. There's something carved into it, a rune or a letter, but my fingers are too calloused to read it in the darkness.

I know exactly what I'm supposed to do with it. Gods know I've had enough time to plan every possible escape scenario from this hole, but they all depended on getting help from outside. The metal shard is all the help I need. I spend the night sharpening it on the links of my chain. I have to be careful not to make too much noise — now that I'm alone in the prison again, every sound I make reverberates in the chambers tenfold. Soon the shard is turned into a decent tool — not good enough for stabbing, but just right for the next stage of the plan.

Properly maintained, the bath house brick walls can stand for centuries. But without someone cleaning and drying them regularly, like the Old Man at Ariminum used to do, the damp and the mould wear them out in no time. Eventually, even the bricks themselves start to crumble and fall apart — they just need a little prodding.

I start scratching at the stones to which my chains are attached. The brick and mortar are of better quality than at Ariminum — this was a rich man's bath, built in the glory days of old Rome. I remember now that Wortigern used to use this place as his prison, too. I fear my blade will break if I push too hard, but it proves a piece of some great bladesmithing. At length, the mortar begins to yield, first in crumbs, then in great flakes.

I have no handle on the blade other than the old rag. My hands are torn to the bone. I hide my scars from the guards, but they're just slaves and care not for my state. It's harder to hide the blood splattered around the brick I'm working on, so I have to smear more of it elsewhere around the walls, pretending I've been taken with some new type of madness. This makes me grow weaker and slows down my work. The blade is slippery in my grip; the mortar deeper into the fissure is harder, more solid. These ancient builders knew what they were doing.

At long last, the brick itself begins to wobble. I can now remove it from the wall whole and free myself from the shackle. Only… what then? I'll be alone, weak, in a hostile city full of men loyal to Wortimer…

I decide to worry about that later. First, I need to get out of this dungeon.

The rat-faced slave grumbles at me, annoyed. He raises his torch to look at the blood-splattered walls. I can see he's wondering if he'll have to clean it at some point if it gets too much. He needn't worry — in all the months I've been here, nobody's ever bothered to clean the cell. The dried residue of all my bodily fluids forms a riddle of stains on the floor worthy of a mosaic master.

"I dun'no why yeh'r still 'ere," he grunts. "Yer brain's turned to mush."

He spits on me, his usual goodbye, and turns to the hallway. I grab the chain at my leg and yank at it. It doesn't take much — I already removed the stone last night, and carefully put it back in so that it would fall at the slightest tug.

The chain makes a hellish racket in the silent darkness of the prison, but I know nobody will come to check it — I've been making enough mad noises these past days for the guards to learn to ignore them. The slave spins around and reaches for his reed cane, but he's too slow. I may have been kept shackled on nothing but thin gruel and water for months, but I *was* a warrior, once, and desperation gives me strength. I flail my chain at his legs; it wraps around his ankles, and he tumbles to the ground, dropping the torch and the bucket. I throw myself at him and reach for the throat with my steel shard. He gives a brief struggle, but I push the blade deeper, halfway into his neck, and tear it out as he pushes me away. He tries to stand up, but the chain pulls him down. He tries to scream, but he only lets out a desperate gurgle. As the flame of the torch expires, so does life in his bulging eyes. Gasping and scratching at the floor, he chokes slowly on his own blood.

I sit down, panting. The fight was short, but it almost exhausted me. I've grown weaker than I thought — a few seconds longer, and the slave would've overpowered me. While I recover my strength, I search his body and find a bundle of keys, and a bread roll which I devour instantly. I embed the blade at the end of the reed cane, creating a mockery of a spear, and climb out of the *frigidarium* into what once must have been the *apodyterium*, the changing room. Fortunately, the layout of all Roman baths is similar, no matter how big or old they are. Beyond the changing room door there must be an *atrium*, and then a way out, into the streets of Londin… There's some light here, creeping through the cracks in the ceiling. I stare at the largest fissure and, for the first time since Callew, I can see the sky. It's dark grey, with an orange glow of dusk.

A flight of several steps leads to the exit door. It's locked. On the other side, I hear two men drunkenly arguing over tumbling dice. In my state, I have no hope of fighting two guards, even drunk. Surprise is my only chance. I unlock the door with the key I found by the slave's body, and make a sound of tumbling down the stairs.

"Rat? Is that you?" one of the guards calls out. *They* do *call him a Rat.* "Fuck, are you that drunk already?"

I moan from the floor.

"Go and see what's wrong with him," the other guard says. "Don't want to have to pick his stinking carcass up in the morning."

I grab my "spear" tight in my hands and crouch, waiting. The guard enters the arc of light of the doorway. He's big and fat. He calls for the Rat again. I imitate the slobbering grunt as best I can. The guard belches and steps down. I spring upwards, aiming the weapon at his stomach. The blade digs into the blubber. The guard looks down in surprise. I pull the spear out and stab again, higher. But the steel shard is too short; there's hardly any blood coming from the fat gut.

The guard swipes a punch. My nose explodes and I fly backwards. He roars and launches at me. I have just enough strength to grip the spear and thrust it up as he comes down at me. The impact of his fat body knocks all breath out of me. I brace for more punches, but the guard lets out a strange wheeze and his body turns motionless. I roll him off me: the steel shard slides out of the guard's heart with a horrific squelching sound.

I rush outside, ready to face the other guard. The setting sun blinds me, and the freezing wind biting at my face takes my breath away. The *atrium* is empty, except for an overturned chair and a dice table, and overgrown with frost-parched vines. The guard must have run for help. I hear the noises of the city beyond the pillars of the *atrium*, voices, carts tumbling on the cobbles, animal bellows. I must be near a busy street. I stumble in the direction of the noise. Something ice-cold falls gently on my bare shoulders. I look up. It's snowing. It hasn't snowed in Londin in years.

I can now look clearly at the steel blade shard. The mark carved into the metal is the Saxon "Ash" rune. The same as it was on my rune stone.

A cloth sack falls on my head and the darkness engulfs me again.

CHAPTER II
THE LAY OF CAEOL

The sack comes off. I blink at the bright light. A bonfire crackles in front of me, and braziers beam all around. Peering past the flames, I see a blurry silhouette of a fair-haired man, sitting in a heavy, sculpted oaken chair. There's maybe a score more men and women gathered around us in a wide circle. We're in an entrance chamber of some old Roman public building, a *curia* of some sort. A cracked *cupola* over our heads lets in the snow and cold wind. I shiver, despite standing next to the fire.

"Give the poor sod a blanket," the man in the chair commands. "And get these shackles off him." I recognise the voice. I rub my eyes and look again: it's Beormund.

Somebody wraps me in thick wool and for the first time in months I feel warm. I close my eyes and almost fall asleep, but I'm shaken awake by the impact of a blacksmith's chisel on my wrists. The chains fall on the marble floor with a loud racket.

"Is that him?" Beormund asks a woman standing next to him. She comes closer. Her red hair and green eyes stir something in my memory, but I'm too weak to dig deeper.

"I thought you said you knew him," she says.

"It was five years ago, and we were in the same war band only a few weeks," replies Beormund. "I needed to be sure."

"Yes, it's him," the woman says, nodding.

"So you *are* the famous Ash," says Beormund. "Or infamous, as the case may be."

"I told you, it's not like that… The Princess…"

He shrugs and laughs. "I don't care. None of us here do. The war is as good as lost; what does it matter what caused it? All we want is to survive. And for that, we need you."

"I don't understand."

"No, of course you don't. I'll explain everything later."

"They will be hunting for me…"

"They won't. The prison guards owed us a few favours. You are dead to everyone outside this place, killed while trying to escape. For now, have something to eat and drink. Rest. Return from Hel."

He gestures to my right. Somebody takes me by the hand and leads me to another, smaller chamber. Now it is used as a kitchen, with a great iron cauldron full of boiling stew in the centre — but it was a library once. One of the bookcases still stands against the wall; the others have been chopped up into firewood. The scrolls are piled up by the cauldron; the cook throws them on the fire one by one. My heart breaks at the sight of all that knowledge being devoured by the flames, but my gut is drawn to the smell of the cooking meat in the cauldron.

The stew is thin and watery, with more roots and tubers in it than meat — and what meat it is, I dare not guess. It scalds my tongue and burns my throat. But it's warm food, real food, and I devour it by the bowlful until I sense a churning in my stomach, grown unused to so much sustenance. I stop shivering.

"Look at you," I hear a female voice behind me. "A courtier in the *Dux*'s inner circle. In love with a Princess. A state prisoner. You've come a long way from a bath cleaner's slaveling."

I turn around. It's the red-headed woman from before. My eyes are still blurry from the flame and smoke, so I can't make out her face. Her voice is hoarse, throaty, unfamiliar.

"You don't recognise me?" she says, with a tinge of sadness. "I shouldn't be surprised, with everything that's happened to you since we last…"

"Ead… gith."

I stand up, walk up to her and embrace her. She stands stiff and cold at first, her bosom heaving with deep breaths. Then she melts and returns my embrace.

We don't need to speak. Everything we would have to say to each other is in that embrace. Ten years of life apart, of wasted opportunities, of family and friendship that could have been. I sense her love for me is long lost, just as mine for her; I sense her life was as hard, if not harder, than mine. I sense her loneliness and confusion, reflected in the darkness of my sins. Her body is tough, full-grown, her hips have borne children and her breasts have fed them, her arm and back muscles have grown used to carrying heavy loads. Her amber hair is cut short, and has lost its lustre. Only the glimmer in her eyes remains.

We pull apart. She wipes her eyes with a quick gesture.

"I heard your village was one of the first to be attacked," I say.

"You — you knew where I lived? And you never came?"

I look away. What can I say? "I was checking up on you from time to time, from a distance. You seemed... satisfied without me."

"I suppose." She nods. "I took over my father's smithy. I had a man."

"And he gave you a child," I add, glancing appreciatively at her hips and bosom.

"The child wasn't his," she says, slowly, looking me straight in the eyes.

"What — what do you mean?"

"Octa will be ten years old this winter."

The revelation takes a while to sink in. Was it really only ten years ago? It feels like a lifetime has passed since Master Pascent tore us apart. Ten years... ten years old...

"I... I have a son?"

"So you don't know *everything*." She chuckles, wryly.

"What's he like?"

"He looks nothing like you — took after me and my father. But he's smart, like you. I couldn't keep up with him in learning."

"Where is he now? Is he here? Can I see him?"

She turns grim. Her eyes grow cold and dark. She calls for the cook to give her a jug of warm ale and downs it in one before starting her tale.

She was in the market in Saffron Valley, selling her knives, when Wortimer's army attacked Orpeddingatun. They came armoured and on horseback. The Iutes stood no chance. The Britons killed all the men in the village, including her husband, Caeol. Burned the houses down, threw the corpses into the well. Then they took all the young women and children away, and left the old ones to die.

"They don't kill children," she says. "Wortimer sends them West. I don't know why."

"Ambrosius," I guess. "He still has connections to the Roman slave markets. A Saxon child would fetch a good price in Hispania or Italia."

Her lips curl in the faintest smile. "Then Octa might yet see Rome. It was always his dream. He wanted to be a priest, like Fastidius."

My hands are clenched in weak fists. In a matter of minutes, I have become a father — and I lost a son. I've had enough reasons to hate Wortimer and Ambrosius before. Now I know I will not rest until I see them both destroyed.

I look at Eadgith again. She seems resigned to her fate. There was no fury in her voice when she spoke of what happened to her family. I look around, and see the same resignation in the eyes of everyone else in the room.

"Is everyone here like you?" I ask. "A survivor?"

She nods. "We come from all over Wortimer's domain. All the villages and hamlets strewn between here and Andreda. This is all that's left — four, maybe five score people at most. We all try to do our bit. I'm their chief bladesmith," she adds, and I realise it was she who wrought the steel shard for me — and carved the *Ash* rune into it. "Not that there is much use for my services."

"Why didn't you join the other Iutes, beyond the Medu?"

"It's safer here," says another voice. Beormund has decided to join our conversation. He looks nothing like the withered slave I remember. In a boar fur cloak, clasped with a bronze pin with silver inlays, with a sword at his side and a band of bronze on his arm, he is again the proud war chief who once hunted Picts on the beaches of Cantiaca.

"Outside, Wortimer's men kill anyone who even looks like a Saxon or Iute, on sight," he says. "The Medu crossings are blocked. There is nowhere left to hide. But here, in Londin, nobody cares about us."

I find it hard to believe. Surely, the first place Wortimer would make certain there were no pagans would be his own capital.

"You'll see for yourself," says Beormund. "As soon as you're back to your strength, I'll take you out on one of our raids."

"Raids? What raids?"

He grins. "Pillage, of course. It's all we have left."

For the next couple of weeks, Eadgith nurses me back to health. She feeds me, helps me train, she even bathes me a few times at first, when I'm too weak to do it myself. She never makes any attempt to rekindle our passion, and for that, I am grateful. I can't bring myself to think of pleasures of women yet. In my heart, no matter how wrong and sinful it may be, there's still only a place for Rhedwyn. If I can't be with her — and I have finally remembered what sin it was that drove us irreconcilably apart — I don't want to be with any other. I'm certain she's still alive somewhere, under Wortimer's watchful eye.

Instead, we talk. We tell each other our life stories. I prefer to listen to Eadgith's. It might not be worthy of an epic; there are no great battles in it, or journeys to far-away lands. But there is something in it lacking from my story: fulfilment. She had a good husband, and a child she was proud of. She learned a trade, and then mastered it. She sold her knives and kitchen tools, as far as Dorowern and New Port, to Iutes, Saxons and Britons alike. If it wasn't for Wortimer's war, I could imagine her dying in peace as a respected elder, surrounded by a loving family.

"I guess I was never important enough for the gods to bother cursing me," she chuckles as I make another of my complaints against Fate. She's a pagan now, as everyone in her village was — it was easier that way; but she doesn't seem to put much thought into which gods were worth worshipping more.

With her help, I'm soon able to wield a sword and climb a four-foot wall without pain. This is enough for Beormund. I'm presented with one of Eadgith's blades, a long battle knife of exceptional quality, and told to prepare for a night raid.

It's hard to fathom how much Londin has changed in the nine months of my imprisonment. The streets are strewn with filth and rubble. Rats and wild cats flee before us in droves. The plaster on the walls of the *villas* crumbles, the hedges are overgrown with weeds and vine. We enter the area by the south-eastern walls, a district of taverns and brothels; one that I remember as full of lights and noises all through the night. It's dark and quiet now, with only a few patrons seeking the pleasure of cheap whores in the back alleys, only to scuttle as they see us approach, just like the rats before them.

"What happened to this place?" I ask.

"I told you," replies Beormund. "Wortimer doesn't care about Londin. At least this part of the city. He doesn't have enough money for the upkeep and services; he spends everything on fighting the Iutes — and on paying his supporters."

"What about the people? Why is everything so dark and empty?"

"Many left north and west, others sailed across the Narrow Sea. Those that remain are shut in their homes, afraid of the night. Night is a time of bandits. Night is our time."

This isn't the Londin I knew. The city may have had its problems — too many to list, one could say — but one thing it never was, was afraid. The night was just like any other time, except you took a torch with you when you went about your business. The taverns and whorehouses were always open, as were the homes of your friends.

"Where are we going?" I ask when we reach a cross-road and stop.

"I was hoping you would tell us," Beormund replies.

"Me?"

"Most of the nobles in this part of the city were exiled by Wortimer," he says. "Their treasure taken to pay for Wortimer's expenses. We take what's left of their *villas*. We're no better than rats," he chuckles.

"We've only been here a few months," adds another member of the raiding party. There's five of us altogether. Only I and Beormund are armed with blades, the other three carry clubs and big cloth sacks. Clearly, they don't expect much resistance. "We don't know the streets very well. We hope you know where the best treasure is."

I take a moment to gather my bearings. In the distance, up on the hill, shines the only bright light, the brazier atop Saint Paul's bell tower. A dotted line of torches marks the edge of the Wall — at least Wortimer has had enough sense to still keep it manned. The city may be in decay, but the grid of the streets is still the same.

"Not in this part, that's certain," I say. "The richest men loyal to Wortigern lived in the north-east, by the Old North Road."

"We know," replies Beormund with a grimace. "But it's not our area."

After nightfall, the city, he explains, is divided between four groups of thieves: Iutes, Saxons, Angles, and native Briton bandits, who control the most profitable area around the Forum and Governor's Palace, Londin's heart. The Angles hold the north-east, and the Saxons — a handful of them — remain confined to the western half of the city, which now, as it always has been, is poorer and more sparsely populated than the rest.

"We dare not start a war over territory," Beormund says. "It would draw Wortimer's attention. There's enough plunder for everyone, for now."

"I thought Wortimer only fought the Iutes. Where did the others come from?"

"After his successes in destroying the Iutes, the others grew jealous. The *Comites* have brought war upon their own allies. There's fighting now brewing on every border — except in the West."

"Some of them have always been here," says one of the sack-carriers. I recognise him from somewhere. "As have many of us. We've been a part of this city for years. We survived the expulsions. I used to sell honey at the Forum."

"We all crawled under the stones, just like the rats, when Wortimer pushed us down," says Beormund. I find his constant comparisons to the rodents disturbing — I've had enough of them in the dungeon. "And like the rats, we crawled out when the streets emptied of guards, and when hunger forced us to steal. We clung to each other, a Iute to a Iute, a Saxon to a Saxon…"

"Not everyone is one or the other," adds the honey-seller. "We will take anyone who's worthy. Even *wealh* beggars have their uses."

Wealh *beggars*. It's an odd phrase on a Iute's lips. The Britons were their masters once; even a beggar in Londin thought himself greater and prouder than a barbarian. Now, together, they roam the streets in search of food and scraps of the rich.

Beormund requests that I focus on the task of the night, and I study the cross-road again.

"Have you been to Postumus's house yet?" I ask. Postumus was one of the Councillors most loyal to Wortigern — and he died at Callew, so I'm sure his *villa* will be empty by now.

"Which one is it?"

"It had a great statue of a naked woman on the porch, with one arm broken off."

"I remember it," says the honey-seller. "The statue is no longer there, but I know the house. We've only scoured the gardens once."

"There would be more statues and sculptures around the house," I say. "Some of them bronze."

"Bronze is good," says Beormund, licking his lips. "Let's go there."

The raid at Postumus's house is a great success. We haul two sacks full of quality bronze scrap, the statues hacked into easy to carry pieces by Beormund's sword. We fill the third sack with some unspoilt grain we find in the larder, and other bits and pieces forgotten by Wortimer's brutes from *their* plunder.

I feel like I'm letting Beormund's Iutes destroy something far more important than just the weight of metal; what they're hacking to pieces, what they're burning under their cauldrons, is civilisation itself. *They're only copies*, I tell myself. The originals, if they still exist, are somewhere in Rome or Graecia. The joy on the emaciated, weary faces of the Iutes when we spill the spoils on the floor is worth more than any statue.

We repeat the raid a few nights later, and then we move on to another *villa*, then another. With my knowledge of Londin, and Beormund's leadership skills, we rule the night in our part of the city. Not only do we no longer go hungry, but now we have food and supplies to spare. Once we even dig out an old pot full of hacked silver coins, forgotten by the inhabitants leaving in a hurry. The word of our accomplishments spreads throughout the underworld. Soon, however, the success turns us into its victims.

More Iutes, Saxons and Angles arrive daily to join us from the countryside, as winter forces them from the forest hideouts where they fled before Wortimer's soldiers. We smuggle them up through the old water gate by the Cathedral Hill, in funeral boats returning from the cemeteries down river. The more supplies we gather, the more mouths to feed we have. Even some Britons show up at our door, begging for scraps.

"This is too much," I warn Beormund. "We're too visible."

"What do you want me to do? Turn them away?"

"We should send them to Robriwis. Hengist needs men to fight Wortimer."

The mighty fortress still guards the Medu crossing, halting Wortimer's progress into the land of the Cants — but everyone expects it to fall in spring, when the war should resume in fullness.

"Look at them," he replies and points to the small crowd, huddling around a bonfire in the *atrium*. It's mostly women and younglings, with a few men between them as thin and shivering as I was upon emerging from my dungeon. "You want to send them to war?"

I shake my head. He's right. If we send this sorry horde to Hengist, we'd only add to his trouble.

"But then, what do we do? There isn't anything more to rob around here."

"Not in the empty houses, at least."

I stare at him in puzzlement, then realise what he means.

"No."

"I have already decided. You can either help us, or stand aside."

"It's one thing to take from the dead or exiled what nobody needs. You want us to become criminals? Robbers? Bandits? That *will* bring Wortimer's attention to us."

He winces. "Everyone else is doing it already. The Saxons in the west have an entire band of brutes robbing carriages in the daylight. Nobody's doing anything about it."

"Greed has blinded you."

"Greed? I don't want anything for myself. I'm just taking care of my people. Besides, we would only be stealing from other thieves. Nobody in this city who still has anything worth stealing has earned it the honest way."

I leave him in a huff, and we do not speak about it for a few days more, until Beormund invites me to another night raid. He doesn't tell me where we're going this time. I grow suspicious as we take a turn into a broad alley leading north to the commercial district. I know there are no more abandoned *villa*s to rob in that direction.

"Wait. What's going on?"

We stop. Beormund pulls me under the eaves of a boarded-up tavern. Snow muffles his whisper.

"It's Yule in three days," he says. "The first Yule since Wortimer's war started. We have no beasts for the *blot*. Not enough food for the feast."

"So you think that makes it right to rob someone."

"Of course it does!" he bursts in a whisper so loud I fear he'll wake up the entire *insula*. "Look, Ash, I know you've been raised a Christian, and you have your strange Roman morality still holding you back. But this isn't Rome. If you're hungry, you have to steal."

"But we're *not* hungry."

"We're hungry here," he says, punching his heart. "My people need a Yule feast to sustain their spirits, and with Wodan's help, I'm going to give it to them. Are you with me?"

I look back at our sack-bearers. They don't hear us, but look back at me, full of hope.

Who are you to tell others what's right and what's wrong?

In my mind, the grey-hooded man stares at me accusingly with his one healthy eye. Wodan is right. I'm being a pompous arse. None of these men would commit a sin as great as I have. Compared to mine, their souls are as clean as baptismal robes.

"Who are you going to rob?"

A relieved smile brightens Beormund's face. "There's a corn merchant who's been hoarding grain in his house and selling it at inflated prices at the Forum. He owns three warehouses in this district. We'll only take what's in one of them."

"If he's friends with Wortimer, he'll bring hellfire upon our heads."

"We'll have to worry about it later."

"No, wait." I look down the alley and spot a stone bridge rising over a small, nameless stream. We're not far from the Coln Gate, where the Wall begins to arch north-west, separating the city from the old burial grounds and marshes of the River Lig.

"How far are we from the Angles' territory?"

Beormund points north. "A few streets that way and we'd risk bumping into one of their roving bands, I wager. Why?"

I point to one of the sack-bearers, a lively girl, with her white hair tied in twin pig-tails.

"You. Run back to the *curia*, find Eadgith, the bladesmith. Ask her to give you her best spear blade and a few ringlets of mail. Tell her I sent you."

The girl nods and disappears in the snow, while I explain the plan to Beormund.

Beormund takes the rope tied to the sheep's neck and leads the beast to the altar strewn with oak twigs and sprigs of herbs. It should be a cow, or a pig, but not even the silver we managed to steal from the grain merchant's warehouse was enough to procure such an animal at short notice.

I was right about the merchant. He did bring Wortimer's wrath on those who robbed him — or, rather, those whom he thought robbed him.

When Eadgith nursed me, she showed off the blades she made in her smithy. I recognised the Anglian pattern and guessed she must have studied with Old Weland, who, after all, lived no more than a day's journey from Orpeddingatun. The mail links we dropped on the floor among the spilled grain were just to make sure the investigation into the crime went the right way. The Iutes wore little mail; only the *Hiréd* warriors could afford it. It was more common among the Angles.

The plan worked and nobody suspected us of the robbery. The city guards spent Yule Eve chasing the Angles in the streets of the northern district, while we prepared for the feast. We had pigeons and ducks for roasting, cheese and honey for bread, and even a barrel of winter ale that one of the new recruits had brewed in secret in a cellar of an abandoned whorehouse.

Beormund slaughters the sheep and sprinkles us with its blood. There is no wassailing this Yule, no music, no song — we need to keep quiet under the cracked *cupola*, like the early Christians I read about in lives of the saints. But we are joyous in our silence.

"This was a tragic year," Beormund speaks, and we murmur in agreement. "Every one of us here has lost someone. Their friends, their family. For many, this will be the first Yule that they spend alone. But today, you are not alone. Your dead friends are with us. Your slain family is watching us feast. Let them see that you are merry. That you are happy. That you are alive."

He raises a tankard of ale and spills it on the blood-splattered floor. "To Wodan, the All-Father," he says in a quiet, solemn voice. The girl with the twin pig-tails pours him another measure of ale, which he also spills. "To Neorth and Frige." The third tankard he drinks himself and raises it above his head in a silent toast to the spirits of the dead.

All through his speech, I feel a familiar tingling at my spine, the goose-bumps rising on my skin. I'm almost certain that I can sense the dead around us. Not just the Iutes slain by Wortimer. That shadow dancing on the northern wall must be Fulco. That cloud of dust — Horsa. The sparks rising from the bonfire — the warriors who fell on the beach fighting the Picts...

Somebody presses a mug of ale into my hand. Eadgith, a sad smile dancing on her face, sits down beside me.

"You heard him. Be merry. Or the *draug* will get you."

"Draug?"

"The living dead, raised from the grave. My mother used to scare me with them at Yuletide when I was naughty."

I shiver, though I know it's just an old wives' tale. I wrap the cloak tighter around my shoulders.

"Octa loved Yule," she says and sighs.

She hasn't told me much about her son; *our* son. I wait for her to continue, but she stays silent. She hides her face in the tankard. All around us, people are drinking and eating, in similar silence. They, too, must now be remembering their loved ones. It is a grim feast. I feel the shadows thrown by the bonfire grow dense around us, as if sensing our sorrow and wanting to feed on it.

"I've only ever been to one," I say. "In Beaddingatun, years ago."

"We only started celebrating after we moved to Orpeddingatun. My father celebrated Theophany until his death. He'd even go to the new chapel at Beaddingatun for the Masses, while health allowed him…"

"So Paulinus finished his little church."

"…but Caeol and I turned to the gods of the Iutes. I could not look at the Roman priests after — after us."

She turns away, ostensibly to reach for a piece of roasted pigeon, but she doesn't turn back to me for a long time.

"I miss them," she says at last. "I miss my man."

I put my arm around her and we watch the others feast. As the night grows long, and the great barrel of ale grows empty, I notice the men and women stand up from the circle of light cast by the bonfire and disappear in the darkness, some of them alone, others in pairs.

"Where is everyone going?" I ask.

"To commune with the spirits in solitude," she replies. "I don't know how they do it — I never needed to try it myself before."

I rise and pull her up. She sways in my arms — she's had a lot more to drink than I have. "I'll help you," I say.

We stagger outside. The crisp winter air sobers me up, but does nothing to help Eadgith. I lead her to her smithy — she's built it inside what once was a small marble pavilion in the gardens of the *curia*, by filling the gaps between the columns with sun-baked bricks. The smithy is also her house, though it more resembles a hermit's cell — the only furniture is a sheepskin-covered bedding of furs and sackcloth, and a wall of pegs where she hangs her tools.

She frees herself from my arms and slides down onto the bedding. She stares at the embers in the furnace, still smouldering and sparkling.

"I miss my man," she repeats.

"I'm sure he's here today, watching…"

"No, he's not," she says in a firm voice. Her eyes are cold and sober. "It's all a fairy tale." She grabs my hand and pulls me down beside her. "Do you not miss your woman?"

"Of course." I think of nothing else every night. I never told Eadgith what I discovered about Rhedwyn, but she knows enough to understand that I've lost her forever; that, although Rhedwyn may still be alive — at least, I still choose to believe that — just as Eadgith will never again be able to lie with her dead husband, neither will I ever again taste Rhedwyn's white skin on mine.

Eadgith leans to me and whispers in my ear. "I could be your Rhedwyn for you, if you'll be Caeol for me."

I don't pull away. Her voice is filled with sadness and longing. "Only for one night," she says. "Nothing more."

I reach under her tunic to touch her breast. She closes her eyes and her body shivers from anticipation at the touch of my hand. Naked and clumsy, we lie on the furs, and she tugs the sheep-skin over our bodies, to hide us from the watching spirits.

The Saxon Might

CHAPTER III
THE LAY OF BIRCH

"The cattle will come through the marsh postern, here, and we will attack between the two ruined tenements, here and here."

I draw a rough schema of the neighbourhood with charcoal on old goat skin, and place two battle markers — painted pebbles — in the positions from which I want to push with the assault.

"Isn't it all a bit much?" moans one of the Iute women studying the preparations. "We're just going to rustle a few cows."

I adapted this way to teach tactics from what Fastidius used when we fought our mock battles at Ariminum, when simply explaining his ideas with sticks and pine cones was no longer enough. The woman is right — for this particular raid, it would be sufficient to just position the bandits in the required locations and let them do as they pleased.

For the first few months after Yule, we stuck to plunder again — we had enough food to last the winter, and neither Beormund nor I wanted to risk drawing the city guard's attention to our little band. In spring, however, a new wave of refugees reached the city, bringing the news we all feared and expected with dread: Robriwis had fallen. It was now only a matter of time before Hengist's Iutes would be forced back to Tanet. Would this be enough for Wortimer and Ambrosius, or would they try to fix Wortigern's "error" and push the pagans altogether out of Britannia, nobody could guess.

There are now so many of us, we no longer fit into the ruined *curia*. The camp spills out to neighbouring, abandoned *insulae* plots. It is now a village of tents and huts not unlike the one I saw on my first visit to Tanet. It astonishes me that the city guards continue to appear oblivious of our camp. We're less than half an hour's walk away from the Governor's Palace. All it would take for Wortimer to discover us would be for him to wander away from the road leading to the Cathedral, or from the Augustan Highway. But of course, he'd never do that — he'd have to enter the empty, filthy, waste-strewn streets of what the Londin folk are now calling the Poor Town.

The city, abandoned by a *Dux* obsessed with his military campaign, crumbled before the onslaught of an unusually harsh winter. In this desperate time the administrative genius of Wortimer's father became apparent in full. Wortigern was not only managing to keep the peace in the streets, but also to feed the people of Londin from his meagre budget, giving away the grain to those most unfortunate, like the Imperators of old used to, in Rome. Now, with the countryside ravaged by war and bad weather, and the supply network all but destroyed, the only ones with grain to spare are the merchants and those who steal from them — like us. Those who could, have left the city to try their fortune with the friends and relatives outside. The homeless squatters, the beggars and the rats fill the dark narrow streets and tall tenements of east Londin, all fighting for the same scraps of sustenance. Nobody ventures here willingly, not even the army.

For now.

With so many new refugees to feed, we soon exhaust every *villa*, warehouse and tenement that can be safely plundered. I have no choice but to yield to Beormund's arguments. From pillagers of empty houses and robbers of abandoned graves, we turn into common bandits.

None of us has any crime experience. But we learn. We start small: rustling cattle heading for the market, or robbing grain carts. We restrict our attacks to the border zone between us and the Angles on one side and the Britons on the other, to throw suspicion on them as much as on us. Wortimer's men can barely tell one pagan from another. It is my idea to dye our hair and smudge our faces with charcoal; everyone stays silent, only I'm allowed to speak and I do it in perfect Imperial, to sow even greater confusion among our victims.

With success comes greed. Even my blood begins to run hot when I think of a new strike. I spend most days preparing and researching for the robberies; I find it lets me forget about my woes, about my sins, forget even about Rhedwyn, at least during the day.

"I told you before —" I explain, patiently. "You need to learn how to follow these plans in case we need one day to fight a real battle. With the way things are going in the city, you never know when we'll have to face regular soldiers."

"This isn't how a Iute fights," scoffs another warrior. He waves his hand. "All this... planning, marking, preparation. This is the *wealh* way. A way of the weak."

"I'm a Iute, and this is how I fight," I say, with force. "Beormund made me your war chief, so it's my job to prepare you for a war as best as I can."

"You're only half a Iute," the warrior says. "And you're more like them than us."

"And what do you mean by that?"

I step up to him. He's a head taller than I am, so I have to raise my head to look him in the eyes, but I'm not afraid of him. I've seen him fight in a couple of raids — he's strong, but foolish. No wonder my tactical plans irritate him.

"You can read, write and speak their tongue. You know all about their customs, their faith. Yet you know next to nothing about ours, and you speak Iutish like a child. Why should we even trust you? For all we know, they've only let you out of their prison to spy on us!"

I grab him by the tunic, hook his leg with my foot from behind and throw him down to the ground. I slip a knife from my boot sheath and press it to his neck.

"Is this Iutish enough for you?"

The fear flashing in his eyes turns quickly to anger. He shoves me off and stands up in a huff.

"*Wealh* tricks," he murmurs, as he limps away.

"You — can't — blame — them. They're — not — used — to — trusting — anyone — from — outside."

Eadgith speaks through the pauses between her hammer striking the anvil. She's forging a butcher's cleaver out of an iron bar salvaged from some abandoned *villa*'s fence.

"They've only accepted me because of my husband," she adds, as she puts the hissing blade into the quenching bucket. "And my skill."

"But I'm *not* an outsider," I protest. "Unlike you, I *am* a Iute. I was born in a Iute village — not even some of them can say that. I was all set to marry their Prin…"

My voice breaks, as I still can't bring myself to say Rhedwyn's name.

"I don't need them to like me," I continue. "But I need them to trust me as their commander."

"Win enough battles and they will forget who you are. It worked for Fastidius."

"I don't have the time."

She puts the cleaver onto the cooling stand, wipes her hands in cloth and turns towards me.

"Why do you care so much what they think, Ash? You don't know any of them. You haven't met any of them before."

"They are my kin."

There's more to this, but I find it difficult to put it into words. I feel like I owe the Iutes for them having to be around me, to endure my curse. Sooner or later, I will somehow bring some disaster upon them, like I have upon everyone in my life.

I can't tell anything of this to Eadgith. She's too practical to believe in curses and dark Fates. I wonder if she still thinks I'm destined for greatness, now that we're both stuck in a city of weeds and ruins, struggling for survival by rustling cattle and stealing grain from others, less fortunate than us.

"Just ignore them, then," she says. "In time, they'll grow fond of you —" Her voice softens. "— they all do, eventually."

"I'm thinking something big," Beormund says one late May afternoon. "The Pentecost is coming, I hear it's a great holiday for you Romans. Would be easy to get away with a bold strike."

Just as Eadgith advised, I'm trying to ignore his jabs at my Roman upbringing — but I can't let this one go.

"You mean like the Easter Market."

He winces. It is a low blow to remind him of the disaster. It was the last raid he commanded in person, trying to prove his worth as a war chief. We struck at a caravan of wagons belonging to the same corrupt merchant whose warehouses we attacked during our first ever robbery, as they were heading for the Easter Market. From the start, I had my doubts — not least because the Easter Market was no longer what it used to be, diminished by war and the economic decline that followed — and I was proven right. The merchant was better prepared than even I expected. There were Legionnaires among his guards, mercenaries hired from Ambrosius's army. Without proper strategic preparation, the battle quickly turned into the violent chaos the Iutes were so fond of — with dire consequences. We lost two men and got away with nothing. In retribution, Wortimer sent a squad of soldiers to burn down many of the huts on the edges of the Poor Town, though the Iute camp, deep in the centre, was never in any real danger.

"This is why I chose you to run the operations," says Beormund, scratching a scar on his cheek from a Legionnaire's sword. "You know these Romans better than anyone here. And for what I have in mind, this knowledge will be crucial."

"And what *did* you have in mind?" I ask, already preparing a rebuke. Beormund has come up with several hare-brained schemes since the Easter debacle, all of which, so far, I have managed to shoot down and replace with something more reasonable and less risky.

"You'll think me mad."

"Yes, I probably will."

"The Bishop's house."

"The Saint Paul's rectory?" I exclaim. He was right — I do believe he's gone mad.

"Whatever you call it. That big stone building at the back of the Cathedral."

"It's almost a fortress! There are always people around! You'd need an army to storm it."

"Even at the Pentecost?" He smiles slyly. This gives me pause. I'm surprised he'd even know what Pentecost is, much less the details of the Bishop's comings and goings during the holiday. I confront him about it and his smile grows even more sly.

"I've had a good tip from a guard," he says. "The Bishop doesn't have enough men to spare to protect him, the Cathedral and his house all at the same time. There'll be crowds at the feast, and we've made everyone around here scared of thieves, so that's where all the soldiers will be."

"And who is this guard? Why should we trust him?"

"He's a Iute."

"A Iute in the Bishop's guard?" I raise an eyebrow. "Sounds unlikely."

"He's one of the hostages who came with Haesta. He's been under the Bishop's protection."

This is the first I hear of any of the young hostages surviving Wortimer's rampage. What happened to the others? What happened to Haesta himself?

"How come we've never heard from him before?"

"He was in hiding. Thought he might be the only one of his kind left in Londin. Then he heard about our plight and wanted to help."

I shake my head. "I don't know. Too many strange coincidences. This all looks like a trap to me."

"Why would anyone want to set up a trap for us? They know where to find us."

"They'd need to purge through Poor Town before coming here. Much easier to trap us on the job. They know we'll send our best men to get this prize."

"And what a prize it would be," he says, wistfully, his eyes gleaming with the vision of the Church's riches.

I have been so involved with the lives of the Iute refugees, I don't even know who the Bishop of Londin is anymore. It could still be Fatalis, having proven his loyalty to Rome at Callew — or that Gaul Severus, who came with Germanus on the ship, which started this disaster; or somebody else entirely. What I do know is that no matter who it is, they're sitting on a pile of treasure greater than anyone in the city, including Wortimer. Most of that wealth is stored safely in the Cathedral's crypts, with the Bishop only partaking in as much of it as is prudent for a man of cloth.

"The last time I was there, there was more silver than a man could carry," I muse, remembering the time Fastidius took care of me after the fight with Wortimer's roughs, ten years ago. "It must be a lot more than that now."

The lure of silver is strong. Beormund goads me with the vision of all the things we could buy for only a handful of what I saw at the rectory. I know it's selfish — the money would be better used to help the poorest of the Iutes, maybe even distributed among the inhabitants of the Poor Town, who have already suffered so much on our behalf; but I have lived among these wretched refugees, in their filth and squalor, for too long. For the past months, I, who feasted at Wortimer's court, have been reduced to eating pea soup and goat stew and simple curds, and frankly, I'm fed up with it all. I want wine, and chicken, and cheese that matured in a cave.

"I still think it's a set-up," I say.

"Fine. Prepare for a trap, then," Beormund replies. "Don't tell me you can't outsmart a few guards?"

"If it *is* only a few guards," I say, cautiously, but my mind is already working on the plan, even as I still hesitate to agree to Beormund's proposal.

I fondly remember the Pentecost Masses from my previous life. It's a festival almost as grand as the Easter, attracting huge crowds from the countryside as it comes in the time of year when the weather is milder and there is less work out in the fields. And since there's less produce to sell, the market is a less important part of the event. This day is all about the Church: the baptisms, the sermons, the Psalms — and the confessions; for many serfs and peasants who can only afford to go to church once a year, Pentecost is when they receive absolution for all the sins of the past twelve months.

The congregation this year is guaranteed to be even greater than usual, boosted by the paupers hoping for a share of the Church's alms. As we climb the Cathedral Hill, I hear them buzz like a nest of angry wasps. For the first time I think this might not be a trap after all. This is the greatest gathering of people since Wortimer came to power, and they are all in a foul mood; neither the town watch nor the Cathedral guards will be able to fully control this famished, incensed multitude. The soldiers will not care about the rectory, way out at the back of the hill — they will be busy trying to halt a riot.

We reach within sight of the rectory, and the buzzing stops, replaced by a loud, harmonious singing. It's the Cathedral choir, doing their best to calm the crowd down with their angelic voices. My baptism training kicks in and I recognise the hymn they chant as Psalm 114, "Bless the Lord, O my soul". Inadvertently, I murmur the words to myself. As the voices rise, the music starts to affect me in an odd way. My hair stands on end, my breath and heart quicken. Standing in front of the rectory, with the massive, Heaven-reaching wall of the Cathedral behind it, I am in awe; a realisation of what I'm supposed to do dawns on me: I will strike against the Holy Church, steal the treasures donated to it by the pious faithful. I might as well be stealing from Christ himself.

What have I become?

"Commander?"

A voice breaks through the haze of my self-pity. It's Birch, the girl with the twin pig-tails. There's only four of us on this mission; I hand-picked them myself from among those most experienced in the robberies. Four should be enough to overpower the few remaining guards, if the Iute was right; and if it's a trap, it's a small enough number to sacrifice. Birch is the smallest of us, fast and agile, able to get into the smallest of holes like a hunted hare. Wulf, carrying a big axe and the big sack, is the muscle of the group, while Raven, once a hunter in Andreda Forest, is our lookout.

The hymn ends, and the angry buzzing resumes. I take a deep breath and remember, of all people, King Drust of the Hundred Victories. He was a Christian, baptised by a living saint, with a loyal Bishop at his service; none of which stopped him or his men from plundering churches and killing priests here in the South — and God did not choose to punish him with anything worse than a minor defeat on a beach of the Ikens. All I'm planning to do is take some trinkets from a rich man's house; if possible without hurting anyone in the process. Does it really matter that the rich man happens to also be a Bishop?

"Raven?" I ask.

"There is only one guard at the back gate," the lookout replies. "This entire part of the compound is empty except for a few slaves cleaning the floor."

"Maybe the hostage was telling the truth after all," I muse under my breath.

I study the walls of the rectory from our base at the top floor of a ruined sandstone tenement. A ring of *insulae* around the Cathedral has been reduced to rubble for security and protection from fire, so this is the nearest building still standing, some hundred feet away from the compound. In the ten years since my first visit, the compound has expanded in all directions, but the window of the room in which I once lay, recovering from the beating received from Wortimer's band of roughs, is still accessible from street level. There are iron bars across it now, a mark of the more dangerous time we've come to live in.

I point it out to Birch. "Can you fit through there?"

"Not even at my hungriest," she replies, her pig-tails shaking left and right. "But I could take a peek."

She doesn't look it, but she's a few years older than me — old enough to remember the Old Country and the sea passage. She came to Tanet with Hengist, the chieftain of her clan. Her back still bears the purple diagonal scar from a snapped rope that cut her during the storm.

"Raven will show you the way."

"I can see it from here!"

Before I can stop her, she leaps out the window and climbs down the wall like a lizard. A red lightning bolt dashes through the rubble; we're all wearing the crimson robes of a Pentecost penitent underneath our dirt-drab cloaks, in case we're caught and have to explain ourselves to the town watch.

A new hymn erupts at the Cathedral, one that I'm not familiar with. Germanus must have brought it from the Continent. This time, the buzzing of the throngs doesn't recede. The chant rises above the murmurs, but cannot overcome them. These people did not come here to listen to songs: they want bread.

The red lightning bolt zooms back.

"Somebody's asleep in there!" announces Birch. "And snoring like a bear in winter."

I frown. "But it's the middle of the day."

"I know, right?"

"Maybe a slave is cutting a nap in his master's bed," suggests Wulf.

"Hmm."

He may be right, but I don't like it. It's a new, unexpected snag in the plan. I knew some of the servants attending at the Cathedral back in the day. I'd hate to have to hurt any of them.

"Right," I say and crouch down to draw a plan in the brick dust on the floor. "This is what we're going to do."

I approach the guard at the door with a grimace of lost hope on my face. His grip on the spear relaxes as he spots my red Pentecostal robe.

"Are you lost, pilgrim?" he asks.

"I — I think so." I try my best to sound like a Briton peasant from the North. "The streets here are so winding and narrow… Our village only has one street, you know."

"If you want to get back to the Mass, it's right that way," he says, pointing in the direction of the murmuring crowds.

"Oh, I just came from there. I'm looking for my friends. They're supposed to be waiting for me at some tavern called the Bull's Head, but I have no idea where that is."

"Bull's Head? I know the place." He looks at me inquiringly. "It's not cheap, though. Are you sure it's the right one?"

Of course, I had to come up with a tavern for the wealthy guests… In my days at Wortigern's court, those would have been the only ones I frequented. "Yes, that sounds like it.

They did say it's a dear one. It's for my nephew's baptism, you see, Lord be praised."

His face lightens up. "Hallelujah!" he cries out. "It's not far. You just need to climb down there, turn right, then left, and you'll find it right by Cardo Street. Can't miss it."

I make my best confused face.

"That's what they told me, but then I ended up right here…"

"You — ugh." He rolls his eyes. "I see what happened. You should — " He pauses, looks at the door he's supposed to watch, then at his spear, then at the searing midday sun, then back at the door again. "You know what, there's nobody here anyway. I'll show you to the crossroads; you can't get lost from there."

He puts the spear by the door. This is easier than I thought it would be. I didn't even need to ask — and I had an entire story prepared, ending with promising him a flask of ale at the tavern. How has the security at the Cathedral allowed to have lapsed so much?

We climb downhill to the shadowy crossroads which should lead me to the Bull's Head. As planned, Raven leaps out at us from a dark underpass, brandishing a long knife, pretending to be a robber. I cower behind the guard. He draws a short sword and rushes to attack Raven, when I thump him in the back of his head with the cudgel I was hiding under the cloak.

We drag his limp body into the underpass, where Birch ties him up. I give Raven the guard's sword and take back my knife — Eadgith's blade. Like the others, I smudge my face black with charcoal, and the three of us run back to the rectory door. Wulf has already cracked it open with his axe.

We cross under the gate into a small *atrium*. A servant shrieks and flees at our sight. "I'll check upstairs," I say. "Birch, you come with me. Raven, go to the left hallway, find a way into the kitchens. Wulf, stay on guard."

The upstairs corridor is windowless and dark, just as I remember it. I hear the snoring coming from behind one of the doors. "That's the room with the barred window," Birch whispers. I nod. The layout of the floor hasn't changed since I was last here.

"That means the Bishop's study should be somewhere... here."

I push the door. It swings gently open. The room is dim and stuffy, like the hallway — the shutters are closed. There's a desk by the window, with a single candle flickering in a silver candlestick. Two leather-bound chairs stand beside it. Bookcases line the walls. A crucifix of gold and precious gems hangs by the shut window, gleaming in the candle's light. Birch lets out a quiet shriek of joy at the sight. I stop her.

There's somebody here, I gesture, silently.

The study extends behind one of the bookcases, beyond our vision. I hear the rushed breathing of someone waiting in ambush. It was a trap after all. I nod at Birch to run downstairs and check on the others, but it's too late: I hear her tussle with someone on the stairs and cry for help. I enter the room, knife drawn.

[70]

"So it *was* you," the voice from behind the bookcase speaks, in high Imperial. "They said you were dead."

The man comes out into the light. He's wearing a rich, ornate white robe, trimmed with gold: the Bishop's vestments. A black curly beard hides the lower half of the face, while a shadow of the tall bookcase shrouds the rest, but I don't need to see the face to know the voice. I've known it all my life.

"Fastidius!"

He opens the shutters, flooding the study with sunlight. I still hold my knife drawn. The sound of combat downstairs dies down.

"Are you going to fight me, brother?" he asks, surprised.

"What's going on? Why are you here, in these clothes?"

"This is my study. These are my clothes."

"*You're* the Bishop of Londin?"

"You mean you didn't know?"

I hear many footsteps rushing up the stairs. "Did you set up all of this?" I ask. "Why?"

"I needed to be sure it was you. I heard the rumours, but nothing certain. We were all told you were dead, slain along with the others by the Iutes. *The Massacre of the Long Knives*, they call it."

"It *was* a massacre," I say. "But not how Wortimer tells it."

The Cathedral guards burst into the room. Fastidius gestures to them to stand down. I put the knife on the table and step back.

"One of them got away," says the captain of the guard. I spot Birch and Wulf, held at the back of the hallway.

"Don't worry," says Fastidius, noticing my gaze. "Your people are unharmed and free to go."

He nods at the guards, and they release the two Iutes. Birch hisses at her captor; he steps back, rubbing a forearm red with bite marks.

"And you can take this with you," Fastidius adds, taking the golden crucifix from the wall and handing it to Birch. "God has no need for such trinkets when there are people starving."

Birch looks at me for orders. I tell her to take the crucifix — and the silver candlestick I swipe from the desk — and return with Wulf to the camp. "Find Raven, if you can."

Both the guards and the Iutes depart, leaving me and Fastidius alone in the study. He invites me to sit down in one of the leather-bound chairs. I push it away.

"First, I have to know," I say.

"I'm still your brother, Ash. I'm loyal only to God and the Holy Church, not to Wortimer."

I stare into his eyes, trying to guess if he's telling the truth, then step forward and give him a quick embrace. I sense the tension flowing away from my muscles, though some of it still remains. The situation is too strange and unexpected for me to feel fully relaxed.

"You must have many questions," he says, pouring each of us a cup of wine.

"How come you're the Bishop? What about Fatalis — what about Severus?"

"Severus got the prize he *really* wanted — the See of Trever in Gaul. It's a far wealthier diocese than Londin, and closer to Rome. Poor old Fatalis couldn't take the strain of what happened and locked himself in a monastery somewhere in Armorica."

"And they chose you? A heretic? Wortimer's last living enemy?"

He bites his lower lip. "I had to renounce Pelagius and accept Albanus's miracles. Germanus thought it would be a good idea to have a 'convert' like me as a Bishop — it would help convince others, especially the nobles."

"And did it?"

"I wouldn't know," he replies with a shrug. "I doubt anyone has the time to care about such things these days. Germanus returned to Rome, and I haven't heard from him since."

"It's not been a good year," I say with a deep nod. "For any of us."

"At least we're both alive."

I clink his cup and take a sip of wine. The choir outside chants a violent *Te Deum*.

"Who's celebrating the Mass if you're here?" I ask.

"I asked the prior of Saint Peter's chapel, the one at the Forum. I told him I was feeling unwell."

"How long have you been planning this?"

"Since Easter. That's when I first realised it might be you leading the robbers. Wortimer still thinks it's some allied band of Britons and Angles."

"Then my ruse worked. How did *you* know?"

"You were using tactics *I* taught you," he replies with a smile of shy pride. "Back at Ariminum, when we were just kids."

"Is that where I got it from?" I laugh out loud. "And here I thought I came up with all of that by myself."

"The way you divided your forces for battle — straight from Vegetius." He takes a long sip of his wine. His eyes glint with amusement.

Outside, the choir stops. The crowd grows silent. The first words of a sermon drift into the room on the wind. I sense once again that ancient pious awe which always shook me to the core during a Mass. The prior of Saint Peter's is no great orator — certainly not in the league of Fatalis or Germanus; but he speaks the words of the Holy Scripture with energy and confidence and it is enough to make my whole body shake. Or maybe it's just the stress of the robbery and anticipation of ambush that is finally receding…

I barely hear Fastidius's next question. He wants to know what I've been up to since we last saw each other, before I departed for the Council with Wortigern and Beadda — and Rhedwyn. He doesn't mention her name, which makes me suspect he knows or deduces more about what happened than he lets on.

I look at the empty space on the wall, where the golden crucifix was hanging. The figure of Christ might be gone, but I still feel its accusing eyes upon me. I grow hot with shame. I gaze down: I'm still wearing the red Pentecostal robes. They remind me it is a holy day. The day of confessions; the day of absolutions.

I step down from the chair and kneel before a startled Fastidius. I bow down my head, raise my hands in prayer, and recite the formula:

"Forgive me, father, for I have sinned."

"This is too much," says Beormund, with a scowl. "Wortimer will find out about this."

He's referring to the long line of huddling, wretched poor, waiting for their chance to get a small loaf of bread, freshly baked from the grain stolen from the noblemen's warehouses. Another, shorter line, stands on the other side of the *curia*'s courtyard, this one leading to a makeshift bathing pit, dug into the mosaic pavement of what was once a dining room for the clerks. Covered with a dome of straw and filled with boiling hot water, the pit is the first chance for a bath most of these unfortunates have had in a year.

"Why are we doing all this, again?" asks Beormund. "The more we spend on them, the less we have for ourselves."

For the past few weeks, we have been working hard to bring back a semblance of civilisation to the Poor Town. We dug new wells, so the townsfolk wouldn't have to drink the poisoned waters of the Tamesa — the only working aqueduct in the city supplies just a few *villas* of the nobles in the West; we cleaned the gutters, so the filth once again flows to the river; we helped settle some of the poorest homeless under roofs, even if those roofs are only made of blankets and straw thrown over crumbling walls of abandoned tenements; and we are sharing more of our food with the needy, so that no one needs to die of starvation anymore.

It's not just the spoils from our raids that pay for all this. Fastidius is helping, too, as much as he can, without rousing Wortimer's suspicion. A few times now he has sent us "hints," leading us to silver and gold he's hidden among the rubble. Without this assistance, we could never have achieved so much for the poor townsfolk.

"These people were here before us, and will stay here when we're long gone. Would you rather fight them, or feed them?"

"I'm not afraid of some half-starving *wealas.*"

"Trust me, it's worth it," I tell Beormund. "They are our wall. Stronger than stone — and less conspicuous. When was the last time you saw a city guard come through here? Or an

Anglian bandit? Every time anyone gets too close to Poor Town, they're pelted with dung and waste. There's nothing here that's worth this bother."

"I'd rather have an actual wall. Of stone."

"That *would* draw Wortimer's attention. And that of his Council. We cannot challenge them so openly in their own city. But this…" I point to the mass of the huddling poor. "Nobody cares about this. The nobles are happy somebody else is taking care of the problem, and keeps the beggars out of their sight."

"Is that really the only reason you're doing this?"

I sigh instead of an answer. I don't want Beormund to know about my conversations with Fastidius — I call them "confessions", but there is never much talk of God and his mercy — and how they're making me feel. I don't know if helping the unfortunate townsfolk does anything to wipe the stain of sin from my soul, but I feel like I need to do *something* to make amends for what I've done.

Sometimes I go down to the courtyard, to look at the poor picking up their bread or bowl of stew. I see gratitude in their eyes, sometimes a smile or even a bow — they know I'm the one responsible for the meal they receive, often the first one they eat in days, or the clean water, or the roof over their heads. I know seeing it should warm me inside, should make me feel something, *anything*. But no matter how many times I witness this brief flash of mirth lighting up their miserable existence, my heart remains dark, cold and empty.

"We need to get our hands on more firewood," I say. "Maybe then we can dig a second bath."

CHAPTER IV
THE LAY OF AMBROSIUS

This is the first time since joining Beormund that I kill someone who isn't a guard or one of Wortimer's mercenaries.

I watch as the blood flows from the Angle's chest into the gutter. His sky-blue eyes are wide open, staring into the dawn sky. Moments ago, he was still gasping, clutching at the air as life escaped him with his last breath.

I check on my men. Wulf ties a strip of cloth around his arm — that's another scar added to his collection. The others are unharmed. I shouldn't worry, we've been doing this long enough. Everyone in the band is an experienced fighter by now; I barely even have to give them orders. But this one may have been the toughest bout we've had so far, so I double check on everyone again before calming down.

Defeating the Angles here will expand our territory to the other side of the Augustan Highway. I long hesitated before making this move, fearing this would spur the Angles and the Briton gangs to unite against us. But we need this land. The Coln Gate is where the richest merchants carry their goods. The land of the Trinowaunts, untouched by the war — since what few Saxons lived in Peredur's domain were friendly and tame, almost Briton themselves — is the only land where the harvest is bound to be plentiful this year. It's almost August, soon the carts will begin rolling into the city, filled with grain on the way in and with goods bought in barter on the way out. Moreover, this quarter of the city is where Wortimer's loyal supporters have built their new palaces, raised from the plundered spoils. The *villas* are crude in design, and built more in wood and daub than reclaimed stone, but immense in size, sprawling over several *insulae*, belying the poverty of the rest of the city; so great in fact, that they must be difficult to defend from robbers all the time. If we can't lay our hands on all those riches, many of the Iutes and the townsfolk of the Poor Town might not survive the coming winter.

The killing is something I will need to confess to before Fastidius the next time we meet. I have been seeing him each Sunday, after the Mass, sneaking into the Cathedral through the rectory door. I don't know if I believe confessing my sins will help me in the afterlife, but it certainly helps me survive in this world. It was such a relief telling him about Rhedwyn and myself, and have him accept the sin, that I decided to confess to him weekly — even though he could not absolve me.

"I don't know what sits in your soul, Ash," he told me. "Not anymore. You do not belong to the Church, and although Pela —" He hesitated and glanced around, wary of eavesdroppers. "— some Fathers of the Church say a good man does not need to be of God to be saved, I… I don't know if you're a truly good man."

The accusation shook me more than I expected. Maybe because hearing it from Fastidius confirmed my own fears and worries.

"Is it because I stood with Wortigern at Callew? He was my master, I had to obey —"

"The Lord is our only Master. But it's not about that, or anything you've done. It's about what you *feel*. I sense no remorse in you for your sins, only anger at God — or the gods — for the fate that's befallen you. The only sin you feel ashamed of is Rhedwyn — and this one wasn't even your fault. Every soul can be saved if there is will enough to serve the prescribed penance... But I see no such will in you."

He's right. I haven't even asked what penance he would prescribe me for my sins. I wasn't interested in this part of the ritual. I only want to drop the heavy load of shame off my chest. I'm using Fastidius as a receptacle for my darkness, and he knows it, but his good Christian heart won't let him stop my weekly visits. I know he's counting on a breakthrough, a conversion that will open my heart to Christ... And I don't disavow him of this notion. Who knows?

"Miracles have happened," I told him once.

"Yes, they have," he answered, raising his eyes to the ceiling. "But you don't believe in any of them."

I wipe blood from my sword and rifle through the dead man's clothes. There's a leather cord around his neck. I rip it and raise it to the light. A tiny wooden cross dangles at the end. I have been seeing these more and more often on the Angles; Germanus's mission at Werlam is proving a great success... Or is this the result of our victory at the beach, and Fastidius's proselytising? I think of Una and her Anglian warlord lover. What must they be thinking of everything that's been happening in Britannia? Are they even still ruling the Ikens — or have their neighbours defeated them in some battle and taken their land?

Most of the Angles in Londin know nothing about what's going on in the North, and those who do, will not speak to us. They have been flowing into the city from the outskirts of

Una's territory, to escape Wortimer's border encroachment, bad harvest, Elasio's slave runners, forced recruitment into the Iken army, rumours of more raids from Drust's Picts… There are no warriors among them, no *Hiréd*; they are peasants and village craftsmen, and they stand no chance against well-trained fighters like my band, no matter to what acts of valour their hunger and desperation drives them.

The Iutes will be starving and desperate too, if we fail here, I remind myself, putting the tiny cross back on the Angle. I add a silver coin from my purse as *wergild*.

"Hide the body somewhere," I order. "We'll send word to his tribe where to find him later. He deserves a proper burial."

Fastidius welcomes the end of my confession with a deep sigh.

"At least I know you're truly sorry for this one. Would it hurt you to take a penance for it, so at least *my* soul was at ease?"

"I've paid my dues already," I reply. "A whole silver *mili*. It's more than the life of a churl like him is worth these days."

He sighs again. "Is this what things are like in the Poor Town? An inch of silver for a man's life?"

"You've no idea. All the coin in Londin has gone to pay for Wortimer's mercenaries. That inch of silver could buy a cow out in the countryside. That pot of hacked up plates you left us a month ago? We're still eating bread from the grain we bought with it."

He shakes his head. "Wortimer has a lot to answer for." He stands up, then sits back down again. "Do you have anything else to confess to? Just — don't tell me who you've lain with since last time. I have enough of this from my flock. Sometimes I think they just come here to brag."

I force a false, bawdy chuckle. "That's not something I'd feel sorry about," I say, though the truth is, I have not been able to lie with a woman, other than the one-time tryst with Eadgith. The pleasure of flesh is no longer enough to warm the cold inside me.

"Good," he says. "Now, come with me."

He leads me out of the rectory and into a lonely, darkened hallway. He leans forward and whispers in a conspiratorial manner.

"There is somebody else who'd like to meet you."

I tense up and look around. *Is this another trap?*

"Not here," says Fastidius. "Come to the Bull's Head tonight at the third vigil."

"Will you be there?"

"I cannot be seen with them."

"Who is it?"

"If I told you, you'd never agree. Do it for me," he pleads. "I vouch for this meeting."

I'm intrigued. "Fine. But I will be armed and with company. I won't make the same mistake as Wortigern."

"Take only those you trust to keep this a secret."

The Bull's Head has changed almost beyond recognition. It was once my home — a luxurious tavern, where the nobles mingled with rich merchants to discuss trade deals and bribes. Now, it's a fortified building, with windows boarded over, iron-bound door and the carriage gate, no longer in use, filled up with rubble. The Cardo Street, once the busiest highway of the city, is now a border land between the Poor Town and the more affluent territory, controlled at night by the Briton band.

Nobody's surprised when I enter the tavern just as the watchmen cry seventh hour — midnight. As a neutral house, it's been used as a nightly meeting place between Londin's rival bands for months. I nod at my three guards to sit down at the great table, where a late-night dice gambling session is still going on. I scan around for whoever sent out the mysterious invitation. I spot several guests who, despite being dressed as commoners, have the sharp movements and bulked-up muscles of professional soldiers — they must be the bodyguards. The landlady notices me and points with her thick thumb to the back.

The man sitting by a small round table in the back room wears a hooded cloak of fine brown leather, and gloves of kidskin. A noble, then. All evening I've been trying to guess who it might be; Wortimer was the obvious guess, but also the most unlikely — he'd know I would try to kill him on sight, even if I had to do it with my bare hands. One of his disgruntled courtiers, perhaps — or a threatened merchant, like Dene. I suspected the aim of the meeting would be some kind of conspiracy against Wortimer's interests; it would be the only reason for arranging the meeting via Fastidius. Nothing, however, prepared me for seeing the face revealed when the fine leather hood dropped.

I sit down and look at him in silence. The last time we saw each other, he was staring at me and Wortigern, red-faced, from the wooden benches of the auditorium at Sorbiodun. Since then, his name became bound inextricably in my mind to that of Wortimer; his face is the face of death and rampage, his armies marching across Britannia Maxima, robbing and pillaging Iutish and Saxon towns and villages alongside those of Wortimer. What could he, the self-styled Governor of All Britannia, the *Dux* of Corin and all lands West, Ambrosius son of Aurelius, possibly want to talk to me about?

Ambrosius speaks first. "We must get rid of Wortimer."

"I thought we'd exchange greetings first."

"I know what you think of me. I don't expect any courtesy."

I have to hand it to him — he certainly caught my attention.

"I know why *I* would want to get rid of him," I say, "but I thought you two were friends and allies."

He scoffs. "Friends? Never. I was a friend with his father. But Wortigern chose badly."

"So you had him killed."

He pauses, mulling his answer. He then reaches into the sleeve of his cloak and produces a piece of parchment. It's in Wortigern's writing.

"I swore on the Gospels no harm would come to him," he says. "I would never break such an oath."

I scan through the letter. The *Dux* is alive and well, ruling a petty kingdom of his own somewhere in the far western reaches of Ambrosius's territory.

"The land belonged to his wife, so it's his by right," Ambrosius adds to the letter's content. "He's busy fighting Scots alongside my brother Utir. But I fear his talents are wasted on those forlorn shores."

"They certainly are," I reply, before realising what he means. "You want him back in Londin?"

"It might be the only way," he admits with a dejected nod. "I —"

"Wait."

I stop the conversation and return to the landlady demanding ale, and lots of it. This looks like it will be a long night.

"I'll need one of you to stay just in case," I tell my men, "but the rest of you can go home. I'll be back in the morning."

With the ale jug on the table, I sit back down.

"Fine. Explain," I say, with an inviting gesture.

"How much do you know of what's been happening on the Continent?" he asks.

"I had other things on my mind," I reply. "I barely know what's going on outside Londin."

This is not strictly true, at least not anymore. As the band of Iutes grew stronger and richer, Beormund and I were able to start sending out patrols beyond the city walls. We even managed to provide some assistance to Hengist in his war with Wortimer, in supplies, reconnaissance and a few trained warriors. I also tried to contact Pefen's Saxons in the South, though so far to no avail.

But Frankia, Gaul and other realms across the sea might as well be beyond the Great Ocean. The only news I've heard in the recent months were Church appointments related to me by Fastidius.

"At the beginning of the year, the Huns crossed the Rhenum and entered Gaul, burning the fields and pillaging the cities. Just after the Pentecost, *Dux* Aetius gathered a great army of all of Rome's allies at a field called Maurica, and defeated the Scourge that was plaguing all the peoples of Earth," says Ambrosius, with a poetic flourish which tells me he must have received the news from some literate nobleman, or a priest, from Gaul. "The Huns have been thrown back beyond the Rhenum. The great war that forced your people to abandon their land is over."

I stare at the ale in my cup, stunned by his simple words. Twenty-five years ago, the Iutes were so desperate to flee the great movement of peoples that they boarded their wobbly little ships and braved the whale-road in the middle of the storm season. That movement of peoples, that war which encroached on their borders, was, I've learned since, initiated by the arrival of the Huns from the East — the Scourge, the army of horse archers who like a plague of locusts burned and destroyed everything in its wake. We had accepted that the Huns were here to stay, that perhaps Rome would keep them at bay in our lifetime, but the war would never truly end until all land was trodden under the hooves of their small horses.

And now… it's all over? And Rome — won?

"What does it have to do with Wortimer?" I ask, still processing the information.

"All I ever wanted was to bring Rome back to Britannia," he replies. "Or rather, bring Britannia back to Rome. But as long as the Empire was busy warring with the Huns, this was only a dream. Now, I could invite Aetius and his Legions to bring peace and prosperity to all… If it wasn't for Wortimer."

"But I thought Wortimer wanted the same thing."

Ambrosius's face contorts in a grimace of deep disgust. "Wortimer doesn't understand Rome. Just like his father never did. They both think Rome is all about power. About who's stronger, who's richer."

"And isn't it?"

"Rome is more than just military might. Rome is law. It's trade. It's peace."

"It's slavery. It's tax."

"Tax is the price of civilisation, you barbarian!" His face turns red to the tips of his receding hair. "You've seen what happens when we abandon Rome's values!" He waves his hand pointing to the outside of the tavern. I have a feeling he's been through this argument with many others before, that he's angry at his phantom opponents, more than at me. "Chaos. Poverty. Famine. Wortimer doesn't care about any of that. He wants Rome's power to himself, he wants to rule Britannia in its name, to use its money and armies, but not to obey its laws and customs."

"This, I agree with. I can't imagine Wortimer listening to anyone but himself."

"And that's exactly the problem! He's become a tyrant. He's turned Londin against himself, with his obsession of destroying the Iutes. You saw what happened at the Pentecost — the only reason the Mass didn't turn into a full-on riot was because I lent him a centuria of my best Legionnaires to keep the crowd in check."

"Next time, even that might not be enough."

He closes his eyes and calms down.

"So you do understand. And now people think Wortimer *is* Rome. Lord knows he's claimed it himself often enough. And they've come to hate, and fear, both."

"And what about you? What would you do if Rome returned?"

He smiles, weakly. "I would retire in peace," he says. "To a farm in Domnonia, or Armorica… Let others take over. Power is overrated. I hold it to serve my people, to protect them from the dangers of this world, not to grow fat on their riches and labour. You can't take gold into Heaven. Wortigern understood it — that's why I respect him."

"You should've let him stay, then."

"He forced my hand. Turning his entire province against the Church would have been a provocation Aetius could no longer ignore — and there would be a great war. A disaster for us — and it would sap Rome's strength in Gaul just when it was needed to deal with the Huns. This was the opposite of what I wanted. Just like now, Wortimer is doing the opposite of what I had hoped he would do."

"Have you thought of simply not meddling in our affairs ever again? Nothing good ever seems to come from it."

"Look, do you *want* him overthrown or not?"

"Wait a minute," I remember. "Wasn't he supposed to marry your daughter?"

"How do you know about this?" He grows suspicious, but quickly dismisses the thought with a wave. "Nothing came out of it in the end. He lost interest in the marriage, and I wasn't pushing. The alliance was strong enough without it, and my daughter deserved better."

There's something in the way he says it that I don't like. I sense he's hiding the real reason the marriage fell through. But it's not as important now as the other question that bothers me.

"I still don't see why *I* should help *you* in this. If you replace Wortimer with Aetius, or yourself, or some other Roman, how will this change anything for my people? I know what the likes of Germanus thinks about the pagans. Are you telling me *this* has changed since last year, too?"

"I can assure you, Rome would not want another war so shortly after the last one. Now that the Huns are gone, the Iutes, Saxons and Angles would be free to return to their homelands. Or stay here, if they so wished."

"Not as pagans, they wouldn't."

"The army of Aetius was half-pagan. The Vandals, the Goths, the Franks, all fought by Rome's side. The King of the Goths fell and was mourned like a saint throughout the Empire. The Bishops have been silenced by the victory. Germanus himself died last year, and his allies have dispersed. There's a change in the air."

"And how long would this new peace between Christians and pagans last?"

"This, I cannot say," Ambrosius admits. "But ask your Iutes what they would prefer — to keep fighting with Wortimer, or to make peace with Aetius, even if it's a brief one."

I appreciate his honesty. He's as well versed in Rome's history as I am, if not better. He knows the Empire is a fickle master, that a new Imperator could easily reverse any policy of his predecessor, start a new war, send a new army to quash the rebels. But he's right about the Iutes. Even a few months of peace would save us, and help Hengist consolidate his defences, especially now, with another winter just around the corner.

"There's still one thing I don't understand," I say. "Why come to me? You don't need me to defeat Wortimer. If only you and Aetius would stop sending him men and supplies…"

"It's too late for that," says Ambrosius. He leans back and the stool under him wobbles precariously. "We — *I* have let him grow too strong. Wortimer… He's not as good a leader as his father, but he can instil fierce loyalty in his men. He's Wortigern's rightful heir, even the old veterans fight for him willingly. They will man the city walls — and you know how strong those walls are… I don't want the return of Rome to start with blood flowing down the Tamesa."

I let out a chuckle. The irony is delicious. "So instead of having to deal with a reasonable Wortigern, you now have his son in the exact same position — except he's a mad tyrant, with the Church on his side. If only you'd waited a year."

He raises his hands in a shrug of futility and sighs. "We've all made mistakes."

You bastard, I want to scream. Your "mistakes" cost scores of innocent lives. Forced my people to live in tents and sleep in the streets, to fear for their lives and mourn their loved ones. They turned Londin into a sewer of filth and pain. And now you dare to come here and ask me for help?

My knuckles on the ale mug grow white. I hold the outburst in. Here is a chance to kill Wortimer, something I've been waiting for all these months. For this, I would make a deal with the Devil — or God.

"You want me to take him out for you quietly."

"That would be ideal. I will, of course, assist you in any way I can — as long as my involvement remains secret. But you know the city. You know the palace. You have loyal, trained men at your disposal, who owe nothing to Wortimer."

"And I'm a godless heathen, so the sin of murder wouldn't stain my soul."

His silence is confirmation enough.

"How soon do you need to get this done?"

"Before the storm season. Aetius will return his Legions South for winter, and then it will be too late."

This gives me less than a month to prepare and execute the attack… Whatever its nature. I'm still having difficulty envisioning how exactly I am supposed to do what Ambrosius asks of me, even with his assistance. If I knew how to slay Wortimer, I would have done it myself a long time ago.

"Fine," I say. "I'll think about it. I'll give you the answer in a week."

I need to see for myself if what Ambrosius said is true. I find it hard to believe that anyone could stay loyal to Wortimer out of conviction, rather than fear or greed, so I ask Fastidius to take me around the taverns and courts of Londin's central hub, between the *Praetorium* and the Forum, where Wortimer's most loyal subjects are frequent patrons.

I disguise myself as his slave, while Fastidius puts on the simple robes of a village priest. Wortimer himself is unlikely to enter any of these establishments, but I hope none of his father's surviving courtiers recognise my emaciated, grime-covered face.

"They're unlikely to look at a slave at all," Fastidius says. "And even less likely to tell one Saxon from another."

"Those who served under Wortigern would," I reply. "We have to be careful."

He shakes his head. "A lot has changed since you've last been in this part of the city. I'd be more worried about whether they'll let you in at all, even when you're with me."

We reach the Forum first. It is a shadow of its old self; less than a shadow, a faint memory. Wortimer keeps it deliberately empty, preferring a vast, open space as background to a giant statue in the centre, of a man in Roman robes, roughly hewn in marble reclaimed from some old column. I'm guessing the statue is of himself, but it's hard to tell, as the head is not yet finished, and doesn't look like it ever will be. There are maybe a dozen stalls still open, all selling the most basic of goods — simple pots, bread, curds, drab cloth. The prices demanded for these in silver make my eyes water, but most buyers don't come with silver. They only have other items for barter. A lot of what's being sold and bought here appears robbed from abandoned buildings: old cutlery, bits of masonry, lead piping, shards of mosaic, quality bricks or roof tiles. This is where the fruit of our nightly plunder ends up, after we sell it to the Briton barterers. The city is being slowly sold to the countryside for food, piece by piece. I imagine a local village chief, somewhere beyond the marshes spreading just outside the Wall, decorating his straw-thatched hut with pieces of old Roman glory: a bronze candlestick, exchanged for a leg of lamb; a marble statue sold for a basket of eggs.

I can no longer watch this. Somehow, the plight of the city moves me more than the plight of my fellow Iutes. Is this how Londin dies? Teary-eyed, I tell Fastidius to get us out of here. He leads me to a small inn attached to the wall of Saint Peter's chapel. I recognise the building, though not the establishment itself.

"Wasn't this a cobbler's shop once?" I ask the barmaid. She gives me a look you give a turd which suddenly speaks.

"Yeah, it was. What's it to you?"

"Just wondering what happened to it."

"People don't buy new shoes, is what happened," she says and turns around so fast the ale mug in her hand spills its contents all over my tunic.

"Don't ask too many questions," says Fastidius. "When was the last time you saw the Forum? This place hasn't been a cobbler's shop for years. Not everything that's gone wrong was Wortimer's fault."

"Then why are we here?"

"Wait and listen. They're bound to come sooner or later."

"Who's *they*?"

He puts his fingers to his lips and gestures at the bowl before me. The food here is the only thing worse than the ale; a pale imitation of the Saxon stew, but with even less meat and herbs in it than what we eat in the Iutish camp. The bread is rock-hard, and it would only have salt if I cried on it. To force myself to eat this, I remember the days of captivity in Wortimer's dungeon and the hunger that I felt back then.

"Did Wortimer really believe I died in his prison, I wonder?" I ask between the bites.

"He didn't, at first," replies Fastidius. "For a while, he was furious, certain some noble, secretly still loyal to Wortigern, must have helped you. He even came to me demanding that I let him search the Cathedral."

"And did you?"

"Of course not. The Church is a sanctuary. You're not the only one of Wortimer's enemies disguised as my servant."

"The Iute hostage you sent to lure us…" I guess. He nods and raises his finger again, this time pointing to the door.

A couple of drunk louts enter, singing a loud, rude song. They both wear red padded leather jackets and armbands of Wortimer's army.

"Drinks are on me!" shouts one of them. "Today we celebrate a great victory!"

One of the patrons looks up from his mug, red-eyed. "Oh? And what village full of women and children did you decimate this time?"

The soldiers stagger up to him. The shouty one raises his fist. "Mark your words, Saxon-lover! If I wasn't in such good mood, I'd give you a handful."

The patron stands up — he's a tough-looking, broad-shouldered Briton, at least a foot taller than the soldiers. A short Legionnaire's sword hangs at his belt. He throws a bronze coin on the table and wraps a crimson cloak around his shoulders: an officer, then.

"We're the ones fighting the real battles. All you do is mop up the survivors. I'm sick of your *Dux* taking all the credit."

Wortimer's soldiers glare after him as he leaves, then turn to the others and laugh.

"Don't listen to him, lads. These Westerners are all talk. They don't fight for God, like us — all they care about is plunder and slaves. And they make good slaves, these pagans, eh? This one knows what I'm talking about." He winks at Fastidius, who smiles feebly. "Hey, don't I know you from somewhere, *pater*?"

"I doubt it," Fastidius replies, putting on his best Northern accent. "I've just come from Werlam to hear about your *Dux*'s glorious victories over the heathens."

"Ha-ha, you've come to the right place, then. We know all about it. We've been with Wortimer since his victory at the Medu Ford!"

I fight the urge to look up. I stare at the table in contrition, like a good slave should.

"Oh, tell me more," Fastidius prods.

What follows is a tale of fantasy; a fanciful retelling of the battle at the Medu Ford in which Catigern died and Pascent, I and the others were taken captive by young Aelle. In this new version, Wortimer is the one to ride to our rescue instead of Hengist; Horsa and Catigern die fighting each other; Aelle is reduced to a minor nuisance. I'm not in the story at all, and neither is Fulco.

They are good storytellers, I must admit — much better than they would be fighters, judging by their scrawny muscles. Even I feel myself drawn into their story, wondering how many lies they can weave into one tale. The other patrons gather around our table, listening with their jaws dropped as the men describe Wortimer's valour. They end their story with a piety-inspiring flourish — Wortimer burying his brother and making a vow to God to do everything in his power to avenge the deaths of the Christian martyrs.

"And he's been doing so ever since," the storyteller ends. "Truly, he is a living saint. Just think of the many churches he's built. And with your help, soon he will be able to wipe the pagans from the land their vile Princess stole from Wortigern. Am I right, *pater*?"

"We pray for the success of his endeavour daily in Werlam," says Fastidius, still with the same weak smile. "As we do for the victories of our *Comes*, Elasio."

The soldier frowns in confusion at the mention of Elasio. He scratches his head, thinking of a comeback. "Yes, Elasio is our great friend and ally, of course... But you'll need to do more than pray. We need money for weapons and armour, food for our warriors."

"I wouldn't know anything about that, kind sir," replies Fastidius. "My village church is only a small and poor one. Nothing quite like the great churches your lord has been building."

The admission of poverty makes the soldiers lose interest. They turn to the rest of the gathering. One of them starts another tale of battle — in which, to my astonishment, I recognise an equally fictitious retelling of the Battle of Crei — while the other begins to gather whatever valuables the patrons have to offer, "for the support of the holy cause".

We pay for the ale and food, and leave before the collection platter reaches our table.

"I don't think I saw either of them at the Medu Ford," I tell Fastidius.

"You wouldn't have seen them in any of the battles," he replies. "They're actors from the Londin Theatre. The tall one was a passable Pamphilus only a few years ago. As you can imagine, there's not much work in theatre these days — unless you're an executioner."

"And people are buying this? All these battles and skirmishes happened within our lifetimes. Everyone should still remember what happened."

"How many people know what really happened at the Medu? How many warriors from Crei are willing to tell of their defeat when they can boast of a victory?" Fastidius pauses to leap over a gutter overflowing with sewage. "And it's not just actors telling stories in inns. Wortimer has chroniclers writing it all down, and sending copies to all his neighbours, to the North and even across the sea. I had priests from Armorica write to me asking about the names of the fallen for their prayers."

"What was that about a *vile princess*? Do they mean Rhedwyn?"

"They say she seduced Wortigern and forced him to give land to the Iutes. But I wouldn't worry. It's one of the new stories; I don't think it will last for long."

I shake my head in disbelief. "That big man — he was one of Ambrosius's, wasn't he?"

"Yes, but you'd be hard pressed to hear anything about them taking part in Wortimer's war. Everything now is about the folk of Londin. It makes them proud to take part in something, something bigger than their own sorry existence."

"And what do you think about it?" I ask, as we stop to make way for a passing cart. "All this talk of pagans and God. Sounds like something you should support, as a Bishop."

He's silent until the Cathedral Hill comes into view, then sighs. "As a Bishop, I have no choice. I insist on baptising the Iutes instead of killing them, and take as many converts as I can into my service, but there's little else I can do. Rome would send someone worse in my place if I opposed Wortimer and Ambrosius openly."

The Cathedral looms over our heads as we climb the hill. He stops and turns south, towards the Wall, the river, and the lands beyond it. "I am a man of Rome now, brother. I serve its interests. And God's."

"Do you want it to come back?"

"Whatever God wills, will happen"

"It's not exactly a ringing endorsement."

"Everyone who wants Rome's return imagines it as something different. Wortimer thinks of it as power and money. For Ambrosius, it's laws and trade. But all I care about is salvation of souls, and for this, all the Rome I need is in this building," he says, pointing to the Cathedral. "But tell me, in all honesty, having seen what you've seen today — can things get any worse than they are now?"

"Not for you and your flock, maybe. But what about the Saxons and the Iutes?"

"If they choose Christ, Rome will do all in its power to help them. But if they stay heathens… Then they are your responsibility, brother, not mine."

He smiles, but the smile is cold. I feel a chasm opening between us, as if the street itself was torn apart by a spasm of earth. I wonder, have I committed one sin too many for him to stand? I'm certain my confessions shook him more than he was willing to show.

"That's not what Ambrosius told me," I point out.

"Ambrosius is not a priest. I have my duty to God."

"Who should I listen to?"

"Listen to what your heart tells you to."

"My heart tells me to kill Wortimer first and worry about the politics and religion later."

This takes him aback. He may be a Bishop now, but I can sense deep down he's still as innocent as the boy he was in Ariminum. I've been surrounded by death and suffering for so long I forgot there are still people like him, who've never so much as harmed anyone in their lives.

"You know I can't endorse this murder," he says. "My conscience will not bear it. And neither should yours."

"Not even a monster like Wortimer?"

"He's still a man and his soul is immortal, like everyone else's."

"I've killed before, you know."

He winces. He doesn't like being reminded of the world he has to live in. "Not like this. Not in cold blood, unprovoked."

"Is there a difference?"

He looks away.

We reach the steps of the Cathedral. "Is this the answer I should give Ambrosius?" he asks.

"Yes. I'll do it. Not for his sake, but for mine. But first, he'll have to do something to prove his honesty."

Even if I am not able to kill Wortimer, I might try to get something worth my while out of this deal.

"More violence, I'm guessing."

"You can try to pray Wortimer away, *Bishop*," I reply. "And I'll try my way. We'll see who's right."

The Saxon Might

CHAPTER V
THE LAY OF MYRTLE

"Here they come."

Beormund nods in the direction of the enemy. From our observation post at the roof of a half-crumbled four-storey tenement, we can see their arrival marked by the line of fires burned through the huts of the Poor Town. A crowd of panicked civilians, beggars, paupers, and petty thieves floods the narrow streets towards our lines. The Iutes pull away the carts to open a passage in the barricades, but we only let the first wave through. Then the carts move back in place. Those who didn't make it, will need to find another way to safety.

An entire cohort is heading our way, if the patrols are to be believed. Five hundred men, split into centuries, just like in the old war manuals. But they are far from the Legionnaires of old. Only Ambrosius's men, less than a third of the entire force, wear any armour and carry shields and spears. The rest are all street fighters, brawlers, bandits gathered by Wortimer from all over the city with a promise of plunder and pay. The Briton gangs are all here, our old enemies in the robbing business, hoping to stake a claim on our territory.

That they have come in such force is bad news, not for us here in Londin but for those fighting for survival outside. Wortimer must be feeling confident to sacrifice so much of his force on dealing with a band of robbers. The last I heard from Hengist's *fyrd*, they were fighting in the marshes around Dorowern, holding on to the last mainland bridgeheads guarding the approach to Tanet. Aelle's Saxons retreated deep into Andreda, barring all approaches to the coast, especially Pefen's fortress in Anderitum. In the North, it is Elasio who's been making more progress against the Angles than Wortimer, but though they may be rivals in the Council, they are allies in this particular battle so it's no consolation. With his flanks secure, Wortimer can afford to halt his operations beyond the Wall to bring peace to his own city — not for the sake of its citizens, but his own wounded ego.

"If only he knew I was here," I say as the column of smoke approaches, "he'd send all his army to fight us, not just this rabble."

"This rabble is enough to wipe us out, if you're wrong," replies Beormund.

"I'm not wrong."

I hope he can't sense how little confidence there is in my voice. I have no idea whether I can trust Ambrosius and his men to hold their end of the bargain. I fear not for myself — if this is how I am destined to die, so be it. I accepted my death a long time ago, in Wortimer's dungeons; everything since then is a borrowed life. But the Iutes who serve under me and Beormund do not deserve to be victims of my foolishness.

It's too late to escape now, and there is nowhere *to* escape to, with the city gates locked down until the battle is over. Wortimer has us trapped between his army and the Wall. There was always a risk we would end up like this, as soon as we'd grown strong enough for him to no longer be able to ignore us. We've been making ourselves ready for this battle for weeks — and still, I fear it might not be enough, if my hope is misplaced.

The head of the cohort reaches within a spear-throw of the first Iutish barricade. The river of Wortimer's men splits into four streams, each flooding down one of the main streets which come from four directions to meet in the middle of the Iute territory. The streets of the Poor Town, bordered with piles of rubble and waste, would make for ideal ambush points — if only we had enough men to spare for each of the approaches; but we are outmanned and outmanoeuvred by the sheer number of the attackers. Focused defence is our only hope.

The skirmishers pull back behind the barricades, their missiles exhausted. Each side measures the other's worth, jeering and throwing obscene gestures at one another. I search for Wortimer among the warriors, but as expected, he's nowhere to be seen.

"Why is the coward not here?" Beormund asks, as if reading my mind.

He doesn't know the details of my bargain with Ambrosius, only that it is somehow related to Wortimer's incoming assault. I told him and the Iutes just enough to prepare our warriors for what was coming. They trusted me enough to not ask any more questions.

"I hear he's never led a battle again after Crei," I reply. "It scared him too much. He's always in a *villa* somewhere, far from the fighting. I bet he's in the Governor's Palace, right now, feasting and humping some slave girl."

"Pity. I would welcome a chance to plunge my spear into his heart even if it was the last thing I did. Maybe we *should* have told him you were here."

I smile, doubtfully. Wortimer's grown too suspicious to show himself in the open like this, even for what appeared like a decisive victory. Ambrosius admitted I was not the first to whom they reached out for help with killing the tyrannical *Dux*. With each failed attempt, Wortimer's distrust grew. He moved only from one fortified *villa* to another. Even his own men now rarely get to see him, always from a distance, always surrounded by a retinue of well-paid Gothic bodyguards. With the war going in his favour, his presence on the battlefield is no longer necessary, so he leaves command to Brutus, his most loyal commander, with him since the campaign in Saffron Valley.

One of Brutus's officers now barks an order, and a column of Briton warriors charges at the southern barricade. The same action repeats to our north. Wortimer's brutes are in front, with Ambrosius's Legionnaires holding the rear in case of an ambush. The barricades, built of overturned carts, sacks of bricks, shards of big oil amphorae and other refuse, hold, barely. The fighters on both sides are armed only with the primitive weapons of bandits and rebel serfs — clubs, flails, kitchen knives — so a breakthrough here is unlikely.

"The main assault will come from the west," I say, pointing to the bulk of the cohort, still halted in front of the third of the blockades. "You'd better go."

Beormund nods. As a chieftain, his place is with his men, in the heat of the battle. I'm his strategist, like Fastidius was once mine, and my duty is here, at the observation post in the centre of the battlefield, sending out runners with orders, as necessary. For now, the Iutes are doing fine without my intervention. The pressure on the northern and southern barricades slackens, and for a moment I fear my warriors are *too* crafty. For the ruse to work, I need the battle to be going against us. What if Wortimer's band proves so incompetent, the Iutes defeat them on their own?

But I needn't worry. The charge against the western barricade starts in earnest, and here Wortimer's officers are throwing his best men. The first blockade falls in a matter of minutes. Beormund orders a retreat to the second line. I turn to the east — here, the fourth and last branch of the attack moves up and probes our defences, but only just enough to tie up the Iutes here from helping their comrades in the west. My attention returns to the main assault. The second line holds, but the Britons spread out and climb over the rubble of the demolished *insulae*, to flank the barricade. I send out an order: retreat to the third, and last, line of defence.

Now the battle will be decided. The third line is crucial. Not just because there is nowhere to fall beyond it — but because reaching it is the signal for Ambrosius.

I count the excruciating seconds from when the first of Wortimer's warriors climb onto the third western barricade, throwing stones and javelins over, wrestling with the Iute shieldmaidens, parrying the blows of the clubs and maces. How long will it take before Ambrosius's commanders realise it's time to give their orders? I count to thirty. Still nothing. Sweat trickles down my forehead as I reach a full minute. The Iute line begins to falter. I order some of the men from the northern and southern approaches to move to reinforce this last stand, even if it means they, too, have to retreat to their respective rear lines. A minute and a half.

A whistle sounds out in the west. Then another to the south, the north and, finally, in the east.

Ambrosius's soldiers drop their spears and draw their long cavalry swords. They are more use in close combat — and there is no closer combat than having to stab your comrades-in-arms in their backs.

Death and chaos spread faster than the panic. It takes time for the head of the column to notice what's going on at their rear guard. When they do, it's too late. The slaughter is one-sided. On my order, the Iutes push forth from the barricades. Now is the time for those hidden in ambush to spring from their hiding places. Raven and his fellow hunters pop up on the roofs, picking out the fleeing enemy with their arrows; young, green warriors leap out from under the rubble, their task — to make sure that not one of Wortimer's roughs escapes to bring word of the betrayal to the palace.

Blood flows down the narrow streets so deep, Ambrosius's men are slipping in it. They hack and slash their way through the enemy from one side; the Iutes smash and club from the other. I climb down from my post and run into the brawl. I reach the front line just as the two sides meet in the middle, the tall pile of dismembered bodies between them.

"Stop!" I cry in Iutish. "Enough!"

The warriors halt, their arms still raised to strike. They eye Ambrosius's soldiers suspiciously. The same order is repeated three times on other sides of the battlefield. Slowly, the fighting quietens down. Only twanging of bows and short cries of agony mark the deaths of fleeing marauders.

An officer, clad in a purple cloak, steps forward from the ranks of Ambrosius's men. He wipes blood from under his shiny brass helmet. He looks at me with a grim, unforgiving expression. I know him — I fought with him against the Picts, on the Iken beach. I'm glad to see he decided to throw his lot with Ambrosius, rather than stay with Wortimer. That was a tough, but glorious struggle, worthy of song. The battle we just fought brought neither of us any joy or glory.

"Are you satisfied, Iute?" he asks.

He may have even fought at Saffron Valley. If so, like me, he must appreciate the bitter irony of Britons betraying other Britons to aid the same Iutes they stabbed in the back seven years ago.

I look around. Moans of the dying fill the air, silenced by whacks of clubs on skulls as the younger Iutes finish off the wounded. My boots are soaked with blood. The tenement walls are splattered with it up to the ground floor windows. The entire slaughter couldn't have lasted more than ten minutes.

How easy it is to kill.

"Yes," I reply. "Tell your *Dux* I will do what he wants."

How did my life lead me to this?

The thought distracts me as I plunge into the raven-black, ice-cold, sludge-like waters of the Tamesa. The darkness is absolute, as if the world had disappeared, leaving me alone in the abyss, the nothingness. I am surrounded by a distinct *lack*

— a lack of light, lack of sound, lack of any sensation other than cold. Am I still alive, or have I died already? There seems to be no difference between the two states. My only connection to the world of the living is the bank of *caementicium* I touch with my right hand as I swim alongside it.

Somewhere around here there's an opening of a sewer leading from the fountains in the Governor's Palace gardens. It's hidden under water during the highest of tides. There are only two days in a month when it happens, one at Full Moon, one at New Moon. The Full Moon is in two weeks — I cannot wait that long, especially since this is only a reconnaissance mission before the real strike.

At least, I hope the opening is still there. I studied the pipes and connections linking the defunct ponds and fountains in the *Praetorium* for many bored evenings, as I waited for Rhedwyn to arrive to our reading and writing lessons. I even tried to make some of the hydraulics work again, but the muck and sediment had grown too thick, the sluices rotted through, the siphons broken apart. Only the main sewer was kept clean by the gardener, to prevent flooding of the palace during the great summer storms. Would Wortimer have still bothered with such details?

My fingers feel like icicles, tracking the cracked *caementicium*, searching for the opening. I can't stay in this freezing water too long; I feel life and warmth seep out of me with every passing second. Something slimy touches my leg. I hope it's an eel. My teeth chatter so loud I fear I will attract the attention of a guard, but there are no guards out in this cold, windy night.

At last, a hole. I touch around. It's the correct size. A slightly warmer current flows out of it. I touch metal, and panic. An iron grate spans the breadth of the outlet. I can't remember if it was there before, or is it a new addition? I grab the bars, press my feet to the *caementicium* and pull. The iron grinds on stone. I rub my fingers and take a sniff: the layer of rust is thick; the metal flakes away in my hands. I take a breath, dive under, grab, pull. I swim out, take another breath, and pull again. My feet slip on the *caementicium*; the rough texture shreds my soles. I'm losing my breath, I'm losing my strength. I pull one last time with all my remaining power and this time, something snaps. The weathered stone crumbles, the rusted-through iron cracks, and the bars fall away. I throw them aside and emerge, gasping.

I kick my feet and dive into the now open channel. I don't remember how long the sewer is. In the darkness, in the cold, with my arms and legs touching the walls of the sewer with each stroke, fear sets in. *What was I thinking?* Was this really the best plan I could come up with? Unlike most Iutes, I'm a bad swimmer — Loudborne was never deep enough to learn, and there was never much reason to swim in the Tamesa other than to cool myself down in the summer. Even if I get to the other side, what if somebody sees me? I have asked Ambrosius to arrange a meeting with Wortimer tonight, so that all the guards would be busy in the main wing of the palace, but there's always a chance someone ventures into the gardens for a night stroll...

I move slowly. I don't know how much time passes in the tunnel. My chest tightens, my limbs grow heavy. In my mind, I regress to the last time I was this long under water. I'm three again, gasping for air, seeing my father and mother disappear in the stormy depths. My lungs hurt just like then. The tidal water tastes the same as the ocean. Bubbles of air slip from my lips against my will. I see nothing, I feel nothing. I'm dying. I see a ray of light at the end of the sewer. I hear an angel, somewhere in the distance, a beautiful voice singing a tragic, solemn dirge. For some reason, the angel sings in Iutish.

I know this song. My mother used to sing it to me and Rhedwyn, back in the village in the Old Country…

I follow the light and reach the surface, splurting, coughing, wheezing. The light is that of a single oil lamp hanging from a tripod. Beside it, on the stone bank of the fountain pond, sits the singing angel, clad in a green dress, her golden hair flowing in long tresses down her shoulders. Startled by my appearance, she stops the song and leaps to her feet. She hides behind a rose bush and watches me clamber out onto the bank, panting and flailing, like a washed-out, dying seal.

The first thing I notice in the flame of the oil lamp is how well tended the palace gardens are. The grass is freshly mown and weeded. The flower bushes are trimmed into fanciful shapes. The trees are pruned. Thin rays of candlelight seeping from the palace windows carve flickering slices of golden and amber leaves out of the darkness. The state of the garden is the exact reverse of the state of the city beyond its walls. It reflects the crucial difference between Wortimer and his father. While Wortigern tended to the city and its people, he abandoned the gardens. His son did the opposite.

She moves out from behind the rose bush gingerly. She calls my name; her voice wavers. I recognise the voice, and the face — but her body has changed. The green dress clings tightly to her form, her taut shoulders, full breasts, rounded hips — and a swollen belly.

[114]

I try to stand, and sway into her arms. She helps me sit down on the edge of the fountain. Her touch is cold, mechanical. Up close, I see now that her face has changed, too. She's grown older than her years, wearier. Her skin is grey and saggy; her eyes have no glimmer to them.

"Is it really you?" she asks. She touches my face as if she was blind.

"It's me." I reach out to her hand, but she pulls away. A shadow flickers across her face.

"I've waited. So long. He said you were dead, but I didn't believe him. But you never came."

"I — I didn't know you were here."

"Where else would I be?"

I'm ashamed to find no answer. I had a year to find her, since escaping Wortimer's prison. I should have found a way. I should have tried harder. I never even tried to spy into the palace before. Did I really *want* to find her…?

I stare at her tired face, her heavily pregnant body. I still love her. I still *want* her. And I'm afraid of it.

"The child —" I start. I touch her bump. She shudders under my hand. "Whose…?"

I don't need to finish the question.

"It's *mine*," she replies.

"Did he — did he force himself upon you?"

She scoffs. "Can a king force himself on one of his subjects? He demanded me and I obeyed. Time and time again."

She looks straight into my eyes as she says it. She wants me to feel her shame and humiliation. She wants me to know that while I could have been humping as many Iutish girls I wanted, she had to endure Wortimer's slobbery lust, for weeks, for months — and all because he promised he would keep me alive in the prison cell. I turn away, unable to stand her stare.

"You really didn't know I was here?"

"I had no idea," I reply. "Nobody knew what happened to you after Callew."

She scoffs again. "For a moment, I thought you'd come to save me. Not that it would change anything... But if you're not here for me, then why —" Her eyes widen in realisation. "You're here to *kill* him," she whispers. "Did Ambrosius sent you? Are you running his errands now?"

"How did you...?"

"He's been sending his assassins here since the Pentecost. Wortimer's too stupid to notice who's behind all those attempts on his life. So now he's hoping you can succeed where all others have failed..."

"Not today," I say. "Today I was only testing the route."

There's something deeply absurd about our conversation. I dreamed about meeting her again, touching her, smelling her. I imagined this moment so many times. But I never thought what we would talk about would be murder.

"I can get you out of here," I say. "The sewer — it's big enough for both of us, I think, and…"

She touches my hand. *At last.*

"You can't kill him," she says. A glint returns to her eyes, but I don't recognise it.

"What are you saying? Of course I can — and I will!"

"No, be quiet, you stupid boy, and listen. You can't kill him — because *I* have to kill him. I am the one he's made suffer the most."

She pushes me gently back onto the fountain's edge. "Help me do this, and then we can escape."

"It's too dangerous for you."

"And it's *impossible* for you. Why do you think so many assassins have failed? He's crafty and cautious. He almost never comes here to the *Praetorium* anymore, always hiding, always moving. I'm the only one he's ever alone with. I'm the only one who knows where he's spending the night. He thinks he broke me — he thinks he's safe with me. I will only get one chance, if that — but it's one more chance than you, or anyone else, will ever get."

"It's not your task. I agreed to do it. I will not have a sin of murder on your conscience."

"*Sin?* Don't talk to me about *sin*." Her words and her eyes cut me like a slap. "I would be ridding the world of a demon. I'll be doing God a favour."

I try to argue more, but she silences me, laying her hand on my mouth.

"You know you can't out-argue me if I put my mind to something... *Aeric.*"

I look up, startled.

"You — you knew?"

Light vanishes from her eyes. "Then it's true."

I freeze. My head spins. An odd booming sound fills the air. It takes me a moment to realise it's my own blood, pumping in my ears.

"I started remembering things..." she starts, slowly. "After we talked — piecing memories together... The rune stone you told me about — you being on Eobba's boat — your strange behaviour at Sorbiodun... I realised you must've found something out."

"I'm... I'm sorry."

She scoffs. "What are you to be sorry about? I wasn't some virtuous maiden seduced against her will. I wanted you just as much as you wanted me. How could we have known?"

"I should've realised sooner."

"There was nothing you could have done. It wasn't your fault."

Her words make sense, but they don't *feel* right. Yes, it wasn't my fault — just like it wasn't my fault that Aelle attacked us on Medu River. It wasn't my fault that Wortimer betrayed us at Callew. And it wasn't my fault that we have committed, unwittingly, the worst atrocity two people could commit... Fastidius wouldn't even absolve me of the sin, refusing to acknowledge its severity. I was alone with it — or I have been, until now...

I'd say she seems to be taking the revelation well, but she's had almost a year to come to terms with it. I haven't been with her to see her suffer. I can't know how many nights she wailed and cursed me. Still, her calm makes me uneasy. Perhaps I *am* making too much of an issue of it? Perhaps compared to what happened to her in Wortimer's captivity, our transgression was too insignificant to wallow in it in fruitless melancholy...

"We're wasting our time," she says. "He will leave the palace soon." I see the haughty pride of a Princess of the Iutes return to her blazing eyes. Her stern voice brooks no refusal. No matter what I say, she will not heed me. I am no *Dux*, no warchief. I'm only her older brother.

"Just provide me with the means to destroy him, and he'll be gone."

"How would you even do it? Stab him with a hidden dagger? Put poison in his drink?"

She grabs both my shoulders. "Poison, yes. Something only the Romans would know how to make. Something that kills slowly and painfully. I want to see him suffer."

Her sudden passion fills me with dread. This is the first time I recognise the expression on her face — it is the same face she made when she was under me, only now it's a grimace of hatred, rather than love. I dread to think what Wortimer did to her to provoke such loathing.

I give in to this passion. I see it's far greater than anything I could muster.

"Yes, I will give you the poison," I say. "Give me two weeks, by the next Full Moon…"

"No!" She almost cries, then remembers we need to be stealthy. "It's too early."

"Too early for what?"

"For this," she replies, patting her belly. "In a month, the child will be born. I can't do anything until then."

"A month is too long. I promised Ambrosius —"

"A pox on Ambrosius!" she snarls. "This has nothing to do with him. He's a liar, like all of them. You can't trust a *wealh*. Trust only your own kin."

A voice comes from the direction of the palace, and a rustling of feet. Somebody's entered the garden path.

"Go away, now." She pushes me towards the cold abyss of the fountain pool. For a moment, her face turns gentle and soft. Her eyes fill with tears.

"If only we could have started again," she whispers. "My dear brother. My beloved."

"We will," I assure her. "Once all this is over… I'll figure it out, somehow."

"Stop it. I've had enough of your promises."

The voice calls for her, an old guard or servant, lost in the maze of shrubs. She steps back and throws the tripod with the lamp into the pond with a shriek of feigned fear. Darkness falls around us like a thick, black blanket. I feel her hands around me and, for the briefest of moments, her lips, salty with tears, on my lips.

"At next Full Moon," I whisper quickly.

"I'll be here."

Ambrosius stands up to greet me. I punch him in the face.

"You knew!" I yell, lifting him up from the floor by the collar. "You knew she was there!"

It took me until emerging back out on Tamesa's shore to connect the dots in what Rhedwyn was saying. She knew Ambrosius; she must have seen him, or even talked to him while she was in Wortimer's captivity.

"Who else knew? Does Fastidius know? Are you both in this together?"

The door to the tavern's back door bursts open. Ambrosius's bodyguards fall in, wrestling with my men in the doorway. I let him go, and he gestures his soldiers to stand down.

"I see you've met the girl," he says, wiping blood from his lips. He picks up the overturned stool and waits for both squads of guards to leave us alone.

"Why didn't you tell me?"

"You know very well why not. Think about it."

I pause. My fists, still clenched, shake.

"You thought I'd try to rescue her instead of killing Wortimer," I say.

"Frankly, I'm surprised you didn't."

"She didn't want to leave."

"Is it because she's with child?"

You know this, too?

I explain what Rhedwyn wants from us. He frowns and shakes his head.

"I'd much rather entrust this matter to you than some pregnant girl."

"She's worth ten men like me. And a hundred men like you."

"What if she changes her mind? What if she grows afraid for her child?"

I glare at him. My fist rises again of its own accord and he flinches, fearing another blow.

"If she says she'll do it, she'll do it."

"And will she make it in time before the storms start?"

"Yes," I lie.

Rhedwyn is right. The Britons can't be trusted. I don't care about Aetius and his Legions; I don't care about Rome. If she needs two months to finish off Wortimer, she will have it. And then together we'll... I haven't planned this far yet. Maybe we will live a chaste, sinless life in the Tanet monastery, raising her child. Nobody needs to know we're brother and sister. Maybe we could move to Armorica, like so many Briton nobles have been doing lately.

"It will be costly to procure the required poison in such short time," he says. This surprises me. Of all the people in Britannia, Ambrosius was the last one I suspected of *milli*-pinching.

"I'm sure you can manage a vial or two with your connections."

"I may not have as much money as you think. This war, and two years of bad harvest, have cost me dearly."

At least this explains why he had to resort to hiring me to kill Wortimer. He can no longer afford paid assassins.

"Are you saying you can't do it?"

He wrings his hands. "I'm just saying, this better work as you promise. I may not be able to help you again. I'm running out of time. If we fail, or take too long, I will have to retreat to Corin and forget about this entire misadventure."

Works for me. *The sooner you go away, the better, you whore's son.*

"You have until Sunday, if I'm to make it before the Full Moon," I say. "And make sure it kills slowly."

I find her deeper inside the garden, by a small, withered tree with fragrant leathery leaves and black berries, frost-dried on its boughs. She's wearing a simple dress of undyed linen today, one that wouldn't look improper on a slave. Her face is expressionless as she greets me.

"Do you have it?"

I take the small clay bottle from the leather pouch I kept tied to my chest as I dived into the sewer. Carefully, I place it in her hand, but do not let go yet.

"It's a tincture of wolfsbane and white hellebore," I say. "The Armorican herbalist who prepared it said it would make a man beg for death for hours."

"Perfect."

[124]

She looks at the bottle with the same gleam in her eyes she used to have when looking at me: lustful, eager. She wraps her fingers around the clay as if it was a part of a lover's body. I hold back.

"Are you sure of this?" I ask. "I can still do it for you."

"Give it to me."

She yanks the bottle out of my hand and hides it into her bosom.

"I don't want you to get hurt," I say.

"I cannot be hurt any more. I am beyond hurt. The only thing that can help me now is watching him die screaming in a pool of his own vomit."

She scowls and bends in pain. I hold her from falling.

"What is it?"

She raises her head. She's smiling. "She's kicking. She wants out."

She takes my hand and puts it on her stomach. I feel her insides jerk and churn under the taut skin. I feel sick, thinking a spawn of Wortimer is within my Rhedwyn, but she doesn't seem to mind. It's clear that the unborn child is one of the only two things she yet cares about in this world. The other — the little clay bottle of poison.

"How do you know it's a she?" I ask.

"A mother knows," she replies with a mysterious smile. But the smile is gone as soon as it appears. "It is not my first."

I make a quick calculation in my head. Is this another child of mine I didn't know about?

"You mean we — I —"

She shakes her head. "It was another one of *his*." The way she says it sounds like the hissing of a snake. "He made me drink pennyroyal to get rid of it. That was back when he still hoped to marry Ambrosius's daughter. A bastard half-pagan was not a helpful thing to have." She scoffs. "He doesn't care about any of that now, so he's letting me keep her. God knows why."

Her gaze turns to the withered tree. She caresses its leathery leaves with a tender touch.

"I will name her Myrtle," she says.

"Myrtle?"

"It's what this tree is called. It was brought into this garden from a far-away land, a long time ago. It doesn't thrive in this climate. It's shrivelled and weak. But it endures, and stays forever green."

She picks a leaf and rubs it between her fingers. The sweet fragrance fills the air. "It never gave up."

A distant voice of a night watchman calls the sixth hour.

[126]

"You have to go," she says, with a sudden urgency in her voice. "He'll be calling for me soon."

The thought of Wortimer spending the night with her right after our meeting fills me with rage. I reach for the long knife in my boot. "Let me go at him," I say. "I will kill him right now. This could all be over in a minute."

"You'd be dead the moment you stepped into the palace. Please, go. I will be fine. I always am."

She puts her fingers to my chest. Her lips are a narrow, determined slit.

"When can I come see you again?"

"You mustn't," she says. "Not while he's alive. He's becoming suspicious already. It's grown too cold for me to stay in the garden in the evenings... And he doesn't like it. He says it reminds him too much of you. He used to watch us, you know."

I feel sick at the thought and look towards the palace windows. I think I see a silhouette in the faint candle flame, but it could just be a trick of the light.

"What if you fail? What if it's the last time I see you?"

She caresses my cheek. "Be grateful for what you have, dear brother. Every time we saw each other could have been our last." A sad smile darkens her face. "In the end, what we did didn't matter."

"What do you mean?"

"Nothing about our lives would have gone differently if we were of different blood, or if we stayed chaste. Wortimer would still tear us apart. All this —" She gestures around the garden. "— still would have happened."

"Maybe the gods are punishing us."

She laughs a short, bitter laugh. "The gods don't care for the likes of us. I prayed every day for their mercy. They never listened."

"They might yet."

She looks at me with pity, mixed with scorn. Though she's the younger of the two of us, there is wisdom of pain in her eyes that defies her age. "Yes, they might," she says; but it's obvious to me she's no longer capable of hope.

She turns and starts walking away.

"Wait," I stop her. "Isn't there anything else I can do to help you?"

"He drinks a lot when he's nervous," she says, not looking back. "Make him nervous."

I need to buy her time. A month is not enough — Rhedwyn must be strong enough to kill Wortimer, and she can't do it from her birthing bed. I ask Eadgith, telling her I need this information for a tribal judgement. "Two weeks at least before a shieldmaiden can fight, and before the child can survive without its mother, if it's born healthy," she answers, eyeing me with suspicion.

A month and two weeks means waiting until we're deep into the storms season. Aetius and his Legions will have to wait until next year if their invasion is to succeed without too much bloodshed. I can only imagine how mad this must be making Ambrosius. It's easy enough to ignore him; all I need to do is to stay away from the Bull's Head until the coming of winter forces him to leave the city — most of his troops have left already — and return to his own capital. It's the increasingly desperate summonses from Fastidius that are the real challenge to overlook. Fortunately, I don't have time to meet him — I have a new war to deal with.

The disastrous defeat at the Battle of Poor Town may have been enough to goad Wortimer into action against us, but I wasn't going to risk just depending on his ill humour. I used his own methods against him, recruiting a bunch of beggars and thieves from the Poor Town to start spreading nasty rumours in the undercurrent of what's still left of Londin's night life.

"He's scared of the Iutes," I ordered them to tell whoever was willing to listen. "He's all talk. He was supposed to throw them back over the sea, but they struck him in the very heart of the city, right by the Cathedral walls — and won! Maybe their gods *are* stronger than the God of Rome after all?"

I thought of poor Fastidius as I taught the rabble their lines. I hoped the words would reach many of Wortimer's courtiers, just like in the times of the first coup, raising doubts in those less loyal to him, and rousing them against the *Dux*. But that would mean they would also reach Fastidius's ears; he would guess at once who was responsible for the blasphemous allegations. I wondered, would he waste his time trying to fight back the heathenry, or shrug it off, knowing it's all just a ruse?

Whatever Fastidius thought of it, the ruse worked. The Council is incensed and demanding action. Wortimer's fury burns bright. Without Ambrosius's help, he can't afford another frontal attack, but he's determined to make our lives difficult, and to show he can still control what's going on inside his own city.

Beormund, not knowing anything about my plans, summons the *witan* when it is no longer possible to ignore the new wave of attacks. It's been a long time since so many people have gathered under the cracked dome of the abandoned *curia*. Since we're an assortment of Iutes of different clans and villages, of all ages, there are no "elders" here — everyone is free to speak, including the messengers sent from other territories.

"The edges of the Poor Town now burn daily. The raiders strike deep along the main streets, pillaging and raping as they go," says a messenger sent by the Briton homeless to the *witan*.

"The plunderer has become the plundered," somebody remarks wryly.

"He pulled troops from Tanet and Andreda," another messenger reports. This one reached Londin through the old water gate, bringing news from the South. He's looking weary; dried blood clumps the hair on his forehead. "I saw them marching on the way here. Entire columns, a hundred men each."

"We need to fight back," I say. "This time he will try to starve us off, rather than finish in one go. Winter is near. All he has to do to cut us from supplies is to turn the Poor Town against us."

[130]

"We would never do that," protests the Briton delegate. "We remember your generosity throughout last winter."

"We can't demand loyalty from you against your own people," I reply. "We will fight our own war. You just have to stay out of our way."

I feel Beormund's glare on my back. He thinks I have said too much, but he can't admonish me right now — the leadership must show unity before the *witan*. I turn to him and bow.

"If it is decided thus, of course," I say.

He summons me to his side. As the *witan* erupts in a debate, he whispers:

"You're not a chieftain. *I* am the chieftain."

"I'm aware of this."

"Then stop acting like one. You are only my advisor."

"Yes, *chieftain*." I try not to sound sarcastic, but judging by his scowl, I fail.

"I don't know how, but I feel like you're behind all of this. You've been scheming with these *wealas* for too long."

"I assure you, I have nothing to do with them anymore."

"Then why is the Bishop of Londin sending couriers to me every Sunday?"

I raise an eyebrow. "He does? And what do you do with them?"

"I dismiss them without a word. Your days of plotting are over."

I answer nothing, only bow and return to my place in the *witan*. The tribal politics doesn't interest me. All I want is for the war with Wortimer to last long enough for Rhedwyn to make her move. Distracted and agitated, he's bound to get nervous, just like she said, to start making mistakes — and one of those mistakes might be his last.

By nightfall, a decision is made. We will take the fight to Wortimer, just as I proposed. Beormund and I are ordered to prepare an offensive in any way we can: ambushes, traps, raids, whatever it takes to stop the Briton army from encircling us in its deadly embrace. A line of communication must be maintained with the outside world and for this, I suggest — to Beormund's irritation — an attack on one of the city gates.

"It's madness!" he scoffs. "Nobody's ever captured a city gate."

"Not from the outside," I reply. "But we'll be charging from the inside. Wortimer already did it once, and succeeded, during his previous coup."

I omit the fact that Wortimer had men among the guards back then — something we will never have. None of the Iutes present at the *witan* knows enough about the coup to contradict me.

"I may not have your experience in fighting in the *wealh* style, or your learning," admits Beormund, "but I know a doomed plan when I see it."

"That is why they'll never expect us. Think of the element of surprise."

A murmur ripples throughout the *witan*. They are getting impatient — and hungry.

"Why don't we just have a vote on it," I propose.

"Fine." Beormund nods, impatiently. "Let the wisdom of the crowd prevail over the haughtiness of youth."

The Saxon Might

CHAPTER VI
THE LAY OF WORTIMER

Beormund is right, of course. A strike at the Wall is bound to fail. We have no siege weapons, no soldiers trained in siege warfare. Wortimer knows the importance of the gates — they were his first target in the brief conflict against his father. Not only are the gatehouses fully manned, but there are new blockades and checkpoints surrounding each of them with a ring of steel and stone.

We've been fighting Wortimer for almost two months now, launching surprise attacks at his caravans and supply camps, checking his advance into the Poor Town, even going as far as raiding the Forum, plundering and burning the market stalls. But all of this has made little dent in his forces — and caused great losses in ours. A third of our warriors lies either dead, unburied, in the streets of Londin, or wounded in the tents of healing. Our supplies are dwindling, our weapons are blunted and, just as I predicted, the people of the Poor Town are turning against us as the circle of burning huts tightens around the abandoned *curia*; those whom we thought friends are now joining the enemy ranks, for the promise of safety and food. The strike at the city gate is our last hope of reverting the tide of war, or so I've made everyone believe — everyone except Eadgith.

"I know when you're lying," she tells me. "That much hasn't changed since we were kids."

She presents me with a sword she's made with the last of her good iron. It's longer than a *seax*, more the size of a Roman *spatha*, and with a hilt and pommel taken from a Legionnaire's sword; it's light, fast and perfectly balanced. It is, without a doubt, her best work so far. The runic letter A is carved into the blade just above the hilt.

"Whatever your real plan is, I pray it succeeds," she says. "I don't want to die yet."

"Even after everything that happened to you?"

I'm as surprised by my question as she is — I didn't mean to say it out loud.

"You think *I've* had it bad?" she asks. "I'm alive. I'm warm and fed. I've never even been hurt. My child is likely still alive. Most women here have suffered far worse than simply losing their friends and family — and they're the ones fortunate to be alive. Yet you don't hear them complain when we send more of them and their men to die in your little war."

I look away, ashamed. "I'm sorry. That's not what I meant. Of course you want to live. We all do. Otherwise... we wouldn't still be here."

She gives my shoulder a gentle rub and looks me in the eyes. "What's bothering you, really? I've never seen you so distracted before a battle. Are you sure you're in shape to lead men today?"

"Today is as good as any day," I reply with a shrug. "I won't be any less distracted tomorrow."

It's been nearly two months since I last saw Rhedwyn, and Wortimer is still alive, still sending troops against us. I've had no news of any kind. I wish I could see her, make sure she and the child are fine, but even if I wanted to risk the sewers again, it's now impossible. There's ice on the river; the floes gather by the shore at low tide, blocking the water gate. Nobody could survive in the water for more than a couple of minutes.

If she's dead, how would I know? At what point do I have to assume something terrible has happened? How long do I have to wait? Maybe that's what Fastidius is trying to tell me through his messengers... If she failed, then all of this is in vain. I have wasted the lives of many young Iutes, and am about to waste many more, for nothing.

No, I tell myself. I would know. Just like I knew she was alive all this time. Somehow, I would know.

"It's no good doubting yourself now," says Eadgith, guessing my thoughts. "It'll only do more harm. Do whatever it is you want to do, and pray for the best."

"I'm fine, really. It's all fine," I say, distractedly. "Thank you for the sword. It's the best I've ever had."

The dawn rises over the battlements, its rosy fingers penetrating the narrow streets where so many lie dead at the foot of the Wall.

It was a prolonged disaster; a slow calamity. Several times through the night we'd broken through the Briton barricades and reached the gatehouse, only to be thrown back every time.

The youngest warriors were the first to breach the defences, and the first to die, their bodies scattered throughout the approaches to the Coln Gate and along the broad paved expanse of the Augustan Highway. Their bright blood stained the ancient Roman cobbles. The older fighters followed in their wake, with the shieldmaidens holding the rear. But no matter how bravely the veterans pushed, how valiantly the shieldmaidens held, how futilely the younglings died, we could not hold the gate long enough.

Beormund finds me standing in the middle of the Highway, out of arrow shot from the gatehouse. There is not a part of his body that's not covered in dried blood. He was the first in every charge, and the last in every retreat. His sword arm hangs limp along his side, but he still holds the axe firm in his left hand.

He looks back at the ramparts, a toothed monstrous shadow, black against the rising sun. Wortimer's forces are also severely depleted. The Briton dead lie among our own. A pile of them lies at the foot of the left tower, where they fell defending the *ballistae* emplacement. Those that remain look in silence at the three delegates marching through the field of corpses under a flag of truce.

I recognise their leader.

"Brutus!"

He looks me over and nods.

"So it was you, half-Iute. I knew these barbarians wouldn't come up with any of this by themselves."

"What do you want?"

"A ceasefire to pick up the dead and wounded. We can continue this slaughter after that, though God knows why anyone would want to."

"That's very generous of you."

"This is the proper way to do things. I'm not one of Wortimer's brutes, I'm a soldier of Londin." He thumps his chest in an old Roman salute.

We agree for the truce to last until the next watch, and the three Britons return to the gatehouse.

"They must be exhausted," says Beormund looking after them, air whistling through the hole after a lost tooth. "If we could only muster one more charge, I reckon we'd take it."

"No," I say. "It is over. Take care of our dead and let's get out of here."

He stares at me, one eye swollen, the other bloodshot. "We never had the chance, did we?"

"There was always a *chance*," I reply.

"It was never about the damn gate."

I say nothing. I'm trying to calculate some way out of our situation, a surprise attack, a strategic retreat, but I come up empty.

Beormund shakes me by the shoulder. "What was your plan, half-Iute? Now you can tell me!"

As I turn to speak, a trumpet fanfare sounds nearby. Astonished, we both watch a gold and silver litter being carried across the field of death. The litter moves slowly, the bearers careful not to step on a severed limb or a hacked torso. At last, they reach us and stop. The door opens and out comes the Bishop of Londin, in full regalia, the silver ray headgear balancing precariously on his head.

He looks past us, upwards, towards the bloodied gate. The trumpeters in his wake sound the fanfare again. He raises his crooked staff and in the trained, booming voice, announces to us all, Iute and Briton alike:

"The Great *Dux* of Britannia, the Commander of the Eastern Armies, the Vanquisher of Pagans, the Blessed Wortimer son of Wortigern — is dead! Cease this senseless fighting and join me in mourning his departure, and rejoicing at his soul reaching the Heavens!"

Only now he turns to me and Beormund. "I would like to speak to my brother alone, chieftain."

"Your brother?"

"He means me," I say. "How's Rhedwyn? How's the child?"

There is a darkness in his face that I've never seen before. He glares at Beormund and waits for the warchief to walk away. Before he opens his mouth, I know what he's going to say.

"The child is fine. The mother… was found dead this morning, next to Wortimer's body."

It's like that time we both first went to the Easter Market. Fastidius is saying something, I can see his lips move through the red haze, but all I can hear is a buzzing in my ear, a thumping, a roaring of blood. Single words break through the haze and noise: *forced to… poison… suffering.*

"How's the child?" I repeat, holding on to the only sliver of hope in what's happening.

"It's being taken care of," he says. "It's in the hands of the Church now. Safe."

"She's… my niece."

"Do you really want the world to know that?"

"There's Hengist —"

"And there's Wortigern." My knees buckle under me. I lean against him. He reaches his arm around me. "Now is not the time to talk of this. You're in shock."

"Tell me… Tell me again what happened."

"She poured poison into Wortimer's wine — but he was suspicious and told her to drink from the cup, too."

"The herbalist said it would make one suffer for hours."

"And it did. I'm so sorry."

"How do you know all this?"

"I was summoned to administer the last rites for them both. She was stronger than Wortimer — she could still speak when I arrived."

"Did she — did she say anything about me?"

"She asked that you forgive her."

The red haze returns. *Forgive her?* For what? I'm the one who failed her. I knew it was dangerous. I should never have let her do this.

The blood roars. I push him away. "You also knew. You all knew. You should've done something. You should've told me sooner."

"It would have changed nothing. It was her own choice," says Fastidius. "She knew the risk. Respect that."

"Don't talk to me about respect! You have no respect for us. We're nothing but useful tools for you and Ambrosius."

His face grows stern. "This is not true. I always had nothing but utmost esteem for your kin."

"Esteem? You wouldn't even pray for her."

He turns red. "That has nothing to do with anything."

"So you admit!"

"She killed a Christian. And then she killed herself. She left her child alone. God may forgive her, I cannot."

[142]

I reach for my sword and, in my rage, I struggle with the sheath and the cord. Fastidius steps back. Finally, I draw my weapon. He raises his hand in defence. "You've lost a sister today. Do you want to lose a brother, too?"

"I've never had a brother," I say. "The Iutes are my only family."

"Then go to them. Take them the sad news. You're not the only one who's lost a loved one today. Console each other."

He takes another step back, and the litter bearers move in front of him, shielding him with their sweat-shined bodies.

"I have to go," he says. "The city is waking up. I am its leader for today. I must prepare."

"This isn't over, Bishop," I snarl.

"I know," he replies, his voice mournful like a funeral lyre.

"The entire city is locked down. All the gates are shut, except this one," says Beormund. "Nobody goes in or out. The streets are empty. Everyone is just waiting."

I nod absentmindedly. The tribe needs me now more than ever, but I cannot bring myself to care. Not anymore. I have done all that was required of me — I destroyed Wortimer, our worst enemy, I have freed us from his tyranny… But my heart is empty and black.

We stand on the southern slope of the Cathedral Hill, watching the funeral boats depart through the water gate. The boats head across the river, to a marsh island designated for heathen burials. The queue now spans almost the entire breadth of the Tamesa. The tide is low, revealing sand banks and swamp dunes along the southern shore. The procession is slow. The watchmen check under every shroud this time, our bribes no longer sufficient to maintain the usual pretence.

There aren't that many guards here. Most of Wortimer's army awaits orders from Fastidius, who's now the highest authority in the city. We could overwhelm them easily if we wanted to. But everyone is too stunned, too tired from the events of last night to even think about any more fighting.

"We've lost so much," I say.

"But it worked," says Beormund, oblivious to my pain; he's suffered enough himself — he will never hold a sword in his right hand again, and his head is one great lump of blood and scars. He leans on a shaft of a broken spear. "That was your plan, wasn't it? Somehow you got Wortimer dead. How did you do that? Was it the Bishop? Is he really your brother?"

"I have no brother. And I did nothing."

"Don't tell me it was all just a coincidence."

I turn to face him. I want him to see the suffering in my eyes. "I need you to listen very carefully, chieftain. And then tell that to the others. The one who killed Wortimer, the one who saved us all, was Rhedwyn, daughter of Eobba, the Princess of the Iutes."

"Rhedwyn? But — she was alive? All this time?"

"She *was*."

His jaw drops. "They killed her! Those *wealh* bastards!"

"She —" I stop halfway through correcting him. In a way, isn't he right? None of this would have happened if only the Britons would have left us alone. "Yes. *They* killed her." I look at the guards, then my gaze moves west towards the Cathedral, a dark monolith standing over the city like a giant mausoleum. "They killed so many of us. If it wasn't for the *wealas*, they'd all be alive. Our soldiers, our families. Horsa. Beadda. Rhedwyn."

A tiny flame lights up in my heart. I don't know yet what it is, but I feel it might grow to burn down the whole world.

I stare out the window at the city below, grey in the rain that came to wash away the blood. This is my study room, a room in the attic of the *curia* that used to be some clerk's office, one of the few with all the walls and roof still standing. This is where I prepare battle plans, but there are no more battles to prepare, and nobody to fight against.

The streets have never been this quiet and empty. Just like Beormund said, everyone is waiting, even though many days have already passed since Wortimer's death. For the first time in living memory there is nobody to take over the seat in the Governor's Palace. It will be long before news reach Ambrosius, and even longer until Wortigern finds out he can return — not that anyone in Londin knows about his survival. The old *Comites* of the neighbouring *pagi* are bound to arrive first to stake their claims — Elasio, Peredur, Worangon, maybe even Catuar from the South, if the Saxons let him. There even might be renewed fighting between the contenders, until Ambrosius arrives with his Legions. And then there's Aetius across the sea, waiting for the winter storms to be over…

But for now, the city is a silent tomb. There is no trade in the Forum, no craftsmen advertising their wares, no noblemen strolling, no beggars wailing. The city belongs to the rats and the cats, and to the dead still waiting for a burial in the marshes.

I should be preparing, too. The Iutes will be leaving the city as soon as Fastidius decides to open the gates. The Saxons and the Angles have already started packing, I imagine. There is nothing here for us. Let the Britons fight over these dead, blood-splattered stones between themselves. But I cannot make a move. The spark in my heart is like a candle in a *frigidarium*; I know it's there, but it's too weak to warm up even the air around it. I feel just like the city outside: dead and cold.

The curtain, hung in place of the door, moves aside. Eadgith comes in bringing a mug of some steaming hot liquid. The scent is familiar, but one I haven't smelled in years.

"Is that hypericum?"

She pushes the mug into my cold hands. I almost drop it. I take a bitter sip. The warmth soon spreads over my arms and chest.

[146]

"I had one of the gravediggers bring some from the marsh," she says. "I remembered Father Paulinus mentioning it back at Ariminum. I thought you could use it."

"That's… very thoughtful."

She sits down beside me. She has purple bags under her eyes and smells of smoke; she was working all night and day in her smithy, mending the weapons damaged in the battle — those that didn't get buried, bent in two, with their dead owners.

"I've heard about what happened," she says. "With… your woman."

I nod.

"I'm sorry."

"Thank you."

I slurp the infusion in silence.

"What are you going to do now?" she asks.

"Do?" I shrug. "Nothing."

"You can't just sit here and look at the rain."

"Why not?"

"Your soul will die if you do."

"Don't I deserve to mourn her?"

"This is not mourning. Where are your tears? Where is the wailing? Why aren't you at her grave, tearing your hair out?"

"You know we're not allowed to go to the graves yet."

"Fine, forget about the grave. But this — this must end. How long have you been stuck in this attic? You mourn to cleanse yourself of death. What you do is wallow in it. I've seen this happen. Women who have lost their husbands and children, they would sit just like you, in the darkness. They might as well have been dead themselves."

I look up from the mug. "I know you've lost your loved ones, too," I say. "And I appreciate your pain. But maybe I'm just not as strong as you."

"This isn't about me. And I know how strong you really are. The people need you. Beormund is out of his depth. There's too much politics. You need to go talk to Fastidius, tell him to let us go from here before the Britons start fighting each other."

"I don't need his permission," I snarl. "The Iutes are a free people, we can come and go as we please."

She smiles.

"What's with the smile?"

"At last, you've shown some emotion."

"It's only anger."

She lays her hand on my chest. "Anger is good. It burns out the sorrow. I was angry a lot after I lost my village. Angry at the Britons, the Fate, the gods. Use it well."

"Use it for what?"

"To help yourself. To help your people. They are waiting for you."

She leans back. "And go talk to Fastidius. He *is* your brother. He was there with you from the beginning."

A sound like a raging of waves crashing against the cliffs disturbs my melancholy. As I emerge from my hermitage into the street, I realise I am not the only one who's chosen anger over sorrow.

A vast crowd of Iutes surrounds the *curia*, overflowing out into the gardens and the surrounding streets. It seems everyone who can still stand is here, men, women, even younglings who can barely hold a weapon. Beormund, standing on a broken pillar base, struggles to contain them. They are crying vengeance. I don't know on whom or for what at first. Then somebody spots me and shouts:

"There he is! She was his woman — let Ash lead us to battle if Beormund is not willing!"

I raise my hands. "Halt! What do you mean? What battle?"

"They killed our Princess!" the men and women howl. "They killed Rhedwyn — and they must pay!"

I let them wail. I am reminded that all of them, except the younglings born in the new villages, have lived for a generation together in a tight community on the Isle of Tanet. They saw Rhedwyn grow up, walk amongst them. She was the last living scion of the three *Drihtens*, a beam of hope in her green dress among the muck, perhaps even destined to be a chieftain herself one day.

I recognise the pain hidden in their wailing. They cry not for the Princess, but for themselves, for their own suffering, their own dead. They demand to avenge Rhedwyn, but what they really want to avenge is their own sorrow and loss; and, somehow, not just the dead fallen in the war with Wortimer, but everyone they've ever lost since setting out in their wobbly *ceols* across the whale-road. There are many here who still remember the crossing and its terror; who remember the filth and squalor of Tanet, the disease and hunger that took so many; the fighting with the Picts and the Frankish pirates raiding the island; the first war with the Britons and those who fell at the Crei. I hear all those dead called forth now, as witnesses to the woe.

"Haven't you had enough of fighting?" cries Beormund. "We've barely finished burying the dead, how many more graves do you want to dig?"

"If they have killed the Princess, they will come for us next," shouts a tall man with a deep scar across his face. The scar is fresh; must be from the battle at the Wall. "We have to strike first, while they're still reeling!"

"*Reeling?* The soldiers are not reeling, they're more ready to fight than you or I!"

"I'm ready!" The tall man shakes his axe. "Are you a coward now, Beormund?"

"Yes, Eadric," Beormund throws his healthy hand up in exasperation, "I'm a coward. That's why I lost a hand at the Gate. Out of cowardice. Ash, tell them what a terrible idea you think this is."

I want to tell him he's right. I want to tell the Iutes to disperse and wait for how the situation develops further. But their howls are like a wind that fans the burning in my heart. It speaks louder to me than Beormund's logic. For them, Rhedwyn is just an idea — but for me, her death is real. I will never hold her again, I will never hear her sing again. We will never figure out how to live together through our pain. Only my pain remains. Only my pain counts. The world without her might as well burn for all I care.

"Gather your weapons," I say. "And torches. Come back here at dusk."

"What?" Beormund turns, stricken with horror. "Have you gone mad?"

"That's right, Beormund. I'm mad with grief. I will lead these men to glory or death, if that is their wish, or I will go alone if need be."

The Iutes raise a cry of triumph and vengeance that shakes the city to its very foundations.

"I've come to warn you," I say. "Tonight, I'm putting the city to the torch."

[151]

He sits with his back to me, at his desk by the window, surrounded by piles of documents. He's reading one of them, a long, handwritten scroll.

"I'd much rather you didn't, brother," he says.

"I will spare the Cathedral. Tell anyone you care about to come here."

"I care about every single one of my flock," he replies. "The Cathedral won't fit all of them."

"Then open the gates and let them out."

"If I do that, you and your Iutes will all die."

I step up to him, grab his shoulder and force him to face me. "What do you mean by that?"

He throws the scroll in his hand at me. "This is Wortimer's last will," he says. "As dictated to me on his death bed. I'm about to read it out in public. And before you try anything, it's not the only copy."

The will reads like a sad joke. Wortimer, aware of the lack of a successor, set up a task to determine who will rule Londin and Britannia Maxima in his place. A contest as gruesome as only Wortimer could have invented. The prize — the jewel-studded diadem, and the throne; the playthings — the Iutes.

"I want to be buried in the grounds of the monastery of Martinus on the Isle of Tanet, my head facing Rome and Jerusalem where our Lord Christ suffered…" the will reads. "For this, the Isle must be cleansed from the vile heathens, who took it by deception and hold to it by force. Whosoever kills the most Iutes, will be granted not only the rule of Londin, but no doubt a seat in Heaven."

I crumple the scroll and throw it back on Fastidius's desk. "Are you going to honour this absurdity?"

"It doesn't matter what *I* think. The *Comites* stand at the gates with their armies, poised to strike. I spoke with them — they've agreed to terms between themselves. It makes more sense than having them fight each other. The Walls are shut not to keep you out — but to keep them from adding your people to the headcount."

"Then we were right," I say. "First you've killed Rhedwyn, now you've come to kill us."

"Have you started believing your own lies, brother? If anyone killed her, it was you, insisting on your foolish scheme. I told you this would end in tears!"

"Don't you dare —!" I grab his throat and raise a fist.

He looks at me calmly.

"If it makes you feel better," he says.

"Fuck you." I push him back on the chair. "Open those gates, I don't care. We will take them all on, or die trying. Your desert God's Heaven may be a place for the meek, but Wodan's Mead Hall only has seats for the brave."

I storm out. On the threshold, I turn around one last time.

[153]

"I was going to let your Cathedral stand, but now I'm not so sure anymore."

We are a snake of fire, a salamander, weaving through the streets of the Poor Town. The heat from the torches is like that of a blacksmith's furnace; it ignites the straw on the roofs of the huts, and soon the entire district is standing in flames. The Britons flee before us in terror, aware that their betrayal will not go unpunished.

I march in front, alone, with a torch in my left hand and Eadgith's sword in my right. Eadgith is not with us — she stayed at the *curia* with Beormund and a handful of others who couldn't, or wouldn't, answer the summons; children and infirm among them. She didn't try to stop me, just stared at me with disapproval. It does not matter. I am the flame, I am the hammer. Donar is in me, and Hel follows after me. I have drunk the henbane of grief and madness.

I don't know where I'm going.

I turn from one narrow, smoke-filled street into another, until I march out onto Cardo Street. Six hundred feet away, a jagged shadow marks the ruined walls of the Governor's Palace. This is where Rhedwyn died. This is where we will have our vengeance. All we need to do is reach it.

There is another angry crowd standing between us and the palace, a dark, heaving mass filling the entire length and breadth of the avenue. These aren't soldiers — they're citizens of Londin, average Britons, poor and tired, mostly unarmed and, like us, incensed into a rage-addled mob by their own grievances. They have no leaders, no strategy, no plan. They, too, howl for vengeance. They demand justice for the death of their *Dux* at the hand of a pagan woman. They want retribution for the long months of poverty and humiliation they have suffered under Wortimer, for which they blame not him but us, the newcomers. They are our mirror image, only vastly multiplied.

I feel no fear. We are the Iutes. Every one of us is born a warrior. They are just some pampered city folk. We will cut through them as if they were reeds on a river bank. I raise my sword.

The low mowing of battle trumpets sends a tremor through the air. The sound comes from the south, where the Bridge Gate guards the ancient river crossing. A line of braziers lights up along the Wall, disappearing into the night. More trumpets play in the distance, to the north and the east of us. A faint echo reaches from the west.

Fastidius has opened the gates. The armies of the *Comites* are pouring in through the breaches to stop us. But I will not have my prize taken from me, not when it's so close. The palace is a bow shot away. We will reach it, and we will raze it to the ground, and then I will drink mead in Wodan's Hall with Rhedwyn, Beadda, Horsa, and everyone else at my side.

I lead the charge. The roar of two hundred throats carries me forward. The Britons hold firm for a moment, but then they falter and fall back. Their hearts do not burn as hot as ours, they did not love Wortimer as much as we loved our Princess. Clusters of them decide to stand and fight, here and there, brave or foolish, or both; but the rest of the crowd flees from our blows and slashes, from our howls, from our pain. Their fear fans our flames. We are death. We push into the streets on the other side of the avenue, and some of the

Iutes disperse to burn and rob the houses along the alleyways leading towards the Forum, but most push with me straight towards the Governor's Palace.

The guards at the entrance flee as we approach. The main gate is barred, but the younglings among us climb the outer wall and open it from inside. We pour into the inner courtyard, setting fire to everything that can burn — straw patches on the roof, hay for the horses, wooden crates, carts, bales of cloth waiting to be weighed. I tell the Iutes where to find the best fuel: libraries, kitchens, heating storerooms, and then release them into the palace. I see their torches in the windows, followed by flame. I hear cries of terror and gurgles of death: not everyone has heeded my warning to abandon the palace tonight; I wonder, briefly, if these are courtiers and guards, loyal to the last, or some poor servants and slaves, not even aware of what is happening or why.

I stride inside and reach the throne room. Here is the seat that Wortimer took from his father. Here is the long table at which I gave council for so many years, the strange curiosity, the half-Iute courtier. Here is the seat where Rhedwyn once sat, in a splendid gown and a sheer veil, when Riotham came to visit. To all of this I put the torch, until it becomes nothing but a bonfire of painful memories.

I want to get to the garden, but the corridors are too hot to get through already. I go back outside. The ruined hallways of the palace's disused wings were filled with waste and debris; all of this is now one giant burning beacon. The flames in the east wing reach the clouds, turning the courtyard into the mouth of a great furnace. The west wing yet stands, but it will soon succumb to the heat. I think of all the riches that go up in those flames; the books and scrolls in the palace library, the gold and silver melted into pools in the treasury, the lead oozing from the brickwork and plumbing. I feel like Rome itself is burning down and falling apart around me.

Most of the Iutes have already left the compound, unable to stand the heat — and are now fighting in the streets. One of the *Comites* armies has reached us at last. In the chaos, I can't tell whose soldiers they are. If they thought we'd be an easy prey, they were sorely mistaken. The Iutes fight as if they have drunk the henbane beer. They shrug off wounds and stand fast until they have no limbs or all blood flows from them. They tear weapons from the hands of the dead and wounded and use them against the enemy. A horse rides past me in panic, its rider thrown off by the mob and clubbed to death.

But we are too few; trapped in the maze of streets, we're split into small groups, each slowly succumbing to the onslaught. I hear the battle trumpets again, nearer this time, marking the arrival of another army to finish us off. I pick up a shield — it's marked with the white horse of the Cants — draw the sword and throw myself into the brawl. A fountain of blood spurts in my face from the first enemy I stab.

The world is shrouded in a purple mist, from which enemies emerge only to end up at the stabbing end of my sword. Sometimes an axe comes at me, and bounces off from the shield, then a spear thrust that I swerve to dodge. A club blow hits my shoulder, shattering the nerves, but I do not flinch. I spin and cut the enemy across the stomach until his guts fall out. My sword arm rises and drops in a monotone motion, like a thresher's flail, each drop ending in somebody's scream. I feel no pain; the spearheads reach me as if they were pinpricks, swords cut like letter openers.

But I have not drunk the henbane, after all. My limbs weaken. My blood flows freely. A powerful mace blow brings me to my knees. I get up and slash, then fall again. An axe crashes through what little is left of the shield. I throw the shards away, grab the sword in two hands and whack a Briton on the head, splitting his skull in two. The sword hilt slips from my hand. I pick it up just in time to parry another blow, but barely.

The enemies around me disappear into the purple mist. All I see in the haze is the laughing face of the bearded, one-eyed man. He beckons me to follow; I see the great Mead Hall, ablaze with warm light, echoing with laughter and song. Among the laughing voices I think I can hear Fulco and Horsa; I hear Beadda singing praises of the women of his village, and many other familiar, long-gone voices of the fallen warriors. They're all here, waiting for me to join them…

A sword cuts through the mist and the vision disappears. Arms reach out to me and help me up: they belong to Eadgith and Beormund. Behind them stands the faint figure of Fastidius, almost translucent in a white robe with a purple trim, looking nervously around him. A troop of soldiers, both Iutes and Britons, surrounds us in a tight circle of steel, their white tunics marked with the crosses and swords of Saint Paul's.

Supporting me on their shoulders, Eadgith and Beormund press through the brawl. Fastidius leads the soldiers ahead of us, out into the open space of the main avenue. A two-horse cart stands here, the beasts' ears anxiously perked up.

"Get him up there," says Fastidius. I notice he's holding a short sword, its edge bloodied. They shove me onto the cart. Eadgith climbs up after me and sits beside me, holding my hand. Beormund gives a sign to the driver.

"We'll meet at Beaddingatun," says Beormund, "if all goes well."

"May Christ guide you, Chieftain," says Fastidius.

"And may Wodan protect you, Bishop," adds Beormund.

The first cold drop of rain falls on my face.

The Saxon Might

[160]

CHAPTER VII
THE LAY OF PAULINUS

Heaven, I'm surprised to discover, looks just like the bedroom in Ariminum that I shared with Fastidius when we were children, all the way down to the musty old bed with sheepskins and woollen covers, the bookcase full of war manuals, and the desk upon which Fastidius took his religious studies.

The angel in this Heaven has taken the form of Eadgith. She puts a cold cloth on my forehead. I moan. She rolls her eyes.

"You're not that badly hurt," she says. "I don't know how you've managed it, but most of your wounds are just bumps and scratches."

"I… I thought I died a dozen times."

"You've got a spear stab on your thigh that would've killed you if it had gone in an inch to the left," she says, putting her hand gently on the wound. "But Paulinus took care of that already."

"Paulinus…!"

"I'm still here."

The old priest staggers into the room. He's changed; he no longer reeks of ale, and his eyes are clear.

[161]

"I did not think I would ever see you two together in this house," he says. "God and his mysterious ways, eh?"

I sit up. The world wobbles. Eadgith lifts me to my feet and helps me to a chair. My right hand feels sore from gripping the sword. My long-suffering left shoulder is burning again, but I've grown so used to it hurting over the years I barely notice.

"Was that really Fastidius I saw?" I ask.

"Yes."

"What was he doing there?"

"He came to us just as you and your torch mob departed," she begins, "bringing a detachment of the Cathedral guards with him."

He told them he prayed all day and had an epiphany. He could not let the innocent die, even if they were pagans. It was too late to save the ones I led to destroy the city. But while the attention of the *Comites* armies was focused on me and my mob, he could spare the ones who stayed behind in the Poor Town. He ordered the water gate open and commanded the funeral boats to take the Iutes across the river to the island of the graves, from where they could wade to the southern shore.

"Where are they now?"

She nods to the window. With her help, I walk out onto the *villa*'s yard. I notice a new earthen wall surrounding the property's perimeter, and a new, smaller, more heavily fortified gate guarding the entrance from the Londin Road.

[162]

The courtyard is full of people, young and old, sitting in the mud or walking around. They huddle in clusters, sheltering from the rain under the trees, cloaks and bits of tent cloth given to them by Paulinus and the *villa*'s servants. I count maybe fifty of them.

"Is that all there is left?" I ask.

"I put the worst wounded and sick inside," says Paulinus. "Maybe a dozen more."

The enormity of what I've done is slowly sinking in. This is maybe a tenth of the tribe's original strength, before the final stage of my war with Wortimer started. Only a day earlier I gave no thought to leading the last two hundred of them into their deaths. All of them perished in the narrow streets of Londin. My hands are bathed in their blood.

I feel Eadgith's hand on my shoulder. "There was nothing you could've done, Ash," she says. "The Britons would've slaughtered us anyway. At least they died fighting."

"I should've asked Fastidius for help earlier," I say. "I let my anger get the better of me."

Just now a cart rides into the courtyard. Fastidius is in the driver's seat, still in the purple-trimmed Bishop's robe. Five men lie in the box, six more run in after the cart.

"This is the last lot," says Fastidius, leaping off. The hem of his robe is splattered with blood. His face is grey, his eyes surrounded by purple rings. His breath is heavy. He must've been riding all through the night.

"Where's Beormund?" asks Eadgith.

"We were ambushed on the island of the graves," Fastidius replies. "Beormund was holding our rear." He says no more. The grim tone of his voice is enough.

I step forth. "You've saved me again, brother."

"It is your mortal body I keep saving," he says. "If only I could save your soul, too."

"It's far too late for that. But… thank you for trying."

A faint sad smile curves his lips.

"I have to go back, before the *Comites* notice what I've done. Londin needs its Bishop. What are you planning to do with your people?"

"Me?" I ask, surprised.

"You're their chieftain now," says Eadgith.

"But, I can't —" I back away. "All I've done is lead them to slaughter. Why don't *you* lead them?"

"I'm just a bladesmith," she says. "I don't know how to command people. There is no one else left. Look, they're all staring at you. Waiting."

She is right. All the eyes in the courtyard are turned in my direction. But unlike Eadgith, I can't see them waiting for my orders. All I see is weariness and grief.

"Whatever your plan is, they can't stay here for long," says Paulinus. "I've given away all the *villa*'s stores already.

There is not enough food or shelter here to sustain this many people for more than a day."

"The *Comites* will be looking for you," adds Fastidius. "I will try to keep them occupied in Londin, but I don't know how long it will take before they figure out you're all here."

I raise my hands to my head. "Enough!" I cry. "I can't do this! All my decisions brought nothing but death and pain. Let someone else choose. Anyone."

Paulinus steps up and slaps me in the face. "Get a hold of yourself, boy! Right now these people need a leader. If I or Fastidius could do it, we would, but it must be one of their own. I know you're clever. You're the second smartest pupil I ever had. So what if you've made bad choices in life. We all did. I'm a drunk, sinful priest, a heretic who denounced his master and will burn in Hell for eternity. But I keep making decisions, as best I can. Otherwise I should just curl up and die."

"Don't give him ideas," says Eadgith. "You don't know what he's been through." She turns to Fastidius. "How much time do we have?"

"You should leave before night."

"We won't need that long. Give me an hour."

She takes me to the shore of the Loudborne, shallow and half-frozen at this time of year. Across the river I glimpse the charred ruin of Beaddingatun, and the whitewashed wall of the chapel, but that's not where we're going. Eadgith leads me downstream until we reach a forest clearing.

"Do you remember this place?" she asks.

It takes me a moment. With the carpet of fragrant ramsons replaced by a blanket of naked dirt covered in hoar, the clearing is difficult to recognise at first.

"I do."

She turns her back to me and faces the river. "That first time…" she pauses, then shakes her head. "*We're both adults*," she whispers, then continues aloud. "That first time, I used you in place of Fastidius."

"I suspected as much," I reply. "Sometimes I think that's what everyone sees in me. A worse substitute for my brother. Why are you telling me this?"

"I didn't see in you then what I saw later."

"And what could that be?"

"Fastidius has a brilliant mind — sharp, inquisitive, quick. I'm not surprised how high he ended up in the Church. But… he's always been so prim and proper. He would never be a master of war — only a master of knowledge."

She turns back. "I don't know much about war — but I've seen enough of it to know you need to be at least a little mad to wage it."

"You think me mad?"

[166]

She puts a hand on my chest.

"There is a madness in you that I never saw in Fastidius. It's as if the blood in your veins was spiked with henbane. It always scared me and drew me to you in equal measure."

"Until it drove you away."

"Yes. In the end, I wanted a peaceful life. The life I had with Caeol and Octa. But that peace was taken from me — from all of us. And this is why we need you, a madman. A warrior. A warchief."

I stand still, stunned. Is this the curse that has followed me all my life? The madness that is in my blood — the heirloom of my father and my uncles, the three *Drihtens* of the Iutes? I know next to nothing about the lives of my kin before their arrival on Tanet. Hengist, certainly, had his share of mad adventures, leading a band of bloodthirsty mercenaries in the lands of Danes and Frisians, sung about in the songs of his *scops*. And my father was said to have been the fiercest warrior of the three, while he lived. I am a spawn of uncounted generations of such war leaders, all the way to Wodan and Donar if the clan myths are to be believed.

I know she's right. I sensed that madness last night, perhaps for the first time with clarity. My blade yearns for blood; my spirit aches for more death. But neither more blood, nor more deaths will save the fifty people waiting for my orders at the *villa*'s courtyard.

I shrug. "Whatever you may have seen in me was burned out long ago. There is nothing left but darkness."

"It is a dark age," she replies. "The light can only take us so far."

We return to the *villa* in grim, sombre silence. But my mind is buzzing with strategies. I have put away the pain in a locked compartment somewhere at the back of my head. This war is not over yet; I can return to my wallowing and brooding once everyone is safe.

"They would expect us to go east, to join with Hengist," I tell Fastidius. "But that would mean crossing the Medu, and marching the entire breadth of the land of Cants."

He nods. Of course, he knows what I'm going to say — he already came to the same conclusion hours ago. There is nothing that I can come up with that would surprise him. When it comes to war planning, there is still no quicker wit than his.

"The army that came first through the Bridge Gate was that of the Cants, not of the Regins." Fastidius nods again. "That means Catuar wouldn't stake his claim to the title?"

"It would seem so. I haven't heard from him or the Regin Council since the war started."

"Then he no longer rules in the South, even as a puppet of the Saxons."

"It is likely."

"If you're thinking of going South," says Paulinus, "the road is blocked at the crossroads by the ruins. If you had your

Iute army you could think of breaching it, but with this lot…" He casts a doubtful gaze at the multitude of children, old and wounded.

"We will go through the woods."

"Andreda?" Paulinus raises an eyebrow. "You'd put your life in the heathen's hands?"

Fastidius and I glance at each other. It's odd to be speaking to someone so unaware of how much things have changed. To Paulinus, time stopped the day we left him alone at Ariminum. To him, I was still the wayward Christian boy, needing guidance not to stray too far from the true Faith. Aelle was a heathen bandit, a murderer, roaming the woods in search of plunder. I don't have the strength to explain the strange new world to him.

I look at the poor wretches gathered in the yard.

"I need a pony, and somebody who could ride with me."

"Don't look at me," says Eadgith. "I hate the damn things."

"I might be able to help with that," says Fastidius. He whistles and waves to one of the huddling groups. A small figure breaks off and runs up to us, pig-tails bobbing in the rain.

"Birch! You're alive!"

I lost track of her after the battle at the Coln Gate. Many of the Iutes have gone missing, and we had to presume them all dead beyond the Briton barricades where our searching parties couldn't reach.

"The name's Betula now," she says, pointing to the little crucifix at her neck. "What is it, *pater*?"

Fastidius smiles at me apologetically. "You can ride a pony, can't you?" he asks Birch.

"If I have to."

"You will ride with Fraxinus."

She gives me a side-eye. "As you wish, *pater*."

"I'll fetch the horses," says Paulinus.

"Ponies!" I call after him. "Iute ones. I know you kept some after Beaddingatun fell."

I duck under an oak bough and brush the twigs from my face. The forest is black and barren here, only a few withered leaves still hold stubbornly to the branches. Clumps of box trees smothered in ivy are the only patches of green, but it's a cold and unpleasant hue.

The pony leaps over a stump and swerves to avoid an upturned tree trunk. It is a clever and sturdy beast, from good Iutish stock, and I soon grow fond of it as it carries me deeper into the woods.

"Betula, huh?" I ask Birch. She rides beside me as much as the narrow paths allow. She's less comfortable in the saddle than I am — I can tell from her stance that she's only ridden a few times in her life, and that a long time ago.

"It means Birch in the Roman tongue," she replies.

"I know what it means. When were you baptised?"

"The day before the battle at the Gate. I knew it would be a disaster, and I did not want to die a heathen."

"You knew — but you still came?"

Her pony moves forward and I see her shrug. "You gave the order. I heeded it."

"You must have spoken to Fastidius prior to your baptism. Gone through all the preparations."

She slows down and tells me she's been meeting with him every Sunday — as did many of the other Iutes of the Poor Town.

"At first, it was his generosity. When he gave us that crucifix… None of our priests or chiefs would have been capable of such a gesture. All they want is more beasts for sacrifices, more silver for their diadems."

"That's just how Fastidius is," I chuckle. "I assure you, the previous Bishop —"

"I know that now," she interjects. "I saw that he was different from the other Britons. The light of God shines through him, and the wisdom of God speaks through him."

I glance at her and see the piety glint in her eyes. Somehow, her words make me feel uncomfortable. I know Fastidius is a good priest, with an impressive record of conversions and baptisms, but I never saw him the way Birch sees him. How disappointed my apostasy must have made him — the one sheep lost forever…

"I saw you several times at the Cathedral," she says. "I thought at first you, too, were secretly a Christian. It made me think better of you. Until His Grace explained what was really going on between you two."

"You don't think well of me now?"

"You're a good commander in the field," she says, repeating Eadgith's earlier assessment. "And it was fun going with you on all those raids." There's a different glint now, less pious, more murderous. Briefly, she's the Birch I know, the little mischievous shieldmaiden, not Betula, the Christian. The moment soon passes. "But before long I realised you would send us all to our deaths if only it served you some purpose."

"I supposed I proved you right last night."

"Even earlier than that. That's why I never returned after the Gate. I joined the Cathedral guards, like so many others fed up with that war."

"There were more like you?"

"Dozens. And all because of you. We tried to tell Beormund, but you were too clever, too convincing, with your fancy words, and your book learning… You treat people like battle fodder. Those map markers you used to teach us tactics… That's all we were to you. That's not what being a chieftain is about."

"I'm sorry."

She stops the pony and turns to face me. "Are you, really? What are you sorry for?"

I need a moment to think about it. Certainly, I was to blame for the death and destruction of last night. But that's not what made Birch angry with me. If it wasn't what I did while succumbing to pain and fury that upset her, then what? What other mistakes have I committed — that she knows of? She can't know I was the one who goaded Wortimer into the war. Nobody does, except maybe Fastidius. And once the war started, there was no way I could've led the men better. Yes, sometimes I sent a squadron to its death as a ruse… Or I knowingly let the enemy spring up an ambush so that they wouldn't learn of my spies… But it was all necessary for our survival. Just like the charge at the Gate was a necessary distraction, to let Rhedwyn administer the poison…

Wasn't it?

It worked — Wortimer is dead.

So is Rhedwyn. And so, so many others. And now the war is lost anyway.

"When Fastidius and I were children," I say, "we used to play at war. At first, all that mattered was who was the strongest or the biggest."

"It used to be like that in the Old Country."

"Then Fastidius came up with tactics, and others started to learn from him. Then the victory belonged to the ones who were the smartest."

"You mean everyone was moving the markers on the map."

"There wasn't a map as such, but... yes."

She nods and waits.

"But sometimes... Sometimes we got bored of the tactics and would just bash at each other however we felt like, just like in the old days. The days before the maps and markers."

"And who would win then?"

"The ones who could make the hearts of their men burn the hottest."

A sudden, brief grin flashes on her face.

"What is it?"

She spurs the pony on. "His Grace disagreed with me when I complained about you," she says. "He believed you could be a great leader — if you'd only understand your flaws."

"He always thought too highly of me. Even when we were kids, he stood up for me. I did nothing to deserve his praise."

The ground grows muddier and more broken up by roots. Our ponies slow down to a slog.

[174]

"Maybe it's time for you to earn it," she says.

"It may be too late for that."

The ground rises in folds and creases as we climb higher up the Downs. "There's still several scores of people back there in need of a leader," she says. "It might as well be you."

"Why does *everyone* want me to be a leader?" I snarl. "All I know is how to lead good men to a slaughter."

We reach an unmarked fork in the forest path. A tall ash tree, bald except a single leaf on the topmost branch, grows between the two arms.

"Do you even know where we're going?" Birch asks.

"I have no idea," I admit. "We just have to keep going deeper into the woods and hope Aelle's men will spot us. Somehow, they always do."

It's almost dusk by the time we're intercepted by three men — boys, really, fair-haired, spotty-faced, in drab grey tunics and dapple green cloaks — on the other side of the Downs. Two hold their bows aimed at us, while the third one points a spear.

"Halt! Who are you; why are you here?" he asks in broken Briton.

"Do we look like the *wealas* to you, boy?" I reply. "We come from Londin. We seek your *Drihten's* help. Urgently."

The boys step back and discuss this among each other. The one with the spear speaks up.

"You'll have to go blindfold."

I look to the sky. "It's almost night. We're in a forest. And we're in a hurry."

"I will let one of you ride my pony," says Birch, shifting backwards to make space before her on the beast's back. This finally convinces the leader of the three boys.

"You're fortunate," he says. "Aelle is camping on the High Rocks today. It's less than two hours from here."

They lead us along a path that only they can see, from ridge to ridge, ever deeper into the heart of the forest. Long past midnight, tired, half-asleep and hungry, we reach a place in the middle of a deep dark wood that must be what the boys called the High Rocks. I've never been here before: a withered edge of a tall sandstone cliff, cut through by the ageless winds and rains into a maze of gullies, cracks and tall, shattered rock faces.

The boy with the spear whistles three times. Somebody drops us a rope ladder. Birch climbs first, nimble like a squirrel. I follow with weary pulls.

At the top waits Aelle himself.

"Ash!" he exclaims joyfully and gives me a mighty bear hug. "I knew I'd see you again!"

"I wish it was in happier circumstances," I say. "This is Birch. Birch, this is Aelle of the Saxons, the chieftain in Andreda."

"Betula," Birch corrects me. "We're starving, chieftain. We've been riding all day and night."

"I like her," says Aelle with a grin. "Straight to the point. Come, come, we still have some of the roasted deer from last week. You will want water. We have good water here. That's why I like to camp in this place. Come, come."

A small, ancient fortress rests on top of one of the bluffs, connected with rope ladders to other clifftops where the rest of the encampment sprawls, lit up with braziers and bonfires. This camp is far greater than any I've been to in Andreda — practically a town. Clearly, Aelle feels safer in the forest than ever, to allow his people to gather in such a large concentration.

He leads us to a small timber building — a mead hall. The logs are freshly hewn. The chimney at the back puffs merrily, filling the air with the smell of roast. Aelle's joviality and enthusiasm, the abundance of food and drink waiting for us in the hall, the bright burning flames in the fireplace, make me feel like I've stepped into a dream. Either that, or the past months have been a nightmare from which I have just woken up. The blood-washed streets of Londin, the dead piling up in the burnt-out city, the sick and the wounded waiting in Ariminum, can't possibly belong to the same world as this lit-up, busy, mellow clifftop fortress.

But which is real, and which is just a dream?

"I remember you once said, if I ever needed your help, I just needed to look for you in the woods," I say, between the bites of a succulent deer haunch, fat dripping down my chin. This is the best food I've eaten since… I rummage in memory — was it the Council at Sorbiodun? "Well, here I am."

"I know why you're here," he says, pointing at me with a drumstick of some forest bird.

"You do? Well that should —"

"You've come to lead us into battle alongside your Iutes. And we're ready for it. We've heard all about you and your war in Londin!"

His face lights up as he speaks. I put the deer haunch down.

"I'm afraid you're mistaken," I say. "There will be no more battles. We're here to ask for sanctuary."

He drops the drumstick. "You mean you've been defeated?"

"I… It's complicated."

"We have eighty souls waiting up in Beaddingatun," interjects Birch. She casts me an irritated glance. "Can we decide on their fate first, before we start discussing who's won and who's lost?"

"Eighty? Is that all?" Aelle calls out to his bodyguard. "Offa! Have the women prepare places for eighty people for tomorrow. Lodgings, food, whatever they need."

[178]

The guard nods and rushes out of the hall. "There's hardly anyone here these days," says Aelle, seeing our astonished faces. "It'll liven the place up. But — eighty? Don't tell me that's all you have left…"

I nod. "We have suffered greatly these past few months. Wortimer brought his full wrath upon us."

Aelle takes a deep breath and reaches for the ale jar. "So that's why we have had an easier time around here. And I thought he was simply running out of soldiers. But… if he's defeated you, he's going to crush Hengist now, and then come for us. The forest is not going to stay safe for long."

"He might have done that — if he was still alive."

He claps his hands. "What is this? A night of surprises! Have all my spies failed me? Offa!" he calls again. "Why did I not know about any of this?"

"It's only been a week since he died," I say. "I will tell you all about it, but first —" I turn to Birch. "How soon can you ride back to the *villa*?"

She shrugs. "I've been waiting for your orders. I'm only worried about the pony."

"Take one of mine," says Aelle with a wave. "They know the forest better than anyone. You'll be back in half the time."

"Tell Eadgith what you've heard here. Have everyone march out as soon as they can. Paulinus will give you the carts for the wounded. And, Betula —" I add when she stands up, "— get some sleep after all is done."

The first cart with the wounded rolls up to the High Rocks perch just as the descending sun touches the treetops. Those of the Iutes who can walk have been arriving in small groups for the past few hours, settling in the shelters of bough and moss normally used by Aelle's warriors. Soon the entire meadow looks like a nomad camp. I stand on the edge of a cliff, surveying the glade below.

"And what will you do when the *wealas* come here after you?" asks Aelle.

"Don't worry," I reply. "We will move again, as soon as we've rested and healed. Further south, if you allow us."

"And if they keep coming?"

"We've always been just refugees here. There's barely enough of us left to man three *ceols*, and sail away again, just like we started. Maybe to Armorica. Maybe back home, to the Old Country. I hear it's more peaceful there than here now."

"Mhm." Aelle grunts doubtfully. "I wouldn't be so sure."

He steps away from the cliff edge and sits sullenly on a rock. He's been sulking in his disappointment all day. One thing I like about the young Saxon, he never tries to hide his true feelings.

He yawns and stretches. We've been talking through the night. Having recounted to him the recent events in Londin, I listened to his tale of what was happening in the South after the Battle of Callew — or the "Massacre of the Long Knives" as the Britons insisted on calling it.

[180]

"Just before he marched on the Iutes, Wortimer had sent envoys to Catuar, demanding he joined his war on the heathens," Aelle explained. "We intercepted those missives, of course — nothing gets past my men on the southern highway. My father decided it was time to stop the pretence of the Regin rule."

"So Catuar is no longer the *Comes*?"

"He's not even in Britannia anymore. We've sent him away to Armorica, along with a bunch of loyal nobles. As far as the *wealas* are concerned, or if Rome ever asks, the *pagus* of the Regins is now ruled by an independent Council of Britons — but they have no power over anything other than the civil administration." He waves his arm. "From here to the coast, it's Saxon land now."

"Under your father's rule."

"Not quite yet — but we're getting there."

"How did Wortimer react to this news?"

"He tried to force his way through our borders once or twice — to 'liberate' his fellow *wealas* — we'd always beat him back," he replies with a grin, but his expression soon turns sour. "We never had enough strength to go on the offensive. We could only watch as he destroyed the Iute villages, and pushed your people back towards Tanet…" He shakes his head. "I feared he and that other *wealh* —"

"Ambrosius."

"— would turn his full attention to us after he'd dealt with the Iutes. But then the winter came — and the fighting all but stopped."

"That was when we started the war in Londin."

"It was a blessing for us. We rested and regrouped. We've built up this place," he says, nodding around, "in preparation for a spring offensive, to regain some of the lost ground."

An offensive? I look around doubtfully. I vacillate between admiring Aelle's optimism, and condemning his arrogance. Even with Wortimer gone, the remaining Briton cohorts are a force to be reckoned with — and Ambrosius, despite his offers of peace, would not hesitate to send his troops to aid his kin to defend from any barbarian attack. There can be no offensive. Only retreat.

CHAPTER VIII
THE LAY OF SOLINUS

"I never imagined it would end like this," Aelle says with a disappointed sigh. The arrival of the Iutes failed to fill the hilltop fortress with mirth, as he'd hoped. We brought with ourselves nothing but the moaning of the wounded and the wailing of the mourners.

"I hoped we'd ride into battle against the *wealas*, you and I, side by side, and drive them before us. And then, one day, we'd watch from Wodan's Mead Hall as our sons charged the gates of Londin itself and shattered them with their axes."

I scoff, though his vision intrigues me. I never suspected he held me in such high esteem. "Life is not a song, Aelle. These people are under my care, and they can no longer fight. I have led them to their doom one time too many. Now I must ensure the survival of what's left."

"*We* will stay and fight," he says. "We, Saxons. Even if you Iutes will abandon us."

"Look down, Aelle, at these poor wretches. Even if I wanted to help you, I could at best muster what, a dozen able men? What use would that be for you?"

He leaps up and pokes me in the head. "You still have your brain, don't you?" he says. "That's all I need. I have men to spare, but none of them know how to fight in the *wealh* way. We can hold our own in a forest, against Wortimer's brutes, but in the open field, against a skilled Roman army, it's a whole other thing."

"Have you fought them before?"

"Once, at the beginning," he says. "We made a stand at Verica's tavern, in the old hillfort. A hundred of us, behind a wall. We expected an easy win against Wortimer. Instead, we fought a *centuria* of the Westerners, all clad in mail and shield."

The grim shadow on his face tells me all I need to know about how that battle ended.

"Then stay in the forest," I say. "You can defend here for years."

"And watch the *wealas* burn down the towns and fields all around us?" He puts a hand on my shoulder. "Remember what I once told you? When all the *wealh* armies unite against us, they will destroy us easily. This is why we, too, should unite against them."

I shake my head and brush his hand off. "It's too late for that. Tanet will fall to whoever controls Londin now, sooner or later. And when the storms end, Aetius will arrive with his Legions to mop up the remains."

"Aetius, you say?" Aelle scratches his head.

"Don't tell me you forgot about him. He is the reason this entire mess started in the first place…"

"No, that's not it." He snaps his fingers. "I remember now. There is somebody I'd like you to meet."

[184]

"Sure. As soon as my people are settled, I'll talk to whoever you want."

"Not here. On the coast, at New Port. You'll have to come with me."

"I can't leave my —"

"It'll only take a few days. Your Iutes aren't going anywhere anyway. Trust me, it'll be worth your while."

We ride for a day across the wintry wood, through files of silvery beech trunks and under a black lace canopy of barren oak boughs. Patches of snow nestle in the cold nooks. Crows laugh at us from the treetops.

This part of Andreda is less desolate than I remembered. We pass tiny villages of several huts clustered on the sandy heathland, huts of lumberjacks and tar-men on the frost-blasted meadows, forges and smithies smouldering on grassy islands in the icy marsh. Saxons and Britons, living together in this harsh land, eking out an existence that is as difficult as it is free.

"How many people now live in these woods?" I ask.

"A thousand at least, maybe two," replies Aelle. "Not counting my troops, of course. They're mostly scattered along the streams that flow from the high lands."

"Why are they here? There's peace in this land," asks Eadgith. "They don't have to hide or flee from anyone." She's riding a pony awkwardly behind us. I asked her to come with us, fearing spending more than a couple of days in Aelle's presence alone.

"Some of them do," says Aelle. "Criminals, bandits, rent debtors, runaway slaves… Others come here because they prefer freedom to safety. There are no masters here, no *Drihtens*, no judges."

He waves to a group of tar-men rolling a mighty black barrel. They wave back. Three of them are Saxons, the fourth has short, curly black hair and skin the colour of a walnut.

"Are you not their *Drihten?*"

"I only command those who *choose* to follow me. I have no power over the Free Folk of Andreda. Nobody does."

We stop for the night in the house of an iron smelter, atop a hill on the edge of the woods, overlooking the Roman highway. His wife welcomes us alone, as the smelter is gathering ore in the bog. She and Eadgith strike up a conversation on various qualities of the local iron in an instant, while Aelle and I prepare our beddings by the furnace.

"Are you still not planning on telling me who it is we're going to see?" I ask. "Or why?"

"Oh, I can tell you *why*, now that we've come all this way." Aelle rolls out a deer skin. "The man we're seeing has come from across the sea. I hope the news he brings will change your mind."

"News — about Aetius?"

"Among other things."

[186]

"Fine. I'm intrigued."

I watch him put the bundle of his belongings at his head.
The black timber shaft of his weapon juts out of the rolled-up
cloth. The weapon that slew Horsa. It sends shivers down my
spine. I look up at Aelle, see his grinning face. Is this really
the boy who fought us at the Medu Ford? A long time ago, I
used to think him a monster, the worst man in all of
Britannia… I've learned since who the real monsters are.

"Where did you get this thing?" I ask.

"The stick shooter? I found it in the ruins of Anderitum.
There was a whole stash of strange old weapons hidden
under the main bastion, most of them no longer working."
He notices me staring at the weapon's deadly tip and the grin
vanishes from his face. "I… I'm sorry, Ash."

It takes me a second to realise what he's talking about. I
shrug. "You've apologised for it before. How were you to
know? To you, we were just another *wealh* caravan passing
through your hunting grounds. We should have been more
careful. We shouldn't have trusted Quintus."

"I still remember that man with the great axe. I've never
seen anyone fight so well."

"Fulco the Frank." I nod.

"It was because of him that I chose Offa as my
bodyguard," he says. "There's nothing quite as deadly in close
combat as a Frankish axe."

I nod, remembering my sparring with the silent warrior.
"Offa is not a Frank, is he?"

[187]

"No — but he fought there with my father, and picked up the skill."

"How long ago was that?"

A pause, as Aelle calculates. "Twenty years. We moved to Frankia when I was a young child."

Now it's my turn to fall silent. I imagine a life Offa must have led. Twenty years ago, he was already a veteran of many wars. And he's been a warrior ever since. Is that why he's now so silent and grim?

"Do you think in twenty years' time, we'll still be fighting in some war?" I ask.

"I hope so," Aelle replies, eagerly. "What else is there in life?"

New Port is barely recognisable. The last time I was here, it was a thriving, bustling harbour, spread in a long and narrow line from east to west along the ridge of the chalk downs. Carts, mules and foot porters laden with fish, sand and foreign goods would leave in a steady stream north, towards Londin, while those with grain, vegetables and iron ore arrived from inland. The sand-dusted marketplace, in the shadow of a tall stone church, was just as loud, crowded and foul-smelling as the Forum in the capital. The broad beaches, covered with wharves, piers, and stone-paved squares, were filled with goods ready for loading onto the waiting ships. A giant treadwheel crane creaked in the wind and heaved under the hefty loads.

Now, half the piers stand abandoned, their planks rotting through. Weeds and moss grow through pave stones. The spokes on the crane's wheel are cracked, and there's no rope on the pulley. Instead, a troop of slaves struggles to carry a giant barrel onto the deck of a galley, bobbing in the waves. The broad-decked galley is the only ship in the harbour that's getting ready to sail — the remaining handful of vessels, including a couple of Saxon *ceols*, seems to be wintering out the storm season, their tack shrouded in cobwebs and dust.

With the harbour in this half-hibernated state, we have little problem finding the room at a tavern in the town's more affluent district, a suburb to the west of the main harbour, where the rich merchants keep their offices of business in the summer. Paying for it, however, proves more difficult.

"A whole silver coin per night?"

"That's the price. It's two coins in high season. Take it or leave it," grunts the tavern keeper. "And none of your clipped northern filth. This is an elegant establishment."

"What's the problem?" asks Aelle. He's already sitting at a table with a flask of Tarraconian wine, having left us to deal with the formalities.

"I… I don't have any silver coins," I say, embarrassed. There are chests full of money back at Ariminum, but I didn't think I would need them going into Andreda. "I only have a handful of *nummi*."

"A silver coin would get you a week in a Londin tavern," adds Eadgith. "It's been months since I've seen a whole one. Maybe we can go somewhere else."

"Nonsense. We have our appointment here tonight. I'm sorry, I keep forgetting what you've all had to go through. Barkeep!"

Aelle strides over to the counter and gives the owner a long, deliberate stare — until he's recognised. The keeper lets out a brief shriek and bends down in a deep bow, murmuring apologies.

"You will add this to my father's tab, won't you?" says Aelle.

"Oh, I wouldn't dare, my *Hlaford*," says the landlord, his voice trembling. "Please, take whatever room you want. We're half empty at this time of year, anyway."

Grinning, Aelle returns to his wine. "Well, that's sorted."

"*My* Hlaford?" My eyebrow goes up. The word is a Saxon term for a noble-born, but used only in the context of a subject speaking to his superior. I would never expect a Briton to use it when referring to a pagan.

"He is the son of a *Rex*, after all," a familiar Gaulish twang booms behind my back. "I didn't expect to see you here until spring, Aelle."

"My father is still only a *Drihten*," Aelle replies. "We are slow to embrace your continental ways, *Decurion*."

Odo's long, curly hair has a few more grey threads in it, his face sports a few more battle scars, and he bears a new diadem of gold and silver upon his brow. The scabbard of his trusted cavalry sword is now studded with precious gems and laced with gold wire fashioned into fighting dragons; his cloak, clasped with a brooch in the shape of a golden deer, is trimmed with purple and has the Imperial Eagle embroidered at the back; but other than that, he is the same tall, proud Gaulish *Decurion* I last saw three winters ago, commanding a troop of mercenaries on the beach in Anderitum.

He is still a commander of a band of mercenaries, a different one, that he'd begun to gather after leaving Britannia in the aftermath of Wortimer's coup.

"Why didn't you stay?"

"I didn't want to join Wortimer's army of roughs and butchers — and nobody else would pay me to join their side."

"You thought the Iutes were a lost cause," I say.

He scowls. "I'm a cavalryman. I don't know how to defend forts and villages." It's clear from his expression he doesn't want me to explore this line of enquiry any further.

"And where is this band of mercenaries now?" I ask.

"Here, in New Port," he replies. "What's left of it. We arrived on that broad-decked galley that stands in the harbour, Solinus's grain ship, the only one that dared to venture the storms."

"How many of you are there?"

"As many as we could fit on the galley. Thirty horses."

"That's even less than we had when fighting the Picts," I say. "What were you planning to do with this handful?"

My scepticism riles him. "These men survived the entire trail of Aetius's campaign against the Hun, from Tolosa to Maurica. Every one of them is worth a dozen best warriors of this poxy island."

"Then why did you bring them here? There's nobody left in these lands who could afford the services of such skilled mercenaries, except maybe Ambrosius, and he's far away — you'd have been better off sailing to Corin."

"I've tried that. We spent a month in the West, fighting the Scots and the Picts — but there was little glory or coin in those mountain skirmishes, and the weather there at this time of year is abysmal. Besides, we've earned enough spoils on the Huns. We just need some place to spend the winter and not let our swords grow rusty."

His eyes shift aside as he speaks. It is clear he's not telling us everything, so after plying him with more of the inn's heavy Tarraconian wine, I prod again, until he throws his hands up in the air and admits the real reason.

"The Huns are back," he says. "As strong as they ever were. And this time, they're marching on Rome itself. Aetius went back to Italia to stop them, and asked his allies to help him, but they abandoned him after the way he treated them at Maurica. And I... was weary of fighting."

The news strikes the table like lightning. I'm less concerned with the return of the Huns — I never believed it was possible to ever truly destroy them. But Aetius was the constant, obvious threat. Everything that has happened since

Germanus's arrival hinged on the menacing presence of his Legions just across the Narrow Sea. It was the catalyst that spurned Wortigern into action; it was the shadow that kept Wortimer's opposition in the Council in check. If the Huns were to defeat him in Italia, or even just bloody his Legions badly enough, this threat might be gone forever...

"Ambrosius said we could go home," I whisper, still trying to wrap my head around the consequences of what was just said.

"I... I'd advise against that," says Odo. "With the Huns and the Legions busy elsewhere, all of Gaul is in turmoil. The lands north of Frankia — your homelands — have been hit the worst. Nobody even dares to go there anymore. The levees are broken, the seas swallowed the fields. Frisia is as good as gone. Some have even sailed to Britannia again, seeking better fortune and filling Hengist's ranks — it was thanks to them that the Iutes managed to hold out for so long. Others gathered into bands of roving marauders, harassing whoever else was left."

"That just means more space for us to get lost in," I reply, staring grimly into my cup. "I can see us becoming one of those bands of marauders. Anything is better than being hunted to death, like animals."

"Help me fight back, and nobody will hunt you ever again." Aelle leans over. I don't think I've ever seen him this serious.

"I've been fighting them for a year!" I cry. "It changed nothing. All I have left is a cartful of wounded men and an island full of graves."

"But don't you see? Things *have* changed. Aetius's Legions are gone. Wortimer is dead. Ambrosius is busy with the Scots and the Picts, his treasury depleted. It's just the few *Comites* and their militias we have to deal with…"

"*Just* the *Comites!*" I laugh, bitterly. "Well, if it's *just* the *Comites*…!"

"If you need a cavalry wing…" starts Odo.

"You know I could never pay your men for their service," I reply. "And no, I don't need a cavalry wing, because we are *not* fighting back. That war is over. I'll just need to find another way for my people to survive."

I stand up. The table wobbles. A goblet falls and the Tarraconian wine spills all over the table, thick like blood.

"You will change your mind," Aelle shouts after me. "You'll see!"

"What is it?" asks Eadgith. "Can't you sleep?"

I'm looking out the narrow window of the tavern room at the sleepy harbour below. The icy breeze blows in from the sea, making my naked skin stand up in goose-bumps. My contemplative mood is disturbed somewhat by the sounds of Aelle humping a bar wench he fancied bringing to his room next door.

I didn't feel comfortable with Aelle paying for separate rooms for the two of us, so Eadgith and I are sharing the bed tonight. Lying close to her radiant, abundant warmth and hearing the excited moans behind the thin wooden wall makes the blood rush boiling hot to my extremities. I'm hoping for the cold of a winter night to calm me down.

"Rhedwyn was here, once," I say, my teeth chattering. "In Catuar's palace," I add, pointing to the only building on the clifftop overlooking the town with the lights still on. "Before Germanus arrived, before everything fell apart."

"What was she like, this Rhedwyn?"

Of course, I remind myself, not being a Iute, Eadgith never had the opportunity to meet my... sister. In my mind, I run through ways of describing Rhedwyn that wouldn't sound too gushing or trite. An angel... a princess... a beauty as there never walked the God's Earth...

"Do you remember — there was a statue in Ariminum... A goddess of marble, supporting the veranda's eaves, clad in nothing but long hair and a bath towel..."

"I remember. I was envious of her growing up. Was Rhedwyn like that?"

"No." I smile. "She was no goddess — she was a real woman. When I first saw her, she was thin and gaunt from living in the squalor of Tanet. Her skin was rough, there was black dirt under her fingernails. Her breath smelled of goat meat and sour milk. She was covered in lice. But I didn't see any of that. To me, she was more beautiful than any ancient statue. She was like the ray of light peeking through the clouds at the end of a summer storm."

Eadgith's answer is a heavy silence.

"Octa was my only ray of light," she says, eventually. "I don't think I've ever loved my husband like that. And with you, well…"

"I know. We were too young."

A stronger gust of wind whistles in the gutters. It cuts my skin with frost. I step away from the window and close the shutters. I sit on the edge of the bed. The moaning on the other side of the wall has mercifully stopped.

"Have you given much thought yet to what Odo told us?" Eadgith asks.

"I try not to. It's too much to take after all this Tarraconian wine."

"Do you think you're going to change your mind, like Aelle said?"

"I don't think so." I lie back down beside her. The noise begins anew in the other room, but this time it's just Aelle's drunk snoring. "And I doubt it would change anything if I did. Aelle's giving me far too much credit."

"He must have his reasons."

"What do you think I should do?"

"I'm just a bladesmith," she replies. She puts her sturdy arm across my chest, and I wrap mine around her shoulders. "I don't know anything about politics or war."

[196]

"And I'm just a Iutish slaveling who's read a few books too many," I say with a chuckle. "I have no right to decide what anyone should or shouldn't do."

She sighs. "We've been through this. You're the best one that's left."

"Is that really a good enough reason?"

"Do you need any other?"

I find Odo washing his lustrous black hair by the tavern's well. His chest and back are pocked all over with small, deep, triangular scars, all pointing downwards.

"Hunnish arrows?" I ask.

He puts away the bucket and looks into the distance. "They blotted out the sun," he says, and his eyes go dark and fierce. "A black cloud of death, like poisonous rain from the sky. Their arrows could pierce any shield or armour at three hundred feet. The only way to survive was to keep riding, charging ahead, as fast as the horse would take you, hoping that you could outrun the arrows…"

He rubs his eyes and laughs. "How many men did we have fighting on that beach in the land of the Ikens? Five hundred? And at Anderitum — a thousand on each side? And these are the battles that will be remembered for generations to come." He sits on the well's rim. "The day before Maurica, we encountered a Gepid vanguard in a forest clearing. We fought them back with ease, it was just a skirmish, not worth noting in the chronicles… Ten thousand bodies were left for the ravens in that wood."

I repeat the number in astonished whisper.

"That's nothing. They say a hundred thousand men fought at Maurica," he says. "A number I can easily believe. Can you even imagine such a thing? That's twice as many as there are in Londin, and all of them bloodthirsty warriors, from every corner of the known world. Alans, Franks, Goths, Gepids, Burgundians, Armoricans… A hundred thousand men at each other's throats, gouging, thrusting, shooting, hacking, dodging, parrying, fleeing in fear and then rallying back to save their comrades." His hands dance in the air, drawing each movement he speaks of. "And the only two men who could make any sense of it all, like two mighty gods, one on each side, Aetius and Attila, lives of thousands in their hands… I thought such battles happened only in myths until I saw the sea of men with my own eyes."

"What was your part in the battle?"

He crouches and sketches a rough plan in the dirt with his fingers. "There was a ridge… The Huns held the north end, we climbed from the south. I led an *ala* of Frankish riders — a hundred men of royal stock, axe-wielding giants, loyal and brave. If I still had them with me, I'd conquer this whole island by myself…"

"The battle," I remind him.

"Aetius ordered the Franks to guard the left of the centre. He had Alans in the middle, fearing they would defect to the Huns… If that had happened, we would have been trapped between the two hammers. So Meroweg, the *Rex* of the

Franks, had me keep close to the Alan chieftain, and kill him if it looked like he was going to betray us."

"And did you?"

He nods, slowly. "I pierced his neck with a Hunnic arrow. Made it seem like the enemy slew him. This rallied the Alans, the centre held — until the Goths rode from behind and fell on Attila's own *Hiréd*, scattering them in the four winds."

"You must have been greatly rewarded for this!"

"You'd think so, wouldn't you?" He scoffs. "But no. The diadem and the scabbard were all I managed to take from the battlefield, and I had to tear it off the Alan chieftain with my own hands. Aetius took all the treasure for himself."

"How did they let him get away with that?"

"He played them all brilliantly. Tribe against tribe, *Rex* against a *Drihten*... In the end, everyone just went home with nothing. But, I don't hold a grudge. He did what he had to do. Rome needed that gold to survive. Or at least try to."

The harbour bell rings out the third hour of the day. The breakfast should be ready. I scoop some well water in my hands and brush sleep from my eyes.

"Why did you really come here?" I ask. "Did you plan to join Wortimer's army against us?"

"No," he replies firmly. "I would never side with that traitor and coward. I met his father in the West, you know — he told me of everything that happened here. And after what

I and my men saw at Maurica… We'd rather stand with the pagans than with Rome."

"Sail to Tanet, then. Hengist needs all the help he can get."

"I told you — my cavalry would be no use there. We'd just get bogged down in the mud."

"Then what are you going to do? Go back to Gaul when the storms end?"

"Maybe. There are rumours of another war in the South, on the border with Hispania. The Goths will be looking for men who know the lay of the land."

There is no conviction in his voice. I sense he's disappointed that I haven't proposed that he join us, but I cannot accommodate his expectations. Instead, I just nod and turn to the dining hall. He calls after me.

"Ash!"

I look over my shoulder.

"I was really hoping we could fight side by side again one day."

I stroll down the harbour beach, passing the empty crates and barrels, piles of wood, rolls of cloth, fishing nets, stacks of sailing gear the purpose of which I cannot fathom. I walk alone, in the freezing rain, with only the sailors and porters from Solinus's galley huddling under wet sailcloth for silent company.

I can't remember the last time I was alone like this, out in the open, breathing in the crisp sea air, listening to seagulls and the rush of waves. The hills roll gently away to the east; in the west, a broad, slow-moving river estuary marks the town's border. It is a pleasant land, even in the cold grasp of late winter.

I reach the market square, where the Roman highway from Londin meets the coastal road from Regentium. Fresh blades of grass sprout from between the flagstones, marking the coming of the spring thaws. With spring, the war will resume, one last time, and Hengist's forces on the distant Isle of Tanet will be crushed forever by whomever gained the upper hand in Londin. And while this might be enough for a while to the exhausted Britons, it's obvious that sooner or later they will turn their attention to other territories not under their control. Britannia has to belong to the Britons.

I keep thinking about what Odo told us. We talked for long hours after breakfast. The *Decurion* described the battle with the Huns in still greater detail, painting the magnificent picture of an alliance of tribes, a confederacy of peoples united in the single goal: to meet Attila's army head-on and inflict on him such a defeat that he would never dare to enter Gaul again. In this, at least, they succeeded — the Huns were now moving on Rome, leaving the Goths, Franks, Burgundians and others alone, to fight for spoils among each other.

Prompted by Aelle, Odo told us what he had learned of the new barbarian kingdoms, explaining at last that strange new term he kept mentioning, one that the Goths and

Burgundians used to call their overlords, rulers of all united tribes and clans: *Rex* in the Imperial Tongue, or *Reiks* in the language of the Goths; I knew the word only from the old chronicles, where it described the monarchs of the small kingdoms Rome had conquered while extending its dominion. Drust of the Hundred Victories was the first *Rex* I've heard about in the West since the days before the Empire. I thought he was an anomaly, an odd relic of the past — but now, it seemed, kings were becoming the new norm; they were the *future*. New kings were popping up all over the place, everywhere the power of the Empire waned: Theodrik of the Goths. Meroweg of the Franks. Gundoweg of the Burgundians. They were more than just *Drihtens*, war leaders like Hengist or Pefen; their power was absolute — they heeded no *witans*, no judges, no priests. And it was clear from Aelle's interest in the matter that he wanted this title for his father — and, eventually, for himself: Aelle, *Rex* of the Saxons.

I had no interest in titles or power. I barely qualified as a chieftain of the handful of survivors hiding in Andreda. But I did find Odo's tale of the great alliance of pagan tribes intriguing. If only he'd arrived sooner with this idea, something may have come from it. If all the pagan tribes of the island had come together, while we were still in control of the swathes of Londin, perhaps we could have crushed Wortimer and his Briton allies once and for all. But now it was too late. The Iutes were spent, Aelle's Saxons were cowering behind their barricades, the *Gewisse* were no doubt banished from Elasio's lands, and as for the Angles, they were too far away to be of any use…

I stop and raise my face to the rain to calm myself down. I've let my thoughts wander too far. There will be no alliance; there will be no battle. I need to focus on the people under my care. The camps at Andreda will only support them for so long, and while they might settle on the blasted heathlands like the free woodsmen we saw on our journey to New Port, it would be a life far more harsh than they've grown used to in their villages and even later in Londin. Aelle mentioned an island off the southern coast, Wecta — sparsely populated now and exposed to sea raiders, but warm and fertile for anyone who might wish to put a plough to it, better suited for us than Tanet, and easier to defend from the Britons; all we'd need is to organise ourselves a transport and hope —

"Young Fraxinus? Is that you?"

The voice comes from inside a litter carried by six olive-skinned slaves, heaving under the weight of their passenger. The small window opens, showing a round, fat, pale face.

"It is my name, yes," I reply. "How do you —"

"Don't recognise the old man, eh? It's been years, but you haven't changed much."

He opens the door and clambers out. The slaves put down the litter with relief; one of them rushes with an umbrella to shield his master from the rain.

I've seen Solinus a couple of times in Londin over the years, but it takes me a while to recognise him. He is even fatter now than I remember, and completely bald except for a few tufts of white hair over his ears. His jowls hang like two chops of meat.

"What are you doing here, boy?" he asks, then lowers his voice. "Have you been sent from Londin to check on us?"

I don't see much point in explaining to him all that's happened to me since we last saw each other, so I just shake my head. "I'm here with Aelle."

"Oh, the young *Hlaford* is here!" He gets all flustered. "Please give him my best regards."

"I will," I say. I raise my hand to wave him goodbye, and stop halfway. "Young *Hlaford*," I repeat. "You've grown used to the Saxon rule, then?"

He laughs. "Used? Can't get enough of it! You know I've always liked your people being here, boy. They keep things clean and safe; they keep the pirates and bandits away. They've lowered the taxes and duties to almost nothing." He jiggles his fingers, showing off massive gold rings. "We've never had it as good as under *Rex* Pefen." He comes over and lays his fat palm on my shoulders. "If only you Northerners stopped fighting among each other and resumed the trade! Any chance of that happening, son? I admit, I haven't been following news from Londin since Wortimer started that silly little conflict with the Iutes."

"Wortimer's dead."

"Oh!" He pulls away. "I'm sorry, I didn't know. Still." He shrugs, "Maybe at least now there'll be peace."

"Eventually. When all the Iutes are dead or have fled."

His face grows even paler, if it's at all possible. His jewelled fingers tremble. "Dead! Fled? No, no, no, this will not do at all."

"I'm grateful for your concern, Master Solinus… But I'm afraid it's too late to help them."

"Don't get me wrong, boy," he says quickly, his fingers dancing, "I'm as much against senseless slaughter as the next man, but I've seen a fair share of wars in my life. My concern is strictly financial. You see, I have interests in the oyster beds on the Iute land — and I've seen what Londin does with those when they get their hands on them…"

"You mean like they did with Master Deneus."

"Ah, so you've heard about poor Dene…"

He wipes the rain from his face and lingers for a moment in thought.

"Oh, but I am holding you out in this darned rain, my apologies," he says. "I need to send out some messengers to the North, figure out what to do with this news. I may need to cut my profits short this year. Dead! Fled!"

He retreats, rear first, into the litter, mumbling apologies and farewells.

"But I have to say," he adds at the end, "I'm surprised at you, Master Fraxinus."

"Why?"

"I thought you would stand up for your people with more vigour. Aren't you a half-Iute yourself?"

I cross the market square and climb up to the church overlooking the harbour from the same low green sand ridge as Catuar's palace. Both buildings are empty now. The tribal Council has little reason to gather anymore. The church is closed on days like this — a regular, middle of the week winter day, with nobody having any business visiting the cold stone edifice.

At least, it should be. Instead, the door is wide open. I hesitate before entering. How would the Roman God living inside react to my presence — an apostate, a baptised heathen? Even the God of Pelagius would not welcome me into His abode — I am no longer the "good soul" Fastidius once saw in me. I am a heathen *and* a sinner, the worst of both worlds...

"Come in, whoever you are," a voice beckons from the stillness.

It's dark inside — only a few candles light up the frontispiece. The sun, already dimmed by the clouds, fails to penetrate through the narrow gable window.

"Why is this place open?" I ask. A lonely echo distorts my voice and sends it flying up to the gables. "It's not a holy day."

"The Lord rewards the hopeful."

"So you just stay here all day, hoping someone will stumble into your temple at random?"

"And here you are."

I peer into the dusk, trying to see who I'm talking to. A young priest, same age as Fastidius, comes out into the dim light, squinting. "You're one of them."

"*Them?*"

"A Saxon. Have you come to rob us?" He waves at the altar. "There is nothing left, as you can see."

"I'm a Iute," I reply. "I have been baptised."

The priest picks up a candle and approaches. He studies my face. "That's a strange turn of phrase. Normally, you'd just say you were a Christian."

"Make of it what you will."

"Why are you here, baptised Iute?"

Why *am* I here? I haven't been inside a church since Germanus's fateful sermon at Saint Paul's Cathedral.

"I needed a quiet place to think."

He walks up to the door and glances outside. He looks at me with a raised eyebrow. The town is morbidly silent in the freezing mist, quieter than the inside of the church, filled with a low hum of reverberated wind.

"I can see you're in some distress, my son," he says. "I would propose a prayer — but I suppose it's not what you're after."

I go up to the altar and look up at the figure of Christ, roughly hewn in local green sandstone. His eyes and face are shrouded in the shadow.

"My people are being slaughtered," I say. "In the name of your god."

"Killing is a man's business," he replies. "Not God's."

"But your god is letting it happen."

"If your people want God's protection, all they need to do is ask."

"Some of them did," I say. "There were many baptised among the dead in Londin."

I look around. The church is very sparsely equipped. There is barely any silver — the dishes are pewter and clay; the decorative cloth is bare linen, dyed only in the simplest of patterns.

"What happened here? Did the Saxons really plunder this place?"

"In a way. We had to sell it all to pay their new taxes. They threatened my parishioners if we didn't comply."

So that's how Pefen was able to finance his lowered duties on the merchants... The Saxon is as clever as any Briton lord. The merchants are the true power in the harbour city; their support is all that matters here. If only Wortigern had had the time to do the same in Londin. I remember the great heap of treasure in Saint Paul's vaults: it would've paid for an army of mercenaries ready to withstand *any* foe.

"Do you hate them for it?" I ask.

"I hate no one," he says. "But I hope you'll understand why I'm not fond of our new pagan masters."

I turn around. "What would you do if a Roman Legion landed today on this beach and started killing them all? Men, women, children alike?"

He opens his mouth and pauses. He then strengthens himself and looks me in the eyes. "I would do everything in my power to stop them."

His words sound sincere — but it took him just a second too long to say them.

CHAPTER IX
THE LAY OF LIVIUS

"Fine." I slam my hands on the tavern table. Aelle and Eadgith look up from their plates. The front legs of Odo's stool hits the floor as he leans forward.

"Let's say we go for it — and that's still a big *if*— how many warriors could you give me by Easter?"

Aelle's eyes grow and brighten as understanding dawns on him. "Yes! We're doing it! I knew it!"

"I haven't decided on anything yet. I need to see some numbers, find out what the *wealas* are planning. I'm not going to go into any battle without a certainty of victory. Not again."

"Why Easter?" asks Eadgith.

"It's the first good time to march out to war this year. The ground should be dry enough for the horses and carts — and I reckon whoever ends up the new commander in Londin will want to wait for a big Mass to get a blessing for all his soldiers. Especially if it's Elasio."

"We won't have much time," notes Odo.

"Neither will they. They'll want to finish us off before Ambrosius arrives."

"Two hundred," says Aelle, so abruptly I have to ask him to repeat it.

"Two hundred warriors are scattered in all the war bands around Andreda. Plus my own *Hiréd* — not as good as my father's, but they will hold their own against any tribal militia."

"That's fewer than I'd hoped for. I thought your father's army was marching with us."

"My father has… plans of his own for the spring."

"He would fight other clans, while there's still a war on with the *wealas*?"

He puts a finger to his lips. "Not so loud. The spies report the chieftains are conspiring against him — he needs to act first. This is a more immediate threat."

"What about the Free Folk?"

He clicks his tongue. "You'll find it difficult to make them fight other than in defence of their own homes. I told you, I'm not their warchief. I will send out a call to arms, but I'll be surprised if more than a hundred answers the summons. Maybe more if we can reach across the Medu — there are some Frisians and Franks on the Cantish coast who, for the most part, have been staying away from all the fighting."

"I see." I rub my chin. "It will have to do, I suppose. Right." I turn to Odo. He sits up almost to attention. Colour returns to his cheeks, and fire to his eyes. "Do any of your men know this land, beside yourself?"

"One or two might. The Franks have always had an interest in this part of Britannia."

"I'll need them as couriers. Will you ride with me to Ariminum?"

He nods, enthusiastically. "Good place for a headquarters," he says. "Close to the road, well supplied."

"That's not why I'm going there. At least, not only. Eadgith —" I open my mouth and realise it's run dry. I lick my lips and reach for the wine.

"Come with me to the stables," I tell her after quenching my thirst. "I need you to ride back to High Rocks. I'll explain everything along the way."

"What made you change your mind?" she asks when we reach the ponies. She eyes the beast with mistrust, still unconvinced about this mode of transport.

"A chance meeting," I reply. "A key to the puzzle lock, if you will. I came up with a way we might have a shot at victory. It's still only a chance — but it *is* a chance."

"And that was enough? All you needed was to know there's a chance we might win?"

"Does that disappoint you? Should I have hesitated for longer?"

She shrugs. "I'm just glad you stopped questioning yourself."

"Oh, I don't think I'll ever stop doing *that.*"

"Why couldn't you tell me my task at the table?"

I help her put tack on the pony and strap the small padded saddle. When our faces meet under the animal's belly, I speak again in a hushed voice.

"I need you to prepare the Iutes in the camp to move again. As soon as Aelle gathers his army and marches out."

"Move? Where to?"

"Here, to New Port. You'll meet with a man called Solinus. He owns most of the ships in the harbour. He'll take you all to the island of Wecta. You'll be safe there, no matter what happens."

"*All* of us?"

I pause. "If you can find a dozen or so fit enough to fight, have them join me in Ariminum."

She ties up the strap and pats the pony on the neck. The animal lets out a gentle whinny. "Then you don't really believe we have a chance," she says, with a sullen expression.

"I don't have to — what matters is that others will believe it."

He who can make the hearts of their men burn the hottest, wins.

"This is why you must keep your task in utmost secrecy, for as long as possible," I add. "The entire plan depends on it."

[214]

She steps back. "I... I don't know. This is a lot of responsibility. Why choose me? I'm only a bladesmith. You're asking me to be some kind of a... a deputy warchief."

"You can handle it, I'm sure." I grasp her hand. "Besides, you're the only one I can trust with this."

"Is this really a good enough reason?" she asks, with a wry smile.

I smile back. "Do you need any other?"

Plataea. Cannae. Salamis. Leuctra. Gaugamela. Battle after battle, chapter after chapter, volume after volume. The pile of books and scrolls on the mosaic floor of Master Pascent's study is rising ever higher, and so does my frustration. There is nothing here that can help me. The Ancients are dead, silent voices, describing hollow, meaningless victories.

I lied to Eadgith. I lied to everyone. I have no plan, other than saving the handful of Iutes sent to Wecta from immediate destruction. I needed them out of the way to have a clear head; I hoped that once I knew they were out of danger's way, I would be able to focus calmly on developing a battle strategy — to forget about the gloom enveloping my every thought. But my mind is like a dark whirlpool, and the ancient books are like flotsam swallowed into its depth without a trace.

"Having trouble?"

Paulinus stands in the doorway with a wooden mug of steaming hypericum in his hands.

"I was a fool to think I could find an answer in these moth-chewed tomes. I'm no Alexander. I'm no Caesar. And I don't have a battle-trained Legion or a phalanx of hoplites under my command, just a band of Saxons and a handful of Franks, who never fought beside each other."

"Your enemy is not exactly Hannibal, either, son."

"I know. But they will outnumber us, by I don't know how much. And they will have veterans among them, officers of Roman stock. Brutus himself will most likely be the commander in chief. This is the battle that will decide everything. There will be no second chance."

I reach for another tome. It slips from my sweaty fingers and goes crashing to the floor.

"Sit down," says Paulinus, pushing me on the chair. "Calm yourself. Have some ale. You can't find every answer in a book, God knows I've tried. Sometimes you just have to give yourself into the hands of the Lord."

I give him a weary look. He waves a hand.

"I know, I know. Wodan, or whatever barbarian demon you believe in." He sighs. "I don't know why I'm even helping you, heathen."

This makes me chuckle. So old Paulinus finally accepted me for who I am. It does not seem to have shocked him as much as I feared it would. I'm guessing, in the brutal chaos of the recent months, it may well have been the least shocking experience he's had to handle.

I touch the leather cover of the nearest book and rifle through it. It's Diodorus — I've read it through twice already, finding nothing of any use to my predicament.

"Shouldn't this wait until you know more about what the enemy is doing?" he asks. "How many of them are there? Who leads them?"

"If I wait until then it might be too late."

He crouches down beside me and takes a slurp from his mug. "Nobody can foresee the future, Ash. Not even Alexander, or Caesar. They learned from their predecessors, yes, but then they adapted that knowledge to whatever circumstances befell them. Every battle they fought was different."

"Then I should just sit and do nothing?"

"You could help me prepare for the Easter Mass," he says, with a mischievous smile.

"You're still doing it? I thought you were removed for sustaining the heresy."

"The villagers don't care about that. And Fastidius, God bless him, never bothered to send a replacement." He raises the mug in toast to the Bishop.

"Is that why you got back to drinking this instead of the mead?"

"I... owe a lot to your brother. More than just letting me back in front of the altar."

He doesn't finish, but I understand that this is the answer to his earlier question. He's helping me because of his loyalty to Fastidius, and to Pascent's line. In this loyalty, he is ready to assist a pagan against a Christian; he's almost become a pagan himself, a heretic, preaching against the orders of his own Church.

I could build a kingdom on such men.

I don't know where this thought has come from. I never planned to become a *Drihten* — the Iutes already have one in Hengist. I find Aelle's ambition to become a *Rex* of the Saxons laughable. All I want is for things to go back to what they were... The Iutes safe and happy in their villages, a stable peace between them and Britons, Londin the prosperous and vibrant city it once was...

This will not bring her back.

No, it will not. And neither will it resurrect all those fallen warriors. But it might make their sacrifice worth *something*. More, at least, than that handful of souls that right about now should be getting ready to board Solinus's grain galley.

"I will help with your Mass," I tell Paulinus. "I think I still remember something from my baptism lessons."

The first of Odo's Franks arrives at the *villa* early on Easter Monday, while Paulinus and I are still sitting at the breakfast table, eating the leftovers from yesterday's small feast. It was a morose event; after a year of war and bad harvest, the countryside is devoid of any mirth. Only a few townsfolk from Saffron Valley came to the Mass, the rest of them stayed at their homes, weary of coming too close to the charred ruin of the Iute village, sprawled like a rotten corpse on the other side of the church fence.

The rider brings news from Aelle: he has gathered his two hundred warriors in a camp on the eastern outskirts of Andreda. From the rider's description I gather that it's the exact same ancient hillfort where I first met Aelle — where he dragged me and other hostages after the slaughter on the River Medu.

Of course, he hasn't done this on purpose — it's the best positioned spot from which to send out patrols to follow the route of the *wealh* army towards Tanet, whichever road they take. Still, the irony is not lost on me — or Paulinus, when he hears the news.

"You knew who you were allying yourself with," he tells me.

"I know. I just don't like being reminded about it."

The next day, another rider comes from New Port. He brings two letters. One of them is from Eadgith. The news is encouraging. Some twenty Iute warriors are waiting with the Saxons at the forest camp. More volunteered but, just as I asked, she and Birch worked hard to choose only those fit enough for a battle.

She continues on another page, in a different hand. Whoever she was dictating the first page to, she must have deemed them unworthy of her trust for the news she brings next. The first column of the Iutish refugees — those most vulnerable, among them children and those with most grievous injuries — has reached the town and boarded the ship to Wecta. The rest are making their way through the forest. As far as she can tell, Aelle did not suspect anything.

"I don't ever want to do anything like this again, Ash," she — or rather, the scribe, writes. "My mind is swirling. If it wasn't for Betula's help, I would never have managed. Choose someone else to be your lackey next time. I wish to go back to my blades as soon as this is over."

The other sealed letter is from Solinus. I burn it without reading. His mission, his *other* mission, is not crucial for the success of my plan, but it might tip the scales at the last minute — and I don't want to give myself false hope. Things have already been set in motion. If I find out he's failed — could I really stop everything? *Would I want to?*

"So far, so good," remarks Paulinus. "Shouldn't you be readying yourself to move out?"

"Not yet. There's one more rider I'm waiting for."

The third and last of the messengers is Odo himself. I sent him out to Londin to pose as a *Decurion* of the mercenaries willing to join with the Briton army, and find out whatever he could about the situation in the city. I was hoping he would arrive early, to give me enough time to analyse the news and prepare, but days pass without any trace of the Gaul's whereabouts. I drown my anxiety in Paulinus's tincture. Was he found out? Has he decided to betray me and go with the higher bidder? Or maybe he's just fallen victim to one of the many accidents that could occur in a city as dangerous as Londin is now — just another prank of the vengeful gods…

[220]

I can't afford to wait any longer. If the Britons marched out after Easter, they'd be well on their way to Tanet now. Maybe already there — even if their war band didn't exactly march at a Legion's pace. I must ride out to meet Aelle and his patrols and ready myself to face whatever Fate brings before me.

I step outside just as Odo rides in through the Ariminum gate. He's not alone. The other rider mounts a grey mare, and wears a woollen *paenula* cloak. An oaken staff is slung over his back. The two approach me in silence, but Odo's face is beaming with hidden mirth. I stare at the other man as he dismounts. The cloak, the staff, the hooded cloak make him seem like Wodan the Wanderer in my dreams. I back away, my hand hovering near the hilt of my sword.

The stranger lowers his hood.

"Why are you always so surprised to see me, brother?"

Fastidius knew something was odd about Odo's behaviour the moment he saw the Gaul in Londin, trying to ingratiate himself with the Council of *Comites*, who have ruled the city since Wortimer's death.

"The man is too honest to keep up a lie for too long," he tells me. "And I knew he would never betray a friend. I had to find out what he was really doing in Londin."

He approached Odo after the Easter Mass to take his confession. It was a rare privilege, one only afforded to the rich and powerful; but there were no rich and powerful left to talk to. Those who were rich, have already fled the war-torn city. Those who were powerful were too engaged in the fight for the throne to bother with confessions.

"It didn't take long to drag the truth out of him. I was his brother in arms too, after all. And when I found out you were behind it all, and that you were back in Ariminum, I... I had to come here in person."

"You saw me just a couple of months ago."

"I realised this might be the last time we see each other."

"It happened before," I reply. "You thought I was dead after Callew."

"I never had the chance to say goodbye then," he replies. "I'm not making this mistake now."

"You don't think I can win this?"

He scratches his ear with a wince.

"I think there's a possibility you might lose."

"Then help me."

"I *am*. There is another reason why I'm here. It would take too long for Odo to grasp the nuances of everything that's been going on in the city right now. I'm in the middle of it all. I need to tell you about it myself."

We enter the study. His eyes fall on the pile of the Classics on the floor and the table. He gets on one knee beside them and picks up the thickest tome.

"My father's books… What are they doing here?"

"I was trying to figure out how best to beat the Britons."

"Found anything?"

"Nothing that would be of any use."

He shakes his head, rifling through the pages. "I forget how many years it has been since I read these."

"Back when everyone thought you'd end up as a general, not a priest."

"I'm still a general, of sorts," he says, standing up. "I fight God's fight."

"And how's that working out for you?"

I make it sound more cruel than I meant to. His predicament is entirely my own fault. By making him help me, I'm putting him in the same difficult position as Paulinus — except he's not some defrocked village heretic, but the Bishop of Londin, the most important position in Britannia's Church.

He stands up and reaches out to embrace me. "Thank you for your concern, brother," he speaks in my ear, "but it's going better than you'd think. Have you heard of the great new church they've built at Wenta of the Ikens?"

I see him grin as he steps away. He waits for me to get what he's saying.

"Parable of the Lost Sheep," I guess.

He nods. "For what woman, having ten pieces of silver, if she lose one, does not sweep the house to find it? And what man, having a hundred sheep, if he loses one, does not go into the wilderness after that which is lost?"

"The Britons are already Christian. You're hoping to gain souls among the Iutes. Will Rome look at it the same way?"

"That depends on how successful I am. We are."

I laugh. I know he wants me to promise him to build more churches on the Iute land if we succeed. This is all that matters to him — to spread the Faith among the heathens.

"Brother, you don't need to bargain with me like this. Come, let's have some food and talk things over. I don't have much time."

Perhaps the most surprising of Fastidius's news is that *Comes* Elasio has not yet won over all the other contenders to the *Dux*'s throne in the weeks since Wortimer's death. Despite having the largest army, and the implied backing of Rome as protector of the Chapel of Albanus, he still needed to consult his decisions with the others.

"I didn't think there would be anyone else left to challenge him."

"Not on their own. But for now, they're all united against him. Old Peredur with the Trinowaunts. Masuna with the Atrebs."

"Are they still playing Wortimer's morbid little game? Counting Iute heads?"

"Not so literally. But they will be assessed on the valour they show on the battlefield when it comes to a decision."

"What about the Cants?" I ask, noticing he omitted one important pawn on the board.

"This is one battle you've already won," he replies, pointing a finger. "Worangon and many of his best warriors perished in the fire you started. The Cants are in disarray. Most of their forces are already tied besieging Tanet, anyway."

"I didn't know the fire was… that bad." I look to the floor. "Did many city folk die?"

"Not as many as we feared, thanks be to merciful God. But the city centre is ravaged from Tamesa to the Forum. At dawn came the rain, extinguishing most of the flames."

"Praise be to merciful God," says Paulinus, raising his eyes piously to the sky. "You haven't mentioned Ambrosius yet."

"That's because nobody knows what his plans are. The *Comites* would rather not have to deal with him until they deal with the Iutes and the Saxons. Masuna blocked the fords and bridges along the Callew Highway to slow down his advance, but so far, there is no word from the West."

"We'll worry about Ambrosius when he's here," I say.

"There is… another one," says Fastidius.

[225]

"Another contender? Who would that be?"

"Brutus. He's gathered Wortimer's roughs and the Wall garrison around him and announced himself the true successor to the dead *Dux*."

I nod. "Makes sense." Brutus, my nemesis, the traitor of Saffron Valley, the general at Crei Ford, the defender of the Coln Gate. Undoubtedly the best of Wortimer's remaining commanders. "But it's bad news. He knows me — he might be expecting me to plan some surprise for them."

"I doubt it. The general consensus is that your Iutes no longer exist as any sort of fighting force. I don't think they've even set up any flank defences, other than the border guard on the crossroads."

"So the armies have moved out already?"

"Yesterday. For now, the entire mass of soldiers is keeping together —" Fastidius pushes the plates aside and rolls out a map on the reading table: a piece of old, torn, yellowed vellum Paulinus found somewhere in the library. There were better maps of Britannia in the *villa* when he was teaching me geography, with more detail, finer decorations. All are gone now. Though most of the bound tomes in Pascent's study have survived the years intact, many of the scrolls did not — eaten by moths, used for kindling in harsh winters, soaked through when part of the roof fell in during a spring storm…

"— at least until Dorowern. I don't know what their plans are exactly, but I expect the main host will march straight to Rutubi."

The Saxon Shore fortress of Rutubi, an outpost across the narrow channel from Tanet, was Wortimer's last conquest, in autumn. Had he lived through the winter, it would have been the base from which he would have launched an assault on Tanet itself.

"From what I've heard, Hengist is holed up with most of his forces in Eobbasfleot," continues Fastidius. He looks up at me briefly — he's the only one at this table to know about my relationship to Eobba. I stare back, showing no emotion. "They fortified it as best as they could, with stone from the abandoned monastery, and now can only wait to make their final stand."

"There's no chance for them to come to our help?"

"Perhaps. But the Cants control the channel, and I doubt the Iutes have many war boats left."

Odo leans down over the map and traces the fading lines of the roads with his finger, until he reaches a barely visible black dot on the northern coast. "What about Reculbium?"

"It's still in Iutish hands, but the garrison there is tiny."

"They will send a small force to keep it in check," I say. "With the weakest of the contenders in charge. Peredur?"

"That's likely," says Fastidius.

"He will try to capture it and kill everyone inside, to keep up with the others in this grim contest."

"Careful, Ash," Paulinus interjects. "Remember what I told you about predicting the future."

"I'm only guessing. Aelle's lookouts will find it all out anyway. Speaking of which, we have to get going. Time is running out on us. Odo, are you ready to ride again today?"

"Always."

I reach into my saddle bag and take out a wax-sealed clay flask. It's the last of the mead from Beaddingatun, before the town's destruction by Wortimer's forces. A gift from Paulinus. He told me he hasn't drunk a drop of it since witnessing the slaughter. It is not for me to drink; it's to pour as libation to the gods in the memory of the fallen.

In the other bag is the gift from Fastidius. He didn't take it with him to Ariminum — he *found* it there.

"By the way," he said, handing me the book as we parted our ways — his grey mare going back north, my pony and Odo's black stallion heading east, down the old Pilgrim's Way, "Livius, Book Twenty-Two."

"Thanks, but I've already read all of Livius."

"Haven't you noticed, the first half of that volume was missing? This is my personal copy. It was still in my room, with Vegetius."

"I've gone through more than a dozen of these tomes, will half a volume really make a difference?"

"This one might."

[228]

I'm eager to find out what it is that Fastidius thought so important about Livius's Book Twenty-Two. Of course, I know what's in its second half — everyone knows; the prelude to, and the aftermath of, the battle of Cannae, Hannibal's most famous victory. But I have neither the men, nor battlefield, nor the skill of command to pull off another Cannae in Britannia. Nor do I have the time to play at slow, delaying war, like Fabius Maximus, the Cunctator. What else have I missed?

The copy, from what I glanced, is a number of sheets of studying paper written in Fastidius's own young, shaky handwriting, bound between two wooden boards with a length of string. I imagine him poring over the volume by night, by the light of an oil lamp, his tongue in the corner of his mouth, while I frolicked with Eadgith or some other girl from the *villa*. Paulinus never had me copy entire books like this — already back then he must have known I would lack patience for this sort of exercise. Did he, too, see the *madness* in me that Eadgith spoke about? Or just the laziness…

We follow the old Pilgrims' Way to the Medu, and stop for the night in the burnt-out remains of the old *mansio*. There's no trace left of the landlord and the landlady. Instead, an empty chapel stands among the ruins, one of Wortimer's many foundations. He's built so many of them, Fastidius told me, in an effort to gain the Church's blessings, that there were never enough priests or even the faithful to fill them up. They're scattered like this all over the countryside, empty monuments to his pride — and perhaps, I entertain the thought for a second, to his guilt?

I take a stroll along the riverbank, to the ruined temple — it still stands, only more overgrown and cracked; it must have escaped the attention of Wortimer's plunderers. It could not be more different from the last time I saw it. The wall is rough and cold to touch. An icy wind blows from the river and weaves between the columns. The stone floor, where the priestess once stood, is blackened with a thick layer of ancient soot and burnt fat. No gods dwell here anymore. Between this ruin and Wortimer's empty chapel, no light of faith penetrates the darkness of this wilderness.

I look south, towards the black wall of Andreda. If there are any gods left in this land, it's there, among the oaks and ashes, greening with the first spring buds, brimming with bird song. But for how long? If the *Comites* win against the Iutes, how long before the Saxons are thrown back to their homelands, and then the Angles — until there are no heathens anywhere in Britannia? Can Wotan and Donar truly be defeated? A few years ago, such a thing seemed impossible. Now, everything hinges on the outcome of the coming battle.

This is the North…

The shadow creeps up on me again. What am I doing here? What do I care about Wodan or Christ, gods and demons? I can barely bring myself to care about my fellow Iutes, men of flesh and blood, facing extinction. Rhedwyn is gone. I have achieved my vengeance on Wortimer. What else is there left for me in life? I'm going through all this effort — organising, planning, marching, fighting — and for what? I could just take my share of the Ariminum treasure and go to Armorica, with all the other nobles, to live the rest of my life in quiet solitude. I would gladly defy the destiny everyone has always tried to force on me. Damned be the *Drihten*'s diadem, damned be the Council, damned be the peace between the Iutes and the Britons.

"There you are."

Odo steps up from the riverbank. He takes one look at me and realises something's wrong.

"You're having second thoughts," he says.

"I'm fine."

"Fastidius told me you lost your woman recently. Something like this can bring down a man harder than a dozen Hun arrows."

"I have no time for mourning."

"That's right." He steps closer and lays a hand on my shoulder, the same way Pascent and Fulco used to do. "Whatever it is that ails your turbulent soul, you must keep it in check until this battle's over, Ash. Lives of too many people depend on you keeping calm and focused. There will be plenty of time for mourning later. Do you understand?"

I look up. "I... I think so."

"I lost many good friends in Aetius's war. I, too, had no time to mourn them properly. I promise you, after the victory, I'll take us to the finest inn in Londin and we'll drown our sorrows in a waterfall of Burdigalan wine."

This makes me scoff a light smile. He pats me on the shoulder. "Come on. Let's get back to the tent. I have some of that Burdigalan with me, as a matter of fact. Let me teach you a song a girl in Tolosa once sang to me..."

It takes us two more days to reach Aelle's war camp. The rest of Odo's mercenary band is already here, as are the twenty Iutes Eadgith promised me. She is also here, to my surprise. She carries two throwing axes at her waist and a spear on her back, and wears a band of mail over her shoulders.

"I… wasn't expecting to see you here," I say. "I thought you didn't want to have anything more to do with this."

"I thought so, too. Gods know why I've changed my mind." She sighs and glances around. Her hand rests on an axe head.

"Thank you. I'm glad you did."

"I'm not."

"Have you seen Aelle? I need to talk to him."

She points with one of her throwing axes. "He was about to leave somewhere. You can still catch him if you hurry."

I wade through the sea of tents sprawled all around the hilltop. I pass by a watchtower in the centre, and pause to remember the bodies that were piled here, in front of the bonfire, Fulco and Catigern among them. I recall being tied to a stake somewhere nearby, with Master Pascent and Lady Adelheid at my sides. I look around to search for the hut where I was kept prisoner, but the layout of the fort has changed over the years. There are more huts, more tents, fewer walls, as Aelle's army grew greater and more confident. Dozens of trees were felled on the edges of the glade, beyond the earthen walls, to make place for more tents than the fort could previously accommodate.

I unclench my fists. Not that long ago, a mere generation, the Goths sacked the city of Rome, plundered its treasure, murdered its people. Now, they are the Empire's staunchest allies in its war against the Huns. If Rome could overlook its own destruction, it's about time for me to forget the Saxon transgressions, for the greater good.

I find the sentries at the new gatehouse, some two hundred feet from where the old gate stood. Aelle has already gone, but another troop has just returned from their mission. To my delight, I recognise them and their leader.

"Eirik! Hilla! You're here!"

The Geat is quick to return my embrace — but Hilla steps back, warily.

"Traitor," she hisses.

"Come now, Hilla. He was just defending his people," says Eirik. "You would have done the same in his place."

I look the Geat up and down. The muscles on his arms have rounded, as has his stomach. There's more silver than gold in his beard and hair, and crow's feet around his blue eyes. He's wearing richer clothes underneath the green dappled cloak, and a jewelled pendant on his neck, which he keeps touching with ringed fingers.

"Have you really been here all this time?" I ask.

"Actually, I moved to the coast a few years ago, to run a shipping business. But I answered Aelle's summons when the Northerners started encroaching on our borders."

"And what about you?"

Hilla looks just as I've always imagined her to look in ten years' time — the same rough, scornful face, covered with more scars, the same rippling shoulders, taut and ready to pounce at the enemy. She carries a long *spatha* at her waist, its tip almost reaching the ground, and a round Saxon shield slung over her back.

"I was always here," she replies.

"Hilla now commands a war band that controls all land west of Arn," says Eirik, beaming with such pride as if Hilla was his own daughter.

"*West* of Arn?"

"There are no more *wealh* bands in Andreda," she says, grimly, leaving no doubts as to what happened to the Briton bandits who dared to stand in their way.

"It's good that you're already here," says Eirik. "We bring important news: the Londin army has reached Robriwis."

"Already? How many?"

"One full cohort, and two *centuriae*. If you count only those that looked like regulars."

Eight hundred soldiers. A number that would once have struck terror in my heart. It still should — it vastly outnumbers anything we could put to the field. But after hearing Odo's tales of Aetius's campaign, it sounds pathetic; no ancient chronicler would ever consider it worthy of inclusion in his work.

I make a quick mental calculation. The Britons are moving slowly; at a Legion's pace, they would already be in Dorowern. Moreover, it looks like they decamped in Robriwis for more than a day, perhaps to wait for more allies to arrive. This means they think they have no reason to hurry. They expect no resistance along the way, or any threat from the southern flank. They know the Cants control all the main roads leading to Tanet. They know Hengist's Iutes are a spent force, and imagine Aelle is safely shut in the woods, unable to go on an offensive.

"Did Aelle leave you any orders?"

"We were told to wait for your arrival," Eirik replies. "Treat your orders as if it were his own."

I turn back to gaze at the war camp. There appears to be a lot more than just two hundred warriors gathered in the fort. Perhaps Aelle's war cry resounded with more force than he expected. All of this power, at my disposal. It's fortunate that Eirik is here — he will vouch for me. Without him, would the folk of Andreda really listen to me, a Iute they've never heard about?

"Tell everyone to prepare to march out at a moment's notice. We go as soon as Aelle returns. We have to reach Dorowern at the same time as the *wealas*."

I don't have a battle plan yet, but I'm almost certain our best chance is to strike at the Briton host in the mud plains east of Dorowern, just after Peredur's centuries split to march north against Reculbium, but before the main army reaches the safety of Rutubi's walls.

With nothing left to do except wait for Aelle's return, I find the hut prepared for me by Eadgith. It's a far more comfortable dwelling than when I was here last time — with a small reading table, an oil lamp and a raised bed packed high with straw. I light up the lamp — it's already dusk outside — and, at long last, open Fastidius's book.

From the first page, I sense a faint memory creeping to the fore of my mind. Of course, I've read this before, a long time ago — how could I have forgotten that there was more to Book Twenty-Two than I found in Master Pascent's study? The beginning of the narrative is strikingly apt: it starts with the onset of spring, and Hannibal and the Romans both marching out of their winter camps against each other. But then follows the tedious description of portents and Hannibal's difficulties with his Gaulish allies, and his march through Italia's marshes, all of which bears little relevance to our situation.

I grow bored and impatient. Where is the fighting? Where is the battle? The Romans holed up in Arretium are refusing to fight. Hannibal provokes them by burning the fertile fields of Etruria. Consul Flaminus marches forth from the city in a long column, towards Lake Trasumennus, where the Carthaginian has laid waste to the land — and then...

I drop the book and reach deeper into the bag, for the tattered map of Britannia Maxima we studied at Ariminum. The Roman road to Rutubi... The line is rubbed out at the end, but I remember it well enough to add the missing details. Past Dorowern it crosses the River Stur and the surrounding marshes, then it swerves sharply to the north-east, to avoid a low-rising chalk ridge to its south, and a swampy sea shore to its north. Instead, the road runs along a narrow spit of sand between the hills and the water.

Just as at Lake Trasumennus.

I leap from the bed and run out to search for Eirik and Hilla. We have to march out *right now*. Forget Dorowern — that chalk ridge is where we must reach before the Britons do. *Long* before. Long enough to prepare an ambuscade worthy of Hannibal himself.

The Saxon Might

CHAPTER X
THE LAY OF HELLRUNA

She arrives in the evening, with Aelle, from Pefen's court. They call her *Hellruna*. Nobody knows her name, nobody even knows what she looks like underneath the goat's skull mask she wears all the time. All we know is that she arrived at Anderitum from Frisia, shortly before her homeland was overrun and ravaged by the hordes fleeing the Huns — an event she claimed to have predicted on the day of the Battle of Maurica, while everyone else rejoiced the destruction of the barbarian army. She strikes a tall, arresting figure, with a cascade of black, unkempt hair falling on her shoulders, clad in a robe embroidered in wild patterns in blue and gold.

"It's been a long time since I saw a proper divination," says Aelle. "The Saxons of old would never go into battle without one."

"Like the Romans, before they turned to Christ," I say. "Now, they just pray."

"Have the Iutes ever performed such a ritual?"

"I saw Beadda search through horse's entrails before Saffron Valley. He found no answers in there."

We gather in a grove of ash trees, below the hillfort, and wait until midnight. The treetops sway in the gentle breeze, bathed in the silver light of the waxing Moon. All is silent, except for the crackling of a small bonfire in the centre of the grove. A clay basin filled with water is hung over the flames on an iron tripod.

The men begin to hum an eerie, low melody. *Hellruna* enters the ring of trees, dancing slowly to the tune. She cuts the ash branch over her head and strips the bark off. She throws the bark into the bonfire, and cuts the branch into nine pieces. The melody intensifies. Somewhere in the forest, a drum sounds, joining with the humming, then, from the other side of the glade, a piercing, ghost-like flute. My skin rises in goose-bumps. The *Hellruna* carves runes into the pieces of wood and throws them into the water basin. She then reaches into her pouch and, still dancing, adds nine handfuls of herbs to the brew.

With each throw, she chants an incantation. This is the first time I hear her voice, haunting and beautiful. *Mucgwyrt, the eldest of worts,* she calls, in a hard Frisian accent. *Wegbrade, the herb-mother.* The crowd repeats after her. *Stune, the stiff, dashing all pain. Maegdhe and Wergulu, the food and the cure.* I look at the Saxons around me — they know the verse by heart, some chanting even before the *Hellruna. Attorlade and Stidhe, against the venoms. Fille and Finnule, the mighty two.*

The music grows frantic. The crowd around me weaves and heaves with the rhythm. *Hellruna* lets out a shriek and tears off her robe. Underneath, she is painted in the same blue and golden patterns as on her robe, from head to toe. She starts to whirl and leap around the bonfire. I'm hypnotised by her swirling feet, her spinning arms, her bouncing breasts. The water in the basin bubbles up and releases steam, quickly condensing in the cold air into a thick, white cloud. She spins and spins, with her right arm outstretched and a finger pointing into the air.

[240]

The music stops.

She stops too.

Her finger is pointing at me.

"You!" she calls. She beckons me with dancing hands. I feel myself pushed into the centre of the glade by somebody from behind. She grabs me by the hair and pulls me to the bubbling basin.

"Look!"

She holds my arms in a lock and pushes my head towards the boiling brew. The heady smell of the nine herbs steals breath from my lungs. I see the nine rune pieces bobbing up and down in the water, showing and hiding the runes. One rune appears more often than others — "*Ride*," for "R". What does that mean, *Ride*? I struggle, feeling the searing heat near my face, but she's stronger, much stronger than me. I shut my eyes. She thrusts again, and shoves my face into the scalding brew.

The water is not hot at all. If anything, it's too cold for comfort. I open my eyes and face the milky whiteness. The runes dance before my eyes, as big as the ash trees, the "*Ride*" rune the largest of them. I do not know what they mean — they form no words, only patterns that I cannot discern.

I hear the music again, the humming, the drumming and the piping, distant and muffled by the mist. I cannot move, I cannot turn, I can only wait for what happens next.

She comes out of the mist, a little more than a wisp at first, then an ethereal form. She becomes solid before my eyes, and now I understand what the "*Ride*" rune stands for.

She looks just like the first time I saw her, young, small, with the white veil on her head and the green gown clinging to her body. She carries the ash wood lyre and sings an ancient song of death and sadness.

"I miss you," I say.

She stops the song. The lyre disappears into the mist.

"You need to move on, Aeric."

"I'm trying. It doesn't mean I'm not going to miss you."

"I suppose." She smiles. "Is my child safe?"

I'm thrown by the question. Talk of a child does not fit her in this younger, less mature form. "I think so. Fastidius took her in. But —" I hesitate. "I… I thought I was here to learn answers, not to give them."

"What answers?"

"About the future."

"I can't help you with that," she says. "I am dead, after all."

"Then why are you here? Why am *I* here?"

"Have you told our uncle about us?"

[242]

"Uncle… You mean Hengist? I can't. He's on Tanet, under siege. Why would I even want to —"

"You were supposed to tell him."

"What does that mean — do you want me to go to Tanet?"

"It doesn't *mean* anything," she scoffs. "Not everything is a prophecy."

"This is."

"Is it? Do I look like a *witch* to you?"

"No, you don't… You look beautiful. As always."

I yearn for her so badly. I almost forgot how much I loved her. I wish I had limbs in this mist world with which I could hold her.

She shimmers in and out of view. "Don't go yet!" I cry.

"I'm not really here. I've never been here, Aeric."

"Call me Ash, like you used to," I plead.

"But that's not who you are, Aeric. Not anymore."

"I'm so lonely. I don't know what to do."

"Yes, you do. I just told you."

"Is this really all this is about? Me going to Tanet?"

"It's about whatever you want it to be."

The music returns, grows louder. She waves a goodbye.

"I will never love anyone else," I tell her. "Not like you."

"No," she says sadly. "Not like me."

I feel a tug on the hair at the back of my head. Gasping, I emerge from the basin, the scalding water dripping from my face. The *Hellruna* throws me to the ground and leans over me, shrouding the whole world with her naked, painted body and her goat's head mask.

"Have you seen it?" she asks.

"I have."

"Do you know what to do?"

"I — I think so."

"Good."

"You — you don't want to know what I've seen?"

"The vision was meant for you only. The gods have spoken and chosen you." She leans even closer, until her mouth is next to my ear. She whispers something, but the goat mask muffles the words. It sounds like "Aeric, son of Eobba…" — but it might be anything else.

In its narrowest spot, the channel separating Tanet from the mainland cuts through a sea of reeds and silt. Easy to hide a single row boat with a couple of men in dark hoods at night, easier still now that the Cants don't have enough men to regularly guard the entire coast.

The same can't be said for the Iutes. As soon as we cross the mile or so of open sea and reach the other side, we're spotted by a patrol at the bottom of the chalk cliff. They point their spears at us.

"Who rows there?"

I throw my hood to show my face and fair hair to the torch's light.

"So the rumours were true. You survived."

The guard lowers his torch.

"Haesta. I'm glad to see you alive as well."

"Not thanks to you or your *wealh* kin. What are you doing here?"

"I need to speak with Hengist," I say. "It's urgent."

"He's resting after a skirmish. We're waging a war for survival here, in case you haven't noticed."

"That's why I'm here. Please, time is precious."

Haesta looks at the other man in the boat — one of Hilla's men. "You, stay here," he orders. "And you — put this on," he says, handing me a blindfold.

"Haesta — I know where Eobbasfleot is —"

"We're taking no chances. The Cants have sent many spies."

He leads me along the muddy shore, the sea lapping at my feet. I stumble on the roots and rocks and splash into the mud pools so often, I'm beginning to suspect he's leading me deliberately into traps.

"How did you escape from Londin?" I ask.

"I'd… rather not talk about it."

"What happened to the other hostages?"

"Some stayed with the Bishop. Those who did not want to be baptised, tried their chance in the waters of the Tamesa. Only I came out on the other side."

I can't see his face, but there's an odd tone in his voice. I can't tell if it's a remorse of the only survivor, or just the grief after his lost comrades.

The mud ends, and I step onto a gravel path.

"Look out, there's a rise here."

We climb up and down a low earthen embankment. I hear Haesta exchange whispers with some other guard, and then a change in the quality of air and a flickering light penetrating my blindfold tells me we're inside a building.

"Leave us alone," I hear Hengist's voice. "And bring us some ale."

"My *Hlaford* —" Haesta protests.

"Leave!"

The blindfold comes off and I see there's just the two of us in the building. It's not Hengist's old mead hall — that one must have been dismantled when the Iutes established their settlement on the mainland — but a small, stuffy hut, illuminated only by a single oil lamp.

"Ash!" The *Drihten* strikes me on both shoulders. "I never thought I'd see you again. How long has it been?"

He tries to sound joyful at seeing me, but a harshness in his voice betrays him. He is a shattered, mirthless man; his face, covered in a deep grid of battle scars, is sunken from hunger and sorrow.

"Five years, at least."

"I've heard about everything that happened in Londin." He gives me a warm pat on the back. "We mourn her every day."

"As do I."

"Why are you here? Rumours say you've been leading a band of Iutes in Andreda, or Wecta, or some such place."

A young woman enters and puts a jug of ale on the table. A bare *seax* hangs at her waist, its blade blood-rusted and chipped.

"I've returned for one last battle with the *wealas*," I say when she leaves. "They're marching on Tanet as we speak."

"I know, boy. I have my spies. But there's nothing I can do about it. Outside of this hut is all that's left of my warriors — maybe a hundred men. You're welcome to take the last stand with us. We will go to Wodan together."

"Thank you, warchief, but I have other plans," I tell him. "And I need your help. How many boats do you have left?"

"We had to burn most of them for fuel, and lost the others to the *wealh* pirates. Maybe half a dozen. Why?"

"It should be enough."

As I explain my battle plan to him, I see the initial excitement die down in his eyes, replaced by disappointment.

"I know a plan devised at the last minute when I see it," he tells me. "You didn't want to involve us in the original strategy."

"I didn't... know how many of you there were, how I could make the best use of you," I lie. I only had a day to come up with the revised plan. I haven't even yet convinced myself that it would work.

Even Aelle, in his unrelenting optimism, wasn't certain that my trip to Tanet was worth the effort. Just a few days earlier, we both believed that the surviving handful of Hengist's Iutes had no strategic value left. It took me some convincing to have him agree to me wasting our precious time on this journey. Of course, he did not know the real reason why I rowed across the narrow strait. Nobody, with the possible exception of the *Hellruna* herself, knew about the vision I saw in her water.

"We will do it," says Hengist. "Anything beats waiting here to get slaughtered like badgers in a sett. If we lose, it will not make a difference. But tell me," he pauses to pour himself the ale — to the last drop, "why are you really here? You wouldn't risk crossing the channel at night just for this — you could've sent somebody with the plans."

He saw right through me. I didn't expect to have to explain myself so soon. I take the mug from his hand and quaff it in one go. I wipe my mouth with my sleeve and take a deep breath.

"Something has happened since we last saw each other," I say. "I found out who I really was."

"This is excellent news!" he cries out. "I will call for more ale —"

"You may want to wait with your celebrations, *Drihten*, until you hear the truth."

"The truth?"

"But first, tell me — why didn't you tell Rhedwyn she had a brother?"

"A brother…" He rubs his eyes with a tired gesture. "For a while, we hoped we might find him. We found some survivors from the other ships, on the slave markets, or in the fishing villages… Rumours of Seaborn children, much like yourself… But never anyone from Eobba's household. In the end, we decided it would be easier not to add to Rhedwyn's suffering. She didn't remember any other family, and having to grow up without her parents was painful enough." He pauses. "What does any of that have to do — by Wodan's Horse — you don't mean —"

"I am Aeric. Son of Eobba. Brother of Rhedwyn."

He reaches to smooth his shaggy beard, but his hand hangs in the air. He turns pale. "Impossible. You must be mistaken."

"I wish I was. But there is no mistake. I have remembered it all. My parents — Rhedwyn — the village — even the coming war…"

"Do you have any proof of this…" He waves his hand. "… claim?"

"Nothing but my memories. Except… When I was first found, I had a blue rune stone around my neck, with an 'Ash' rune carved into it, inlaid with gold."

"Those were Eobba's colours." Hengist holds a hand to his mouth, and I remember that these were also the colours of the *Hellruna's* robes and skin paintings. Was that just another coincidence…? "Rhedwyn would have received a similar stone, had her parents lived long enough to name her."

And if they called her Rhedwyn, the rune on her stone would be "Ride"…

He reaches for the jug and shakes it empty. He drops it and lets it roll on the floor.

"Horsa would've known," he says. "I wasn't there when Eobba's ship sailed — I'd been fighting in Frisia for five years before then. I didn't see either of my brother's children being born. Maybe then — maybe then…"

"There was nothing you could've done," I say.

As the silence prolongs, I realise there had been hope, still, in my heart all this time: that it was all a mistake, that he would now say something like, "Rhedwyn was never your sister, you were a foundling", or "a poor couple gave you away to Eobba as a mewling newborn" — but the dull greyness in his face tells me this is not going to be a fairy-tale ending, and the last sliver of hope shatters into dust.

"Did Rhedwyn know?"

I don't know what to tell him, with how much of my pain I should burden him. His spirit needs to stay strong for him to lead his people into this one last battle. I fear my story could be the last straw.

"It doesn't matter," he says, as I keep silent. He shakes his head. "What is done cannot be undone. Wouldn't be the first time the gods have played such a cruel trick, if you believe the sagas."

He stands up. "This is a bittersweet day to me. With Rhedwyn's death I was certain I had lost the last of my family. Now, I discover another child of my brother still lives — and I cannot share this news with anyone."

He looks into my eyes. "Fight the darkness within you, Aeric, son of Eobba," he says. "Forget about the past. There is still much life for you to live."

He reaches out to me. "And you can start by helping us defeat the Britons who killed your sister."

As I sink myself in his fatherly embrace, I feel a heavy block of ice slowly melt away from my heart.

That night, for the first time in months, I do not dream of Rhedwyn.

All through the night, Aelle's troops trickle towards the assembly points scattered along the south side of the long chalk ridge. It has been, so far, a masterfully executed operation. He and his men have learned much about being stealthy since the time of Saffron Valley, when my sentries had no trouble spotting his army marching through the forest. This time, the warriors travel down field paths and forest tracks, avoiding villages and main roads, in groups small enough to be undetected by the Cant patrols or, if caught, to avoid suspicion: just another band of barbarians, fleeing before the great Briton army. I hope all of this is enough to lure the Britons into my trap. They must suspect nothing.

I survey the assembling force. They huddle in the darkness in the shadow of the chalk ridge. There are no campfires, no songs, no pre-battle celebrations. The only flicker of flame is a cluster of huts at the edge of a nearby forest, where the Iute contingent is busy brewing the henbane wine. I raise my hand to cover a yawn.

"You should go back to sleep. You'll be tired for tomorrow," says Eadgith. She, too, looks weary, having arrived only recently in one of the trickling warrior groups, alongside Birch and Raven, the remaining two of my old

Londin war band. It feels good to have them all here, as well as Eirik and Hilla. I feel strangely elated, as if the presence of my old friends alone was enough to win the coming conflict.

"If these men don't sleep, neither will I. Besides, if all goes well, I'm not going to be doing any fighting. I'm a strategist — I need to oversee everything from a distance."

"Even Fastid fought in the battles he devised."

"When there were a dozen of us, each spear made a difference. When there are hundreds of better warriors, I would only be getting in the way."

She looks at me. "Something's changed," she says. "Your eyes are gleaming again. Your death wish is gone."

"Perhaps."

I don't know how long this elation will last — I don't know for how long I can keep the darkness at bay. Maybe only until the end of the fighting, as I promised Odo. Or maybe Hengist's words struck deeper than I thought…

"Was it because of your visit to Tanet? Something Hengist told you?"

"I suppose." I lay a hand on her shoulder and feel her tense up. "I'd like you to do something for me."

"What is it?"

"I need you to stay by my side during the battle."

"Where else would I be?"

"I thought maybe you'd prefer to take part in the actual fight, seeing as you've already come all this way."

She laughs. "Idiot. I'm only here to look after you. Somebody needs to bury your body once this is all over."

From our hideout inside an ancient yew tree atop a bald hillock, Odo and I watch the two centuries led by Peredur leave Dorowern through the northern gate.

"There are far too many of them to deal with Reculbium," I say. "Half that number would be enough. They're not even all Trinowaunts, I see some Cants and Atreb colours among their ranks."

"The others fear betrayal," says Odo. "Like Aetius did with the Alans. They want Peredur as far away from their rear as possible."

"How many do you think we should send after them? Fifty?"

"No more. We don't want to defeat them, just slow them down."

The main cohort is slower to move out of the city. Elasio's standard bearers march in front. Wortimer's banner is risen at the rear. I know he's not risen from the dead, I know it's most likely Brutus, leading those who chose him as Wortimer's heir, but still, I shiver at the sight. Between the two banners, an assortment of soldiers in all sorts of armours, colours, armaments. They march in fours and threes down the metalled highway. The lookouts were right — this is a full cohort, six hundred men, if not more. There is even a semblance of formation in how they march, with archers on the sides and some twenty horsemen — I hesitate to call them "cavalry", as this would be an insult to Odo and his troops — as front guard. The rest are all footmen, most of them with spears or staves slung over their backs. Maybe one in ten wields a proper sword, the rest carry axes, long knives and iron-bound clubs for close combat.

I struggle to keep the doubts at bay. The Britons outnumber us four to one. This alone would give pause to any commander, regardless of how good the warriors on either side were. Aelle may vouch for the quality of his men, but I haven't seen them in open combat yet. The last time I saw the Andreda bandits fight was nearly ten years ago. I have no way of knowing if they have got any better since then. Other than his *Hiréd*, and some warriors Aelle "borrowed" from his father, after much pleading, who's to say his men are any better than this lot? Will they even be able to perform the manoeuvres I invented for them, rather than turn into a mindless rabble as soon as they're let loose?

The cohort is followed by an unruly crowd of roughs and marauders not tied to any of the leaders, just hoping to take whatever spoils are left after the battle. I feel sick imagining them let loose on Tanet, among the children and the old. Losing warriors in battle is one thing; but Wortimer's brutes will make no distinction between armed and unarmed Iutes, just like their leader never did.

"I don't like those bandits at the rear," says Odo. "They will slow me down."

"I'll think of something."

It takes half an hour for the entire host to trickle out of the city gate. Several empty wagons close the procession, destined to be filled with plunder — if there is anything left to plunder on Tanet — or bodies.

The wagons, however, give me an idea. Or, rather, remind me of another story I read in one of the ancient scrolls.

"I think we've seen enough," says Odo. "It's a slow ride back through those hills."

By the time the Briton army has reached our last lookout, in the ruins of an old smithy at the top of the chalk ridge, its column, orderly when it marched out of Dorowern, has turned into a thin, nearly half a mile long, fragmented snake of men, moving in a slow, erratic manner along the narrow seashore road. With the Rutubi fortress almost in sight, the soldiers are relaxed, careless. I can hear their laughter and chatter even up here on the hilltop. I'm surprised their commanders have let the discipline grow so lax. This is a perfect place for an ambush, and I'd expect at least Brutus to have prepared his men for one. It seems our subterfuge worked — the Britons remain fully confident that there are no more threats left to disrupt their assault, other than the remnant of Iutes on Tanet and in Reculbium.

But even this complacency is not enough. The enemy is still too compact for my liking, too organised. I turn to Aelle.

"Send out the first *turma* of the *auxilia* to Rutubi."

I taught him the names from Livius to describe the various troops, to better remember the tactics I've "borrowed" from the Carthaginians. The words are hundreds of years old, and I'm not sure I'm using them correctly, but it doesn't matter. We're not in Italia, and they are not Legionnaires. Today, the words mean whatever *I* want them to mean.

The *"auxilia"* are the Free Folk volunteers who've answered Aelle's call to arms from all around the Andreda Forest: Saxons, Iutes and Frisians alike. They are hunters, lumberjacks, beekeepers, ore gatherers, but most have seen their share of fighting in the defence of their homes. They know they're not here to gain any glory or trophies — none of them expect to live through the battle. They're here to die so that others may live. I don't want to make their sacrifice light.

There are almost as many of these *auxilia* as Aelle's regulars, now that we've sent fifty of his men north to harass Peredur. I can't see from the smithy whether my command has reached them and whether they've marched out to fulfil it — but I trust their commander, Raven. His orders are to join Hengist's Iutes in a sudden attack on Rutubi from the cover of the dunes in the east. All through the night the six boats plied the channel back and forth from Tanet, loaded to bursting, bringing the Iute warriors to the mainland, with Hengist himself coming last to lead their charge. There aren't enough of them to capture the fort, but that was never the plan. We only need them for a ruse. All I can do now is wait and observe the reaction of the Briton column to our trick, minute after excruciating minute…

"It has begun," says Aelle, pointing east. A plume of smoke rises from the direction of Rutubi. The horsemen at the front guard grow agitated, huddle together to discuss the new development. I see Elasio's standard move forward, and then half of the horsemen ride out to investigate the fire.

"Send the second *turma* to intercept. And then the third, as planned."

Aelle waves his hand over his head twice, then points east. Another runner leaps out of his hideout. Things are now beginning to proceed at a swift pace. The second squadron of the *auxilia* runs downhill, making all sorts of wild noises to get the attention of the Briton riders. Seeing that, the rest of the front guard charges ahead, along with some spearmen. As soon as all the horsemen are engaged in fighting the *auxilia*, Raven sends out the third and last *turma* into battle, to position itself between the front guard and the rest of the host, as a dividing screen.

"The head of the snake is cut off from the body," I say. I look to the west. The rear guard has not yet noticed anything amiss in the front, but the entire column has slowed down. The band of marauders at the back grows denser, tighter, more confused. It is time.

"Now!"

Aelle picks up a bolt wrapped in a pitch-soaked rag, puts it to a burning torch and sets it aflame, before loading it onto his weapon and shooting it into the air. The missile leaves a thin black line of smoke after it, striking against the bright sky.

Battle trumpets roar all along the ridge to the left and the right of us. But before any of our warriors are allowed to charge down the slope, on the farthest edge of the ridge, off the very end of our left flank, the hay wagons are let loose.

It was in Arrianus's *Anabasis of Alexander* that I first read about this manoeuvre, in the chapter on Thracians. Whether the ancient Thracians really used it, and whether it was at all successful, I can't know, but the idea seemed sound. Filled with burning hay, the wagons, commandeered in secret from a nearby village, tumble and roll down the slope. Some fall apart along the way, others get stuck on tree roots, but enough reach the marauders to throw them into disarray and send them panicking away from the road. They may be just brutes, but they're not simple. They realise immediately that the impossible has happened: somehow, the heathens have sprung an ambush. I hope most of them will simply flee. I pity those who decide to stand their ground, knowing what's coming for them next.

Just as the flaming wagons hit the road, Aelle draws his sword and, with an ear-piercing battle roar, leads his men in a lethal charge. A hundred and fifty men against six hundred — the odds are badly stacked against us, but the hundred and fifty are the best of Aelle's forest band, hardened by years of fighting, and determined to defend their homeland, armed with fine steel and clad in heavy armour, produced by the smithies and kilns of Andreda, while the six hundred thought, until a minute ago, that they were marching through a peaceful land towards the friendly camp, from which they would execute the final destruction of a few surviving pagan villages.

Trapped between the hill and the sea, the Britons have nowhere to go, no space to line up, no time to even draw their main weapons. The archers on the hill-ward side are simply swept away when the Saxon charge crashes into them, without shooting a single arrow. The spearmen fall with their spears still on their backs.

The shock is complete. In a matter of minutes, the column is cut into two unequal halves, with Elasio and his northern centuries on the eastern flank, and Brutus and his rear guard in the west. The western mass is bigger and stronger; Brutus *was* expecting an ambush, after all. He's wasted no time on being surprised, and rallied his men around him in a ring of spears and shields in what looks like a well-trained manoeuvre. Aelle, thinking quickly, leaves only a third of his forces to check him, and commits the rest to face Elasio in a brutal onslaught.

The Northerners are now trapped on the narrow road, between the Saxon regulars and the Free Folk skirmishers. Slowly, Elasio orders them to push eastwards, correctly guessing the skirmishers, though greater in number, are the weaker threat. With the initial surprise gone, Elasio's resolve hardens. The Britons thrust towards the walls of Rutubi, knowing therein lies their salvation. The hunters and lumberjacks of Andreda fight bravely but fall in their dozens before the Briton swords and spears.

I leave the outpost and rush to my Iutes. These twenty battle-scarred warriors gathered around the barrel of henbane wine, grim-faced and silent, many of them missing various parts of their bodies, are the only reserve we have left.

"We must help them," says Birch. The two-handed battle axe in her hands is almost as big as she is, yet she handles it with morbid precision. "They're getting slaughtered."

"Not yet," I reply. "They knew what they signed up for."

"What are we waiting for?" asks Eadgith.

I raise my hand. "Hold it. Listen. Here they come."

Over the din of battle, the clashing of weapons and the cries of the dying, another sound breaks through, like an approaching roar of thunder: the thumping of heavy shod hooves on the ancient pave stones. Odo's Frankish cavalry, all thirty of them, rages down the highway from the west. They sweep through the remnant of the marauders without even slowing down, pushing any who dare stand against their stallions into the sea. They pass the smouldering wagons and, still in full gallop, form into a perfect wedge, with Odo in front. The diadem on his brow gleams silver and gold, his long black hair flows in the wind, his long *spatha* blade gleams like a lightning bolt. The wedge strikes into Brutus's circle of spears, like a hawk's beak punching through a hedgehog's skin.

Odo and his Franks have become masters of war during their time with Aetius, but Brutus and his veterans are almost a match for them; it is a battle of wits and movement as much as of brute strength and skill of arms. The riders break away, leaving one dead horse behind along with a dozen or so fallen Britons, then turn almost in place — the narrow sand spit leaving little place for manoeuvres — and charge again, at another angle.

Reluctantly, knowing I will not witness a fight like this in Britannia again in my lifetime, I tear myself away from this spectacle, and turn my attention back to the right flank. Here, the battle is fierce, and in fine balance. The Saxons gnaw at Elasio's rear; the Britons push ever closer to Rutubi, and instead of them being entrapped, it's the skirmishers and Hengist's Iutes who are now in danger of finding themselves in the pincers, if the Cants at Rutubi decide to sally. Indeed,

[261]

I'm surprised they haven't already — the battle is clearly turning in their favour. I draw my sword and wait for my men to let the henbane do its evil work in their veins. It doesn't take long for their eyes to mist up, and all the sinews in their limbs to bulge up.

"Go!" I call, before the rushing in their ears deafens them to my orders. The Iutes all let out a wolf-like howl and tumble down the hillside, to tear out a chunk out of Elasio's side.

"This is it," I say to Eadgith. She and Birch are the only ones who remained with me on the ridge-top. They didn't drink the wine. Like me, they watch as the slaughter below unfolds beyond my control. "There is nothing else we can do."

I have no more orders to give, and no one to give them to. I tell the remaining few runner boys — too young to take part in the fighting — to find some place to hide until the battle is over. Even the handful of archers we had positioned on the ridge have by now run out of arrows and rushed down to join the fighting. It is now up to individual commanders to make the best of the battle I have set in motion. In the east, Raven and Hengist have each found a defensive position — Raven a spur of sand dune to the north of the road; Hengist, the small ruined amphitheatre to the south of Rutubi — and gathered the surviving warriors around them in two tight packs. Their number has fallen by half already; they are melting like spring snow. But Elasio's forces are too scattered to make good use of their demise. The hole punched in their ranks by the blood-maddened Iutes has grown into a breach, almost slicing the column again into two, even smaller, chunks.

[262]

In the centre, Aelle regroups his men again. Now it's the western flank that requires his attention. Odo, having lost a third of his Franks already in the repeated charges against the Briton spears, pulls back to let the horses rest and to finish off the marauders. This gives Brutus a chance for a counterattack. His soldiers switch from spears to swords and axes and throw themselves into close hand-to-hand combat with the Saxons.

I think I can spot Eirik's tall, golden-hair-topped frame among the green-cloaked warriors of Aelle's *Hiréd* on the front line, but it's too far to be certain. I try to count those still standing on either side, to see if all of my careful planning made any difference in the numbers. The Briton army has lost maybe a third of its strength in the initial series of Saxon assaults, and the rest has been scattered all along the length of the narrow road, into small, isolated groups — with the exception of Brutus's Londin host. I can only pray that it's enough. The time for manoeuvres is over. Even Odo's Franks can see that. They leave their horses among the burnt-out wagons and charge into the brawl on foot. The battle is now just a bloody mess of bodies and weapons, hacked limbs, cracked skulls, pierced chests. A cloud of red dust rises from under the feet of the warriors and shrouds their deaths from my sight. The battle has entered that slogging, confused stage at which ancient chroniclers would lose their interest and skip to the end. But I don't have that power. I have to stand here at the top of the ridge and watch as one by one, the Saxons, the Iutes and the Franks fall, vanish from my sight into dust.

I can't help wondering, would Fastidius have fared any better today?

CHAPTER XI
THE LAY OF BRUTUS

A small group of Britons breaks out on the western flank and starts climbing up the hill towards us. They haven't noticed us yet — but they can see the ruined smithy, and must think they can defend themselves better within its walls.

We move out of the ruins to find another hiding place. Eadgith trips over something. She picks up the long, black object.

"It's Aelle's stick thrower!"

There's a bundle of bolts lying nearby. The Saxon must have assumed he would not need the weapon at close quarters. I pause to study its precise, intricate mechanism, almost beautiful in its verbose practicality. The bolts are a foot long, half an inch thick, and tipped with a razor-sharp piece of steel. There is a winding apparatus of pulleys and gears at the rear, which makes drawing the sinew string a child's play.

I insert three bolts into the wooden box on top, wind the machine up as I saw Aelle do earlier, and aim carefully at the nearest of the Britons. A squeeze of a trigger and a twang of string later, the enemy falls back with a cry. I shoot again. The weapon is so well balanced that it's almost impossible to miss. By the time the third bolt lands in the shoulder of a third Briton, the rest halts and scatters, seeking shelter from what they must think is a squadron of archers.

I have never before held in my hands anything so deadly. I count the bolts — there's nine left. I could kill nine more Britons — it wouldn't sway the tide of battle, but it would give me a satisfaction of actually *doing* something. Or… I could finish what I started at Crei.

"How close can you get me to that man in the plumed helmet?" I ask Birch, pointing to what I believe to be Brutus, commanding his soldiers from a risen sandbar. I can see now that it was never a coincidence he was at the heart of the fiercest fighting in every battle we met. The man is the best general I've ever encountered. Somehow, not only has he managed to rally the men around him, but turned them around to counterattack despite Odo continuously gnawing at him at the rear, and is now dangerously close to overcoming Aelle's southern flank. Elasio, on the other side of the battlefield, shows none of his skill or tenacity; his northern militias still haven't even broken through Raven's *Auxilia*. One way or another, Brutus must be stopped — for good this time.

It's just like the real Lake Trasumennus, I remember. The Romans would not succumb to Hannibal as long as their Consul lived. It took a Gaulish lance to bring him down, and with him, the entire army. A *ballista* bolt should do the job just as well.

"How close do you need?" Birch replies, licking the edge of her axe.

"Enough to get a clear shot." I glance at the dead Britons and assess the weapon's effective range. "Two hundred feet should suffice, downhill."

[266]

She grins and before I can say anything, she leaps forth from our hiding place. Eadgith and I follow; I barely have the time to reload the weapon with three new bolts. Birch moves like a small silver fox. She reaches the Britons who tried to hide in the smithy. With swift strokes of her axe, she fells two of them and sends the others fleeing down the slope. I raise the "stick thrower" aiming at the back of one of them, but Eadgith stops me.

"Don't waste the bolts."

Birch slows down and looks around her. There's no point in her crashing into the main brawl — she'd get lost in the fighting crowd. She turns to us and points to a black pine tree to her right, growing at an angle from the slope. From its boughs I would have a perfect vantage point — but there are nine Britons between her and the pine, pinning three of Odo's Franks to the tree's gnarled trunk.

"I'll help her." Eadgith launches forward, drawing the throwing axes from her belt. Birch challenges the Britons — they briefly turn their attention to her, but seeing it's only a lone small woman, they laugh and return to fighting the Franks, all except one who points his spear at the shieldmaiden to drive her away.

We strike at them all at the same time. Birch's axe blade slices the spear shaft in half, before landing in the spearman's neck. Eadgith throws her axe — she doesn't have Fulco's skill, but her target is big and with his back turned to her. The axe lands below his left shoulder blade just as I squeeze the trigger and let the bolt fly through the third enemy's neck.

One of the Franks falls among the roots of the oak, but even with him dead, there are now six of us against five of

them, and suddenly the odds don't look as favourable.
Another two pulls on the trigger make it five against five.
One of the Britons throws a long knife at Birch in
desperation, and the rest soon make themselves scarce,
looking for easier prey.

The two remaining Franks carry the body of their fallen
comrade away. I recognise him as one of the couriers I used
in Ariminum and stop them. I know he was baptised in Gaul,
so I close his eyes with my fingers and whisper a quick
Christian prayer — but I'm interrupted by Eadgith calling my
name in despair.

She's kneeling, holding Birch in her arms. The pig-tailed
shieldmaiden is bleeding from a brutal wound in her
underarm. The red-splattered knife lies on the ground beside
her. A chance throw, one in a thousand, hit her in some vital
part and stuck the landing.

"You'll be alright," I say, though it's clear in an instant
that even if, by some miracle, she survives, she will never be
able to use her right arm again. "We'll get you to safety and
patch you up."

"Leave me," she pleads. "There's no time."

"Nonsense. Eadgith, pick her up, while I —"

"She's right, Ash," says Eadgith. "Kill that bastard. I'll
take care of her. Don't just stand there, move before it's too
late!"

She pushes me away, towards the pine. With slippery
hands I climb halfway up the tree and find a bend in the
trunk stalwart enough to support me. The moment I raise the

weapon to my eye, I grow aware of the foolishness of my entire plan.

I'm no archer. I have no instincts of a hunter, no experience with Aelle's weapon — with *any* range weapon. The Britons I shot earlier were less than twenty paces away — a child could kill with this *ballista* at that distance. Brutus is more than a hundred and fifty feet from my oak, surrounded by a multitude of other warriors; all I can get a clear shot at is his head in a plume helmet, and neck. A target the size of a pinhead.

This is insane. There's no way I can hit him.

I load three new bolts. My hands are shaking; the tip of the bolt is swaying all over the place. The first two missiles fly too far, landing somewhere in the sea. The third hits too close, bouncing off somebody's mail coat and disappearing in the crowd.

I pick up the bundle. Three final bolts, the last load, and I'm none the wiser as to how I'm supposed to hit my mark. I shoot again and this time the bolt flies maybe a foot off the plumed helmet. It hits a man standing next to Brutus on the shoulder. In the heat of the battle he hasn't even noticed the missiles flying around him. My hope rises. I shoot the next one too quickly and it flies into the distance. I'm left with my final shot. I take a deep breath. I whisper a prayer to Donar and Wodan. I ask the spirits of my ancestors to help me; I beg my dead fathers, Eobba and Pascent, I appeal to the ghosts of Fulco, Catigern, Beadda, I call on my poor sister… Please, I cry, make this last arrow fly true! I press the lever and…

It's only a matter of an inch or two. The bolt hits the helmet at an angle and bounces off, throwing it off Brutus's head. He staggers, concussed; but there is no other injury, as far as I can tell. I missed. It's over.

Just then I spot a ship entering the channel at full speed, followed by two more. Fast merchant vessels all, cutting the waves on the southern wind. Those fighting below me can't see it yet, and I doubt they'd care if they did, but I know what this means. *Solinus. He's kept his part of the bargain!*

What I requested from Solinus — in exchange for the rights to oyster beds and salt flats in all the future Iute territory — was simple: send out a few of his ships far north, to the land of Ikens and Angles, in hope of them returning the favour they owed us since we helped them fight off the Picts. I put little hope in the scheme succeeding, and even less in the Ikens reaching us in time. And yet, here they are, heading straight for the blood-splattered beach.

Except… something's not right.

As the prow of the first boat grinds on the sand, banners unfurl on all three boats. Banners of an Imperial Eagle, bound in purple, on a crossed field of red. Banners of Ambrosius Aurelianus, *Dux* of the West.

Ambrosius himself descends from the first ship, to the sound of heralds' trumpets, under a banner of truce, surrounded by a retinue of thirty of his Legionnaires. Moments later, another thirty or so warriors disembark from the second ship — these are also Britons, but they don't bear the colours of Ambrosius; instead, they march under the sword and horse banner of Peredur and his Trinowaunt *centuria*. Finally, the third ship releases its sorry load. There's only a dozen of them. They are fair- and red-haired, dressed in a variety of barbarian gear, from torn mail shirts to simple tattered tunics. They all look wretched and haggard, covered in cuts and bruises. They carry no banner, but there is little doubt where they've come from: the forlorn Iute garrison of Reculbium.

They all wade through the surf of the receding tide and stand together, waiting until the fighting stops. The battle doesn't end everywhere at once; the silence spreads from the vicinity of the ships like a ripple from a thrown stone until it at last it reaches both Odo's men, still pushing against Brutus's rear guard on one side, and Raven's hunters, desperately holding to their last dune on the other. It's an odd spectacle, a battle unravelling itself like that, as one by one, the warriors pause to see what made others around them turn and stop the killing.

I can now take full stock of the battlefield. To my surprise, the situation was not as dire for the Saxons as I believed. Between Aelle's warriors, Hengist's Iutes and the skirmishers from Andreda, we slew more than two thirds of Elasio's men, and if our armies had a chance to regroup, they may have stood their ground against Brutus yet. The Cants from Rutubi are still stuck in their fortress, afraid to peek out. Not that any of it matters now...

Once all is quiet, and anyone who can still stand stares at the newcomers in utter amazement, I climb down from my pine. I stop by Eadgith. Birch lies unconscious at her feet; Eadgith tore her shirt into bandages and did her best to wrap up the wound, but the situation is still precarious. A Saxon shieldmaiden runs up to us and carries Birch carefully aside, to further tend to her wounds.

"She needs a surgeon!" I call after her. "The *wealas* will have one."

"The *wealas*?" The shieldmaiden asks, confused. "Why would the *wealas* help us?"

"Just keep her alive for a while longer. You'll see."

"What is this?" asks Eadgith, wiping tears from her eyes. "What's going on?"

"Come with me," I tell her. "Everything should be clear soon."

The other commanders are all marching towards Ambrosius, and the ships sway as well, in eerie silence: Odo and Brutus approach from the west, Aelle, Elasio and Hengist from the east. Brutus's left eye is covered in fresh blood seeping from a bruised forehead; was it my arrow that did so much damage, even from a glancing blow? The Britons give me surprised looks as they spot me, but nothing surprises them as much as what happens next. As we reach Ambrosius, one final passenger appears on the deck of his ship, an old man wearing a purple-trimmed robe and a jewel-studded diadem of a *Dux* on his head. Elasio and Brutus gasp aloud at the sight.

It's Wortigern. He's holding a swaddled child in his hands. A young, strawberry-haired boy holds onto his purple-trimmed robe.

"Octa...?"

Eadgith steps forward, clutching her hand to her chest.

"It's Octa!"

The boy spots her in the crowd and wants to run to her, but Wortigern grasps his hand and holds him back. Is this really Octa, my son? I stare at the boy, the fruit of my loins, trying to see the resemblance. He looks more like his mother than me. Maybe it's in the shape of his eyes, the bridge of his nose...

I push in front of the other commanders and stand in front of Ambrosius before they start asking their own questions. "What's the meaning of this? Why do you have my son — and whose is the child?"

Wortigern replies instead. "The boy we found at one of Ambrosius's monasteries... As for the child, I'm sure you can figure it out — and if you can't, maybe Hengist will help you."

I glance at the Iute *Drihten*, and realise the truth momentarily.

"Myrtle," I say. Of course, now I see it. The child has Rhedwyn's blue eyes and a touch of golden hair on its tiny head. Whether it has any of Wortimer's features I can't see from this distance.

Fastidius must have helped get the girl to her grandfather. He would also tell them to look for Octa — he wasn't bound by confession on this secret, unlike on my relationship to Rhedwyn. Hengist and I look at each other, knowingly.

"Why did you bring those children here?" asks Brutus. "A battlefield is not a place for the younglings."

"We brought them here to ensure both sides keep to the truce," says Ambrosius.

"*Hostages?*" exclaims Elasio. "But why? And who are they, anyway, that we should care for their well-being?" He points at me. "Obviously Fraxinus here knows, for some reason, but the rest of us are none the wiser."

"The boy is mine," I say. "The girl — the child…" I choke, unable to finish.

"Wortimer's the father," says Wortigern. "Rhedwyn was its mother."

He doesn't need to say anything more. The child is the last to hold the lineage of both the Londin and Iutish ruling houses — as far as everyone except me and Hengist is aware, at least. And even though Wortigern is not a monarch in the same sense as the barbarian kings, his bloodline still matters greatly to the Briton pretenders.

Elasio and Brutus exchange glances. They look back to their troops.

"Why do we need a truce?" asks Brutus. "Let us finish this battle, and let the survivors worry about the future of these, and any other, children."

"We did not ask for this war," I say. "I will gladly accept a truce, if it means less death. It would be a godly thing to do."

"Godly!" Brutus scoffs. "You don't know what *godly* means. You're just afraid to lose."

"Anyone can see the battle was going our way," says Aelle, boastfully. I almost forgot about him. He still commands the greatest force in the field. He doesn't care about Wortigern's or Hengist's lines. I must not let him provoke the Britons any further.

"Aelle, stop. Think about it. Even if we defeat them, how many men would we lose? Wouldn't they be of better use to your father alive?"

"You could never defeat me," says Brutus.

"We beat you at Crei," I say. "We'd have beaten you in Londin, if you hadn't hid behind the Roman Wall."

"Cease this prattling!" Wortigern calls. "As your *Dux*, I command you to stand down, Brutus!"

"You lost your title when you allied yourself to these pagans!" Brutus cries. "Yes, Wortimer told me all about what happened at Callew."

Elasio steps forward. "Wait, what do you mean?" He glances at Wortigern. "And how are you here? We thought you were killed at Callew."

"He means Wortimer lied to you all," I say through teeth. "The only massacre that happened there was of the Iutes and Wortigern's loyal courtiers — at his hands."

"Is this true, Brutus?"

"What does it matter? Does the death of a few barbarians and traitors bother you so?"

Elasio throws his sword to the ground. "I take the truce," he says. "Clearly, there are matters that need to be explained before I resolve to sacrifice any more of my men."

"Fine!" Brutus draws his sword and raises it in the air. "I still have enough warriors to take you *all* on! I'll beat the heathens on my own, and then I'll take that diadem off your head, Wortigern. You were never the leader this country needed. And neither was your son."

Aelle steps forward to take on the challenge, but I shove him aside. "This one is not yours to fight," I tell him. In two quick paces I stand before Brutus and Wortigern, my *seax* in hand. "You'll have to go through me, first. Duel me! Let's finish this in the ancient manner — champion to champion!"

"Ash, you don't have to —" Ambrosius raises his hand, but Brutus ignores him.

"*You?*" He laughs. "I've seen you fight Wortimer. You're a terrible swordsman!"

"Then it should be an easy victory."

I can see in his eyes he enjoys the prospect of fighting me man-to-man, the prospect of defeating me personally, something that eluded him so many times. He is a born warrior — in a different life, he would have made a great Saxon chieftain.

"What will I get when I win?"

My confidence, on the other hand, wanes quickly. Why have I never noticed how tall he was, how far his sword

[276]

reached? His *spatha* is twice as long as my *seax*. It will be a challenge for me to even get close enough for a strike…

"*If* you win," I reply, "the Iutes will leave Britannia and seek another home."

I glance at Hengist. Of course, with him present on the battlefield, I am no longer anyone's warchief. It is not *my* place to make any decisions — not here, not today.

Wearily, he nods. There is no strength left in him, or his people, to fight any more. With the battle rush gone, everyone is on their last legs. They will gladly welcome a chance of a respite — even one as brief as our duel.

"And the Saxons?" Brutus stares at Aelle.

The Saxon chieftain bites his lower lip and sheaths his sword. "I was looking forward to ending this today," he says. "But Ash is right. My father could use the men I brought here. I will pull back to Andreda. We'll finish this some other time."

"Works for me, heathen."

"But if *I* win," I say, encouraged by Aelle's surrender — and by the twitching of Brutus's bloodied eye, which tells me the wound on his forehead is still causing him pain — "it is *your* men who will leave Britannia — and anyone else who would wish to follow you — and let the rest of us negotiate a peaceful solution to this conflict."

"Very well." He shrugs. "Doesn't matter — without your tricks and your secret weapons, you stand no chance against me."

[277]

He takes off his coat of mail, thrusts his *spatha* into the sand and raises his arms in prayer, as the onlookers form a tight ring around us. I have no one left to pray to.

I can only see his eyes, narrowed, peering above the rim of the great oval shield, and the tip of the blade of his *spatha*, held close to his head in a tight grip. We circle each other in careful steps, not just to gauge our stance, but to study the sand beneath our feet. Tripping over a root or slipping on a wet patch would be a fatal mistake; this duel must be solved by the strength of our arms, not by a dumb stroke of misfortune.

The one thing working to my advantage is that Brutus has agreed to fight the duel with shields. I shouldn't be surprised — he's a Legionnaire veteran, for whom a shield is just as important a weapon as the sword. But it means his range is only as long as the reach of his shield arm. I wonder if it's still weakened from the javelin I threw at him at Crei. My round Saxon buckler, which I borrowed from one of Aelle's men, is smaller and lighter; it will not last as long under the blows of Brutus's sword as his great shield, but it should enable me to reach further and faster...

I open up and bump my fist against the shield to goad him into the first strike, but he's far too experienced to fall for that ruse. I feel doubt creeping in again. Brutus was right. I'm a poor swordsman. I didn't turn out to be as good with the *seax* as Fulco had hoped. I barely survived facing Wortimer, twice, each time coming out of the fight with injuries. I have trained fencing since then, and I've improved somewhat, but it was never something I had a talent for.

[278]

What was I thinking? Do I actually *want* to die at this man's hands?

Maybe I do.

I bite the edge of my buckler, like the henbane warriors, to take my mind off the dark thoughts. Brutus is strong, but he's not a skilled swordsman, either. His Legionnaire's training would have emphasised fighting as part of a greater force, instead of individual swordsmanship. He must be like me, a better strategist than a warrior. Every time I saw him in battle, he was at the rear, giving orders, rather than in the middle of the brawl. I may have a chance yet.

I pounce forward and clash shield against shield, then leap back again before Brutus's thrust can reach me. We exchange a few testing blows over the shield rims, which helps me appreciate Eadgith's blade: it may be shorter than his *spatha*, but it's faster in a thrust. Brutus's reaction is delayed by a blink of an eye; his left shoulder must be aching under the strain of the heavy shield, and his head wound must be slowing his reflexes. But he's not slow enough to afford me an opening.

It's his turn to charge now. He raises his great shield high and pushes forward, like a one-man battering ram. There's no way I can reach him with my *seax* now. All I can do is set my right foot back, to stop myself from sliding in the sand. He's using his superior strength to wear me out. If this keeps up, my legs will give way... I buckle my knee, and roll aside. He flies forward a couple of paces, just out of reach of my slashing blade. I leap up and stab at his back, but he's quick enough to turn around in time to intercept my thrust with blade. His parry is clumsy, but powerful. My sword arm trembles. I pull away, panting, just as the tip of his blade flies in front of my chest. He follows through with another shield blow. I dodge the main impact, but it still sends me back a step. He pushes again, and I leap away again. I struggle to recover my footing; without it, I can't meet his attacks with full force. I spread my arms apart and shout a challenge in Iutish. Instead of striking, Brutus hunkers down, expecting some new trick; this, at last, gives me a moment of respite.

I glance at my hand, gripping the buckler, and have a flash of inspiration. Brutus is bound to his heavy shield by a leather strap. He can only use it as a moving wall in defence, or to pin me down with it in a charge; my buckler, with its thin, iron-bound edge, is almost like a second sword. I expect most Iute warriors are well aware of this advantage, but it's a revelation to me.

I taunt Brutus again. This time, he reacts. He thrusts forth once more, still hidden behind his shield. This time, instead of clashing board against board, I meet him with the rim of my buckler, striking at the side of his shield; Brutus's shield pivots to the left, exposing his right flank. I jab with my *seax* and hit the flesh. His sword comes down and scratches my leg before we separate again.

The wound is shallow — I barely penetrated his thick leather tunic — but it unnerves Brutus that I managed to draw the first blood. His eyes narrow. His breath quickens. He must be more tired than I am — he was fighting all day in heavy armour, while I watched the battle from the safety of my lookout. I need to act quickly, before he recovers his strength. There's more at stake than just my own survival, I remind myself; Birch is bleeding out somewhere, needing help that only a Briton field surgeon can offer her. I strike down with the buckler again. He's ready this time, and doesn't give me an opening, but the blow pushes him away.

It's my time to go on the offensive. I jab again and again, each time forcing him back a step.

One last thrust from above, and the buckler slips from my hand; it bounces off the rim of his shield and hits him on the forehead, just where the *ballista* bolt hit him. He cries out in pain and staggers away, raising his shield high. I cut at his leg again. He roars in anger and bashes me with the shield, but I pull back at the last moment and he only grazes me. Half-blinded, he slashes wildly from side to side. The pain turns him into a raging wild boar. Without my buckler, I can only parry and retreat; at least, that's what he'd expect me to do.

I grasp the sword in both hands and feint a final, broad, open swing. He spots the opportunity he's been waiting for, and, revealing himself from behind the great shield at last, takes a mighty stab. I twist to the right, just enough to protect my vitals. I let his sword reach my body. The blade digs a deep furrow through my left side, just under the ribs; the pain is unbearable. But in exchange, I finally get my chance. I lunge forward, reach inside his shield and, stretching my right arm as far as possible, plunge the end of my sword into Brutus's exposed neck. I thank Eadgith for making the blade longer and sharper at the point than the usual *seax*; it goes in only by an inch, but in just the right spot to slice through all the blood vessels inside. Blood spurts in a mighty stream when I pull the blade out and leap away. A flash of panic in Brutus's eyes tells me what I already know: the wound is fatal. We both step back and let go of our swords — but I manage to stay upright, holding on to my bleeding side long enough to see Brutus, his eyes bulging, gasping for air and grasping at the crimson fountain at his neck, fall to his knees and slump face down on the quickly reddening sand.

The sight of Eadgith running towards me with outstretched hands is the last thing I see before the world goes dark.

"A surgeon…" I manage to whisper. "…for Betula."

The Cantish guard at the door stares at me with suspicion and scorn. To him, I'm just another Iute, an enemy he's spent all of last year fighting against, here in this muddy outpost of an ancient, crumbling fortress.

"Just tell the *Dux* I want to see my son," I say, wearily.

"Let him in, for God's sake." Wortigern's voice comes from beyond the door. "I know him."

The guard gets out of my way with a reluctant scowl. I push the door open, taking care not to throw it out of its rusted hinges. The building we're in was once an old *mansio* for visiting nobles, built on the road leading to Dubris, overlooking the beach and the harbour spreading north of the fort's walls. Now, half-ruined, it was, along with the rest of the fort's remains, patched up with wooden boards and ox hides to accommodate the parties gathered in the grounds of a crumbled amphitheatre for the truce talks.

Wortigern sits on a rug on the floor, watching Octa play with a toy chariot made of wood and silver wire. In the corner by the sea-view window sits a Saxon wet nurse, with Myrtle at her breast.

"Good morning, sir," says Octa. He speaks the Vulgar Tongue with the same rugged accent as Eadgith.

"You may call me Ash," I tell him. "I'm… a friend of your mother."

"I know who you are," he says. "You're from Ariminum. My mam told me about you."

"Yes, that's right." I pat his head and look to Wortigern. "Was Eadgith here already?"

"She left an hour ago. Ambrosius doesn't want her spending too much time with the children while they are kept…" He shades his mouth with his palm and mouths, "*hostage.*"

"How's your side?" he asks.

"Just another scar to add to the others," I reply with a weak smile. "The surgeon from Dorowern checked on the stitches today, said they're healing fast. For a while, I feared my old injuries from the stag hunt would open up, but it seems my body is stronger than even I thought."

"Lord be praised."

"Quite."

I pull up a chair next to the wet nurse. The child gurgles and laughs. I force myself to remember who the father of this little wonder was. How could something so innocent have come from a crime so vile?

"I just heard the last ship with Brutus's soldiers departed from Dubris," I say. "I'm surprised they all went so willingly."

"They'll be better off there than here," says Wortigern. "Fastidius and I helped arrange their transfer into the Roman army in Gaul. The new *Magister Militum* is in desperate need of fresh fighting men after Maurica."

"You still know how to deal with Rome, after all these years." I shake my head. "Why aren't you at the deal-making table? They could use your expertise."

"I would have nothing to say there." He sighs and picks up a clay warrior from the rug. The toy is stained with age and missing an arm that would have been holding a dart or a spear. "You know, I realised something in the West. I've been doing this for too long. If Catigern was alive, I would have ceded the rule to him years ago. And now, look at me." He chuckles. "I'm a *grandfather* now."

"Are you not going back to Londin, then?"

"I might, for a while — if Ambrosius can't find anyone else in my place."

"Ah yes, Ambrosius…" I look out the window. The waves crash against an earthen wall shielding the fort's ramparts from the angry sea. In the remains of a harbour, Solinus's three ships bob at high tide, alongside several fishing coracles.

It was a long shot when Ambrosius sent out messengers to the harbours of the southern coast, seeking ships. No longer able to count on the threat of Aetius's presence across the Narrow Sea, he did not feel strong enough to force his way through *Comes* Masuna's blockade of the Roman highways and needed to find an alternative way to transport his army, or at least a part of it, to Londin. But the storm season having just ended, most of the seaworthy boats were already out in the ocean, to make up for the trade lost over the winter. There was only one merchant with enough ships ready to sail, but still at harbour, in New Port — Solinus.

It took some considerable persuasion to make him not only change his mind, but to divulge what the ships were originally supposed to be for; still, Solinus was never a man to turn down a profit, and Ambrosius could promise him as much as I had, and more. What the *Dux* learned at New Port made him quickly modify his plans. It was too late to bring Wortigern back to Londin and end the quarrel between the pretenders there. He now had to make it to Eobbasfleot, in time to prevent the slaughter of the Iutes on Tanet.

This was not how Ambrosius had imagined the return of Rome to Britannia — more innocent deaths, a destruction of a people in the name of some sick game of Wortimer's invention. Having hosted Odo earlier, Ambrosius, too, knew now what happened at Maurica and afterwards. He may not have been yet fully convinced of the worth of having the Saxons and Iutes as allies, but he knew better than to antagonise them and their kindred across the sea. The *Comites*, he decided, had to be stopped.

The winds and currents forced the three ships to pass by Reculbium first, where a brief battle between Peredur's two centuries, the besieged Iutes, and Aelle's Saxons was reaching its bloody conclusion. Peredur had been grievously wounded in the attempt to capture the fortress, but the Saxons, as outnumbered here as they were on the main battlefield, had been driven away by the time Ambrosius arrived. Taking on board the survivors from both sides, he learned from them that the *real* battle was taking place ten miles south, on the other end of the narrow channel. And that, if he hurried, his arrival could still turn its course around...

"And why aren't you there, now?" asks Wortigern. "The talks couldn't have ended so soon."

"Why should I be there?" I shrug. "I'm a nobody. Hengist still leads the Iutes. Aelle speaks for his father and the Saxons. I got everyone to promise that they will leave the colony on Wecta in peace, and that was the end of it as far as I'm concerned."

The truth is, I can no longer bring myself to care about any more treaties or peace talks. I have done what I set out to do: prevent the destruction of Tanet. We fought the *wealas* to a stalemate. As Elasio himself admitted at the beginning of the meeting, what remained of the Briton army that set out from Londin was now in no shape to invade the marshy island. They would need to gather again next season — and by then, a new Saxon army would be ready to face them, mustered in the South by Aelle's triumphant father, "*Rex*" Pefen, while the Iutes, buoyed by their successful resistance, would recruit new allies from Frankia and further north to their side... At least, that was a vision we painted before the *Comites*. How much of it would really come to pass, I didn't know, but neither did they, and after the beating they just took at the hands of what they had believed to be an already spent force, they weren't in the mood for taking that gamble.

Either way, there is still a matter of Ambrosius's Legion, nearly a thousand men, or so he claims, waiting to pour through Masuna's borders to ensure whatever peace we struck at Rutubi would hold — and nobody wants to see *that* happen. Britannia is tired of fighting, the war chests are empty, the fields lie fallow; it's seed-sowing time, and if the

[286]

men don't return to their villages, it would mean another autumn of famine. There is nothing to be gained by renewed conflict between the *wealh* factions except more death and suffering.

"If I return to Londin, will you come back with me?" asks Wortigern. "I would need a trusted man at my side. How would you like to be a *Praetor*?"

I raise an eyebrow. As a *Praetor* I would be the *Dux*'s second in command: the position Brutus occupied under Wortimer, and Wortimer under Wortigern. A clear candidate for succession once the current *Dux* died or retired. One could hardly imagine a finer end to a career that started out in the sewers of a bath house at Ariminum.

I have received a similar offer from Hengist: to lead his *Hiréd* house guard, in Beadda's place. I know better than to let all these honours get to my head. Fate and fortune have banded together to ensure I have nobody left to compete with for either of the positions, no sons or obvious heirs surviving either of the two leaders.

I have skimmed all my life on that thin edge between a Briton and a Iute. I thought I had made my choice already, when I led the Iutes into war against Wortimer — but how much of it was out of my personal hatred of him? Would I have fought Wortigern so eagerly? Of course not — I was content to serve as his courtier for years; I served him so well, in fact, he wanted to reward me now with the greatest gift in his possession.

But few Britons are like Wortigern. And all I once knew who were, are now dead. The glorious generation led by men like Pascent and Postumus, the generation of peace and prosperity, is gone, replaced by one of Wortimer and Brutus. I have seen up close what Londin has become. Courtiers playing against each other, without a care for the people they ruled, busy filling their coffers and rising ever greater palaces among the rubble; townsfolk easily roused into fear and hatred, blaming everyone but themselves for their woes; a city of death, decay and darkness, with only Fastidius's Cathedral standing as a lonely beacon of righteousness and honesty. I want nothing to do with it anymore.

"I'm sorry," I reply. "I don't think I could ever go back to that place again. The memories are too painful." I look at Myrtle, then back at Wortigern. He nods.

"I think I understand," he says, and I remember he's one of only three people in Britannia who know enough to *really* understand my pain. Though I have to wonder, how much does he know or suspect of my involvement in his son's death?

"But then, what next for you after this? You're still a youngling, from where I'm sitting. Your whole life's ahead of you."

"I don't know," I reply, and we're both aware how much it is true. "Too much depends on what they decide among themselves." I nod towards the amphitheatre, where the leaders of the warring armies are quarrelling over the peace terms. "I might go to Wecta. Or stay with Hengist on Tanet. Or maybe I'll sail to the Continent with Odo. I've never been to Gaul. It might be the last moment, before the Huns return to ravage it for good."

Octa raises his head. "I want to go to Gaul, too!" he exclaims. He picks up a lead cavalryman, with a broken lance. "They have the best horses!"

Wortigern and I laugh. "God willing, you will," says the *Dux*. "Who knows, you might even get to Rome one day."

"If it's still standing when you're grown up," I murmur, remembering what Odo told me of the Huns approaching the city's walls.

A triumphant trumpet calls from the roof of the keep.

"Sounds like they've come to an agreement," says Wortigern. He picks himself heavily from the floor. "We'd better get ourselves ready. For whatever comes."

PART 2: 455 AD

CHAPTER XII
THE LAY OF HILLA

I step out of the boat and take a deep breath. The tide is out, the shore stinks of rotting seaweed and waste thrown into the river for centuries. A cormorant sits on the remains of an old pier, spreading its night-black wings in the spring sun, unperturbed by the noises of the workmen, hammering and chiselling away on a nearby building site.

I help Octa disembark and we set out to search for Fastidius. We find him in the middle of the Iutish burial ground that gives the tidal islet its name — the Island of the Graves.

"Ash!" he cries out, then pauses and gives me a mischievous look. "Or is it Aeric? Or maybe Fraxinus? Which one would you prefer?"

"Don't be a fool," I reply. I still can't get used to people calling me *Aeric*. Only the Iutes know me by that name, adopted in memory of Hengist's lost nephew, according to the story we told everyone. It goes well with my new title — the *Gesith*. The *Hiréd* — rebuilt after the war — is now mine to command.

To Britons, I am still Fraxinus — Fraxinus the Bastard or Fraxinus the Half-Iute, depending on which side they're on. But to my friends, and those who knew me in Londin, I would always be just Ash.

"I see Hengist has kept his word," I note, after we've exchanged our greetings. The construction site on the edge of the islet is a small chapel, one of several being built throughout the Iute territory. Unlike the ones founded by Wortimer, these ones are filled with light and song. "Just what you've always wanted."

"Some of those buried on this island were Christian," he replies. "It is right that there should be a chapel here, alongside your Iutish shrine," he adds, pointing to a *weoh* raised on the opposite side of the island: a sculpted oak pole surrounded by a circular palisade — the first such building I've seen raised this close to Londin.

We come down to the strip of mud and gravel that counts as a beach. The builders stop their work and bow. Some of them cross themselves; though, I notice, not all.

"You know, they've started calling this place Beormund's Isle," says Fastidius.

"Is he buried somewhere here?" I ask, looking around.

"His body was never found — the river must have taken him."

"Who's Beormund, uncle?" asks Octa.

In Fastidius's presence, the boy speaks Imperial Latin with barely a hint of an accent. He's learned it during his stay in the West, and continued practising at the Cathedral school. He now sounds more like a Roman than I do.

Ambrosius never sold any of the captured Iute children as slaves — that turned out to be just a nasty rumour spread by

[294]

Wortimer; instead, he took as many as he could into a monastery on the western coast of his domain, where they were taken such good care of that many decided to stay there, rather than return to their ruined homes.

I catch Fastidius's eye. There's a question in his stare: *you haven't told him?* I shake my head. "Maybe when he's older," I whisper. "When he starts asking questions."

Octa looks more and more like his mother. His hair is now the same fiery red, and his eyes have the same intriguing glint, but the nose and ears are mine, of that there is no doubt.

"A great Iute warchief," replies Fastidius. "He fell here defending your people as they were fleeing Londin from Wortimer."

Fastidius's servants approach us, bearing trays with bread, cheese and wine. I tear off a chunk of flat bread and chew it slowly, as we stroll along the lazy river.

We reach a small monument of reused marble, all but buried under freshly laid flowers, fruit and other small sacrifices. A cracked inscription mentions some ancient *Praetor*, but he's not the one commemorated by the tomb. Fastidius raises his hands in silent prayer. I drop to my knees, bow down and let my tears flow.

I am once again beset by darkness and pain. They never truly left me. Most days, I throw myself into the duties of a *Gesith*: helping train new recruits in Roman and Frankish ways of war, visiting the settlements, both new and those rebuilding after Wortimer's madness, and attending to various feasts and ceremonies at Hengist's court.

But when there's nothing else left to do, when I'm alone with my thoughts and nightmares, it's all too easy to succumb to despair. I yearn for Rhedwyn's touch almost as much as I yearn for the release of death. I let myself be torn apart between lust and shame, I wallow in painful memories and in sinful thoughts, until there is no spark of light left in my soul — or until a servant comes to wake me from my stupor with a summon to some new duty.

This time it's Fastidius who brings me back into the light, laying a hand on my shoulder and giving it a brotherly squeeze. I look up; through a wall of tears I see Octa's confused face. I wipe my eyes and stand up.

"Hard to believe it's been three years already," says Fastidius.

"It feels like yesterday," I reply.

He smiles and rustles Octa's hair. The boy may be confused by my outburst of emotion, but he doesn't need it to be explained who lies under the cracked marble. Like every Iute child, he has learned the Song of Rhedwyn, the Iute Princess, by heart.

"Not in Londin," says Fastidius. "A lot has changed since you were last here." He points to a Frankish merchant galley landing at the wharf on the shore opposite. It's been a long time since so many foreign ships have been anchored in the harbour. "The peace is working out for everyone, though it will still take time to rebuild all that was lost."

"Yes, but for how long?" I wonder. "With the land carved into so many tiny domains, how can the peace endure?"

The old province of Britannia Maxima is no more, and with it, gone is the *Dux's* throne. Such was the price of peace, agreed after a lengthy negotiation: to end the contest for power among the warlords and tribal chiefs, the power itself had to be destroyed. The Council of Londin — meeting in Saint Peter's Chapel at the Forum, rather than in the burnt-out ruins of the *Praetorium* — now only rules the city and its nearest vicinity. The *pagi* have been largely left to their own devices, as have the barbarian tribes that share their lands. So far, the system remains stable — not least because Ambrosius and his Legions are never far away; but nothing has been done to address the resentments and prejudices that still simmer under the surface.

The peace came with many conditions. Wortigern's domain was divided among the pagans as well as between Britons. The Iutes are free to settle wherever they please on any abandoned land in Cantiaca, up to the line of the Medu in the South, and Crei in the North. The Saxons, united under victorious Pefen, now acknowledged as a *Comes*, retained control of the *pagus* of Regins. Even some villages in Peredur's domain, east of Londin, long inhabited by the Saxon levies, gained autonomy, even though they took no part in the fighting at Eobbasfleot, such was the fear of the rising Saxon power.

The rest of the country is mixed like a stew pot; there are now more Saxons and Britons living in the rebuilt Beaddingatun than there are Iutes. New arrivals from Frisia and Frankia continue settling along the coast, in the vicinity of old harbour towns. But the stew pot only reaches so far. Anywhere north and west of the existing line of settlements, and in any of the walled cities like Dorowern, no pagans are allowed to settle. Travel, trade, work, visiting the graves, even serving in the city guards, all these activities are open to us, but only as long as our homes are at least a day's march away from the Wall. Fear and envy drive the Council's decisions, and impact the way the "fair-hairs" are perceived in the city. Wortimer and Brutus may be gone, but their way of thinking prevails. One day, it's all bound to burst again. Fastidius must know this as well as I do.

"We must do all we can to make sure the war never returns, at least in our lifetime. You on Tanet, me here in Londin ... I'm sure there are others like us among the Saxons or the Cadwallons."

"And in Corin."

"Ambrosius is as dedicated to peace as Wortigern was. I'm certain of it."

"I hope you're right... Though I fear the news from Anderitum might be a harbinger of more bad tidings to come."

The cormorant launches into flight, a black dart in the clear sky, then dives after a fish it spotted.

"How soon do you leave?"

"Tonight. I already have the carriage ready," I say. "You're not sending anyone to the funeral?"

"A pagan rite," Fastidius replies with a wince. "It would be unseemly."

"So you wouldn't come to my funeral, either?"

"You, my dear brother, are just a lost sheep." He smiles. "I trust you will find your way back one day to the home of your shepherd."

The first to enter the avenue, lined with wooden posts and banner poles, are the wailers: a dozen men and women crying, moaning, and tearing their hair out as they crawl in the dust towards the pyre. Behind them, march the animals: first, the live ones, two fattened sheep, a goat and a small dog; then the already slaughtered, carried on bronze plates: a roe deer fawn, a couple of grouses, hares and squirrels. There would be a wild boar, too, but the priests have deemed it inauspicious, since the death we mourn today was an accident on a boar hunt.

There has been a feast for the last three days here on what the locals call a Hill of Death, a long, lonely dune on the Regin shore, where the Saxons and Britons alike have been burying their dead for generations. The feast lasted as long as it took to build the great pyre; to hew the mighty oaks and the slender pines, to chop them into beams and pile them up into a heap the height of a grown man; to build the house of the dead, to set up the avenue of posts linking it to the pyre; to paint the cloth screens that would be hung between the posts, to embroider the banners with the ubiquitous symbol of the white *seax*; and to hurriedly write the songs that celebrated the life of the deceased, to be performed by the best Saxon *scops* during and after the rite.

I was one of the first to come to the mourning feast, leading a gathering of Iutes from Tanet representing Hengist — part of my official diplomatic duties as his newly appointed *Gesith*. The Regin Council was already here, having arrived in its entirety from New Port. Soon more came: from Londin, delegates of the new Council; a few of them I recognise from Wortigern's day, the others have been elevated to the position following Wortimer's downfall. A *ceol* of Angles, sent by Angenwit to pay his respect, sailed from the land of Ikens around the Cantish coast. Even a small group of Saxons from the Continent have crossed the Narrow Sea to witness the passing — a mark of how far the name has reached of the one who purported to become the greatest of their kind in all of *Bretland*: Pefen of Treva, the man who would be king.

The number and rank of the guests, the distance they travelled to the feast, proves not only the importance of the deceased — but also the stability brought to Britannia by the hard-won peace we've all been enjoying since the Battle of Eobbasfleot. A peace the Britons, weary of the fighting in years past, have grown to call *Pax Ambrosiana* — ignoring the men who really made the peace possible, myself and Aelle among them.

I find Aelle by the deer roast, just as the eldest of the *scops* climbs the dais to begin the song of Pefen's arrival in Britannia. I stop to listen — I've only heard snippets of this tale before — but the *scop*'s voice is drowned out by the baying of the animals brought to slaughter on the steps of the pyre.

"How are you holding up?" I ask Aelle. He received the terrible news when he was with me in Cantiaca; we were celebrating the alliance between the Iutes and the Saxons, forged in blood and guts on the shores of the Stur River, and the three years of peace. At the same time, Pefen was celebrating his own triumph: the defeat of Bucge, his last enemy in the long struggle for uniting the Saxon clans. The boar hunt was part of the preparations for the great *witan* of all clans, one that would at last grant him the diadem of the *Bretwealda* — the All-Ruler. But the gods, and the tip of an unfortunately thrown javelin, had other ideas.

"My father lived a dangerous life," Aelle replies. "It's a wonder he survived that long. We had always assumed he'd die before his fiftieth birthday."

"How old was he, then?"

"Forty-nine," he replies with a wry smile. "Now we're both orphans. Free to forge our own destiny."

"What about her?" I nod towards Flaed, standing next to the pyre, weeping almost as loudly and ostentatiously as the hired wailers.

"Flaed was my father's second wife."

He doesn't elaborate, so I don't ask what happened to his mother. A young woman approaches us with a pitcher and two mugs. Aelle wraps his arm around her. She's wearing a long, dark mourning dress, and even though her hair is cut in her usual short, manly manner, it takes me a moment to recognise her.

"*Hilla?*"

She hands me one of the mugs with a smile and pours mead from the pitcher.

"We were going to announce our betrothal," says Aelle. "But now we need to wait until the mourning is over."

"Con… congratulations," I say, choking on the sour mead. "I didn't think anyone would ever tame Hilla."

"*Tame?*" Hilla scoffs. She pours herself the other mug and gulps it in one.

"No mead for me?" asks Aelle, in a wounded tone.

"I'm not your serving wench," she replies. "You can get it yourself." She turns to me and flashes her teeth. "Don't let these mourning robes fool you. Just because I found a man worth getting into my breeches, doesn't mean I won't kick your, or anyone else's, arse just as soundly as ever."

"I have no doubt about that!" I laugh.

The sound of my laughter surprises me even more than Aelle's news. This might be the first time I have truly laughed since Rhedwyn's death. I turn grim again. We are at a funeral feast, it is not the time for merriment.

"Don't you turn sour on me now, Ash," says Aelle. "Tonight, my father departs for Wodan's Mead Hall. It is a joyful day for all."

"You should find yourself a girl," adds Hilla. "A live one, to take your mind off the dead. Whatever happened to that red-head that was with you at Eobbasfleot? She seemed reasonable."

"Eadgith went to Wecta…" I reply, surly.

"Leave him be, Hilla," Aelle pulls his betrothed away. "This Rhedwyn of his must've been something special. He hasn't stopped brooding after her for three years. He'll be done when he's done." He waves towards the pyre. "I have to go. Soon, they will be sending my father on his way. Find me in my tent after the feast. There's more we need to talk about."

The blaze of the burning pyre turns the night outside the tent into daylight. We barely need the small oil lamp to see each other's faces. The day of mourning and feasting took a heavy toll on Aelle: his face is flushed, with a sickly tinge of grey, dark bags hang under his eyes, his hair is speckled white with the ash from the bonfire. Hilla is here, too, sitting on the bedding, picking at her nails with a long knife.

"How's Octa doing?" asks Aelle. "I know you passed through Londin on the way here."

"The boy's fine," I say. "He's growing fast. He misses his mother — but he'd never get the kind of education on Wecta as he's getting at Saint Paul's."

"He wouldn't get *any* education on Wecta," says Aelle. "Aren't you afraid what other ideas Fastidius will put in his head?"

"It will be his own choice to receive them," I say. "As it was mine."

"He's your only heir."

"And he will remain so. Even if he ends up as a priest or a monk."

He shakes his head. "I could not leave such a decision to my son. His faith might determine the fate of a kingdom."

"What are you talking about?" Hilla scoffs. "You don't even have a son."

"Maybe it's time we make one," he replies with a laugh and leans over to kiss her. I still find it odd, disconcerting even, to see the two of them together. "I will need an heir."

"You haven't invited me here to discuss your family plans," I say.

He turns back to me. "Tell me about the *wealas*," he says. "What's the mood in the city?"

"Better," I say. "The new Council is doing a good job of running the everyday business. The loan from Ambrosius helped, too. But they're still all a bit…" I weave my fingers in the air. "…you know."

"Fearful?"

"Something like that."

The Britons of Londin have never fully recovered after Wortimer's rule and the Battle of Eobbasfleot. It wasn't just the devastating loss of life, or the defeat inflicted upon them by the combined Iute and Saxon armies — though I could never be sure that we would have prevailed without Ambrosius's intervention; it wasn't the fact that even after three years of peace, the city was still only a shadow of its old self, the trade routes never fully restored, the exiled nobles never coming home, the markets never as bustling and busy as before.

[304]

It was the sense of isolation that was making the life of the cityfolk the most difficult. The pagans, banished from the city itself, have formed a ring of alliances around it — Hengist, Angenwit and other minor leaders of the barbarian settlements — and Pefen, too, before his death — have all been exchanging messengers between each other, ignoring the old Roman structures of power, no longer heeding any Briton laws on their own land. The pagan alliance was not a formal one, merely an understanding of common interest. It wasn't directed against the *wealas*, in principle, but it was enough to make the Britons want to lock themselves behind the city walls and wait for someone to save them.

Nobody's heard from Aetius and his Legions since they departed to Italia, to deal with one barbarian threat after another. But the initial chaos left in the wake of the Battle of Maurica eventually quietened down; a new *Magister Militum*, sent in Aetius's place, was content with keeping peace in Gaul in alliance with Goths and Franks, and had neither strength nor interest for a fruitless expedition to Britannia. Thus, the only salvation for those who felt trapped in Londin could come from the West or the North: Ambrosius and Elasio. But Elasio was perhaps even more of a threat now to the city than the barbarians; despite the losses suffered at Eobbasfleot, his was still by far the greatest of the tribal militias of Wortigern's old realm. He continued to threaten the fragile peace, claiming the seat of the *Dux* should belong to him, as should the entire province. He even convinced old Peredur and his Trinowaunts to his side, all but completing Londin's encirclement.

Somewhat ironically, it was Elasio's opposition that persuaded Ambrosius to desist from completing the takeover of the city. His man, Riotham, held a prominent position on the Council, and the pro-western faction often held a majority of the vote in the most crucial matters; but the *Dux* of the West, having burned himself twice trying to help Wortimer subdue Londin by force of arms, was wary of trying it again any time soon.

And there was still old Wortigern; though ostensibly retired to his wife's lands in the West, to guard Ambrosius's northern frontier from the Scots, the threat of his return still loomed like a shadow over the city. Every decision of the Council was made under the assumption that, sooner or later, Wortigern will lead an army to retake his throne — and if not himself, then, in his name, whoever gets to marry his granddaughter.

In ten years, Myrtle is going to be of betrothal age. I haven't seen her in two years — and I doubt I'll see her any time soon. Since nobody knows of my relation to her, I would have no say in whom she marries — and neither would she; her bloodline is too important to leave its passing to chance. That would be a decision between the two old men, Wortigern, her grandfather, and Hengist, her great-uncle.

I tell all this to Aelle — except my troubles with Myrtle — and he nods along to my tale.

"You must know some of it yourself," I say. "Your father had an extensive network of spies and informers."

He scowls. "They reported to him, not to me. It will take some time before I can gain their trust. Besides, with all the expulsions in recent years, there are barely any men left I can count on beyond the Walls."

"I don't think you need to worry about the *wealas*," I say. "They are a spent force, too busy bickering among themselves to threaten us again."

"For now," Aelle replies, mirroring my own earlier worries. "They will grow strong again, if left unchecked."

"*Unchecked?*" I scoff. "Don't tell me you're itching for another war. This peace has been the best three years for my people since we arrived in Britannia. We've just had the best harvest in living memory. For the first time, there have been more babies than graves this spring. Your Saxons must be tired of all the fighting, too. Your father has barely finished off the last of his enemies."

"No Saxon is ever tired of fighting," says Aelle, boastfully. "But no, I wasn't thinking of a new war — at least, not yet. I was wondering how we could strengthen our alliance. Make it more formal."

"More formal? In what way?"

He stands up and walks over to the tent entrance. He stares at the blazing flames of Pefen's pyre, the light reflecting in his face, his piercing eyes.

"My father was a great man," he says, "but his ambition reached only the borders of the Regins. All he cared about was uniting the Saxon clans so that the *wealas* wouldn't exploit us — and he'd never do anything that could risk his position at the *witan*."

"I know you two have often argued about this," I say. "But don't you think he was right not to be overly ambitious? The Regin land is easily defended — you have the sea to one side, and the Andreda to the other, almost as fine a barrier as the Londin Wall. If you move beyond it, you'll only expose yourself to all enemies."

"This is why I need allies." His hands grab at the air. "Look at what's happening across the Narrow Sea. The Goths and the Burgundians have divided between themselves half of Gaul, and Rome is powerless to stop them. The Franks took the North. Meanwhile, we still cower before the Britons, begging them to let us stay on their land."

"It *is* their home," I remind him. "You can't just get rid of them so easily. This is exactly what the horse archers did to us back home."

"I don't want to force them out. I just want them to acknowledge us as the new masters of this land." He bumps his fists together. "If the Saxons and the Iutes forge a united kingdom, we will be an unstoppable force."

I'm taken aback by the scope of his vision. Not that long ago, our sole aim was to survive in the face of the Briton onslaught. Before that, we strove to simply live beside the Britons, on parcels of land they handed us. Now he's talking of carving out a kingdom of his own, and of further conquest, as if the Britons were already defeated.

"There are too few of us," I say. "And the Iutes can't hide behind a forest wall."

"There are more coming."

"Those Saxons from the Continent… They didn't come just to pay respects to Pefen."

He nods. "The Old Country is poor and overcrowded. The land here has been cultivated for generations, and most of it lies empty. Now that we can settle as we please, without waiting for the Regins' permission, we will have new settlers coming by the scores."

"Good for you." I shrug, but his words chill me. The Saxons may be our allies for now, but if they grow too strong, will they still look at the Iutes as friends, instead of another foe to conquer? Hengist has nowhere to look to for more men — the Frisians and Franks are but a trickle. The Saxons have always been more numerous, a people made up of many clans and tribes, spread wide throughout the vast woods of Germania — the Iutes were few, hugging the coasts, islands and marshy peninsulas. No kingdom can be ruled by two kings at the same time. How long before this "union" of Saxons and Iutes becomes simply a kingdom of Saxons — of Aelle — with Iutes as his slaves?

"Hengist will want no part of this. All we want is peace."

"I'm talking to you, not Hengist."

"Hengist is the *Drihten*. I am merely his *Gesith*."

"One day, you will rule the Iutes in his place."

"That has not been decided yet. It is up to the *witan* to choose the next *Drihten*."

He rolls his eyes. "*Witans*, Councils... All those factions, all that bickering, who needs any of that? When we are *kings*..."

I stand from the table. Hilla looks up, and gives Aelle a meaningful stare: *now you've done it.*

"I'm not interested in becoming a *Rex*. Certainly not by overruling the *witan*. If you want to be a tyrant over your own people, so be it — but the Iutes obey the laws of their fathers, and of their hosts."

He reaches out to me and puts his hand on my shoulder. "Calm down, Ash." He waves towards the pyre. "It's been… a difficult day for me."

"Your father's ashes are still smouldering. You should be mourning him, not plotting new conquests."

"I know. I'm sorry." He gestures towards the table. "Please, stay with us. Have more wine. There's something else I need to tell you, maybe then you'll understand why I have no fondness for the *witan*."

I sit back down. "What is it?"

He leans forward. "My father's death," he says, quietly. "I don't think it was an accident."

The revelation surprises me less than it should. "How do you know?"

"Something about the way he was hit: precisely, in his vitals — something about how quickly he died… None of it adds up."

"Poisoned javelin?"

"I wasn't there to examine the blade, but it's possible."

[310]

"Do you suspect anyone?"

He shrugs. "He's made so many enemies here. Bucge is most likely, but it may just as well have been someone from the Regin Council, trying to prevent my father from gaining too much power. Whoever it was, they were too late. A few days before his death, the *witan* confirmed me as my father's heir. I will continue his work, and if they thought I'd be easier to deal with than my father, they're all sorely mistaken!"

His fists clench and tremble.

"Yes, so I've gathered," I say, wearily. He notices my sour mood and waves his hand.

"Forget about it. I have my problems to deal with, I'm sure you have yours." He pours me more wine. "Now, we can talk about anything you want. How about you and Hilla reminisce the good old days when you were in Eirik's band?"

"Where is Eirik, anyway? I didn't see him at the funeral."

"He's busy counting coins and growing fat at his *villa*," scoffs Hilla. "He never cared much for Pefen."

"He did send this bottle of fine Tarraconian for the feast, though," says Aelle. "He's turned out as good a merchant as he was a warrior."

"I preferred him as a warrior," says Hilla. She pulls up a third stool and presents her empty mug to Aelle.

"I'll have to visit him next time I'm here," I say. I take a sip and nod. "It is a fine wine indeed."

"Actually, Eirik sent me *two* of these," says Aelle. "And the night is still young. Tonight we drink to my father's memory. *Was hael!*"

"*Was hael!*" Hilla and I repeat.

It was once the main harbour of Cantiaca, and one of the greatest ports in all of Britannia. The mighty warships of the Roman fleet, *Classis Britannica*, once stood in its deep harbour, protected by immense breakwaters, watched over by a fort of the Legions, and serviced by not one, but two mighty lighthouses, beaming flame by night and smoke by day from their rocky promontories.

When the Iutes first arrived in Tanet, they hoped they would be employed to guard the fort's walls, as other *foederati* have in other parts of the Saxon Shore — but by then, there was nothing left to guard. The lighthouses are still there, but they are dead and withered, like remnants of great tree trunks struck by lightning. The sea broke through the breakwaters and silted up the approaches. There are no *liburnae* anchored at the piers; the last of the Roman fleet was used to transport Constantine's departing Legions on their one-way journey to Gaul. All that is left of the once mighty city of Dubris is a small market town: a cluster of huts surrounded by a city wall so ludicrously oversized compared to what it defends, it makes the place look like a child wearing a grown man's cloak.

But recently, things have changed. The silted canal was dredged; a brand new pier was raised over the remains of the old wharf; a row of storage huts lines the beach along the chalk cliff. Among the withered fundaments of an old stone church once serving the community in its heyday, stands a

[312]

wooden chapel, its wood still wet. The harbour, once a dark and empty ruin, is full of noise and light again, though it is all still only a fraction of what it once was, a distant shadow of its former glory.

With the Huns and Romans now fighting in the distant East, with the Frankish king in control of the Friesian coast, and a new, energetic *Magister Militum* in Gaul, there is a semblance of peace on both sides of the Narrow Sea. Once again, the merchant ships are plying the ocean, safe, for now, from pirates and raiders. Once again, it is easier to travel from one side of Britannia to the other by boat than by road. But the reason why Dubris harbour — and another, smaller one, in Leman — is alive again is not just the renewed trade and coastal traffic.

As I step off the small *ceol* which brought me from New Port, I witness a familiar scene. Two Britons stand on the pier, next to an ocean-going galley, arguing. One of them is a balding, bearded noble, sweating under several layers of fine robes; a train of porters awaits his orders by a pile of luggage. The other is a shifty-looking Cantish merchant in seafarer's tunic and cloak. I have seen their argument played out many times already.

The trickle of nobles fleeing Britannia had been flowing even as far back as the Serf Rebellion, but it grew into a torrent in the aftermath of Eobbasfleot. Barely a week passes but some nobleman packs up all their movable belongings, finds merchants willing to provide them a passage overseas, and sells them his entire land, usually along with all the slaves, serfs and other tenants they weren't keen on taking for the ride.

What the merchants did with all that land is anyone's guess. Some have sold it on, to other landlords, looking to cheaply expand their property. Others, somewhat misguided in their optimism, held on to it in hopes of selling it at a better price in the future, when the nobles decide to return. Others still, if they could find no buyers, leased it to the barbarians, in exchange for protection; at least in Iute hands, the land would be kept safe from going fallow and falling prey to bandits and raiders. Several new settlements in Cantiaca started this way.

I stop to listen.

"I told you, I can only get you to Armorica for that kind of money," the merchant explains, rubbing his hands.

"What am I going to do in Armorica?" The nobleman raises his arms. "I don't know anyone in Armorica! My family's in Gallaecia. You promised to take me to Gallaecia."

"Do you have any idea how dangerous the Cantabrian Sea is at this time of year? The Suebians no longer guarantee safe passage, and the new king of the Visigoths…"

"I'm giving you all of my land! How is it not enough?"

"That muddy field full of rocks? It's not even on the right side of the river. You should be happy to get that much for it."

"And a swathe of prime hunting wood!"

"Only a mad man would go hunting in Andreda."

I step closer. "Hey," I call, "what land are you talking about?"

The merchant eyes me with suspicion, but the nobleman is eager to share his indignation, even with a barbarian. "Two villages and a hunting grove on the west bank of the Medu, not far from Aelle's Ford."

Aelle's Ford?

"Where the road narrows?"

His face brightens. "You know the place!"

It can't be a coincidence. It must be the gods, offering me some kind of omen. A chance for redemption, perhaps…

"How much are you asking for the passage to Gallaecia?" I ask the merchant.

"Four gold solids."

Four gold solids is an annual salary of a Council clerk — or an equivalent of the yearly profits from a small *villa*. The price is staggering, even to a nobleman. Few people outside of Londin's rich elite have ever even seen a whole gold solid, the most valuable of old Roman coins. I recall a handful of them lying buried in a pot somewhere on the grounds of Ariminum, to be used as a last resort in a crisis. Naturally, what would change hands here would not be the coins themselves, but their equivalent in hacked silver, clipped bronze or, in the worst case scenario for both sides, farm produce.

"You could *buy* a ship for that money!" I say.

[315]

The merchant shrugs and smiles slyly. "You might, but who would man it? I and my friends own the only crews capable of crossing the Cantabrian Sea at this time of year."

"I'll give you four solids for your land," I tell the nobleman. Both men guffaw. It's a ridiculous offer for what amounts to a scrap of muddy field and a few clusters of mud huts.

"If I knew the Iutes had that kind of money, I'd drive a harder bargain with you," says the merchant.

"Not 'Iutes'," I reply. "Just me."

"And you are?"

"Someone with four gold solids in his chest."

"What do you want with my land, heathen?" asks the nobleman. "Your lot are not allowed to settle west of the Medu, anyway."

"What do you care? You're sailing to Gallaecia. You'll never be back. Your land is mine now."

There is an ominous double meaning to my words — a Iute, saying this to a Briton — which doesn't escape either of us. Silenced, the nobleman looks to his feet, while the merchant extends his grubby hands towards me, to seal the deal. I nod at my servants to bring my travelling coin chest from the boat. I do have a couple of actual gold solids from Pascent's treasure wrapped in a bundle around my waist, but those are for emergencies. An equivalent weight of hacked silver will have to suffice instead.

"Send the deed to the Bishop at Saint Paul's," I tell the merchant, after he's studied the contents of my chest to his satisfaction. "And don't think of cheating, I *will* check if he got it."

The merchant winces. "A Church grant. There's been a lot of that lately. As if the priests weren't rich enough already."

"You're a man of Faith?" the nobleman lights up. "Forgive me, I didn't know —"

"It's none of your business," I reply to both of them. "Now go, before I change my mind. The gods know there are better things I could spend four gold solids on."

I wave at the servants, and we depart north, past the ruined Roman fortress, towards the new Iute lands.

The Saxon Might

CHAPTER XIII
THE LAY OF BETULA

I lower my sword. At the signal, six Iute spearmen charge, in a wedge formation, at a double line of round shields held by another ten Iutes on the other side of the arena: our field of practice is the ruin of the Rutubi amphitheatre. The two groups clash with great clamour; the front line buckles where the end of the wedge smashes in, but doesn't budge, supported by the second row of shields. I wave a hand. Five more warriors spring up from their hiding place behind a low-sprawling yew tree growing out of what once was the entrance for the gladiators, and strike at the flank of the shieldsmen. The shield wall pulls back, but one of the shieldsmen at the back loses his footing and falls, pulling the others with him, and the wall breaks apart.

"No, no, no!" I raise my hands in despair. "You're supposed to fold away, cover each other's sides! Betula, show them how it's done."

I stopped calling her 'Birch' after she and Raven agreed to join my new *Hiréd* as officers. She hesitated a long time; after recovering from her wounds under Fastidius's care, she was considering joining the Church as an acolyte, hoping in this way to repay God for what she saw as miraculous healing. In the end, loyalty prevailed over faith — not to me, but to Hengist, her old clan chieftain.

The shieldsmen groan when Betula starts to line them up again. I know that groan. It welcomed me in Londin, whenever I tried to train the Iutes in the *wealh* ways. But back then, I didn't have Betula at my side, ordering the men around. If it was up to me, she would be the one commanding the entire *Hiréd*. Though small in stature, and with her right arm cut off above the elbow — even Fastidius's prayers could not save all of it — she is the fiercest of my warriors, and the quickest to pick up on my ideas.

I have an ambitious aim: to train this *Hiréd* into the finest fighting force this island has seen since the Legions; while Betula and Raven deal with most of the combat training, I bury myself in the military books I brought from Ariminum, inventing tactics and strategies. After the insight I found in Livius for the victory at Eobbasfleot, I'm eager to discover more ways in which the Ancients can inspire a modern commander.

Hengist and the other elders praise me for my diligence, but their praises ring hollow in my ears. I only do this to keep my mind occupied; to forget. I could be drowning my sorrows in ale, but I don't want to end up like Paulinus — drunk *and* bitter. Hard work is all I have left.

"Can't we just drink henbane and charge at the enemy?" asks one of the spearmen. "That always worked."

He is a veteran from Crei, one of the oldest and most experienced warriors under my command, but also, the most annoying in his obstinacy.

"There will be no more henbane," I tell him. "Unless we're forced to defend our homes again. Our enemies, even our Saxon allies, don't know our secret. I intend to keep it that way. Now if you're finished, I —"

My voice trails off. A young girl appears over the ridge of the amphitheatre, picking up cowslip, which grows in abundance among the crumbling stones. She's wearing a green dress, and her hair falls in long golden tresses down her shoulders. For a moment, I think I'm seeing an apparition, a wraith, come to haunt me from my past. But the girl is real. As she comes closer, I recognise her — she lives in the nearby village; I've seen her many times before. She bears only a passing resemblance to Rhedwyn.

It doesn't matter. The darkness returns, and hits me like an axe blow. My arms slump. I drop the sword and raise my eyes in a daze towards the warriors. I see no point in continuing their training. I see no point in doing anything anymore.

They stare at me in confusion, awaiting further orders. Betula is the only one who knows what's happening. She's seen it many times before. She reaches out with her only hand to rub my shoulder.

"Maybe we should call it off for today," she says. "You seem tired, *Gesith*."

"Yes," I muster a reply. The aching is physical, spreading from my heart to my limbs. I feel that I need to lie down — and never rise again.

A morning bell rings out a melancholy wail, stirring a family of crows into flight. They clash into a flock of seagulls coming from the sea and, for a moment, the birds battle confusedly in mid-air.

The dawn rises grey and pallid over the narrow channel and the mud cliffs of Tanet beyond it. The island is now all but empty of Iute houses, except a couple of fishing villages and a few farms where the land remained fertile enough. The Iutes had no regrets about abandoning the squalid isle and moving to the mainland as soon as they were allowed.

My new house is a far cry from my rooms at the Bull's Head or the chambers at the Londin *Praetorium*. It's a single-room wooden hut, its floor dug into a grass-covered dune overlooking the beach, with a hole in the wall for a window. Even my servants have better homes. As a *Gesith*, I could have ordered my warriors to build me a great Hall worthy of my title, but I see no point. Its empty space would only remind me of my loneliness. The only luxury I afford myself is a chest filled with books and scrolls from Ariminum, for my evening readings.

Were I to go outside of my sunken hut, I would see below the first of the string of new villages, spread along the old road from Rutubi to Dubris. The land here, once protected by the *Litus Saxonicum* fortress at Rutubi, had long been abandoned by the Cantish landlords, exposed as it was to elements and raiders; the serfs that remained, plying the sand-dusted fields and casting their nets to catch the bottom-dwelling fish of the Narrow Sea, were glad to welcome their new masters. They knew the Iutes well, and have grown to like them, despite the difference in faith; some time after Eobbasfleot, I learned that many of them manned the walls of Rutubi during the battle — and were responsible for the Cantish troops staying idle when Hengist's men charged at the Briton army. At least, so they claimed later.

The bell rings out one last time and falls silent. From my small window I can see only the far corner of the wooden chapel, raised on the walls of the Rutubi fort by Hengist to placate those of the locals who frowned on heathens settling on their land. Betula and a few other baptised Iutes have made it their home. Once a month, an acolyte from Saint Paul's arrives to say a prayer for the slain.

I turn to stare at the sea again. This is the worst time of day; I wake up long before dawn, from dreams of sorrow and anguish. It's too early for anything to occupy my mind, so I just let it wander from one dark place to another. I sense the despair creeping almost physically, a tingling at the top of my nose and an itching under the eyes, and I know I'm about to weep once again. These days, I don't even need to think about Rhedwyn; just staring at the blank, dull expanse of the hazy-grey waves is enough for tears to start flowing down my cheeks.

A half-eaten bread roll and a dried piece of cheese rest on the table, untouched since yesterday. I wash my throat and my pain with stale ale, a barrel of which stands in the corner, almost empty. At some point, a servant will come from a nearby inn to replace it. Since I have no official duties planned for today, this might be my only human interaction for the rest of the day. I'm fine with that.

Somebody knocks at the frame of the door.

"Go away," I moan. "You're too early."

"My day is busier than yours, young *Gesith*. I don't have much time."

I wipe the tears and rub my eyes clear. I throw the bread and cheese out the window and wipe the crumbs off the table. I rush to open the door.

"My *Hlaford Drihten*," I say, and bow, more to hide the last of the tears than out of respect. "I wasn't expecting to see you here today."

"I was on Tanet, to see the old mead hall finally being dismantled."

I peek outside. Hengist's pony grazes moodily on the dune grass.

"You've come alone? Don't you think it's dangerous?"

"Shouldn't I feel safe among my *Hiréd*?"

"Pefen thought the same."

"Funny you should mention him." Hengist takes a glance inside, sniffs and winces. "Let's go for a walk down the beach. The breeze is nice and cool at this time of day."

"I hear you've been brooding again," says the *Drihten*. "You let your warriors see you like this?"

My face must be red and swollen. I let the wind from the sea squeeze out the rest of my tears along with the salt of the breeze.

"I have not been neglecting my duties."

"I never suggested you were." He takes in a deep breath. The breeze tears at his beard, more silver now than golden. His hair is tied with a thin silver band in place of the *Drihten*'s diadem, and his arms jangle with silver and gold armbands.

[324]

"From what I hear, the new *Hiréd* is already as fine a band of warriors as the old one."

"That's far too generous. I've only had a couple of years to train them, from scratch. Beadda's men had years of war in them."

"But they never trained in the *wealh* ways. Our people have never been better protected."

Protected from whom?

"Still, I sense you're not satisfied with me, uncle."

Instinctively, he glances around to make sure I wasn't heard. No man except himself, Fastidius and Wortigern know that we are related. But we are alone on this wind-swept spit of dark sand.

"I worry. It's been three years. I can't have my heir succumb to the darkness of the soul for so long."

I look up, startled. "Heir?"

"Why are you surprised? You knew this day would come."

"It's just… It's been two years and you've barely mentioned it. I thought…" *I hoped.*

He crouches down and takes some sand in his hand. He lets the grains fall through his fingers.

"What happened to poor Pefen got me thinking. I have been waiting for too long. I need to gather the *witan* soon and have them approve you as my successor."

"I am not ready."

He laughs. "And I'm not going anywhere yet! But should Fates decide otherwise, I would like to leave the tribe's future in capable hands. And I can't think of more capable hands than yours."

"Are you sure there isn't anyone more suitable?"

"More suitable than the Hero of Eobbasfleot? More suitable than the *Hlaford* of Poor Town?"

I scowl. The titles he cites come from the songs he's ordered the *scops* to write about my exploits. "I never claimed to be any of those things. Beormund was the chieftain in Londin. Aelle was the one who led us to victory at Eobbasfleot."

"And if Beormund lived, and Aelle was a Iute, perhaps I would choose them over you."

He stands up. "But you're right." He wipes his hands from sand. "In your current state, you are not fit to lead anyone, much less an entire tribe. You are no longer a boy. I need you to act like the man you are. You can't stand before the *witan* like this."

And if I don't want to…?

"I will try to keep my… brooding under control, uncle."

[326]

"See to it that you do." He looks me over. "Do you need me to find you a woman? Is that what this is about?"

"No, uncle. I don't think I will need your help in this matter."

He runs his fingers through his beard. "I'll take your word for it." He looks to the sky. "I'd better go back to Tanet, before the wind picks up. I will send out for the *witan* to gather at next Full Moon. I expect you to be back to your old self by then."

"Yes, my *Hlaford Drihten.*"

He gives me an impatient glower. "I can never tell when you are jesting with me, Ash."

"I assure you, uncle, I'm in no mood for jests."

"You'll need to work on that, too. People need a leader who can lift their spirits in time of need."

It is my spirit that needs lifting, uncle... I think, but I say nothing. Instead, I force my mouth into a weak smile and nod, silently.

The last time I saw the Iutish *witan* gather, before the Battle of Crei Ford, it only took a couple of days for all the elders and wise men of the tribe to arrive at the meeting point. Back then, with the exception of Beadda, all members of the gathering still lived on Tanet, in the vicinity of Hengist's old mead hall.

Now, though diminished in numbers after the war, the Iute clans are scattered all over Cantiaca, and with them, their elders; it takes weeks for the messengers to reach them all, and for them to make their slow way back to Rutubi, and that's not even counting the representatives of the Wecta colony, far to the West, under Eadgith's rule — if they are coming at all; their presence is not necessary — the *witan*'s approval of Hengist's decision should be a mere formality.

The moot circle is drawn within the walls of the old Rutubi amphitheatre. It takes up only a fraction of the ruined arena — enough space for twenty or thirty men to shout at each other for a day or two, in between gorging themselves on mead and game, trading gossip and arranging market deals and marriages. It might be a great event in the life of the Iutes, but to me, it is just another village feast. As I observe these preparations, and compare the meagre size of the *witan* circle with the massive crumbling ruin around it, a doubt creeps in my mind, one which I have recently been finding difficult to push back.

Once, I was a Councillor at Wortigern's court; one of the highest ranks one could hold in Roman Britannia, below only that of the regional *Comites*. Once, not that long ago, I took part in the great Council of all Bishops, as equal with the mightiest and noblest of this country. As the sole heir of Master Pascent's fortune — most of which I had to give up when I joined Hengist's court — I would have been richer than all the Iutes in Cantiaca combined, including Hengist himself. And had the Fates been kinder to me, and to all of Britannia, I would maybe have even succeeded Wortigern as the *Dux*. Sometimes, in rare bouts of feeling good about myself, I imagine I could have brought peace between the Britons and the barbarians, not through the fear of war, but through mutual respect and cooperation... But these are mere dreams. Nothing is left of my old life, except a handful of golden solids in my chest and a few influential friends in Londin.

I gave up all of that — and for what? Rhedwyn was the only reason I ever considered moving to the Iute lands. Without her, there is nothing in my life that would fill me with joy. For the past three years, I have been performing my duties diligently, but with no passion, like one of those walking metal men described by the ancient Greeks. Leading a small band of elite Iute warriors would have been a dream come true for a younger, more immature me, but it holds no appeal to me now. I shrug even at the prospect of being confirmed Hengist's heir. What if the real reason I don't want to accept his offer is not that I don't feel strong enough to do it — but because I think it beneath me?

I feel like all my choices have been made for me, simply because I couldn't decide either way. If Londin now wanted me back, would I refuse? I don't know, and it's foolish to speculate. Wortigern's not there, anymore. There's little use for a Iute on the Londin Council these days. Maybe I could persuade them to let me back if I asked Fastidius to vouch for me, but in all honesty, I cannot be bothered. And so, I stay here, in my dug-in hut, among the Briton serfs and Iute farmers and fishermen, doing my best to train Hengist's warriors for him.

What else is there for me to do?

"You know, Haesta," I say, reaching wearily for a roasted pigeon's breast, "when I dug my hut here on this desolate dune, far away from the nearest hamlet, I was hoping I could at last have some peace."

He smiles and tears into the bird's wing with a satisfied crunch. The pigeon is his gift to me, as is a bottle of sour wine of unknown provenance.

"It is not the house that makes this place worth riding all this way, but who lives in it, *Gesith*," he replies.

My title is burdened heavy with meaning on his lips. There is a hint of grudging respect, but it's barely discernible under the thick coat of resentment. I know he believes the *Hiréd* should be under his command. And, perhaps, that's how it would be — but I could never give him the satisfaction of knowing what I really think.

The last time I saw him, he was storming out of the harvest feast at Hengist's mead hall, furious with the *Drihten* for one too many perceived slights. My appointment as the *Gesith* was a great blow to his ambitions; even granting him the rule of one of the surviving clans, in recognition for his prowess during the war with Wortimer, wasn't enough to placate the youth's anger. Soon after that quarrel, Hengist decided to send him with a handful of followers across the Narrow Sea, to Meroweg's court, to repay the Frankish king's support in the war. Haesta eagerly welcomed the opportunity to lead his own war band and seek his own glory, away from Hengist — and myself.

"That is quite the mount you've got out there," I remark. He arrived at the *witan* not on a sea pony, like Hengist and all the other warriors, but on a sturdy warhorse, a dark chestnut mare with a beautiful wide blaze. "Is it Gaulish?"

[330]

"Thuringian," he says. "I got it from *Rex* Meroweg for my service."

"Are your men with you?"

"A few. The rest are staying in New Port."

"Didn't you leave with only a few men in the first place?"

"My war band grew. Frankish mercenaries. Some of Odo's men joined me, too, after he retired to his farm."

Odo, retired? I find it hard to believe — but I suppose he, too, must have decided he'd had enough killing after Eobbasfleot...

"There can't have been much work for mercenaries in Frankia these days, surely?"

He licks his lips. "You'd be surprised. The frontier along the Rhenum smoulders with a quiet war. The Alemanns are itching to have revenge for their defeat at Maurica. The Saxons pretend to be friendly, but they raid the riverside farms when they think no one's looking — and the Gauls..."

He pauses. His cheeks are flushed red.

"No, please, go on," I urge him. "You've clearly been enjoying yourself. *And* you've seen the world. It must have done you good."

"Don't patronise me."

"I'm honest, I assure you. You make me think that I should travel to Frankia myself."

"Maybe you should," he blurts.

"*Ah.*"

We chew the pigeon meat for a long while in silence.

"You know why I'm here," he says.

"You've always disagreed with Hengist's choice of heir. It's no secret. Perhaps you even think you deserve to be the next *Drihten*. Whichever it is, you fear this moot is your last chance to change things around." I shrug. "You will have the chance to present your case before the *witan*, but I fear…"

He raises his hand. "You misunderstand me, *Gesith*. I do not wish this burden upon me."

"Enlighten me, then — why have you come?"

"Because I have seen something in Frankia that made me rethink everything I knew." He stands up — as tall as the low ceiling of my hut allows. "The Saxons and the Alemanns we fought with still live under the old freedoms. They have no *Drihtens*, no kings. They'd only call for a war chief when they were out on a raiding party, which would dissolve once the fighting was over. The rule of the tribe belongs to the elders, the priests and the *witan*."

I nod. "This is how it used to be in the Old Country, I understand. Before we came here. What are you saying?"

"We have been at peace for three years," he replies. "A true peace. We no longer live in fear of the *wealas*, on a tiny, plague-ridden island. We are no longer a people on the move. What need do we have for a *Drihten* in peace time? What need

[332]

is there for all this talk of succession, of leadership — we should go back to the old ways!"

"I agree."

This stops his peroration abruptly. He turns to me, struck dumb.

"What?"

"You're right, Haesta. The Iutes no longer need a *Drihten*, just like the *wealas* have no need for a *Dux* in Londin. Yes, we would still have use for warriors, to defend ourselves from the bandits and pirates, but we would no longer have use for a *warlord*. It would show our people that we live in our own land again, according to our old laws. And it would show the Britons that we mean the peace to be permanent this time — unlike Aelle and his Saxons."

I tap a pigeon bone against the rim of the wooden plate. "Is this what you were going to say?"

"I… yes," he stutters. "How did you —?"

"You're not the only one who's noticed how the world has changed." I lean back in the chair. "But, if you didn't think I'd agree with you, why have you come to see me? Did you think you could convince a *Drihten*'s presumptive heir to abandon his throne?"

"I came to warn you," he says.

"You mean, you came to *brag*." His back slumps. "I take it you have enough supporters in the *witan* to force this matter to a vote."

"But not enough to win."

"So you just wanted to humiliate Hengist and myself by refusing us the acclamation."

"I wanted to make the elders *think*. Maybe rouse some of them to my side. We could force some concessions out of Hengist."

"You should've come to me, first. With me on your side, you could achieve a lot more."

"You — on my side? You would stand against Hengist?"

I laugh at his incredulity. To me, Hengist is just another barbarian chieftain, albeit one to whom I am closely related, and happened to have sworn allegiance to. To him, born and raised on Tanet, Hengist must once have seemed a demi-god, a scion of ancient warlord clans, with Wodan's blood coursing in his veins. It must have taken enormous courage for Haesta to rebel against his *Drihten*, again and again.

For a moment, I allow my spirits to rise. Haesta arrived just in time with his preposterous idea. Perhaps this is how I can escape my destiny, not by defying my bloodline and throwing away my inheritance, but by rendering them meaningless. After all, if there were no *Drihten* and no *Dux*, then no one would expect me to take their place...

"The *witan* gathers in two days," I say. "You'd better get to work on those elders. Tell them what I have told you."

"What about Hengist?"

"Let me deal with him."

"You shouldn't be telling me this," says Hengist with a heavy sigh.

"I thought it decent to give you a warning. Give you time to prepare. I didn't want to insult you with a surprise. It would not be honourable."

He snarls. "And is it honourable to abuse our ancient laws just because you're too cowardly to take on the diadem that is rightfully yours?"

We stand on the rim of the ruined amphitheatre, weathered into a narrow stone rampart by the same salty wind that now tears at Hengist's beard; below us, the serfs are clearing out the arena from market stalls and refuse in final preparation for the gathering. A couple of elders are already here, studying the surroundings, as if they were choosing their seats before the spectacle, even though all that is left of the seats are piles of rubble and rotten wood scattered around the arena, and the only spectacle that awaits us is a handful of bickering old men.

"You know there is sense in Haesta's words," I say.

"And this, this!" He shakes his hand in the air. "Is what surprises me the most! That you would ally with that rash youngling. You know all he's ever wanted was to usurp me."

"Maybe he's changed."

He scoffs. "You don't believe it for a second."

"He's seen more of the world than either you or I have in these past two years. He saw the Saxons and Alemanns return to the *witan* rule. He saw the ancient freedoms they enjoy once again."

"And has he mentioned what he saw at Meroweg's court in Frankia? The throne room in the old Roman palace? The circlet of jewels and gold upon his head? The armies at his sole command?" He shakes his head. "There is no *witan* in Tornacum, I can assure you. Only the *Rex* and his advisors, like a little Imperator. There are no limits to Meroweg's power, no 'ancient freedoms'."

"Is this what you want for the Iutes?"

"Not in my time — I am too old to wield the circlet, to hold that kind of power. But you…"

"Frankia is in a constant state of war with all its neighbours. They need a strong hand. As soon as that threat passes, they, too, will revert to the old ways. And there is no more war in Britannia."

"*There will always be a war!*" he roars and slams his fist on the wall. Spittle flies from his mouth, and dust rises from the crumbling *caementicium*. "You of all people should know that. It will take one bad harvest for the *wealas* to turn against us once more."

It is my turn to reel in shock. Not because of the outburst of anger — I have seen Hengist lose his temper many times before, in the three years I served under him; the *Drihten* has always been as quick to anger as he was to laughter. It's hearing him utter the same arguments as I've heard from Aelle that stuns me.

[336]

"I thought peace was what we both wanted," I say, quietly.

"I am grateful to the gods for these three years we've had, and long may they continue," he says, calming down. "But I remember the name of every man and woman who perished at Eobbasfleot, and in all the fighting before that. Most of them came with us on the first ships. An entire generation, wiped out on a whim of a *wealh* chieftain."

"I know, uncle. I was there."

"Then you should also know that we could never survive a war like it again, if we are not ready. What if there is a new *Dux* in Londin — that Northerner, Elasio, for example — who decides to get rid of us? You've seen how long it takes to gather the *witan*. We'd be destroyed before they even decided on who should lead the war band."

Did he talk to Pefen and Aelle about this, I wonder? The two *Drihtens* met a few times since the war, but if the matter of kingship ever arose in their private conversations, they kept it quiet from me.

Why does everyone want to be a ruler so badly? All these men and boys, vying for power for power's sake… I see no appeal in being a monarch, and see no reason why I would make a better one than anyone else. What's more, I see no way of *becoming* one, other than through force. The *witan* would never agree to grant me a *Rex's* diadem. Is this what Hengist is making me train his warriors for? Is his real plan to force the elder's decision?

I give him the same answer I gave Aelle.

"I did not want to be a *Drihten* — what makes you think I'll want to be a *Rex*?"

"You'll have no choice," says Hengist. "Unless you want to see the Iutes perish under someone like Haesta."

I stand up. "Let us see what the *witan* has to say about *that*."

"It seems you do not remember our customs as well as you should." He stares at me. "A *Drihten* can call the *witan*… But he can also call it off, if he thinks there is a threat to the tribe."

"You would call off the gathering of the elders just because your title is in danger?"

"Because the future of all the Iutes is in danger."

"Not all elders will see it that way."

"Do not test me, boy. I have wrangled with the *witan* all my life. I know how to bend these men to my will."

"And *I* am in command of your best warriors."

"You *dare* threaten me?"

He steps closer, his fists raised. I reach for the sword at my side. For a while, we stare each other down in silence, broken only by cries of seagulls and the gusts of wind.

He unclenches his fists with a sigh. I let go of the sword, but I remain tense and watchful.

[338]

"You're making a mistake, Aeric."

"I'm used to that."

He picks up a piece of eroded *caementicium* and crumbles it in his fingers. Wind picks up the grey dust.

"Fine!" he says. "Let Haesta humiliate himself before the elders. I'm not afraid of him. He's never been much of an orator. And as for you — I know you're better than this. You'll soon see the error of your ways."

If first impressions count for anything before the *witan*, Haesta has certainly won quite a few hearts to his side before he's even opened his mouth. He stands at the centre of the circle dressed in mail and dark leather, with a shiny new helmet of foreign design under his arm and a cavalry sword with a jewelled pommel at his side.

He begins by describing his adventures in Frankia; Hengist was right, he is no public speaker — he stutters and runs out of breath; he meanders into unnecessary details; he pauses for effect where there is none, like someone who's seen orators speak, but hasn't quite grasped the necessary technique. He'd be laughed out of the Forum the moment he spoke. But this is no Forum, and the elders — and they are all literal "elders" these days, since most of the old *witan* who were young enough to wield weapons perished in the war with Wortimer — are more easily impressed than the folk on Londin's market.

He spends a bit too long recounting his encounters along the Rhine with the Alemanns and the eastern Saxons — mere border skirmishes, though embellished in Haesta's retelling into bloody battles — and a bit too much boasting about how many enemies he personally slew; even some of the elders grow impatient. "Get to the point," shouts one of them. "I was fighting Saxons in the Old Country when you were just a splash in your father's balls. I could tell you a dozen stories like that."

Haesta grows red as the elders laugh. He clears his throat and puts the helmet on the ground.

"Freedom," he says. "Freedom is my point. The tribes of the Old Country have returned to the old ways, now that the threat of the Horse Archers has passed. They are not ruled by *Drihten* tyrants anymore — they heed their wise elders instead."

A few of the *witan* nod with satisfied smiles. They must be the ones Haesta has already convinced. I look to Hengist. He stares at the nodding elders with disdain.

"Even the man whom our *Drihten* has chosen as his successor agrees with me," says Haesta, looking towards me. "Do you not, Aeric?"

I am struck by the sense of having lived through all of this before, in some other life, and suddenly feel terribly tired.

"Oh, fuck that."

A silence falls on the *witan*. The gathering is so small, everyone heard me loud and clear.

"*Gesith* Aeric?" the elder standing next to me recoils at the vulgarity.

"I may have let myself be a puppet of a man like *Dux* Wortigern," I say, "when the fate of all Britannia was at stake. But I won't be played by the likes of you, Haesta. Nor you, *Drihten*. You two must perform your little play without me."

"But I thought we agreed…" Haesta stares at me with a confused, angry look.

"For what it's worth, I do agree with what you said," I say. "You've let yourselves be ruled by one man for too long." I raise an accusing finger. "Hengist wants me to be a *Rex*, like Meroweg of the Franks, or Theodrik of the Goths. An absolute ruler, one that no longer needs a *witan*. And even if I tell him no, he'll find another in my place. As for you, Haesta, I don't believe your honesty for a moment. If Hengist offered you my position, you'd take it in a heartbeat, forgetting all your lofty talk of freedom and peace."

I pull off the thick silver armband that marks me as the *Gesith* and throw it in the dirt at Haesta's feet. "Have yourselves a vote now, or just shout at each other for the rest of the day," I scoff at them. "I want no part of this."

The *witan* erupts in a mighty quarrel. Some of the elders call for Hengist to step down, others argue his side, and a few are simply calling for calm, to discuss the new information. I glimpse Haesta stoop down to pick up my silver armband. As I glance to Hengist, the *Drihten* snaps at the warriors at his side. They barge into the circle, pushing the stunned elders aside.

This, too, is a familiar scene, repeating itself like a bad dream. But this time, I am better prepared. Hengist is no Wortigern, and I am no longer that lost, wounded boy I was five years ago. I wave a signal to Betula.

The night before, I called her to my hut and explained what we might expect to happen at the *witan*. She was as unperturbed as ever by the news.

"I do not ask for your loyalty," I told her. "I ask for your friendship."

"You will have both, Ash," she replied. "Though if you ask me, I don't know why you're so opposed to Hengist's idea. You would make a good *Drihten*. Or a *Rex*."

"I pray we'll never have to find out."

She now stands before me, along with the rest of my *Hiréd*. The two bands of warriors face each other off, weapons drawn.

"Then the fate of our tribe will be decided by a show of force, after all," Hengist says, with a wry smile.

"Never," I reply. "I will not be the one to draw the first Iute blood. I just want to make sure the *witan* is free to debate and vote, without your spears at their backs."

"Don't pretend this is about upholding our laws," Hengist scoffs. "You never gave a damn about who ruled the Iutes and how. You've only lived among us for three years. This is all about you doing as you please, without a thought for your people's future. You're just as selfish as Haesta — only not as ambitious. I don't even know why you joined us in the first place."

"Do not let bitterness cloud your judgement, *Drihten*," says Betula. "We are all Iutes here. We are all brothers. Let our words resolve this conflict, not swords."

[342]

"I will obey the *witan* in whatever decision it makes," I say. "If you swear not to intervene in its proceedings. *That* is my word. Will you promise the same?"

"You would speak an *ath* on that?" Hengist eyes me with suspicion. "On the gods and your ancestors?"

I pause, my mouth open half-word. I feel the familiar goose-bumps that rise whenever the Iute gods are invoked in my presence. Nothing good ever came from my dealings with them. The fear of the cursed fate that shattered my life so many times, returns; am I making another terrible mistake?

"If you lack conviction, then step back," says Hengist. "And let me deal with Haesta and the *witan*."

I straighten my back and stare back at him, proudly. "I will speak an *ath*," I say. "And so will Haesta — will you not?"

The boy looks from me to Hengist, then back again. His hand hovers over the jewel-studded pommel of his sword, but he grunts a grudging agreement.

With a swift, well-trained move, Hengist draws a knife and cuts across his palm. He raises a bloodied hand.

"So be it. Let the gods and ancestors hear our oath!"

The Saxon Might

CHAPTER XIV
THE LAY OF DUNN

At the end of a long day, eleven elders vote to keep Hengist as *Drihten* and me as his successor. A dozen others support Haesta's motion to return to the way of peace.

There are none more surprised at the result of the vote than myself and Haesta. We hoped it would be a close one, maybe even a stalemate that would show the strength of our argument. It would've been enough of a humiliation for Hengist to make him consider changing his mind. But it seems the threat of Hengist bearing a circlet of a *Rex*, and the showdown of our opposing forces at the *witan*, proved too much for many of the elders, who still remembered how the tribe was ruled back in the Old Country.

"It's over, uncle," I tell Hengist. "You've lost."

"It's not over yet," Hengist says, between clashes of his *seax* against the training dummy. The wooden pole is half-smashed by the slashing blade; the straw head lies in the grass at its feet, sliced neatly off.

"You would break your *ath*?"

"All I need is for one more elder to vote my way. Then we have a stalemate — and you know what that means."

With the *witan* so diminished in numbers after the war, a stalemate is not an unusual occurrence. There are rules for dealing with such situations, inscribed in ancient laws transferred from generation to generation by the clan *scops* in long, repeating rhymes. When the exact same number of elders vote for opposite motions, the decisive vote belongs to the one who commands the *witan*. In peace time, it would have been the most senior of the gathering. But when a *Drihten* rules the tribe, the final decision is his…

"There are no more elders," I say. "Unless —"

He strikes a blow so hard, the sword embeds itself deep in the wood. He strains to push it out, but when the blade doesn't budge, he gives up.

"The Wecta colony," I guess. "Eadgith's new clan. But it's been so long. How do we know they're even sending anyone?"

It is a long and arduous journey for a Iutish ship, and no one truly expects the newest of the clans to send their representative to the *witan*. Any news coming from the distant colony has been scarce and unreliable, brought by random passing merchants, or a handful of pilgrims coming once a year to join the Yule celebrations on Tanet. All that we know for certain is that Eadgith's people — those who fled Londin after Wortimer's war, and many more who have joined her since — have established several farmsteads and villages along the island's northern coast, and on the mainland opposite. There are maybe a hundred houses there altogether, most of them on the fertile land abandoned by the Briton landlords more than a generation ago.

"*I* know," says Hengist. "I sent my riders to the coast. The ship is on its way, it's just going to wait out the storm in

Leman. We're not in a hurry. As you keep saying — we have peace."

"Keeping that lot fed and sheltered for weeks is going to be costly."

"You caused all this — you pay for it." He shrugs. "One of those *wealh* gold coins you like to flash would be more than enough."

Gone is the fatherly warmth. I can't wait for this preposterous conflict to be over, so that we can be family again, rather than political rivals. I bite my tongue to stop myself from telling him that one of my *wealh* gold coins he so flippantly referred to would be enough not just to feed the guests to the *witan*, but to buy the land under all the Iute villages from Rutubi to Dubris.

It would be an empty boast, of course. The nearest place where I can spend my coin is the Briton market at Dorowern. Gold and silver are of little use in the Iute land, other than for working them into armbands and diadems for the chieftains and jewellery for warriors and their maidens. A Iute serf wouldn't even know that his land was something that could be sold or bought; it was given to him and his household by the local clan leader from the greater whole granted to the Iutes by an agreement with the Cant landlords. The Iutes neither use nor mint money — the only trade that occurs between the villages is a simple exchange of goods: a goat for a set of clay pots, a jar of honey for a new horseshoe.

I was trained in basic Roman accounting; I know how to run a *villa*'s books; in my days as a Councillor, I witnessed and countersigned trade deals between the richest of Londin's merchants. Now I'm surrounded by people who count the value of their house in duck eggs and straw sandals, and haven't even the slightest clue what price the patch of dirt under their farm would fetch at Dorowern's land exchange. No Iute ever needed to buy a square foot of their land. There's enough of it abandoned and fallow in Cantiaca to accommodate everyone.

Sometimes, I swear I can almost feel my brain shrivelling and dying in this place.

I look to the east, as if I were to see a sail of a *ceol* coming from Wecta right this moment. To my astonishment, I *do* spot a ship.

"I thought you said they were still in Leman," I say.

A plain grey cloth sail leaps over the waves, rushing on the eastern gale. If it wasn't for the sail, I'd guess it was a local fishing boat returning to port before the night. But the fishermen of Rutubi use only row boats. A merchant would head in the direction of Dubris or Leman… What other ship could be coming here, to the Rutubi coast? A pirate raiding party? We haven't had one in months…

Hengist has spotted the vessel now, too. He raises his hand to his brow. "It's either them, or some Saxons lost in a storm," he says. "Either way, we'd better go see what's going on."

The boy's face is the colour of winter grass; his tunic is torn on the shoulders; his hair is clumped with salt. There's a twitch in his right hand, and a burn mark on his forearm, which I recognise as the result of grabbing on to a rope too hard in a storm.

Naturally, he is not the elder we've all been waiting for; but he is the only one of his crew still able to stand and speak. The other four are laid under the wall of the village barn where we've all gathered to listen to the boy, among dry nets and empty fish barrels. Two of the men were already unconscious when the boat landed, the other two soon fall into uneasy, exhausted sleep. I recognise one of them from my Londin war band.

"We were blown towards Frankia as we passed Leman," the boy, Dunn, tells us. Outside, the storm still rages on, making the barn's thick walls tremble. "The wind took us north, out onto the whale-road. We fought the storm for three days. We... lost the elder."

I peer into his eyes, staring dead into the distance as he speaks, trying to see in them my own memory from all those years ago, when my father's ship was being torn apart by the furious ocean.

"Why couldn't you just wait the storm out?" asks Hengist.

"We waited a week in New Port — but we couldn't wait anymore, we needed to bring our news before the *witan*."

"And what news was so dire that you risked a spring storm on the Narrow Sea?"

"We've been attacked." The boy takes a gulp of warm mead and wipes his mouth. In the pause, an anxious murmur spreads throughout the gathering.

"A raid on Wecta?" I ask. My mouth runs dry. Wecta was supposed to be a land away from any danger or conflict, a safe haven for those tired of Wortimer's war and the uncertainties of life in Cantiaca. What new nightmare is this?

"Not Wecta." Dunn shakes his head. "Some of the families moved back to the mainland, into the river valleys… We thought the land was empty — but then the raiders came."

"How many dead?" asks Hengist, straight to the point.

"A dozen," replies Dunn. "Three whole farmsteads wiped out, in the course of one week."

Hengist gives me a meaningful glance. *So much for peace*, his eyes are saying.

"Are you sure they weren't just some bandits from Andreda?" I ask.

"Nothing was taken, not even the livestock… *Hlaefdige* Eadgith thinks it was a warning against us settling in that valley, but… We made sure no one was living on the land we took."

Hlaefdige Eadgith — "Lady Eadgith"… Once a bladesmith's daughter, now a clan leader. In any other circumstances I would find this amusing.

"It could be that the farmsteads were built on some ground sacred to the *wealas*," I ponder.

"We talked to the local *wealas* — it's not that. They don't know who could have done it, either."

[350]

"Why not just move somewhere else? There must be plenty of land on that coast."

My question rouses another round of angry murmurs, but I ignore them. It's a good thing Haesta's not here. He left as soon as the vote went his way, to hunt deer in celebration of his victory. The hot-headed young warriors under his command would be clamouring for action, but I see little that can be done other than simply finding a different place for the Wecta clansmen to build their homes. Indeed, I'm slightly confused as to why Eadgith felt it necessary to send her men on the dangerous journey in such a hurry. If any other Iute warrior ruled the island, I would expect them to request Hengist to send a war band to seek out the attackers and wreak revenge upon them; but I know Eadgith is too reasonable for that sort of thing. There must be something else — what does she really want us to do?

"*Hlaefdige* Eadgith requests the *Gesith*'s presence," says Dunn, when I pose the question to him. "To assist with the search for the culprits."

"Only the *Gesith*?" asks Hengist. "Not the *Hiréd*?"

"We have fighters of our own," Dunn says, pushing his chest out proudly.

"I would take a few of my men, just in case," I say, quietly.

Hengist stands up and turns around to the small crowd of onlookers thronging around us. He puts on his diadem, and a hush falls on the gathering, as this is a mark of him making an official pronouncement.

"Iutes! We have been attacked! The peace is broken again! By the authority invested in me by the ancient laws, I declare this *witan* suspended until the matter is resolved!"

The silence erupts in a flurry of questions and panicked shouting. "Are we at war?" "We must gather the *fyrd!*" "Man the walls!" "Are the *wealas* coming?" "It's the Saxons, I tell you! I never trusted them!"

I stand on the table and raise my arms in the air. "Calm down!" I shout. "We don't even know what really happened. For all we know, it *could* have just been some bandits, trying to scare us off their land. Or maybe it's all just a mistake. When the storm clears, I will sail to Wecta myself to find out. I will return as fast as I can with more news."

I wait until the crowd calms down. I step down from the table and as I pass Hengist, I whisper to him:

"Watch out for Haesta. I leave you my *Hiréd* under Raven. If he tries anything, no matter our differences, you can count on them."

"Don't worry," he says with a nod. "I have no soft spot for the boy. I won't repeat Wortigern's mistakes. Just... don't take too long over there."

"I remember when I came here with my father, as a child... There was still a pier large enough to accommodate a *liburna*, but it was already crumbling, not used for decades."

The ship's Captain stares at the ruins of the harbour with a wistful gaze. There is barely any trace left of the old Roman port — a row of wooden posts, blackened with age, a few feet of cracked stone pavement, a windbreak torn apart by the storms. Whatever town or village there was that serviced the port, is mostly gone, too, apart from a few streets of oyster dredgers' huts by the beach. Further upstream, where the river is too narrow to navigate, another small collection of houses stands on a spur of a hill. A remnant of a *villa*'s boundary wall protects the settlement from the northerly winds.

Not willing to brave the Narrow Sea storms in a Iute coracle, I hired a merchant ship to take me from Leman to New Port, and another one from New Port to Port Adurn, an old Saxon Shore fortress guarding the inlets and bays that were once known as Great Havens, the Regins' main harbour, before the dwindling sea trade and silt left to gather on the waterways turned them into just more haunted ruins.

I hoped to find another boat in Adurn, but the Saxon clan who made it their dwelling have locked their gates and didn't respond to our calls, so I threw another handful of bronze into the Captain's purse and asked him to take me straight to the only harbour remaining on Wecta.

I feel a tingle of excitement, something I haven't sensed in a long time. I've never been to Wecta — I've never even seen that part of the coast, beyond the Regin land. This stretch of Britannia was struck hard by the years of hardship after the Legions left, the civil war and the Serf Rebellion. Like Masuna's *pagus* bordering it from the North, this was once part of a disputed border land between Ambrosius and Wortigern, but one that was even more remote and desolate. The Captain tells me that when tribal divisions introduced by the Romans still mattered, the woods and moors along the coast belonged to the people called the Belgs, and I remember the name from my days in Aelle's band.

"There were some bandits in western Andreda who called themselves the Belgs," I note.

We killed them all.

"Sounds about right," the Captain agrees. "All that's left of them are roving bands of starving serfs and runaway slaves. A few nobles are still trying to make ends meet around Clausent, and further inland by Belgian Wenta, pretty much the only bits of this land that remain more or less civilised."

I wonder, is that the source of the mysterious attacks? A band of Belgs, desperate in the memory of their wounded pride to keep the barbarians off what they still see as their land? It sounds too obvious. Eadgith wouldn't make me journey all this way just to solve so simple a riddle.

"This was the only town on Wecta?" I ask, pointing at the ruined harbour.

"If you can call it that. The rest of the island was divided between several great landlords, each owning vast stretches of farmland. Wheat and barley grew as tall as trees on Wecta, some say."

"What happened here?" asks Betula, studying the empty wharf. She's one of the six *Hiréd* I brought with me on the journey as guard — and company. "A plague? Saxon raids?"

"Nothing so dramatic." The Captain laughs. "In my grandfather's days, Roman ships would anchor in this harbour, heaving with wine headed for Londin's market, and grain that would travel to Gaul, Iberia, and beyond… But then the wheat trade collapsed, and the nobles in Londin could no longer afford fine wine. The ships stopped coming, so there was no more reason for the rich to stay on Wecta — and once they were gone, the poor soon followed."

"Just like that," I muse.

"Just like that," the Captain says with a thoughtful nod.

With the pier gone, his ship is too large to try a landing on the beach, so we must wait for one of the fishermen to gather enough courage to approach us in a wobbly boat.

"Are ye lost?" the woman in the boat asks, in rustic Briton.

"We're here to speak to Lady Eadgith," I reply.

"There ain't no ladies or lords on Wech't, sir," she says, the island's name mangled in her mouth. "They've all gone long ago."

"What about the Iutes? Where is their chieftain?"

She glances over her shoulder, to the ruined *villa*. "The pagans took over the Master's palace up the hill," she says and spits. "But they have naught to sell ye," she adds, eyeing the bulging hulk of the merchant ship.

"Will you take us there?"

She shrugs and rows up to the side of the ship. Her boat is only big enough for two people at a time — Betula and I go first. Once we board the boat, the woman extends a hand.

I put two bronze coins on her outstretched palm out of reflex, but I'm surprised when she accepts the payment without a word.

"You still use money here?" I ask.

"We're no barbarians," she scoffs. "The pagans tried to buy our fish with eggs and beans, but we soon taught them how civilised people do trade."

She's dismissive, but I can see how her eyes gleam at the sight of the coins. I imagine the few Briton families left in the town have been circulating the same handful of old money between themselves for years, as meaningless tokens.

"Are you selling your oysters at the Clausent market?" I ask, as we row away from the ship.

"Clausent, Clausent…" She repeats, confused, and nods to herself. "I haven't been there since I was a li'l one… Is that where ye came from?"

"We come from New Port," I reply. "To the East."

She shakes her head. "Never heard of it."

There is no "palace" on the spur of the hill — there's barely a house.

Judging by what's left of its *domus*, the hilltop *villa* must have once belonged to one of the lesser landlords of Wecta. It's certainly a lot smaller than Ariminum, and is made even more cramped by the congregation of Iute huts built on the

[356]

courtyard, whose inhabitants come out to observe me and Betula — we left the other five in the fishing village below — climb the cobbled road.

I recognise their faces from Londin days, and they, of course, recognise me too. They are wary of my arrival. I don't blame them. The last time many of them saw me, I was leading their kin to slaughter at the gates of the *Praetorium*. I am trouble; I am death. What must they be thinking of my return? Did Eadgith consult with them before she sent for me?

Warriors hurriedly line up to welcome us along the final approach to the *domus*, five on each side. They wear new helmets of simple design, and hold swords in outstretched arms, the blades of which I recognise as Eadgith's work. As I come nearer, I note a curious detail — the *villa*'s bath, with its unmistakable three vaulted roofs, is just another chamber attached to the main house's outer wall, rather than a separate building. Instead of a grand porch leading inside, there's only a tiny atrium, with three small rooms opening to it. Where in Master Pascent's house there was marble and mosaic, here there is wood and plaster, rotten and peeling off in great chunks, revealing raw flint underneath.

The eastern wing shows signs of recent repair — timber planks fill out the holes in the walls, thatch covers the roof where the limestone tiles fell off. A buckled bronze door protruding on the side indicates that this wing, too, was once heated by its own hypocaust, which means this must have been the master's bedroom. A new brick chimney at the back puffs out black smoke. A broken statue — missing its head and arms — has been dug up from somewhere and put up against the wall for decoration. Surprisingly, the gable window still has a full pane of bluish glaze in it.

These few details tell me who's responsible for the repairs, and I can't help but smile. Eadgith is the only inhabitant of the Iute colony — perhaps the only person on the entire island — who lived in a Roman *villa*, who saw one still in its full glory. She knows what it should look like; in the only way she could, she must have tried to recreate what she remembered of her old life as the bladesmith's daughter.

"How do you like my Venus?"

She comes out of the *domus*, wiping white powder off her hands with a wet cloth. She wears her red hair long now, tied in a tall bun. The sleeves of her tunic are rolled up high, revealing arm muscles, tight and rounded since I last saw her. She dons a roughly cut apron of heavy leather, so thick that it could double as armour, and a pair of bracelets of stout bronze wire around her wrists.

"It's the only old thing we found when we came here," she says. She reaches out to embrace me and Betula. "That and the mosaic in the master's room. Everything else was pillaged long ago."

"Are you a baker now, instead of a blacksmith?" I ask, pointing at the white dust.

"That's plaster," she laughs. "I was just fixing up my furnace." She nods towards the brick chimney. "The owners of this place would get quite the shock seeing what I've done to their place."

"What are you making there," asks Betula, "new swords?"

"Just some farming tools," replies Eadgith. "We have no steel for swords — other than what I managed to gather for

[358]

my household guard from various scraps we brought with us." She nods towards the ten warriors standing down the path. "And until recently, we had no use for them, either."

"That'd be why we're here," I say. "How soon can we talk about what's happened?"

"You'll need to wait in Puna's house," says Eadgith, nodding towards the nearest of the huts. "While I clean up the smithy. I'm afraid there is no feast waiting — not like you'd expect at a *villa*, at least — and the dining room is full of ingots and charcoal right now," she adds with a tired smile. "But Puna's stew should be ready soon."

"We'll gladly have the stew," I reply. "We've been eating nothing but salted fish and hardtack for the past three days."

"We should never have tried settling on the mainland," says Eadgith, between slurps of the watery stew prepared by Puna, a grey-haired old man who does various odd jobs around the *domus* that Eadgith made her home. "There is more than enough good land on Wecta. The Britons were fools to abandon it."

"The Britons only care for land if it brings them profit," I say, noticing she still hasn't started using the term *wealas*, despite living among the Iutes for so long. "But then, why *did* you move?"

"There's an old Iute village on the coast, established by one of the boats the Iutes sent from Tanet in search of a better place to settle, a generation ago…"

"I remember." I nod. "I always wondered why they didn't just land there, instead."

"The Britons turned them away. There were more of them back then, and fewer Iutes — when we arrived three years ago, they just hid in their huts and waited until we settled up here."

"This can't be the only settlement?" I ask. "I heard there were a hundred houses on Wecta."

"We're scattered all over the place. There's almost too much land for our needs. We're still exploring the island — we haven't even touched the southern coast."

"So why couldn't these old Iutes move here, too?"

"They spent the last twenty years draining the marshes around their settlement, at the mouth of the River Meon — they didn't want to just leave it all to the sea. You know how it is with old folk. It was they who asked if some of our younglings could move to their village — to help them with the irrigation, logging and such like."

"How many are we talking about?"

"Five families last autumn — and ten more this spring, when the first ones brought the good news."

"What good news?" asks Betula.

"Ponies," says Puna. "A great herd of feral ponies, out on the moor a few miles inland. Better than ours — if you can tame them."

[360]

"From what we've learned from the Britons, they used them for everything around here — farming, riding, hunting, even racing," adds Eadgith. "But once the *villas* disappeared, they were just set loose on the moors."

"And how long were you planning to keep this bounty to yourself?" asks Betula.

"We needed to see how easy it was to tame them first," replies Eadgith. "We expected the first foals this *Thrimilce* — if it wasn't for the attacks…"

"I can see why you wouldn't want to just be scared off that land now," I say. I scratch my chin and take a bite of the steaming hot bread that Puna just brought onto the table. "But it seems to me even more now that it could just have been some local bandits, trying to steal your ponies."

For a moment, we all chew the bread in silence — well-risen bread, made of a mixture of fine wheat and rye, I notice, not peas and oats as is the norm among the freemen in the East. If this is what the Iutes on Wecta eat on a daily basis, I'm only surprised that more of Hengist's subjects haven't packed up and moved here already.

"Didn't Dunn tell you they haven't taken anything?" says Eadgith. "Besides, in the past twenty years the villagers of Meon haven't suffered a single bandit raid," she adds. "This place was well and truly abandoned by whoever lived here before us."

"Then I will need you to tell me all the details about the attacks."

"I can do better than that," she replies. "We will sail to Meon tomorrow. You'll see everything for yourself."

As evening comes, and Betula settles in Puna's hut, nestling by the hearth like a tired cat, Eadgith invites me to the ruined *domus*.

"I have a surprise for you," she says.

She takes me to the smaller, western wing, past what once must have been the Master's office, and is now a wind-swept, roofless space, into the bathing chambers added on to the building's side.

Two of the chambers, the towel room and the *tepidarium*, are cold, dark, filled with rubble and waste of decades past; but the *caldarium* is cleared out, and lit up with candles. Eadgith tells me to take of my sandals. The floor is warm; the pool at the far side is filled with water.

Eadgith smiles, seeing my surprise.

"I've built my forge on top of the hypocaust furnace," she explains, "since it had the best bricks. One day, I discovered that most of the old system still worked — whoever built it, knew what they were doing. There's a pipe going somewhere at the back that still hasn't silted up, even when everything around it has crumbled."

She unpins her hair and lets it fall, then slips off her tunic and breeches. "I don't fill it up often," she continues. "It's a bother to carry all that water from the river by myself, so I only do it on special occasions."

[362]

"You should get yourself a slave to do it," I say, not taking my eyes off her body.

She laughs. "Just because I live in a Briton noble's house, doesn't mean I have become one. Now, are you coming in, or are you going to just stand there and ogle me? I haven't grown any younger or more beautiful since you last saw me naked."

I join her in the pool and moan with bliss as I submerge my tired body. I close my eyes.

"How is it?" she asks.

"Not exactly Ariminum, but it'll do," I reply. We both laugh. It feels good to laugh.

"I suppose this isn't such a rare luxury to you as it is to me."

"It's a rare luxury to anyone these days. The last time I was in a bath was when I visited Fastid last month — the Cathedral still has one working. But other than that, it's bathing in a tub dug into the floor, serf style, like that time we…"

I stop myself. *That time we bathed in the Briton hut, and then made love on the straw-covered floor at Robriwis…* That was Rhedwyn, not Eadgith.

"You still mourn her," Eadgith says. It frightens me how well she can read me, after all these years.

"I don't think I'll ever stop."

"I take it you haven't got yourself another woman."

I take a deliberate look around the room. "Your bedroom is empty, too."

"Not always," she replies with a mischievous smile. "But I've had my share of family life. Something you've never experienced. Aren't you at least a little curious what it's like?"

"I have Octa."

"You spawned him, but you're never going to be his father." She moves to the far edge of the bath. It's a small pool — our legs touch. "Have you seen him? How's he doing? I haven't heard from him in a year."

"He's doing great. He's a clever boy. Fastid already has him read bits of the Scripture. And he's grown handsome — he'd have all the girls in Londin chasing after him, if Fastid wasn't keeping him under lock and key."

"He'll have plenty of time for that later."

"I am a little concerned with his physical prowess, though. I'll need to send one of my *Hiréd* to train him in combat."

"And Fastid? How is he?"

There's a soft, longing tone in her voice when she asks the question, that would have annoyed me years ago. "He's the same as ever," I say. "Always fighting for the souls of everyone around him. With no *Dux*, he's the most single powerful man in Londin — though you could never tell when you meet him, except that now he's even busier than usual. He started martial training now," I add. "In case the

Cathedral needs defending again — I don't think he believes in this peace as much as he professes…"

"And do you believe in peace?"

"I believe we may have a chance, if enough people see that peace is more rewarding than war. I hope these few years of prosperity are proving to everyone that it's better to trade goods than blows."

"As long as there are goods enough to trade," she says.

"So you, too, think this will not last."

"It might — if we are fortunate."

I reach for the chunk of soap lying on the bath's edge. It smells of yarrow.

"Let me wash your back," she offers. I turn around.

"Why did Hengist call for the *witan*?" she asks, as she lathers my back with the strength and skill that tells me she's done it countless times for her husband and son. "It surprised us all here. For a moment, we thought you somehow found out about the attacks on Meon."

"I'm afraid it's my fault, again."

I tell her of my conflict with Hengist, of Haesta's proposal and of the stalemate vote. Her hands stop. I turn back to see her surprised face.

"You refused Hengist?" she asks. "Are you still having the same doubts you had three years ago?"

"It's not just about me doubting myself," I say, though she's painfully right. "I believe Haesta's assessment is correct, even if he's doing it only for his own benefit. Don't you think the Iutes should be ruled by the elders, rather than just one man?"

"I don't know much about politics, but I know Hengist is not a man you should slight."

"Come now, don't play the village fool with me. You're *Hlaefdige* Eadgith now. You rule Wecta. You were the one who brought me back from the edge of darkness back in Londin. Yours is the only opinion I trust."

She sighs and pulls back. I reach for the bucket and wash the soap off my back.

"They made me the head of a clan," she says, "because nobody else wanted the job. Even though I'm not a Iute, I don't know the Iute laws or ancient customs, other than what I glimpsed when I lived in Orpeddingatun. When two families come to me for judgement on a farm boundary, or a trade dispute, I just use my common sense. So far, I'm managing to keep everyone happy. But that's completely different from leading an entire tribe — I'm more like a mother to these people, than a chieftain."

"I've been watching Hengist closely these past three years. All that a *Drihten* does in peace time is the same thing as you do here. Deciding cases between the clan heads, settling disputes, applying the law. There's no reason why these tasks couldn't be performed by the elders, as it was in the old days."

"I don't know anything about these *old days*," she reminds me. "I was raised in a Briton *villa*. And so were you. Isn't it a bit presumptuous of you to think you know what's better for the Iutes than the man who ruled them for thirty years?"

"You think I should have agreed, then."

"I don't know what to think. I told you, I don't have an opinion. Only you can decide your fate. Now wash my back, before the water gets all cold."

She turns around. I touch her back with the soap, then with a towel — then with my hands. Feeling her heat under my fingers, I can't help myself; I reach around to touch her breasts. She shivers, and puts my hands away.

"No," she says. "This isn't why I invited you here. I just wanted to talk."

"Why not? We've done it before."

"I was drunk and lonely then. We agreed it would be the last time. If you're having urges, there'll be girls in the village who will gladly accommodate a *Gesith*."

"I'm sorry." I pull away. "I misunderstood."

I'm as surprised by my action as she is; maybe more. I haven't felt the need to be with a woman since Rhedwyn's passing. I thought that part of me was dead forever.

She wraps her arms around me and kisses me on the cheek, then lays her head on my shoulder. "I love you, Ash," she says, in a matter-of-fact way. "But I don't need this in my life. I don't need *you*. And you don't need me — or Rhedwyn. You need to figure out your life on your own."

"I've tried. So many times. It always ends badly."

"Then you just need to keep trying. What else can you do?"

"I did think about not... doing anything anymore."

She pulls away with an angry scowl. "Don't be a fool, Ash. Your song's not over yet." She turns her back to me again. "Now finish what you started and let's go to sleep. I set up *two* beds."

CHAPTER XV
THE LAY OF CROHA

She is the most wonderful beast. She's almost as tall as a Gaulish warhorse, but sturdier and stockier. With its long, flaxen mane flowing in the breeze, slim legs and a chiselled muzzle, the chestnut mare brings to mind a beautiful Saxon woman, enchanted into the equine form.

Other ponies in the enclosure are smaller and not as striking in appearance, but they are all a pleasure to look at. There's still a fire in their eyes, of free pasture, of wind blustering through the moors.

"I see now why you wouldn't want to ever leave this place," I say.

"How many of them are there?" asks Betula. She's just as transfixed by the ponies as I am. She reaches out her one hand to stroke the mare on the forehead, but the pony brays and walks off in a dignified sulk.

"Nobody knows," replies Eadgith. "These moors stretch beyond Clausent, maybe all the way to Sorbiodun. There could well be thousands of them."

"Have you backed any of them yet?" I ask.

"A few. But not her," Eadgith nods at the chestnut mare.

"I will tame her," I say.

Betula laughs. "When did *you* become a horse-tamer?"

"I haven't. But I've seen it done — how hard can it be?"

"It takes years to learn the skill. And even a trained tamer would need weeks to break a wild beast like her."

"I will tame her," I repeat. It is a foolish boast. I've only ever ridden horses a few times in my life. I have no idea how to approach a feral beast. But from the moment I saw her, I've felt a strange connection to the flaxen-haired mare.

"Just don't go calling her 'Rhedwyn'," whispers Eadgith, reading my mind again.

"I… wasn't going to."

"Of course you weren't. Her name is Frige — at least that's what Haegel called her, when he first tried to back her. It seems she's destined to break all men's hearts."

"And who's Haegel?"

An old man, bent in half, approaches the pony enclosure from the direction of the village; he's wearing a grey hooded cloak and supports himself with a long, straight staff of ash wood.

"That'll be me," he says with a broad grin. "Haegel of Hléseg," he introduces himself with a bow. "My family built the first house in this marsh," he adds, pointing to a substantial hut in the middle of the village.

"Doesn't that make you the elder here?"

He scratches his head. "I suppose so. I never paid much attention to these matters. I hear old Eadwin didn't make it to Cantiaca?" he asks Eadgith. "I told him it was too dangerous for someone his age."

"You know how he insisted, Haegel," says Eadgith. "And now you're the eldest that remains. This is *Gesith* Aeric, he arrived yesterday from the East," she adds.

"I gathered as much. Admiring my horses, I see."

"They are magnificent beasts," I say.

"And gentle, too. Unless you want to ride them, that is."

He clicks his tongue and the flaxen mare trots over to the fence. He pats her on the nose and gives her half an apple.

"We hoped she would foal this spring," he says, growing serious. "But the attack scared her and she miscarried."

"You were attacked even here?"

I look around. The village of Meon, named after the river on the banks of which it stands, is at least ten households strong, and surrounded by a shallow ditch and a wooden fence. It seems unlikely that any small band of roaming roughs would ever try to attack it.

"Frige and a few others were kept in a camp in the northern moors. It was the second place to be burned down."

"I'm sorry," I say, both to him and to the mare.

"We have other foals coming," says Haegel. "If there are no more of these… attacks."

"We're here to see to that," I say and point to my men, lined along the enclosure's fence. Haegel nods politely, but I can see he's surprised and disappointed there are only six of us. I can see he expected an entire war band would be sent to deal with whoever caused his favourite mare to lose a foal.

"Show us what happened here," says Eadgith.

He gazes north. "It's best if we go to Tova's place. It's about a mile up the river. It's where everything started."

"They kept the goats here. The whole place stank like a giant's arsehole. But they made good cheese."

Haegel closes the small, charred door. A futile gesture, since the house has no roof and only one wall still intact. The rest of the farmstead, including a smokery and a small grain store, is all burned to the ground. The only thing left standing is the stone chimney of the smoking hut.

"Dunn said the attackers haven't taken anything," I say. "How do you know, if everything's burned down?"

Haegel reaches into his cloak and takes out a small silver trinket, carved in the shape of a horse's head. "Tova wore this brooch — it was her only treasure — she brought it with her from the Old Country. She still had it on her."

"Five people lived here," adds Eadgith. "Two of them children. They were all found in a pile by the smokery."

[372]

"We found the goats out on the bracken moor," adds Haegel. "Frightened out of their wits, but untouched otherwise, just like the ponies after the second attack."

I crouch down by the smokery chimney and root through the charred rubble. There's an air of menace around this place that I last felt in the destroyed village of the *Gewisse* refugees in Masuna's country. Whoever did it, wanted to send a message — but if so, why were they so cryptic?

"And there were no signs left? No tribal markings, no… *crosses?*"

"Crosses?" Eadgith frowns. "No, nothing like that."

"How did they all die? Were they burned?"

"Sword cuts and spear stabs," says Haegel. "All of them. Just like in the other two farms."

"Swords — are you sure?"

Haegel smiles bitterly. "I was with Hengist in Frisia. I have seen enough corpses to know what killed these ones. Now, whether it was a *seax* or one of the *wealh* swords, I couldn't tell you, but it sure wasn't an axe that slit poor Tova's throat."

I stand up. This doesn't make sense. Swords are not the usual weapons of bandits. If these are trained warriors — or even soldiers — why not simply wipe out all the villages in the valley? On our way here I studied the sparse Iutish settlements scattered along the River Meon. There are no warriors here. They have no weapons, other than farming tools and knives. They wouldn't stand a chance against any sort of organised attack. The entire colony could be destroyed within a day.

Somebody wanted to make sure we got the message.

"Who else lives around here?" I ask.

"The nearest *wealh* village is three miles east, by the sea," replies Haegel, pointing with his twisted staff. "Good, peaceful folk. Sometimes we do a little trade. A few scattered farmsteads here and there. It's moor and marsh every other way, until Clausent."

I paint a vague map of the area in my mind. "Three miles — isn't that towards Adurn?"

"About halfway there." Haegel nods.

"Ever had any trouble with Aelle's Saxons?"

"They don't bother us, we don't bother them."

"Until now," I murmur.

"What's that?"

"Well, isn't it obvious? It had to be them."

"No," says Eadgith, firmly. "We'd know."

"Know — how?"

"I've had sentries posted around Adurn from the day we landed on Wecta," she says. "I never trusted the Saxons, and there's a whole war band of them locked up at that fortress.

[374]

In fact, they've been strangely quiet this past couple of months."

"I noticed something was odd," I say. "I tried to lease a boat off of them coming here." I scratch my chin. "I wonder if —"

I stop, as I spot a column of thick black smoke rising over the wooded hill to the east.

"What's that?" I ask.

"That's Spring Farm!" cries Haegel. "Saba's house! It's only on the other side of the ridge."

"Eadgith, go back to the Meon, see if they're all safe there."

"I'll gather the men," she says. "We'll meet you up there."

"No time. Wait for us on the ridge. *Hiréd*, to me!" I shout an order, and launch in pursuit, with my six men in tow.

The ridge is steeper than I expected, and by the time we climb down the other side, I fear we might be too late. I tell the men to let out battle yells as we approach, hoping to frighten the attackers away. I can see through the gaps in the trees that the farmhouse is already fully ablaze, the thick thatched roof burning like a well-oiled torch.

"Look for survivors," I tell Betula once it's clear that whoever assaulted the farm is already gone. It seems our loud arrival worked — the farm is not as thoroughly destroyed as

Tova's place; only the farmhouse is damaged, the outhouses are all intact.

"There's something here," calls one of my warriors from the other side of the burning house. I rush to him. He stands before the trampled remains of what looks like a dog kennel. A small creature is crawling and whimpering inside.

"It's just a dog," I say. "Keep searching —"

"No, wait," Betula pushes me away and stoops down to the kennel. "Help me with that board."

I tear out a plank from the rubble to reveal what's hidden within: a small girl, five or six years old, curled up in the dark hole. She cries out and hides her face in her hands.

"It's alright," Betula reaches to calm her down. The girl yelps and tries to hide even deeper into the hole. "We're here to help."

"Her parents," I ask the men. "Where are they?"

One of them looks to the burning house in dismay.

"No — they're here," shouts another. I leave Betula with the whimpering girl, and join him at the cabbage patch. Among the young green shoots lies a man — the girl's father, no doubt — face down in the dirt, his hands thrown apart, and a throwing axe in his back. His wife is pinned to a nearby cherry tree by a javelin. She's still holding an adze in a tightly clenched hand. There's blood on the blade.

I kneel down to examine the dead man and the weapon in his back. He's only been dead a few minutes. The blood is cooling quickly in the spring air. I pull the axe out.

"This is Saxon work," I say.

Something here doesn't add up. Nothing about this attack resembles what Haegel told us about the previous ones. I stand up and look around. The cabbage is trampled all around us. There must have been a dozen men here. Their trail, splattered with blood of the man injured by the woman's adze, is easy to follow.

"Betula!" I cry. "Take the girl and go back to Eadgith — and meet us at Meon!"

"Meon? We're not going after the bastards who did this?"

"We are — they're heading for Haegel's village. I just hope we're not too late this time."

The first two huts on the outskirts of the village are already on fire — though the second one is merely smouldering on the corner; the attackers didn't bother to raze it properly before assaulting the village itself.

Out by the pony enclosure, old Haegel is fending off three attackers all on his own, whirling his ash staff like a spear, with the skill of a seasoned veteran. The rest of the enemy band pushes at the village fence, trying to force their way through a narrow opening. The men and women of the village are waving farming tools and kitchen utensils, except Eadgith, who is slashing at the attackers with her *seax*. One of the bandits lies dead on the other side of the shallow ditch, but so do two of the defenders, and it's clear that any second now the attackers will push through and destroy the rest of the village.

I gesture at my men to stay quiet as we rush to Eadgith's rescue. Only when we're within a javelin's throw, do I let out a war cry. The attackers turn around in confusion. Just as I suspected, they're all Saxons. They don't belong to any war band — they wear long tunics, and no armour, except simple helmets. Only two of them have swords, the rest hack their way through the handful of Iutes with axes and spears.

I struggle to think why they're attacking the village in the first place. Their heart is not in the fight. I slay one of the two swordsmen with a fortunate first thrust before he manages to raise a weapon to parry. Another warrior soon falls to my men's blows. There are still more of them than us and the villagers combined, but for the moment, they're uncertain whether they should flee or fight on.

"Eafa, Penda, leave that old man and help us!" shouts the surviving second swordsman, clearly the leader of the band. He urges his men to stand against us. "There's only five of them!" he cries. "Deal with them first, then we'll deal with the villagers."

The tide of battle turns swiftly. With the three warriors charging at us from the pony enclosure, it is we who are now trapped between two groups of enemies. There are no orders I could give my *Hiréd*; all they can do is fight, to the best of their abilities, and hope that's enough to defeat the Saxons. We have training on our side; they have numbers. I can't count on the help of the villagers — they're already tired of the fighting, and most have pulled back from the fence to rest.

Eadgith leads a few of them in an attempt to break through to us, but one of the Iutes falls with a spear through his stomach, and the rest are forced back.

I'm struck by the hopelessness of my situation. I have survived great battles; I have led entire armies; I fought in wars that will forever be retold in song; and now I am to die on this plot of midge-infested marshland, defending some tiny village nobody's heard of, at the hands of a handful of nameless Saxons…

Isn't this what you wanted? To end it all, no matter how…

I shake my head to silence the grim voice inside my mind. I parry a spear and thrust again, cutting through leather and meat on my opponent's arm. He yelps and drops the weapon. A mistake that marks him as an inexperienced warrior; I follow through with a diagonal slash, slicing him from heart to chin. His blood draws a red arc in the air. *Don't think, just fight*, I tell myself. If more of the Saxons are as green as this boy, we can still win this. One of my men pulls back, with a wound to his side. He, too, didn't think he'd die in this place — but the wound is shallow, and he soon returns to the brawl with renewed strength. Another Saxon throws his arms in the air and falls on his back with a woeful cry.

I reach the Saxon chief. Sword clashes against sword. He's no Brutus, or Wortimer; he lacks skill and finesse with the *seax*, slashing and waving it around like an axe. I would overpower him with ease, but he leaps back and hides behind one of his men. He's a better commander than a fighter: he orders his men to change formation, and some of them do so. It's a poor show, but it's enough to cut us off from both sides. I glimpse Eadgith's red hair again, leaping in the gaps between the warriors, but there's no chance for her and the villagers to reach us, so I yell at her to stop before she hurts herself.

I groan, annoyed at how long this is taking. I grab a dropped spear and push through, but the Saxon line holds even as another of their rank drops to the ground. The spear gets entangled in the limbs of one of the attackers and the shaft breaks. I use it as a club and whack a nearby Saxon on the head, stunning him and throwing his helmet off. One of my men finishes him off with a blow to the neck. We still hold, but barely. I dream of a shield; we left ours on Wecta, not imagining we'd need them today. If we had shields, we'd make short work of these Saxons…

I hear a whirling, whistling flutter of an axe flying in the air. I duck, instinctively, but the axe flies past me and lands straight in the chest of the Saxon chieftain. His men watch in astonishment as their leader staggers back, the impact pushing him away by several steps, and he falls. This is too much for them; the panic finally sets in. The Saxons howl and push us out of their way, fleeing towards the forest line. I scan the field to our north and spot Betula, a second throwing axe in her only hand, looking for another target. The little girl is hiding behind her, clutching on to Betula's tunic.

I order my men to halt the pursuit — we don't know if there aren't more enemies hiding in the wood — and crouch down by the fallen Saxon chief.

"Why did you attack us?" I cry at him. "What have we done to you?"

He splutters and spits blood in my face.

[380]

"You… reap… what you… sow… Iute…"

His face twists in pain one last time and he gurgles his last breath.

I help Eadgith pick up a dead Iute's body and put it by the wall of the village hall with the others. They will be buried in a peat field by the forest, together with the fallen Saxons, as soon as old Haegel performs the necessary rites. There is no time for ceremony, with the spring sun beaming hot from the afternoon sky.

It was pure fortune that Eadgith returned to the village just when her sentries came with news of a Saxon war band on the move from Adurn. If she'd arrived any earlier, she'd have taken all the capable defenders with her, leaving Meon to the mercy of the attackers.

"It seems your suspicions were right," says Eadgith. "It was the Saxons all along. I don't know how they kept getting past my sentries…"

"It's because it wasn't them before."

"What do you mean?"

"The pattern of the attack, the weapons used… Everything was different today. Something else happened here — and I'm going to find out what."

I drop the body on the ground and wince. I touch my aching side. My tunic is cut, but there's no blood.

"You're wounded?" asks Eadgith.

"Just a bruise — but in a bad place. I don't even know when that happened." I stare at the dead bodies, rubbing the bruise. It's in almost exactly the same spot where Brutus's *spatha* cut me at Eobbasfleot. "We could all be lying here now."

"It was close." She nods.

"Too close." I look up. "Why did you insist only I come? We'd all be dead if I hadn't taken my men with me."

"I didn't think we'd need an entire band of Hengist's best warriors. We couldn't even afford to feed and shelter you all here. Besides, it's not like I don't have any fighting men at my disposal."

"And where are they now?" I look around.

"On Wecta." She laughs, bitterly. "I know. I never said I was a good chieftain."

"Is this why you asked me to come here? To help you with running your clan?"

She scoffs. "I would have asked for someone with actual experience."

"Fair enough. But then, why me?"

"We are surrounded by Britons and Saxons. You know how to talk to both of them — if this was some kind of border misunderstanding, as I hoped, you'd have been the best equipped to deal with it. Now, I fear the time for words might be over…" She nods at the corpses.

"It's not too late yet. Let's not do anything rash. I will go to Adurn tomorrow, maybe I'll find something out at the source."

Betula comes up to us, with the girl still behind her. She picks up her flying axe and puts it next to the other one behind her belt.

"We owe you our lives," I say, and bow. "There'll be a brand new silver armband waiting for you back home."

"And with your left hand, too," says Eadgith. "Is it me, or have you actually gotten better in throwing axes since you lost your arm?"

Betula flashes her teeth. "God guides my aim," she says and makes the sign of a cross. "I could've hit either of you if you weren't so fortunate."

"Nothing 'fortunate' about it," I say. I crouch down to the level of the little girl. I see now that she's older than I first thought — maybe ten years old, just small for her age. "What's your name?" I ask. The girl puts her face in Betula's tunic.

"I asked her already," says Betula, "but she's not saying anything."

"Her parents called her *Croha*," says Haegel, approaching from the peat field. "Saffron flower."

"Her family was from Beaddingatun?" I guess.

[383]

Eadgith nods. "They were part of the original fifty that came with me to Wecta," she says.

"Then I would have feasted with the girl's parents, more than once," I muse and stand up. "Survived Wortimer's war, only to perish on this empty moor."

"She's not the only one made orphan today," says Haegel. He crouches down, lays his hand on the forehead of one of the slain Iutes, and whispers an incantation.

"Was that — a prayer?" Betula asks, astonished.

"Bedca was baptised in Clausent," replies Haegel. "I'm not a Christian, but I thought someone should say something."

"I will help you bury him," says Betula. "I know the rites."

"Take both children to Wecta," Eadgith orders her men. "Wait." She stops them. "Take *all* the children to Wecta. We can't risk losing any more."

Port Adurn, the last outpost in the old Roman shield wall — the westernmost in the long line of fortresses guarding the *Litus Saxonicum*, the Saxon Shore — still stands strong at the tip of a narrow peninsula, jutting into the largest of the Great Haven bays. I can see how Eadgith could easily keep an eye on what goes on in the fort: only one road leads in and out of the single gate, a narrow street linking it to a remnant of a highway that once ran from Regentium to Clausent and further west, but now disappears into the moors on either end.

I approach the fort down the middle of that single road, making sure the guards on the gatehouse notice the flag of truce slung over my shoulder. I see two of them on the wall; it's a hot, lazy day, and they must be dozing off, for they fail to notice me until I'm less than a hundred paces from the gate. At once, one of them draws a bow and aims it at me. I'm concerned with how his hands tremble; I'm sure his aim is terrible, but I don't fancy being killed by a stray arrow released by an idle Saxon guard.

"Who are you?"

I draw my sword and raise it over my head.

"I come from the Iutes," I call. The archer draws the bow further, his hands tremble even more. "I'm here to talk! There's no need for bloodshed."

"You should've thought about it before you slaughtered our women and children," shouts the guard.

"Let me in. I need to speak to your chieftain."

The guards murmur to each other. "Stay there," the one without the bow tells me and disappears behind the wall. I shrug — where else should I go?

"Can you put that bow away?" I say to the remaining guard. "I'm hardly going to breach your fortress all on my own."

The archer hesitates. "I've heard the Iutes brought a witch in from the East," he says. "I'm not risking you putting a hex upon me."

A witch? I stifle a laugh.

"Do I look like a witch to you?"

He bites his lower lip. Careful not to release the arrow, he loosens the string and aims the bow down, but keeps it in his hands. We stare at each other for a few intense minutes, until at last the gate of the fortress begins to creak slowly open.

"Leave the sword at the door," the other guard tells me. "We don't want any of your Iute witch tricks."

"So that's where you've ended up!"

I look around the small hall, built into the south-eastern, seaward corner of the fortress. I hear the waves crashing against the cliff outside. Seagulls shriek loudly on the roof, mocking any attempts to scare them off. The stench of rotting seaweed permeates even inside the building.

Hrodha stares at me for a long while, before finally recognising me.

"What in *Hel* are you doing here, half-Iute?"

"I could ask you the same, chieftain. Last I saw you, you were leading a rebel band on Anderitum beach."

[386]

Hrodha winces and leans back in his chair. He has the demeanour of someone who hasn't had to welcome any guests in a long time. His beard is long and unkempt, as is his hair, falling on his shoulders in clumps, grey with age and dirt. His tunic is untied at the neck, revealing a hairy chest. But despite his appearance, and the desolate surroundings, he is not yet a poor man: two golden bracelets wrap his right shoulder, and his goblet is silver, studded with a little halo of ambers, though the cup is dented and scratched in places, and some of the jewels on the rim are missing. It looks curiously like one of the pieces I stole from one of the Londin *villas*.

He raises the goblet and a slave girl — a Briton, I notice — pours him some mead.

"This is as near to his court as Pefen would suffer me," he says. "The farthest edge of the Regin land. Stuck between the moor and the sea, with nothing but bracken and fish to eat."

There is a dish of salted herrings and onion lying before us, but neither of us has an appetite for it. The smell is making me nauseous, and I bury my nose in the mug, to cover the odour with that of the mead. I remember that the Saxons, unlike the Iutes and Angles, are not all sea-dwelling people — some of them have come from the dense woods deeper inland. Hrodha and his household must have belonged to one of those forest clans.

"I'm surprised he let you live at all," I say, my voice echoing inside the mug.

"I still had my men with me," he says with a boastful smile. "We would have made a fine last stand. But Pefen was a coward. He had the *witan* banish us here, instead."

A sudden thought strikes me. "Was it you who killed him?"

"Killed him?" Hrodha raises an eyebrow. "Didn't he die in a hunting accident?"

Damn it, I forgot it was supposed to be a secret.

"Forget I said anything," I say. I reach for the salted herring and dab at it with a piece of bread. The juice from the onion and herring tastes surprisingly fine, once I get over the smell.

"So, somebody had more guts than I did. Curious." Hrodha gulps some more mead. "Now then, you've heard my story, what about yours?"

"I was asked by the Iutes of Wecta to help them with the recent attacks."

He slams the goblet on the table and glares at me with sudden fury. "They don't seem to be needing anyone's help killing my men."

"Please, chieftain." I raise my hands. "Whatever you've been told…"

"I didn't need to be *told* anything. I've seen the dead. I've seen the burned huts. I've seen the hoofprints."

"*Hoofprints?* What hoofprints?"

"Your cursed moor ponies!" He bangs the table with both fists. "Nobody else around here rides horses into battle."

[388]

"The Iutes haven't backed any of their ponies yet."

"Is that what they told you? They'd lie even to one of their own."

"Hrodha." I lean forward and put as much conviction in my voice as is physically possible. "Listen to me. It — wasn't — the Iutes. We have also been attacked."

"I don't believe you."

"I could show you the ruined farms. I could show you the mutilated bodies. Whoever is doing this, is attacking us both."

He shakes his head.

"Why?"

"That's what I'm planning to find out. But I need you to stop sending your men to harass us. In exchange, I promise we will not seek vengeance for what you did in Meon. We buried them together with our fallen. You can send someone to pick up their belongings."

He raises the goblet to his mouth, but it's empty. He throws it at the slave girl, who dodges it with a skill which shows she's used to this sort of abuse. I see now how the goblet got its many dents...

"When we first came here five years ago, I thought, this didn't look so bad," he starts. "A Roman fortress all to ourselves, with well-kept walls. A *wealh* village to trade with. Good fishing harbour. The soil is poor, but we are managing... It was the boredom that started killing us. For five years, *nothing* happened. We were too far away to take part in the war with Londin, too remote to get involved when Pefen started uniting the tribes." He stares at the salted herrings. "We are a warrior clan, not fishermen or farmers. Men grew weary with the daily tedium. They would wander off, trying to get back into Pefen's good graces, join other chieftains. This clan is half of what it was when we first arrived."

I wait patiently until he finishes his story, wondering where he's going with it. Clearly, he hasn't had much chance to vent his woes to anyone like this for a long time.

"When our villages were attacked, many of my men rejoiced at a chance of a fight. I did try to hold them back at first, until we knew for certain what was happening. I didn't think it likely that the Iutes would all of a sudden start raiding our farms. I couldn't figure out why. But my men wanted blood — they've waited so long for this. I couldn't stop them. And now, you tell me they slew some innocent people..."

"You couldn't have known," I try to placate him. "Whoever did this, knew what they were doing, how to rile us against each other. They didn't use horses to attack the Iutes, so we would suspect you or the Britons."

"We are being played." His clenched fists shake on the table's edge. "Is it the *wealas*? I always suspected they'd fight back with some trickery when they couldn't defeat us in battle."

"If it's the *wealas*, they're not from around here. I'm hoping we can catch whoever it is in the act, if we work together."

[390]

He scratches himself across the chest. A family of fleas leaps out from his hair onto the table.

"What did you have in mind, half-Iute?"

The Saxon Might

CHAPTER XVI
THE LAY OF FRIGE

Our eyes meet. Hers are large, beautiful, brown and sad. They reflect the light of the Moon shining over the moor on a cold, winter night, and hoar frost twinkling on ice-blasted heath.

Slowly, I extend my hand with the gift: bits of apple wrapped in mint leaves. Haegel told me it's her favourite treat. She takes them gently from my palm and chews slowly, as I rub her forehead above the eyes.

I don't quite understand why I feel so determined to tame Frige. The reason I gave others is that I need a good mount now that we know the attackers themselves ride horses; if we are to hunt them, I need to be able to catch up. But I could have picked any other pony, some of them on the verge of breaking. Indeed, a couple have already been backed since our skirmish with the Saxons, and are now being trained to carry two of my *Hiréd* into battle. I could have those — but no, it must be the flaxen-haired Frige.

I was never as fond of horses as I became while living among the Iutes. In Londin, a horse was just another workman's tool. A beast for pulling carts to the market, or to deliver a message from one end of the city to another faster than on foot. In the writings of the Ancients, Briton horses were admired for their quality, and looking at Frige I can easily imagine why, but all of that was a long time ago, before the Legions took all the suitable war mounts North, to the Aelian Wall. Odo's Gauls were the first cavalry I ever saw, and they, along with their animals, had come from across the sea.

To the Iutes, horses are everything. They are their gods; their friends; they name their children after them — even Hengist's name means "stallion" in their language. Losing so many sea ponies on the whale-road was a blow almost equal to losing the children. There was no space for breeding ponies on Tanet — there was barely enough space for humans; so they've only started recovering their herds after moving to the mainland, and that slowly. Discovery of the moor ponies was to them like finding a pot full of gold solids in a latrine. More so, since the gold coins were no longer of any use to the Iutes...

Frige is, as far as Haegel can tell, a mare of three years. That means she was born roughly at the same time as Myrtle — at the time of Rhedwyn's death... If I believed in these matters as strongly as other Iutes do, I could easily convince myself that Rhedwyn's spirit has somehow inhabited the mare. But I don't need such superstitions. The connection I have with the animal is not mystical, but it is real, nonetheless. I can feel it through my hand stroking her head, and through our entwined stares. Any other horse would look away by now, or grow annoyed; Frige doesn't even stir, just keeps chewing the apple in silence.

Somehow, the mare has given me the sense of purpose I was lacking all those years. I feel more drawn into the task of taming her than I have been into anything since Rhedwyn's death. I care not for the job given me by Eadgith. I will find out who the mysterious attackers are, and endeavour to defeat them, because it is my duty, and because I feel that I owe it to Eadgith and her people — most of whom were once *my* people, back in Londin; but my heart does not stir when I think of battle in the same way it stirs when I think of riding across the moor on the chestnut mare's back.

"I will now go to your side," I tell the mare. I have been leading her around the enclosure on a line for more than a week now. She's grown used to my presence beside her, and to the touch of reins on her neck. I move to her flank slowly, keeping my hands on her hide all the time. I close my eyes and let my breath slow down until it's one with Frige's breath. My chest rises as her flank rises; it falls as her flank falls.

I leap up and mount her. I grab the reins tight. For a moment, she doesn't move, as if stunned by my impudence. Then she neighs, and rears high up; I slide down her back and fall on my arse into the mud. She looks over her flank and snorts, mockingly.

"We'll do this again tomorrow," I promise her. "And again the day after that — until you're mine."

A quarrelling of chaffinches in the cherry tree announces the morning's arrival. The man of the farm strides across the barley field, spreading muck from a weaver basket on his back. The woman goes to the goat pen to milk the animals. The goats welcome her with a cheerful bleat. A dawn breeze picks up, rustling the leaves in the trees.

I peek at this arcadia from under the straw blanket that covers the only window in the hut. The man and the woman are not the usual inhabitants of this farm — those have been evacuated to Wecta, together with all the other Iutes living in the households scattered along the River Meon. Haegel's village is the only one left, with its fortifications strengthened by a new perimeter of fallen trees and fascine fencing. The man spreading manure is Huf, one of my *Hiréd*; the woman with the goats, Ermen, belongs to Eadgith's household guard. There are more of us here, hidden in the huts and shelters around the farmstead: six Iutes and four Saxons altogether. There is a similar group waiting in hiding in another, Saxon, farmstead near Adurn, led by Hrodha. We don't know which of the two our mysterious enemy will choose to attack. Both of us hope its's Hrodha — he, for the glory that the battle will bring him; me, hoping I can avoid bloodshed. I don't mind the Saxons getting all the fame and credit for defeating the attackers, if it means the matter is solved for good.

All this is assuming the phantom enemy doesn't have a spy in our midst. If the attackers know of our plan, all this is for naught. They will either wait us out, until we grow bored with waiting, or attack Meon itself. Despite the new makeshift fortifications, the village is still vulnerable to an assault, and we could only spare a few trained warriors to defend it. It would be a disaster if the village were to fall… But I can't help thinking it would also be a way to end my mission. An attack on such scale, a murder of an entire settlement, would obviously provoke Hengist and the *witan* to revenge. The entire *Hiréd* would be sent to aid Eadgith and her people, to wipe out the menace — and, more importantly, retake the moor ponies for the tribe.

Hengist would have his war. And I would be free.

She is here, too, tied loosely to a pole by the goat hut, absentmindedly chewing the grass around her. I'm anxious about using her as bait like this. I have already mounted her a couple of times, and she's learned to tolerate me on her back — but we haven't galloped together yet, and I can only hope she will be patient enough to carry me into battle if it comes

[396]

to the worst. According to Hrodha's men, prints of only two or three horses were found at each Saxon attack site. If this pattern repeats, our band of spearmen should be enough to hold the farm. If the enemy comes in greater force, we are doomed anyway...

We've been stuck here for four days now. Huf and Ermen have grown used to their daily routine, and fond of the livestock they have to take care of in place of the farm's real owners. But we did not come here to grow barley and milk goats. The farm is not large enough to sustain ten warriors for long. Today, we expect a cart full of supplies to reach us from Meon, and it makes everyone doubly concerned. If the attackers do have spies, or at least patrols set up around the moor, they will notice the cart's suspicious arrival.

Frige raises her head and turns her gaze towards the forest path. She snorts, anxiously. Ermen returns from the milking. I tell her to call for Huf; something — someone — is coming.

It takes another minute before we hear the clattering of wheels on the sand. The single-axle cart, loaded with sacks and crates, rolls out from beyond the bend, pulled by a moor pony led by a driver wearing a hooded cape. Huf puts his spear and shield on the inside of the door and comes out to greet the driver, glancing intently all around.

The two men begin unloading the cart when the forest on the other side of the farm, beside the barley field, erupts in war cries.

The driver draws a *seax* from the sheath at her side. The hood of her cape falls, revealing the unmistakable storm of red hair. I grind my teeth. Eadgith was supposed to be with her clan on Wecta, not here, fighting. But I have no time to scold her. I wait for the enemy to charge nearer before I nod at Ermen. We leap outside on three. Ermen throws a spear to Huf and picks up her own shield and axe to defend the house.

There are only two horsemen among the attackers; they ride not the local ponies, but tall warhorses in full cavalry tack: a chestnut and a dun. Both riders wear iron helmets of foreign make, with bronze nasals and bronze-rimmed eyelets; the face of one is hidden behind a dense curtain of mail. Behind the riders, I count six more men on foot, running towards us with lit torches in their hands.

I whistle. All over the farm, our warriors spring out from their hiding places. The ambush gives the attackers pause, but not for long; the masked rider grunts an angry order and spurs his horse to charge towards Eadgith. His men throw the torches at the farm buildings and draw swords, but in confusion, most of them miss their targets. In the far corner of the field, three of my men and two of the bandits are already engaged in combat. The others follow their leader in the assault on the cart.

I make a quick decision. To my left is the goat hut, with Frige tied in front of it; to my right, and nearer, is the cart, with Eadgith and Huf bracing themselves for the enemy charge. I rush towards the cart. The masked rider spots me, grabs a lance slung over his shoulder and aims it at me. There is no stopping a charging warhorse. I shove Eadgith to the right, and roll away to the left. I look back to see Huf, standing before the beast with his spear raised in a thrust; the shaft of the weapon simply shatters on the impact. The horse smashes into Huf, throwing him into the air and trampling him under its hooves.

The rider circles back. I scramble up.

"What are you doing here?" I shout a question at Eadgith.

"I thought you might need help. Looks like I was right."

I look around the farm. Over by the main house, Ermen and another Iute warrior are holding the door against three of the attackers. The other horseman, who tried to ride around the house to flank us, stumbled into the fight in the corner of the field, and is now surrounded by four Saxon spearmen. He whirls his lance from side to side, the silver blade flashes like lightning and with each flash, one Saxon falls. I have no time to see what happens to the other two. The masked rider charges again, over Huf's unconscious body. With only a *seax* and a small shield in my hands, all I can do is keep dodging the lance and the thousand pounds of thundering, steaming warhorse flesh coming my way, hoping for a timely stab that would unseat the rider. My only chance of a fair fight is to get to Frige — still tied to her post on the other side of the farm, unperturbed by the chaos around her…

Eadgith slices through the traces that tie the pony to the cart, and slaps the animal on the flank with her sword. The panicked pony bucks forward, between me and the charging warhorse. The two animals crash; the poor pony is thrown off its feet and falls to the ground with its back snapped. The warhorse slides on the gravel and goes down on its side, too. The rider cries in pain as his leg is crushed under the beast's weight, but holds onto the saddle.

"Run!" cries Eadgith. I cross the farm while the masked rider struggles to raise the horse up. I cut the rope and leap onto Frige from the back. Despite my hurried urgings, she turns slowly towards the storming stallion. The masked rider changes the grip on his lance and raises it over his head, like a javelin. I raise my feeble shield to take on the weapon's thrust and get ready to make a sword blow — I will only have one chance, if I can even survive the impact of that lance. Frige ignores my heels in her sides and moves only a few steps forward before lowering her head to chew the grass again. The ground shakes under the stallion's hooves, dust rises in a cloud. Just as the rider is within a spear's reach, Frige finally raises her head.

She rears, violently, and kicks forth with both front legs. Her hooves meet the rider squarely in the chest. We both fly off our mounts. The warhorse gallops past me; Frige lands back on all fours, her head lowered in an angry glare. It is now a race as to who stands up first. The masked rider, with his leg injured, is slower, but not by much. I pick up the sword I dropped while falling. The rider staggers up. We both assess the situation around us. Only two of his footmen are still standing. Most of the Iutes are also dead. Ermen lies in the door, spear in her chest. Others are scattered around the other rider. But there are still more of us than them, and my men are pushing the surviving two against the wall of the main house. The house roof finally caught fire from the few torches that met their target, the flames adding to the chaos. Eadgith is running towards us from the direction of the cart.

The masked rider decides he's had enough. He puts his fingers to his lips and whistles. His horse turns a circle and rides back. He mounts it at the same moment as I leap back on Frige. The other rider jumps over the two Saxons before him to join the leader in his escape — but a Saxon spear cuts through his mount's chest and stomach, and the animal tumbles down, throwing the rider off. The bay horse stands up and starts off across the moor in panic. Its rider stays on the ground, motionless.

"I'm going after him," I tell Eadgith. "Try to keep one of them alive," I add, nodding towards the two remaining bandits fighting for their lives by the burning house.

"Be careful."

I click my tongue on Frige, and this time, to my surprise, she listens, launching into a mad gallop.

She is naturally slower and weaker than the chestnut warhorse — but here in the moor, she is in her element. The man I pursue must keep to the dirt tracks and sand trails; Frige can ride right across the heath, free like the wind, leaping from one patch of bracken to another, finding shortcuts through short grass, splashing over puddles of mud, leaping over shallow brooks, turning so quickly left and right to avoid quicksand and uneven ground that I'm in constant danger of falling. I hold tight to her mane, my bottom bouncing heavily up and down on her back. I have no chance of steering her in any way; I can only hope she understands that we're chasing after the warhorse, and doesn't decide to suddenly run off in some other random direction.

In this way, we manage to keep up with the masked rider for over two miles of level moor. But then the ground begins to fall and undulate, and the moor makes way to a seaside landscape of grass-covered dune tops amid brackish swamp. This slows us both down, but the warhorse traverses the deep mud with ease, while Frige is forced to wade across, submerged in places up to her hocks. The distance between us and the rider grows. Momentarily, he disappears behind the grassy dunes, hidden from my view as I ride up and down the slopes. I glimpse the sea between the hilltops and begin to wonder where the masked rider is fleeing; there are no settlements here, no harbours, no roads, nowhere to hide. Is he just leading me here because he knows he can lose the moor pony in this unsuitable territory?

We emerge onto a broad sandy beach. He's now a good half a mile ahead, and I can tell Frige is growing slow and tired. Both of us are. We've been galloping for ten minutes straight now; she's not used to having a load on her back, I'm not used to having my bottom smash against an animal's spine for that long. I look up. The rider has also slowed down now; his injured leg must be killing him after that race, and even a warhorse can't keep up a gallop in difficult terrain for long, having already fought a battle before. But there's no chance of me catching up to him now.

Not that I need to. I already see where he's heading. Far ahead on the beach, a small distance into the sea, a large, red-sailed *ceol* stands at anchor. The rider throws off his helmet and shouts something to the ship's crew; the wind carries his voice away from me. The crew lowers a broad gangway from the deck into the shallow water. I try to spur Frige to one last dash, but my effort only slows her down.

An arrow hits the sand a few paces before me. A moment later, another. Launched from the ship against the wind, they fly too far to be any threat beyond a scratch, but the message is clear. I pull on the reins. Frige stops and abruptly lowers her neck, causing me to slide down and fall painfully on my arse.

"It's alright," I say, wincing and stroking her on the neck. "You did well. I've seen enough."

I watch the warhorse wade into the waves and climb out onto the ramp. The ship's sail is lowered, the anchor is raised, and soon, the vessel is launched into the waves of the Solu. There are no markings on the wine-red sail, but I've seen enough of the *ceol* to tell it's a Iutish design. This only confirms my suspicion.

From the moment I first saw it emerge out of the forest, I had a nagging feeling that I had seen the chestnut warhorse before. And now, at last, I remember.

A grey-sailed *ceol* departs on the first ripple of the high tide from the Wecta beach, pushing aside the small fishing boats of the oyster dredgers with its hull. It is the same boat that brought Eadgith's messengers to the *witan* — the only ship of this size on the island. Refitted and manned with fresh crew after its return from Cantiaca a few days ago, it now departs on a new mission: to discover Haesta's hidden base.

Eadgith and I watch the ship's departure from the top of a low hill overlooking the narrow estuary that cuts the island almost in half. Below us, the fishing village prepares for the return of the fishermen from an afternoon sail. Smoke rises from the hearths in grey wispy columns, as fishwives make hearty stews ready for their hard-working men. The tides change often and swiftly in the narrow strait — for one half of the day, the current flows west, for another it flows east, and for an hour between each, the Solu becomes a whirlpool of torrents and slacks, that no experienced sailor dares to enter, if they can help it.

I turn the mail-curtain helmet in my hands — I picked it up from the beach after the masked rider's escape. The helmet is the same Haesta wore to the *witan*; the mail is a new addition. It is not the work of anyone in Britannia — only on the Continent could there still be craftsmen capable of weaving mail so dense and so light. It's yet another indication of who our enemy is. Not that there was ever any real doubt, once we gathered the dead and examined their possessions. The attackers all wore this peculiar combination of Iutish and Frankish equipment and clothes that they could only have obtained as mercenaries in the service of the Frankish king. The dun horse that we found later bleeding out on the moor bore the unusual high-backed saddle that I only ever saw on Gaulish and Frankish riders before. Unless there was another band of mercenaries roaming the desolate moor for some mysterious reason, led by some other warrior on a similar-looking chestnut horse, the only possible explanation was that we were fighting Haesta and his men. The only riddle left to solve was — *why*? And... *how?*

It would have been easier to discover the truth, if any of the bandits had survived the attack on the farm — but the fighting at the end was too fierce, and before Eadgith managed to stop her men from finishing off the surviving two foes, it was too late to save them. The last one succumbed to his wounds the day after the attack, never coming out of the dying sleep long enough to answer our questions. From his murmurs, we could only learn that the bandit base was on one of the myriad small islands scattered at the entrance to the Great Havens — but this, we could have guessed ourselves. The archipelago of reefs and islets, some only existing as patches of rock at low tide, others as marshy scraps of mud and reed, made for an excellent hiding place, no doubt used in the old days by pirates and raiders fleeing from the Roman fleet's pursuit.

"Do you think he's got some of your men working for him?" I ask Eadgith.

"Why would you think so?"

"It takes great knowledge of the local terrain to execute an operation like this. This winter, Haesta was still in Frankia. Until a few weeks ago, he was in Cantiaca, at the *witan*. He had to work with somebody here earlier, to execute the first attacks, and make everything ready for his arrival."

"I don't know," Eadgith admits. "I'd like to be able to say they are all loyal — but I wouldn't be surprised if he found help among the villagers. Life here isn't easy. It wouldn't be difficult to lure some poor farmers to his side with promise of wealth or glory."

"And he *is* a Iute." I nod. "One of Hengist's household. It's not like they're selling us to the Saxons or the Britons."

"Why is he doing all this? What is his plan?"

"I've no idea. But I'm sure we're going to find out soon."

It would be easy to assume that what Haesta is doing was some sort of provocation, an attempt to stir a conflict between the Iutes and the Saxons, maybe even the Britons in the long run — but I can't quite reconcile this with his quest for peaceful transition of power at the *witan*. Why provoke a war, when all he claimed to be wishing for was peace? He got what he wanted; the *witan* voted his way, Hengist and I were no longer to rule the tribe on our own. Why throw away this achievement, destroy everything he's worked for?

I'm missing something. I feel like, somehow, Haesta's original plans, whatever they were, have been ruined by some unforeseen circumstance, and he's now forced to improvise. Was it my arrival on Wecta — or was it the landing of the Wecta ship in Cantiaca, bringing the news of the attack sooner than planned, that put his scheme in jeopardy? Perhaps Haesta underestimated Eadgith's leadership skills, thinking that she would be too confused and frightened by his attacks to react so quickly... If she had taken just a couple of weeks longer to send the message, there would be no *Drihten* in Cantiaca, only a *witan*, slow to gather and slow to respond to the crisis...

Not that any of this matters to me anymore. My role here is over. Haesta's presence means this is no longer a local quarrel. As soon as the grey-sailed *ceol* returns from its mission, we'll send it with news back to Cantiaca. It's time for Hengist to send troops here, to deal with his unruly cousin once and for all. I will no doubt be ordered to lead the *Hiréd* into the battle alongside Hengist's warriors, but that's where my involvement will end.

"Do you think he recognised you?" Eadgith asks.

"Of course he did. But I think he was as surprised to see me here as I was to see him. Otherwise, he'd have planned the attack better. He'd know I'd have prepared an ambush for his men. We were fortunate." I turn to her. "*You* were fortunate," I say. "You shouldn't have been there. It was too risky."

A western breeze brings a gust of icy breath. Eadgith tightens her cloak.

"Let's go back," she says. "Help me run us a bath."

[406]

"That's the second time you've avoided the subject," I say, when at last we enter the dark, hot pool. A bit too hot for my liking, even, despite the cold wind howling outside and through the cracks in the brick wall. I'm already warmed up and sweaty from chopping the firewood and shoving it into the furnace.

"What's it to you, where I am and what I do?" she asks.

"What if something happened to you? Your clan needs you here, leading them, not out on the battlefield. You should leave the fighting to your household guard."

"Now you want to teach me how to lead people?" she scoffs. "You should've accepted the diadem, if you know about it so much."

"I refused the diadem precisely *because* I don't know anything about leading people."

"That's not true. I saw you in battle. The Iutes never had a better commander than you."

I submerge myself to my chin for a few seconds, then jump out and sit on the edge of the bath, careful not to splash water on the single oil lamp illuminating the room. The evaporating water cools my skin.

"There's more to being a ruler than command in battle," I say. "I can do that as a *Gesith*. A ruler needs to give hope. To inspire. The only time I've ever inspired the Iutes to anything, half of them lost their lives, and half of Londin got burned."

"You're being unfair to yourself. You were driven mad with grief."

"And what if it happens again? What if I lose control of my emotions again? What if the darkness inside me wins? With enough power, I could destroy the entire tribe, just like I've destroyed everything else I've ever touched."

"You're overthinking this, Ash." She pulls closer and rests her arms on the bath's edge. "I don't think being a *Drihten* is all that complicated. Most of the time you just need to use your common sense."

"I'm not famous for my common sense." I laugh, bitterly. "You should know."

"Come on. You're a grown man now. A clever man. Do you think Hengist was *born* a leader? He was just a commander of a war band, like yourself. From what you told me, he wasn't even supposed to be the *Drihten*."

"That's true." I nod. "It would have been my…" I stop myself. For a moment, I panic: I can't remember if I've ever confessed the truth to Eadgith or not. I decide to play safe. "It would have been Eobba, if he survived the journey."

"See? It's all just random fate. Gods, playing with us. If they want you to be a *Drihten*, who are you to stand against them?"

"It's Hengist who wants me to be the *Drihten*, not the gods." I sigh and lean against the wall. I hiss — it's freezing cold. "All I want is to be left in peace."

"You have a funny way of achieving that."

"What do you mean?"

"You could have just remained at Ariminum, run the *villa* like Master Pascent intended. You could have refused a seat on the Council. You could have stayed away from politics, from war. Ignore Wortigern, ignore Wortimer, ignore Hengist, live an ordinary life of a Briton noble, and at the end leave for Armorica, like so many chose to. Didn't Lady Adelheid's family have property there? None of... this —" She waves her hands around. "— need have happened."

I'm eager to dismiss her with a scoff, but I'm struck by the truth in her words. I turn away from the lamp, to face the darkness. I run all of my life back in my head, seeking for ways in which things could have gone differently if I had made a choice to stay in Ariminum, away from politics, away from the Iutes, the Saxons, the conflicts and intrigues... away from Rhedwyn...

"There is no *curse*," I whisper. "I brought it all upon myself."

"You don't want peace. You've *never* wanted peace. You were always ambitious beyond your years. How many boys your age decide to elope with their loved one and seek a pagan priest to bless their union?" There is a trace of bitterness in her voice. "You are weary with grief now, but it will pass. I can see it passing already. And when it does, you will regret you've refused Hengist's offer."

"I sincerely doubt that."

She shrugs. "I know what I know. Maybe you really have changed since we lived in Ariminum — but as far as I can tell, you're still the same Ash, except for that melancholy that hangs above you like a storm cloud. And let me tell you something about that…"

"Yes?"

"For someone who professes to not care whether he lives or dies, you fought damn hard for your life on that farm."

I have nothing to reply to that. She slaps me on the butt. "This water is making me sleepy," she says. "You put too much wood on the fire."

"I know. Me too. Let's go." I stand up and help her out.

"You're sleeping at Puna's today," she says, putting on a tunic and the bronze bracelets. "I need to talk to Betula about something."

"Betula?" I raise my eyebrow. "What do *you* need to talk to Betula about?"

"Women secrets," she replies with a mysterious smile. "Now go, Puna's waiting with the stew."

I put on the breeches, throw the tunic over my shoulders and go outside without towelling; I nod at Betula as she passes me by in the entrance to the *domus*, wearing a fine shirt of white linen. For a moment, I enjoy the cool breeze on my chest, and let my mind run clear from the storm of thoughts stirred by Eadgith's words. Soon, though, the breeze becomes too cold and, shivering, I struggle to slide the woollen tunic back over my wet skin.

As my ears emerge at last from under the cloth, I hear a sound that doesn't belong in the quiet countryside night: distant cries for help.

A blaze lights up the dark sky in the direction of the fishing village.

The Saxon Might

CHAPTER XVII
THE LAY OF ALATUC

"No way. This time, you're definitely staying here," I tell Eadgith, as I strap the sword belt to my waist. "Let me do my duty."

"Defending these villagers *is* my duty."

The fiery blaze has spread further up the hill. Any minute now, we should expect the first survivors of the disaster to reach the *villa* — if there are any.

"We've *just* talked about this. Betula!" I call. "Get the rest of the *Hiréd* and meet me at the milestone."

There are only six of us left altogether — Huf perished the night after the battle, coughing blood from a crushed lung. The remaining five live in a camp they've built for themselves in an old ruin on top of the hill overlooking the *villa* — a remnant of some old Roman watchtower. They've been busy fortifying the camp with a fence of sharpened stakes, Legionnaire-style — not out of any sense of danger, more to prove to themselves and me they still remembered the *wealh* training I gave them.

"You're not going there by yourself," Betula opposes. "At least wait for me!"

"I'll just check what's going on. It might be a normal fire. Eadgith, send your guards our way as soon as you can — but *stay here* yourself."

[413]

"Fine!" Eadgith throws her hands in the air. "Go, be a warrior. So much for wanting to be left *in peace.*"

I mount Frige and trot off towards the blaze. It's soon clear that this is no accidental fire. The entire fishing village is in flames: not just the homes, but the boats on the beach, the net huts, the traps; all have been covered in straw and oil and set on fire.

The attackers don't seem interested in pillage — not that there is anything here to rob. Armed men run from house to house, dragging out the sleeping inhabitants and beating anyone who opposes. Soon, the unfortunate Britons are all standing on the beach, naked, shivering, forced to watch as their entire livelihood goes up in flames.

Out on the water, illuminated by the blaze, a *ceol* bobs on the gentle waves. I can't be sure — I can't see the colour of the sail in the fiery darkness — but it doesn't look like the one I saw Haesta depart on. It looks more like the one we sent out in search of his base…

I'm joined by Betula and the other four warriors. Eadgith's guards arrive soon after, in full force, armed and armoured; I'm relieved to see Eadgith kept her word and remained at the *villa.*

"I count only eight men down there," I tell them. "The rest must be on the ship. If we surprise them, it should be an easy fight."

"Then what are we waiting for?" asks Betula.

"Something's not right." I tie Frige to the milestone — there's no way I'm going to force her to ride into these flames. "Why are they here?"

"Maybe Haesta wants to draw the Britons into the conflict."

"It might be an ambush."

I send two of Eadgith's men to check for enemy hiding in the tall grasses and undergrowth around the village.

"And in the meantime, we're just going to stand here and watch them destroy that village?"

"We can't do anything to help — the place is as good as burned down already. As long as they're not killing anybody…"

Just as I say that an enemy warrior drags one of the Britons out in front of the others and forces him to his knees. The warrior raises a sword and looks up, vaguely in our direction, as if searching for an audience.

"Get down!" I order. The *Hiréd* drop to the ground, but Eadgith's warriors are slow to heed my command. Confusedly, they lie down on the cobbles.

"What's he doing?"

"Do you think he can see us from there?" asks Betula.

"I don't know — but he's expecting an audience…"

[415]

The blade flashes, the sword hits the neck, the Briton's head rolls on the sand. I punch the ground with my fist.

"Fuck. Go!" I cry. I stand up and draw my *seax*. I've had enough. "Just kill them all."

I thrust my sword in the heart of the last of Haesta's warriors and pull it out with a bloody squelch. The man drops to his knees, gurgling. I end his suffering with a slice to the neck and throw his lurching body to the ground.

All around me I hear shouts, cries and moans of the enemy warriors being finished off by my and Eadgith's men. Even without the element of surprise, the battle was fierce, but short. Trapped between us and the sea, outnumbered and outwitted, Haesta's men were soon overpowered. They perished one by one on the bloodied sand, until the last two of them leaped into the waves in an attempt to swim back to the *ceol*. Wary of the archers on the deck, I order the men to hold back and let the enemy flee.

The fishing village is smouldering down. The Britons wail and curse; some try to extinguish the flames with sand and sea water, but for most houses it's already too late. They spit and shout obscenities at us, claiming we're to blame for the attack. I want to tell them that at least they're alive — but I know this isn't the right time. For now, I let them grieve; tomorrow, they will need to be reminded who saved them from death.

"Is everyone alright?" I ask Betula.

"Some wounded, but nothing too serious. It was a clean fight."

"Thank Donar," I say, absentmindedly. Now that the battle rush is gone, I'm wracking my brain as to what was Haesta's plan. "They provoked us, didn't they? They knew we'd attack."

"It certainly seemed so." She nods, as she wipes blood from her blade.

"But then they just fought and died. There was no ambush, no surprise. What was that all about?"

"I don't know, but we better go back and tell Eadgith what happened."

I gather the men together. Two of Eadgith's warriors are too weak to march, bleeding from several wounds. I leave a shieldmaiden to take care of them and the rest of us departs back up the cobbled path.

I first notice something is wrong when we reach the *villa*'s boundary wall. The settlement, busy preparing for the evening meals when we left, is now eerily quiet, the silence broken only by the anxious bleating of a goat in a pen somewhere. There are no lights anywhere, except in the windows of the *domus*. I raise my hand to stop the men and dismount. Betula and I draw swords and enter carefully.

Betula lets out a quiet gasp. She pulls on the sleeve of my tunic and points at something in the darkness. It's a dead body, lying on the threshold of one of the huts. I stoop to examine it — it's one of the Iute villagers, pierced through his side with a spear thrust.

I hear a sound of clashing arms coming from inside the *domus*.

"Eadgith!" both of us cry in distress.

No, no, no…

The door to the *domus* is shattered open. A man lies dead on the porch, with his head crushed by a smith's hammer. I leap over him, into the narrow corridor. There's another dead body in the hallway; I take a quick glance and recognise old Puna, a firewood hatchet still in his grasp. The noise of clashing blades is coming from the forge room. I barge in, and face the backs of two of Haesta's men, clad in mail, standing over Eadgith with bloodied *seaxes*. Eadgith leans against the wall, her clothes torn, a deep red gash in her side, and a bloody line across her brow. She's holding a sword in an outstretched arm; her grip weakens with every parry.

I stab the nearest enemy in the kidney. The other turns around and slashes me on the wrist before I can pull my blade out of the first one. I shove him to the wall and punch him in the stomach with the hilt of my sword, then whirl the weapon around and hit him on the head with the pommel.

Betula bursts into the room and rushes to Eadgith. She helps her down to the floor.

"Water!" she cries, "Cloth!"

I run to the bath house — passing another body along the way; I can't tell if it's one of Haesta's men or a villager.

The water in the pool is still tepid. I grab towels and a bucket and rush back to the smithy.

By the time I'm back, Eadgith is unconscious.

"Help me get her to bed," says Betula. We carry her over to the bedroom, and Betula washes Eadgith's wounds. Blood pumps out of the gash in her side with each heartbeat. Whispering prayers mixed with swears, Betula tries to stem the blood flow with the wet towels, but it doesn't work. She takes out a knife and cuts the sleeve of her tunic into strips, but they're not long enough to serve as bandages.

"Here," I offer my shirt. "Is there a pantry in this place?"

"A pantry?" Betula looks up confused. "Over there — what do you need…?"

I open the pantry and find a flask of vinegar. "Take this," I say, giving it to Betula. "Wash the wound with it. It's what Romans use."

Betula splashes the vinegar all over Eadgith's side. Seeing the wound clear now, I can tell there's no way for Eadgith to survive this. If we had access to a surgeon, like in Eobbasfleot, then maybe she'd stand a chance — but the nearest one would be in Clausent, if not further. We couldn't possibly get her to help in time.

The stinging of vinegar on raw flesh wakes Eadgith up. She looks around with foggy eyes. She grasps Betula's shoulder.

"Leave us," she rasps.

"What? No! You need help. We can save you."

"No, you can't. It's too late. I'm beyond help, I can feel it inside. Don't waste my strength." She gasps and looks at me. "Ash knows it. I see it in his eyes. I need to talk to him, alone."

The pain gives force and clarity to her words. Betula stands up slowly from Eadgith's bed. She wipes her eyes. "I will be praying outside."

"Check on that man I stunned," I tell her. "We need him alive."

I kneel down by Eadgith and take her by the hand. She squeezes, weakly.

Why is this happening?

"You're wounded, too," she says. The blood from my cut wrist mixes with hers.

"It's only a scratch."

She wheezes. "Don't you dare mourn me, Ash," she says. "Or blame yourself for this."

"I should never have told you to stay."

"Shut up. My decisions are my own. They always have been. There is no curse, there are just choices we all made. Some were good, some were terrible. Most of yours were… not great. I'll be the first to admit it. But everyone else around you made their choices, too — to be with you, to flee from you, to follow your orders, or to oppose you… This is what your life is made of. The decisions you and others around you make. And now, you must choose again."

"Choose? Choose what?"

"Choose who you really are."

"I'm not ready. Don't leave me. Don't make me go through this alone."

"But you're not alone. You have Octa. You must tell him the truth. And you have your people, an entire tribe to take care of. You will have to become a father to him, and a chieftain to them… Or…"

"Or…?"

"Or you can go back to being a Briton noble's son and keep running away from responsibilities for the rest of your life."

"I don't know how to do any of the things you want me to do."

She coughs blood. I reach to wipe her mouth with the wet towel, but she pushes my hand away. "Nobody knows. Do you think I knew how to be a mother? You'll keep making mistakes. You will cause more pain. But eventually, you'll learn, just like I had to. Just like you've been learning all your life."

"I haven't learned anything." I smile, weakly. "I'm still the same hot-headed youth that first fell in love with you, all those years ago."

She reaches out to stroke my cheek and wipes a tear with her thumb. "It was a lifetime ago," she says. "You're not that youth anymore. I am not a bladesmith's daughter."

"I *will* mourn you," I tell her. "You can't tell me not to."

"Fine — but don't do it on your own. I know you think you don't need other people, but there are two things you can never do alone — rejoice and grief."

"There hasn't been much rejoicing in my life."

"Christ's wounds, Ash, are you really trying to make me feel sorry for you on *my* death bed? Not *everything* is about you!"

Her laugh turns into another bout of bloody cough. I hold her head up. She bites her lip and winces. Her skin begins to turn a sickly blue.

"Call Betula back," she whispers. "Hurry. I don't have much left."

There's no need for paid wailers at this funeral. The gathered crowd is small and largely silent, but the sadness filling the *villa*'s small forecourt is like a coat of lead on my shoulders. I can barely force myself to walk behind the bier. My legs are heavy, as if I was walking through quagmire, my head is filled with grey, gloomy thoughts, my eyes are glued with the dust of dried tears.

In her dying moments, whether on Betula's urging, or of her own accord, Eadgith returned to the Faith she was brought up to in Ariminum. She asked to be buried under the *villa*, near her smithy, in a room which the owners of the house, judging by the remnants of the frescoes on the crumbled wall, once used as a Christian shrine — albeit a Gnostic one. Betula is conducting the burial, reciting prayers as best she can — I helped her remember the correct words, but I could not face taking part in the rite itself. As soon as Eadgith, clad in her finest white tunic and wearing her bronze bracelets, is lowered into the hole, dug into the floor decorated with a geometric mosaic, I leave the *domus*, lean against a pillar of the porch, and take a deep breath.

The mourners outside are Britons and Iutes alike, come to pay tribute to *Hlaefdige* Eadgith, the last lady of the *villa* — and, in the last minutes of her life, their saviour. All but a few inhabitants of the settlement have survived the night ambush, thanks to Eadgith, who spotted the attackers approaching in the darkness soon after our departure and, together with Puna, drew them towards the *domus*; she made her last stand while her people fled towards the stockade my men have built up the hill. Without Eadgith, all the old men and women, and the younglings of the *villa* settlement, including the children brought from Meon, would have perished at the hands of a handful of attackers, while all the warriors were dealing with the assault on the fishing village — just like Haesta had planned.

Once again, he disastrously underestimated her.

I close my eyes and try to clear my mind of the dark clouds, even as inside the *domus* Betula's voice rises, breaking, in a sorrowful hymn. She sings alone — I am the only other person on the island who knows the words to the prayer. I promised Eadgith that I would not wallow in grief, and I intend to keep the promise, not just for her sake, but for myself. If I let myself succumb to another bout of mourning, I might never get out of the pit of despair again.

The news is not all bad, I tell myself. Eadgith's death aside, the raid was costly for Haesta. He lost twelve men in both attacks, killing only a handful of serfs in exchange. The *villa* was clearly supposed to be the main prize of the raid, with the assault on the Briton village a mere distraction — but something other than just Eadgith's courage stood in the way of his plan. There was no need to sacrifice eight men to plunder the fishing village. Some must have disobeyed Haesta's orders and went for an easier, more promising target. This tells me that, perhaps, Haesta does not have such a strong authority over his band of mercenaries as he thinks…

I walk past the *villa*'s wall, down the cobbled path, to the charred remains of the fishing village. The damage doesn't look as bad during the day. It's not easy for eight men to burn down an entire settlement this size. The houses on the outskirts are intact, and of those in the centre, only four are burned down completely. But the livelihoods of the fishermen are gone. The boats, the net huts, the storage warehouses, have all been destroyed with a kind of vicious wilfulness, the point of which I find difficult to understand. If Haesta counted on turning the Britons against us, he miscalculated. For now, at least, the villagers are grateful to us for saving their lives.

It is up to the new chieftain of Wecta to make sure this gratitude persists, before they think of blaming us for the raid. And they wouldn't be much wrong. The only reason Haesta would even think of attacking the island is because of the Iute presence. Whoever succeeds Eadgith, will need to help rebuild the village, repair the boats, feed the villagers until they can fish again… All the while, preparing for the next assault from Haesta's bloodthirsty war band.

Whoever they are, I wouldn't want to be in their shoes.

The little girl kneels down and puts a bunch of daisies onto a mound of flowers, fruit and other sacrifices piled up on the porch of the *domus*. I pat her on her head gently.

"Croha, is it?" I ask. She nods.

"I knew your parents — I think. Back in Beaddingatun."

She says nothing.

"Who's taking care of you now?"

She points to a hut that's being dismantled by a young Iute family. All around us rings out the sounds of hatchet and saws, as the Iutes dismantle their huts. The Iute houses are built to be easily portable in time of danger — such as now. The entire village is being moved to the top of the hill, beyond the palisade my men built. The only remnant of the past life will be the *domus*, retained as Eadgith's mausoleum.

How many times has this child been forced to flee, or move, in her short life? Beaddingatun to Poor Town, from there to Wenta, then to a farm on the River Meon, and back to Wenta again, her life always in danger… What a unique experience this must have been, even in these troubled times. Despite all the wars and rebellions that ravaged Britannia, most Briton families, nobles and serfs alike, haven't moved from their ancestral homes in centuries. Entire tribes have been frozen in time by the Roman rule, like the Ikens and Cadwallons, still living through their ancient grudges and myths of former glory, as irrelevant today as their ruined temples and crumbling cities grown over with vine. How can the *wealas* ever understand a child like Croha; how can they comprehend what her generation has gone through?

She is a child of a new world, even more so than I am, born into this life of constant strife. I find myself wishing there was something I could do to help her spend at least some of her childhood in the kind of peace I was afforded back in Ariminum…

You could do so much more than this.

I look up; though the voice is coming from inside my head, I fancy it coming from inside the *domus*.

I don't have the strength, I reply.

I made my decision after the funeral. I've made the choice Eadgith demanded — though it's not the one she wanted. I will tell Betula to lead the *Hiréd* in my stead. I will go back to Ariminum, to live the rest of my days in peace, like I've always wanted. Eadgith's death was the final straw. I am broken, in no shape to command anyone anymore.

Are you sure?

[426]

Of course I am, I scoff at my own doubt. How else could I react to another death of a loved one, to another life destroyed, another soul burned by getting too close to me…?

But something is different this time. I search my feelings and, to my surprise, I find that not only does Eadgith's death not darken my thoughts, even the black hole left by Rhedwyn has mostly disappeared. I feel strangely energetic. It's as if Eadgith took all my sorrow with her into the afterlife. This confuses me. I was certain her death would only add to my melancholy, but I actually feel as if I was released from its shackles.

I'm slowly beginning to realise something, as I stare at the mound of flowers on the porch: Eadgith's death doesn't belong to me.

Croha looks up.

"Will you kill the people who did this?" she asks. This is the first time I have heard her speak. The question would be cruelly out of place in the mouth of any other ten-year-old girl.

Here is one life that wasn't ruined by me. No matter what I did, whether I was dead or alive, living among the Iutes or the Britons, Haesta would have come here to harass the Iute farmsteads. In a way, it's almost a relief. All this time, I thought that it was just me bringing disaster on everyone around; that it was my fault that everyone I ever loved died. But I was wrong. Eadgith was right. It's not all about me. Sometimes, people just die. Not because of anything I do. Because of how cruel and dangerous the world is. The world that turned little Croha's childhood into a nightmare. That turned *my* life into a procession of disasters. Master Pascent didn't die because of me; he died because Aelle was still foolish and inexperienced enough to torture the life out of him instead of preserving him for ransom. Rhedwyn didn't die because of me, but because she chose to sacrifice herself to kill Wortimer. None of this absolves me from the blame of the mistakes I've made along the way — but those mistakes alone were not responsible for all the lives lost and ravaged by the people I was close to. To think so, I realise, was incredibly arrogant. I am not a god. I don't have the power over anyone else's life and death. None of us do.

Why did it take me witnessing Eadgith's death to discover that truth?

It wasn't just her death, I tell myself; it's the mourning. The people of Wecta have more reason to mourn Eadgith than I ever have. She saved them from Wortimer's wrath, ruled them wisely for three years, and then died defending their lives. They loved her more than I did — my love was just a youth's lust, theirs was the love of a people for their leader. I have no right to take her death for myself — nor anyone else's.

In this, too, she was right. It is better to mourn together.

"We will," I tell Croha. "I promise."

"The people want you to lead them," Betula announces.

Four days have passed since the funerals of Eadgith and the other fallen in the night raid. Normally, there would be a further period of mourning, but there's no time. Something

[428]

has to be done about the continuing threat from Haesta and his warriors.

"No, they don't."

"There wasn't even a vote. The *wealas* of the fishing village do, too."

"The *wealas* only know me as a captain of a war band. The Iutes remember me from Londin."

"This is why they want you to lead them."

I look at her in confusion. "They remember how I led them all to death… And they still want me as their chieftain?"

Betula sits down and shrugs with one shoulder. "That was then. This is now. We are at war. There is nobody else here with your experience."

"What about Haegel?"

"Haegel is ancient, and on the other side of the Solu." She leans closer. "You knew this would happen. Eadgith knew this would happen. There is no one else — and this time, I mean it. You will save everyone's time if you stop this vacillating."

A couple of days ago, I would have refused her outright. I'd have told Betula to lead the men herself. Now, my resolve has weakened. I may not feel strong enough to be a leader of men — but I think I have enough energy to command my warriors for a while yet. If only to fulfil the promise I made little Croha.

"Fine, whatever you say," I reply. "But only until this sorry matter is over. Once I deal with Haesta, I have to go back east — they are aware of it, aren't they?"

She nods. I tap the table with my knuckles.

"It's irrelevant now, anyway. I don't know what we should do next. We have no ship. We can't send for help. I take it we haven't heard from the other side of the Solu."

"No word from Haegel or anyone else. I pray they also haven't been attacked."

"We must assume the worst." I glance out the window at the labouring Iutes. The village is almost gone. "Right, if I'm to be a chieftain, I suppose I'd better start giving out some orders. First of all, send the *Hiréd* over to the fishing village, to help with whatever rebuilding they require."

"Why? Shouldn't we focus on our own needs?"

"We need to keep the *wealas* on our side. There are too few of us on this island, we have to stay together. And we're going to need their boatwrighting skills."

Betula smiles.

"What's so amusing?"

"Eadgith was right about you."

"Is that what you were talking about at nights? Me?"

She laughs, with a twinkling of tears in her eye. "Women don't talk about men nearly as much as men would think."

[430]

"And not as much as men talk about women, I bet. What did Eadgith say about me?"

"She said that if you didn't succumb to melancholy after she dies, you'd soon start acting like a true *Drihten*."

I scowl, impatiently. "I only do what's necessary. Leave me now, I need to think of what's our next move."

She stands up with a mocking bow. "As you wish, *Hlaford* Aeric."

Back in the island's days of prosperity, the Roman landlords had turned every square foot of Wecta's fertile land into fields or vineyards. As a result, the nearest patch of woodland with trees big enough for boatbuilding is half a day's journey away from the *villa*. It takes the Briton boatwrights four days of hard work to transform the two oak trunks, and the remains of the least badly burned boat, into a wobbly, broad-bottomed vessel, sturdy enough to take me and Frige across the five miles of water separating us from the mainland. By the time their work is finished, the patrols sent out along the coast bring back more bad news.

"Our *ceol* is back," the warrior reports. "Every morning it stands at anchor at the mouth of the river, and stays there until dusk."

From the mumbling of our single captive we soon figured out what happened to the grey-sailed ship we sent out to discover Haesta's whereabouts. Searching for the secret base, it stumbled upon Haesta's red-sailed vessel, which lured it into the maze of reefs and sandbanks off the Regin coast.

Stranded on a sand bar, both the ship and its crew were easy prey for enemy warriors.

"They must have caught wind of what we were planning to do," says Betula. "What do we do now?"

"I row at night," I say and wince at the thought. I am not a great seafarer at the best of times. The memory of the whale-road crossing returns every time I'm aboard a ship. I have managed to overcome my fear of sailing enough to travel on the large merchant vessels, preferably in calm waters. But this is different. The Solu may be narrow, but its currents can be fierce, and I have little experience in rowing in the open sea. It would be difficult enough to cross by day — at night it's going to be an ordeal... Inadvertently, I close my eyes and sway.

"Do you want someone else to go?" Betula asks. "You've gone a bit grey."

"No, it has to be me. I will put my fate in the hands of the gods — and those *wealh* fishermen."

It will take four men rowing to get the boat across at reasonable pace. At dusk, I'm joined by Alatuc from the Briton village, and his two sons; we take the boat down to the mouth of the river, as far as the beach allows before it turns into an impassable cliff. We put it on the water, and I lead Frige aboard. The moment she steps onto the wobbly deck, I realise the madness of our undertaking. We're not ferrying Frige across the river; we're taking her out to sea. The pony takes up over half the length of the boat. It wouldn't take more than a ripple to overturn us. Although Alatuc assures me that all signs in the sky and water foretell an exceptionally calm night, and that he has ferried ponies like this before, my mind is filled with images of us drowning in the unfathomable depths.

The fisherman and his sons do not seem as anxious as I am. I do my best to keep up, but often I feel as if my oar is being pulled along with the boat, rather than helping propel us forward. They all hum a merry tune as they row; if it wasn't for the secrecy, they'd likely burst into song. Frige, on the other hand, is as terrified as I am. She flicks her ears back and forth and swishes her tail from side to side. She's got enough sense not to fidget too much on the boat, but I fear she may bolt at any time, taking us with her into the sea.

"These be our oyster beds," says Alatuc, proudly, nodding into the darkness. I have no idea how he's able to tell where we are; I lost any sense of direction as soon as we left the cliffs behind. All I see is the rippling beam of a crescent Moon reflecting in the black water.

"Who is buying them?" I ask.

"Nobody — we pick jus' enough for ourselves. When the season comes, we eat nothing *but* oysters. Oyster stew, steamed oysters, oysters with lovage, oysters in vinegar…" He chuckles. "By the time the spring comes, we all be sick of 'em."

I wonder if he knows what treasure an abundant oyster bed like this really is. When was the last time a ship came to buy the village's produce — fifty years ago? A hundred? I remember Deneus, the merchant from Caesar's Market, who made his fortune on delivering these tasty morsels to the tables of Londin's nobles. Once, the oysters of Britannia were renowned even in Rome. The villagers from Wecta might as well be eating gold for dinner…

"Look out," says Alatuc. "'ere comes a wobble. Hold on!"

Before I can ask how he can tell, a gust of wind hits us from the side. I grab the edges of the boat. Alatuc and his sons row frantically to compensate for the tilt. Frige neighs in panic. I grasp her reins and stroke her nose, whispering calming words. A moment later, the wind passes and everything is as quiet as it ever was.

"That was the breeze from beyond the Cow's Head," explains Alatuc, though his explanation means nothing to me. "We should be fine for an hour or so, until we reach the current from Ancasta."

"Have you ever crossed here at night?" I ask.

"Once, in me youth, as a dare," he says and laughs. "Almost made it, too."

His cheerfulness is beginning to annoy me. "For someone who's just lost so much, you are in surprisingly good mood."

I can see the faint outline of his shoulders rise in a shrug.

"Twice in me life I saw a storm ravage the village whole," he says. "The sea took me brother, and me gran'father. No point worryin' — we be fishermen," he finishes in a sombre tone, the last word containing within it a lifetime of hardship and sorrow.

The sulk doesn't last long, and soon the three Britons return to humming the same rhythmical rowing tune as before. I lose all track of time as we row ahead. The only variation around us is the Moon, moving slowly from one side of the sky to another, and an occasional rocky reef appearing in dark outline on the water. Even Frige falls asleep, eventually. She farts in her sleep.

An hour, or two, of this passes, when something changes. The aft of the boat is being dragged to the side by a sharp current. Alatuc and his sons start to row faster, mumbling curse words.

"What's happening?"

"Damn Ancasta," replies Alatuc. "The tide came sooner than I thought. Must be a strong wind pushing in somewhere in the West."

"What is this Ancasta?"

"It's what we call the river that runs past Clausent. The pagans in the city used to pray to her back in the day." He spits. "Ne'er did them much good."

It seems we are now close to land, in a country of weeds and reeds. Sand patches gleam golden in the moonlight underneath us. I see seaweed tugged by the strong stream at the bottom.

"It looks shallow enough to walk," I notice.

"It's only shoal. We be still a good 'alf a mile off shore," says Alatuc, gruffly. "Row faster."

Gone is his merry mood. Frige wakes up, and I am forced to focus my attention on calming her once again.

"If that beast gets afeared, throw 'er overboard," says Alatuc. "She be a better swimmer than any of us. She'll find her way 'ome."

The bottom of the boat grinds against a patch of shingle. We jerk back and forth. A powerful stroke of Alatuc's oar propels us away. For a while, we struggle with the current, pushing us deeper into a reed bank, until, at last, with a sweep and a swirl, we emerge on the other side, in sight of the beach. I breathe out in relief. Alatuc lets go of the oars to take a moment's rest as the boat bobs calmly on the rippling tide.

"I think we be safe now," his older son says. He takes a lantern and a fire striker from a small waterproof box at his feet. The lantern is made of some sheer material, bound with bronze rings, ancient and weathered. The boy lights a wick and inserts it into the oil at the bottom.

"I've never seen a lamp like this," I say. He hands it to me — the translucent sheet is ox horn, polished until it is see-through. There are marks of the Roman fleet along the bronze band, but too eroded to read it all.

"It's me gran'father's," says Alatuc. "And 'e got it from 'is gran'father before."

"It's a treasure."

Alatuc takes up the oars again, for one last stretch of the journey. He whistles now, merry again. The foreshore is no more than a hundred paces away — I could swim the distance. I stroke Frige on the nose. "We're almost there."

An arrow falls from the night sky and splashes into the water inches from the boat. Another one hits the deck.

[436]

"They found us!" I drop the lantern — the horn shatters and the oil splatters over the boards. "Get down!" I cry. I hear another arrow fly past my head.

This is too much for Frige. The pony rears up with a panicked neigh. The boat flips, and we all fall into the water. I thrash about in terror, until I feel my feet touch the bottom. The water is only chest deep. Frige, instinctively, starts swimming towards the shore. I look for Alatuc and his sons, but I find only the father, holding onto the overturned hull, using it to shield himself from the falling arrows.

Alatuc lets out an anguished howl. A few feet from us, his older boy floats on the surface; face down, with an arrow sticking in his back. The water darkens around him. The younger one appears too, still alive, but terrified out of his wits.

"Hide under the hull and keep quiet," I tell them. "They can only aim by sound."

But Alatuc is too grief-stricken to heed my advice. He wails and curses, himself, me, and Ancasta. The arrows start falling again around us. I need to make a decision, and it's a callous one. As long as the fisherman is making all this noise, he's drawing the archers to his location. As quietly as I can, I wade towards the shore. As I get closer, I see a man with a torch on the beach, and two archers standing beside him, releasing one arrow after another in Alatuc's direction. I crawl out of the water beyond the light's edge. I draw the *seax* and sneak towards them from behind.

I hear a neigh and clopping of hooves on the sand. Frige emerges from the night and gallops past me with madness in her eyes. The archers look around, disoriented. I make good

[437]

use of their distraction. I leap into the light. The fight is over in two strokes of my sword. The third man defends himself with the flaming torch, as he struggles to draw a knife from a sheath at his side. He thrusts the torch at my chest. I ignore the burning pain, cut at his hand, then at his throat.

I kneel down, panting, and examine the bodies. Only the man with the torch looks like he could be one of Haesta's mercenaries; the archers, wielding good quality hunting bows and long *seaxes*, appear to be forest bandits from Andreda. The arrow bags at their belts are almost empty; they must have shot at least a dozen missiles between them in the brief time it took me to reach the beach. Did they know we were coming here, or was it just a random shore patrol we stumbled upon by a mishap?

I pick up the still-burning torch and light up my surroundings. Frige appears to have calmed down. She trots towards me with her ears perked up. Out on the foreshore, the waves wash out an oblong shape. It's the boat, turned on its side. There's no sign of Alatuc — or either of his sons.

CHAPTER XVIII
THE LAY OF MUCONIUS

The gates of Adurn are closed again. This time, I carry no truce flag, and the guards on the gatehouse are not aiming their arrows at me, but the gate remains firmly shut.

"Why won't you let me in?" I ask. "I thought we were allies."

The two guards look to each other with uncertain expressions.

"We have orders."

"Orders? Let me talk to your chieftain."

"It was he who gave us the orders."

"Can you at least tell me what's going on? Have you been attacked again?"

The senior guard hesitates. "We have, but we drove them off this time," he says. He leans over the battlement. "Are the Iutes alright?" he asks with concern. I now recognise him from the battle at the farm.

The Meon village was intact when I finally reached it, after a morning of wandering among the dunes and reeds, avoiding another of Haesta's patrols sent to check on the missing archers. Indeed, Haegel's people have had no trouble in days. His only worry was that he hadn't heard from Wecta. The dire news shocked him. The period of peace gave him reason to hope that, perhaps, we had scared the enemy off for good.

"The ones in Meon are, for now," I tell the guard. "But there's been an assault on Wecta. Many died. We need help."

The guards whisper to each other.

"I'll relay your message to Hrodha."

A few minutes later, the gate opens, but not to let me inside. Instead, I see Hrodha stand in the doorway, beckoning me to him.

"This is a fine beast," he says, nodding at Frige. "Worthy to be Wodan's steed."

"The best. What's going on here, Hrodha? I need your help. I know who we're fighting."

"It's too late for that, *Gesith*. We've been attacked one time too many."

"But it wasn't us. It was Haesta, my *Drihten*'s cousin. I don't know what he's plotting, but this sounds exactly like something he'd want you to think."

Hrodha shrugs. "They were Iutes. You are Iutes. I was forbidden to even talk to you. If word gets out, I might be forced out even of this hole," he says, glancing at the walls of his fortress.

"Forbidden? By whom?"

"Who do you think? Our illustrious *bretwealda*," he says, sarcastically.

"Aelle knows about this already? You've heard from New Port?"

"He's not in New Port. He's here, in Regentium."

"Regentium? What's he doing in that pile of ruins?"

"I'm… not sure. But if you want to sort this out, you'll have to raise it with him. That's as much as I can tell you."

"Aren't you at least interested in what we found out?"

His eyes dart around. "Be quick about it. Aelle's got his eyes and ears even within these walls."

"Haesta brought his band of mercenaries back from Frankia. They have a ship — two ships now, maybe — and are hiding somewhere along the coast. They're now brazen enough to send out patrols along the shore. *Your* shore."

"Mercenaries, huh?" He scratches his cheek. "Do you know how many?"

"The band itself would have been a dozen strong at least, all horsemen, trained and experienced… But he must have recruited some men here in Britannia as well. Some of those we killed on Wecta turned out to be just armed serfs."

"A dozen warhorses take a lot of fodder," he says, nodding in thought. "It would be difficult to hide such a force for long, even in these midge-ridden swamps. I'll tell my men to keep an eye out. If you ever manage to convince Aelle

[441]

to let us help you get rid of this menace, you'll have all that's left of my clan at your disposal. In the meantime, I'll see what I can do about those patrols. I will not have some Franks trespassing on my land."

I grab his shoulders and shake him firmly. "Thank you, Hrodha. This means a lot."

I have little problem finding Aelle and his retinue once I reach the outskirts of Regentium. The noise of hammers, axes and saws rings out all over the ruined city. Following the bustle, I reach a construction site in the foundations of the old basilica. The work has only just started. For now, the labourers are busy clearing the area from rubble and bringing in great logs from a nearby forest. In the remains of the Forum, banners of the white *seax* flutter over a cluster of tents, an unmistakable marker of Pefen's — now Aelle's — army.

There are no fortifications around the tents and the construction site, not even a fence; no guards man the crumbling city walls, and the gates are wide open. Nobody stops me as I ride through the dead streets, until I reach the edge of the Forum, where a fallen red brick wall of the city's bath house forms a natural barrier across what was once the *decumanus*, the main east-west avenue. But there are enough warriors gathered here to thwart any but the most determined of attackers. My heart rises. If I can convince Aelle to spare even a fraction of this force, we should have no trouble dealing with Haesta's band.

"What are you doing here, traveller?"

The guards stare at me suspiciously, but I can see they're excited to be of any use. There can't be that many people passing through the empty city, on their way to the fishing villages and abandoned harbours in the south — the last time I was here, the city's only inhabitant was a stray dog…

"I need to talk to Aelle."

"And who might you be, to speak of our *Drihten* with such familiarity?"

"Aeric, the *Gesith* of the Iutes."

This takes them aback. "You're far away from home, Iute."

"So are you, Saxon." I nod at the ruins around us. "How long did it take to march here from Anderitum? Four days?"

"Five," the guard replies with a disgusted wince. "It rained from New Port, and there were no inns past Arn."

"No inns anywhere around here," I agree. "Unless that's what you're building over there."

"I wish!" The guard grins. "I don't know what this is. Some new palace for *Hlaford* Aelle, I'm guessing."

"If you let me in, I'll find out for you."

He shrugs. "I'll let you in either way. We have no orders to halt lonely travellers. Just leave the sword and the pony here. Gardulf will take you to the *Drihten's* tent; they'll check if you really are who you say you are."

I tie Frige to a flagpole. "I'll have your heads if something happens to her," I warn them.

"Don't worry," says the guard. "I will guard her as my own girl."

"She's prettier than your girl, that's for sure," says Gardulf, with a bawdy laugh.

I need to wait awhile for Aelle to return from a latrine. He's still tying up his breeches when he spots me in front of his tent.

"Ash!" he exclaims. "It is you! I've heard rumours…"

"Yes, it is me." I return an impatient embrace. "Never thought I'd meet *you* here, though. What are you doing in this sea of ruins?"

"Come inside, I'll tell you everything. Gardulf, bring us wine. Or would you rather have ale?"

"Depends," I reply. "Is the wine any good?"

"It's one of Eirik's."

"I'll have that, then."

The inside of the tent is sparsely furnished, reminding me of Aelle's old headquarters in the woods. The only luxury is a small silver mirror standing on the table next to a bronze candlestick.

"So, what is it that you're building here?" I ask, as we wait for Gardulf to pour us the wine. "A fortress?"

"A palace," replies Aelle. "Worthy of a king."

"You're moving to Regentium?"

"Not me; I have enough mead halls all over the land to accommodate me and my court. And I will need to move around to keep the clans in check, at least for a while. But the Regins like to keep everything in one place. I will have the *pagus* Council relocate here from New Port, and the *quaestor*'s office, as soon as we finish repairing the *curia*."

"But it's so far away from everywhere else. And the only good road goes to Londin, rather than anywhere in the *pagus*. Why would you do something like that?"

"Authority," says Aelle, jabbing the table with his index finger. "People believe in symbols. And what greater symbol than to restore the old capital of the Regins?"

"You do this for the *wealas*? What about your own people?"

"My people already obey me. The *witan* heeds my every command. Soon they will give me what they didn't manage to give my father."

"The *Rex*'s circlet."

He nods. "It is the Regins that I need to keep happy. I need them to acknowledge me as their ruler as well, if my reign is to last." He sighs. "I tell you, Ash, it's no fun being in charge of an entire *pagus*. Most of the days I'm just sitting there counting money! Everyone's just talking about taxes and how empty our treasury is… Roads, wharves, guards — nobody told me how expensive all that was going to be!"

"What about the money you took from the churches?"

"All gone a long time ago. The only reason the Regin nobles were happy was because my father lowered their taxes. Now I need to fill the treasury again, somehow."

"And this…" I wave my hand around. "Is helping you, how?"

"I was thinking about our conversation at my father's funeral. I could just try to beat the Regins into submission, now that all the Saxon clans are under my command… But that would be just another short-term gain, like the Church silver. There are other, more lasting, ways to subdue a people than by force."

"So you want to make them come to you, instead of you coming to them."

"Oh, they will moan and groan, at first," he says, waving his hand. "But they will not be able to resist the lure of this place. I've heard them tell their stories at feasts. They all claim to be this practical race of merchants and accountants, but deep down, they miss the glory of Rome. I would give it back to them. I would rebuild their old capital, if they only give me their coin."

"Well, good luck with that. You certainly never lacked in ambition." I take a sip of the wine. Wortigern never managed to squeeze enough gold out of his nobles and merchants to fill Londin's coffers, and he was a Briton — I doubt Aelle will succeed where the old *Dux* failed, but I don't have patience to argue this now. "Where's Hilla?" I ask.

"At Anderitum," he says. "She can't travel far in her state."

It takes me a moment to grasp his meaning. "Oh. How long?"

"Four months."

"So she was with child when I last saw her."

"It would appear so — of course, we couldn't know then."

"Congratulations." I raise the mug. "*Was hael.*"

"*Was hael.*" We both gulp the wine. "Now, I think I guess what brings *you* to this unhospitable place."

I wipe my mouth. "You've heard of the attacks on the Iute villages?"

He grows serious. "You mean *Iute* attacks, on the *Saxon* villages. Yes, Hrodha told me all about it. I was planning to send a complaint to Hengist."

"You know very well my people had nothing to do with it. The Iutes have suffered, too."

"So you say."

"I do," I say forcefully. I will not have my word doubted. "It's Haesta that's our enemy."

"Hengist's rebellious cousin."

"You know him?"

"He passed through Anderitum a couple of weeks ago." He taps the rim of his cup with his fingers. "What do you want me to do about him?"

"Help me stop him, of course. A small detachment of your warriors…"

"And what makes you think I would want him to stop?" He smiles.

"I… I don't understand. He's raiding your villages."

"*Hrodha*'s villages," he corrects me. "Haesta and I had… an interesting conversation at Anderitum. I liked his ideas, and he liked mine. We have come to a certain… understanding."

"So you *knew* it was him?"

He shrugs. "I wasn't sure. And I didn't care. The end result is the same, whoever is causing this conflict to ignite."

I pour myself more wine. I can never stand talking to Aelle sober. I hold my forehead in my hands, trying to figure out what exactly is going on here.

"You *want* this," I say at last. "You want a war with the Iutes."

"I want *a* war. I don't much mind with whom."

"Why not attack the Britons, instead?"

He shakes his head. "I can't be seen starting the war. Then everyone would understand what I'm trying to do. And I can't risk angering the *wealas*. Not yet. I need their money. And I need to keep them placated. If they ask for help from the others... A defeat in battle, when I'm so close to winning the peace, would be unthinkable."

"Then what was all that talk about an alliance for? A union of kingdoms? I was right all along — all you want is more conquest for yourself."

"You were wrong, and you're still wrong." He smiles again, more slyly this time. "But I feel like I've told you enough of my plans. Anything more would endanger our friendship, and I hold it too dear. Guard!" he calls. Gardulf peeks through the tent door. "Escort the *Gesith* out of here. Make sure he leaves the city safely. And call the post rider. I will have some urgent messages for him..."

I'm sitting with my back against the mud wall of a Iute hut, chewing a straw, and watching Frige pinch at the low grass growing along the edge of the gravel path running from the village to the beach. I pick up bits of grit and throw them into the sand, to see them bounce like stones skipping on the surface of a lake. A dark rain cloud hovers over the southern horizon. Judging from the distance, the rain is falling on Wecta.

"Any good news?" asks Haegel. Leaning on his ash staff, he, too, is watching the rain fall on the distant island, with a sorrowful expression. I look up at him with a scowl. "That bad, huh."

"We are not getting any more help from the Saxons," I reply. "We have no boats to send a message to Wecta, and we have no ship to bring back my warriors. Haesta's *ceols* control the Solu. Any day now, his men will attack again, and we'll have nothing to fight him off with except your stick, my sword and Frige's hooves."

I do not share with him the worst news; this one does not concern a village elder. It is a matter between me, Aelle, Haesta — and, if I'm not mistaken, my uncle Hengist.

I figured out Aelle's plan the moment the guard left me outside the gate of Regentium. It took me a bit longer to guess Haesta's role in it; I'm still not certain if the two of them have coordinated their actions in advance, or whether their paths met through a fortunate accident. What I am now sure of, is that Haesta's entire performance at the Iutish *witan* was just a part of this plot.

He never wanted peace; and he never wanted the return to the rule of *witan*. Not for good, at least. All he wanted was for Hengist to give up his diadem, and for the *witan* to prove itself impotent in the face of a real threat — a war with the Saxons. He would then sweep to power, take over the throne and, if all went well, agree to a fragile peace with Aelle; fragile enough to forever keep the tension between the two tribes, fragile enough to be disturbed by an occasional border skirmish, fragile enough for there always to be a need for a *Drihten*, and then, eventually, a *Rex* — himself. No wonder Aelle found him so agreeable. With this ever-simmering conflict forever threatening the borders, no clan would think of challenging the *Drihten*'s rule. Even the Regins would fall into place, to support a leader who could protect them from barbarian raids and maybe even, from time to time, extend their territory.

I wonder how far ahead Aelle has thought this through. He made it clear that the rule of the Regins and the Saxons was not enough for him. In time, his men and Haesta's Iutes would be ready to face Londin's armies in battle again. It wouldn't take much: another series of provocations, this time aimed at the *wealas*, at a convenient time, maybe after a bad harvest or death of some Briton commander... The two rulers, their armies having honed their skills against each other, put their differences aside, to unite, at last, against the common foe. A kingdom united, just like Aelle planned, forged in blood. More war, more death, without end; not to win — I now doubt if this was ever in Aelle's mind — but to forever maintain the need for a strong ruler. Who knows, maybe they'd even manage to convince some Briton general to join their secret triumvirate, and divide the entire province between them. Someone as ambitious as Elasio, looking to take over as *Dux* in Londin, who has the same need as them, for peace to be only a useful, ever elusive memory of the past, never again a reality...

And what, then, would become of Hengist — and myself? It pains me to admit that my uncle might go along with this plan. He doesn't believe in the *witan* any more than Haesta. And he knows that I would never agree to fight this pretend war. Would he join the conspiracy, and turn against me? Gods know I never gave him much reason to like me. I would be stripped of my command, maybe exiled from Cantiaca, told to go back to Londin, from where I could only watch, just another helpless Briton noble among many, as the plan unfolds and engulfs the entire island in flame of eternal war.

Only one thing can stop this terrible future: killing Haesta and destroying his band of mercenaries. But I can't think of any way to do it. I'm trapped in this little village on the moor, with no contact with the outside world, no troops, no information on Haesta's whereabouts, and no plan how to obtain any of those things.

"I know where you could get some boats," says Haegel.

I look up and take the straw out of my mouth. "Where?"

"The fishing fleet at Clausent," he says.

"I need more than a few fishing coracles," I say, "if I am to face Haesta and his *ceols*."

"The *wealas* at Clausent sail for pilchard far out into the Narrow Sea," he says. "You might be surprised at what you can find there, if you know how to look."

"When was the last time you went to Clausent?"

"Ten years ago," he admits. "They're not much fond of pagans over there."

"A lot could have changed in ten years."

"It's still worth checking. Unless you have a better idea, of course."

"I don't think I do." I stand up. Frige flips her ears, sensing we're about to ride out again. "How do I get to this Clausent?"

"Use the road you took to Regentium, but in the opposite direction. It can't be more than ten miles." He scratches himself behind the ear. "I just hope the ford is still passable..."

If it wasn't for the imposing remains of a tall, sturdy wall, topped with round towers, cutting across the muddy promontory, protecting it from any threats from the land, the settlement would barely qualify as a village. Even when it was a Roman town, Clausent would have been tiny, contained entirely within an area smaller than a Saxon Shore fort. It must have been greater once — I spot a few ruins of large buildings protruding through the grass along the road, and an earthen embankment marking out the old boundary — but the only stone structure still standing inside the wall is a warehouse by the old waterfront, on the northern shore. Other than that, the hamlet consists only of a few collections of huts, no larger than the Iute houses in Meon, raised on the foundations of ancient tenements — and a small chapel, built into one of the round towers.

Just like the merchant who brought me to Wecta said, the locals are managing to cling to what few remnants of the Roman past still remain. There is still a marketplace set out between the newer wall and the remains of the old boundary, where the roads meet — not a Forum as such, just a square of sand with a few stalls selling fish, bread and produce of the drystone-walled farms scattered along the old Roman roads. Two men wearing old Legionnaire armour stand guard before the gatehouse, holding spears. Rusty, empty sword scabbards hang at their belts.

As I pretend to loiter among the market stalls, I wonder how I should explain the purpose of my visit to the guards. How much do they even know of what goes on outside these walls? I'm staggered by how their world has shrunk since the times of their grandfathers. It was more like fifteen miles from Haegel's village to Clausent, and the road was barely passable in places — the family that lived in the remains of a *mansio* by the ford had neither interest nor means to maintain it. Still, the distance is not much greater than that between Ariminum and Londin, and it only took me a day to get here on ponyback. Yet to the villagers at Meon and on Wecta, even tiny Clausent is already a legendary place, one they're vaguely aware of, but have no reason or interest in visiting. Why risk a long journey through a desolate, unhospitable land, to sell wares for coins they can't use, or buy produce they don't need, when they have enough fish and grain to feed themselves, and their craftsmen can make all the tools they need in the village?

This is worse than anything I've seen in the lands of Ikens or Regins. The mental horizon here reaches only as far as a day's march, or half a day's sailing. The Iutes are more eager to pursue the ponies on the moors than they are to meet with their Briton neighbours — and I can bet the lack of interest is mutual.

On my way to Clausent, I passed a cross-road, with a trunk road splitting off to the north. I found a moss-covered milestone that told me the road once led to the Belgian Wenta and, further on, to Callew. It must have ended at one of Callew's seven gates that I know so well. Masuna's capital can't be much more than thirty miles away — a Legion would reach it in a day of forced march. I wonder if any of Clausent's inhabitants have ever been that far in their lives?

The two guards see me as no threat, and wave me through the gate without a word, but I stop to ask them a question.

"Where can I find the ruler of this place?"

The guard removes his dented helmet to scratch his head. "A ruler? If you mean the Council, they be in the stone house at the docks."

"You have a Council here?" I look around with a raised eyebrow.

"Of course," he replies, with a scoff that I've already grown familiar with in my interactions with the local Britons. "We're no barbarians."

I follow the guard's direction and find the Council with no trouble — it really is a very small town — but they're not quite what I expected.

"You're the 'Council'?" I ask, trying to not sound amused.

The two of them look up from the dice table. The one on the left missed a *Venera* by one point. A small pile of bronze coins lies before the one on the right.

"Who you be? One a' them pagans from the East?" asks the "Councillor" with the winning hand. "There's nothing 'ere for the likes of you."

The entire place stinks like nothing I've ever smelled before. The stone building doubles as a fishing warehouse.

The floor is covered with a simple mosaic, with motifs of reeds and sea waves. Barrels of rotting fish stand all around us, oozing a slimy paste through the cracks. With astonishment, I recognise the substance in the barrels as *garum*, the Roman sauce of fermented fish guts — or, rather, a poor imitation of *garum*, made by someone who's only heard about it, but hasn't quite perfected the recipe.

"I come from Londin," I say. I speak in a Londin accent — not quite the high Imperial Tongue, for I doubt they'd understand it, but lofty enough to make an impression on this lot.

They jump to their feet. The one who lost at dice trips over his chair and falls, then stands up again.

"Londin?" they exclaim, excitedly. "Londin sent you? Then — the Legions be back? Rome has returned?"

"Rome?" Now it's my turn to be confused.

"We be ready," the one on the left proclaims, proudly. "We remained faithful. Never friends with pagans. Never forgot the old ways." He looks around with ashamed face. "The Council is… not what it used to be, I admit. But it wasn't easy, after the Legions left…"

"I'm sure it wasn't. Why don't you two sit down, calm yourselves… When was the last time any of you have been to Londin?"

"My father went there to help Father Germanus fight the Picts," says one of the Councillors, proudly. Judging by his age, his father's journey must have happened the first time the Bishop visited Britannia — which means they haven't had

[456]

any contact with the capital in… I calculate quickly —
twenty-five years!

"I come from Londin, but I wasn't sent by Rome," I say.
"I am Fraxinus of Ariminum, of the Council of Britannia."

"How do we know you be telling the truth? You look like
a pagan, though you speak like a priest."

I dig into my money belt and take out one of my golden
solids. I flash it before their eyes briefly, knowing they would
not have seen a coin like that here in a generation.

"Is this proof enough for you?"

They nod, greedily.

I put the coin away. "And you two are?"

Deflated, they drop back on the chairs. The one on the
left introduces himself as Muconius, "*Comes* of the Belgs."
The other one is Sualinos, his "*Praetor*".

"I would think I'd find the Council of the Belgs in Wenta,
rather than here."

Sualinos scowls. "There are no Belgs in Wenta. Not real
ones, at least. They forgot the old ways. "

"They're no better than the Atrebs!" adds Muconius,
clenching his fists. "Traitors. Surrounded themselves with
pagans, succumbed to all sorts of debauchery and heathenry."

"There are Saxons in Wenta?"

I wasn't aware Aelle's power reached this far west. If there are Saxon settlers here, they must have come here on some different arrangement to the ones in the land of the Regins.

"Aren't they everywhere these days," Sualinos scoffs. "They were supposed to help us defend from the Atrebs and the Regins. A fat lot of good they turned out to be."

"How come?"

"They proved better farmers than soldiers. We gave them our land, and they grew fat on it — but when the war came, they were as useless as old women. And then the traitors at Wenta gave away all the land in the West. All those great cities. We were left with nothing."

"A war? Which war?"

"*The* war." Muconius looks at me with suspicion. "The one our fathers fought in."

"You mean the war with Aurelius? The Serf Rebellion? The Saxons have been here for so long?"

I can see by their expressions that they have no idea what I'm talking about. They preserve a memory of a war — but they remember no details. The treason of which they accuse the Council at Belgian Wenta must be the Treaty of Sorbiodun, which ended the civil war, but they are not aware of its significance beyond what land their own *pagus* was forced to cede — likely to the west of the river that marked the new border between the two Britannias.

I doubt if even the reason they give for the Saxon settlement is true. It might just be something they've been telling themselves as the only possible explanation for the pagan presence. If the Saxons have been here for so long, their arrival couldn't have had anything to do with the conflicts between the local tribes. They must have come here as a band of *foederati* in the days of the Imperators, to guard the Saxon Shore; they may even have been settled here as veterans of the Legions, like the ones in Trinowauntia. They would now consider themselves as Briton as the two men standing before me.

"Have you had much trouble with your neighbours, recently?" I ask.

"They come ever closer," says Sualinos, grimly. "The Atrebs from the North. The Regins from the East. Adurn was once ours, now it be in the hands of the pagans."

"So you do know a little of what's happening beyond your borders," I note. I pick up one of the bronze coins from the pile and rub off the patina. The coin, its edge clipped out of existence, bears a portrait of some stern-looking Roman and an inscription of "Flavius Valentinianus". The only Imperator of this name that I can remember from my history lessons ruled over a hundred years ago.

"I know enough to not want to have anything to do with it," says Muconius. "There be nothing waiting for us outside except sin and death."

"But enough talk of the past," interjects Sualinos. "Let's talk about the future. What does Londin want with us? Is *Dux* Wortigern gathering an army to finally throw out the barbarians?"

Dux Wortigern... I stifle a bitter laugh. I feel as if I stumbled into a children's tale. A town of myth, stuck forever in the past. But there is an advantage to their ignorance — I can tell them anything I want and they will have no way of finding out the truth.

"I do need your help in dealing with the barbarians, *Comes*," I say. "But we have enough warriors. What I require are your ships."

"Our ships? But we have only a few fishing boats..."

"You're being too modest. The fame of Clausent's pilchard fleet has reached even Londin," I say. Their eyes gleam with pride. "Our main fleet is engaged in battle elsewhere, and all the harbours from Adurn to New Port are, as you know, in the hands of the pagans, so you are our only hope. Can you spare us a few boats, with crew?"

"You will have all the boats you need, Councillor," says Muconius. He makes a sign of the cross. "In the name of our Lord, we will do all we can to help you vanquish these pagans!"

"Our Lord be praised," I say, raising my arms in prayer.

A shooting star crosses the night sky, dragging a lingering tail of green light. In a puddle in the middle of the cross-road, where the cobbles have been torn up by centuries of turning wagons, a toad croaks a hoarse, lonely love dirge. Three men with torches approach down the path from the east. I step into the light to welcome the arrivals.

[460]

"You got my message then, Hrodha."

"I did," the Saxon chieftain says. "Didn't you have anyone better to send than old Haegel?"

"I'm short on trusted men here," I say. "I hope you took good care of him."

"He's feasting on pigeons and ale," says Hrodha with a laugh. "He might not want to go back to his village after this."

He orders the two warriors accompanying him to stay at the crossroads. We walk back towards Meon until we're out of their earshot.

"I found something out," he says. "But I would hear your news, first."

"The Britons have promised us boats to scour the coast for Haesta's stronghold."

"The Britons from Clausent?" He nods with approval. "That's quite an achievement. They hate us 'barbarians'."

"I'm hoping I can convince them to transfer my warriors from Wecta, too, but it will require even more shrewdness. What about your news?"

"My men found the horses — as I thought, it wasn't that difficult."

"But…?"

"The horses are kept on land, in a fortified enclosure and under guard — but Haesta and his men are hiding somewhere among the shoals and reefs off the coast. We daren't risk getting any closer."

"Their base can't be far off. Where did you find the horses?"

"At the end of a marsh promontory, ten miles due south from Regentium, where the seals dwell."

"I think I remember. We sailed around it on our way here from Cantiaca."

"That would be it."

"I will let the Britons know. They should be familiar with the area."

"Do you trust them?"

"I trust them to believe my lies." I smile.

"Sometimes it must be good enough."

"There is one more thing I wanted to ask you."

He looks back towards the crossroads, then to the sky. The torch drips a large drop of burning oil on the cobbles.

"Make it quick. I need to be back before dawn, or Aelle's spies will begin to suspect something."

"What do you know of the Saxon settlement at the Belgian Wenta?"

[462]

He bites his lip. "Not much. They were here long before us — brought in to defend Adurn, I believe, when it still needed defending. They're practically *wealas*."

"They're not subject to Aelle, then?"

"No. Not yet, at least. But if you're thinking of recruiting some to the fight, I wouldn't bother. They're no warriors."

"The Britons at Clausent said pretty much the same. Still, we have twelve horsemen to deal with — we may need all the men we can get, especially now that I can't count on your help…"

"I've heard tales about how you helped defeat the *wealh* army at Eobbasfleot." He taps himself on the head. "If anyone can figure out how to beat this Haesta with what you've got, it's you."

"I was rather hoping you'd change your mind."

"Maybe I could talk to Aelle again about this. But I wouldn't hold your breath. I disobeyed him once already, and look where it got me," he says, nodding in the direction of Adurn.

CHAPTER XIX
THE LAY OF HAEGEL

The gentle rippling of the water under the bow makes me sleepy. We've been following Haesta's red-sailed *ceol* since dusk, when it abandoned its patrol route in the middle of the Solu and set sail on an easterly course. We tried to keep as near as possible without our single-masted fishing boat being spotted by the *ceol*'s crew, but at length, the ship vanished into the reed swamps around the tip of the headland. By then, however, we knew enough of its position to know at least in which area to look for Haesta's base…

We are not alone. For the past few days we've been scouring the edges of the marsh for possible entries. Now five other boats have entered the various inlets with us. One of us is bound to discover the secret hideout tonight. Like a pod of orcas hunting for seals, we are tightening the net around the promontory, sneaking throughout a labyrinth of grassy knolls, sandy shoals and barren rocks. We move slowly in the darkness, by the light of the Moon and a small oil lamp held by Muconius over the prow, to help him spot the hazards.

"How well do you know this part of the coast?" I ask Muconius. When he's not performing his duties as "Councillor" — which is most of the time — he's a fisherman, like almost every man in Clausent; quite a decent one, it turns out.

"Not well at all," he replies. "Seal Isles, we call it. The seals scare the fish, so we do not sail here, if we can help it."

As if to confirm his words, a loud splash to our left announces one of the blubbery beasts sliding from its rocky perch into the sea. I have only seen the seals of the Narrow Sea a couple of times before, and I wish we were sailing by day so that I could observe them some more.

"There be a legend of this place," remarks Muconius.

"What legend?"

"A sunken fortress, covered by the waves, appearing only at Full Moon."

I've heard this story many times before. All over Britannia's coast, ravaged by storms and threatened by silt, people have been imagining sunken cities, ancient forts, swallowed by the sea, punished by God or demons for some perceived transgression. Sometimes, the legends were true — I was once shown the ruins of such a sunken fort off the Trinowaunt coast, ravaged by a storm in the early Roman days.

Muconius raises his hand. The oarsman stops.

"What is it?" I whisper.

"Listen."

"I can't hear anything."

"The sea be deeper between these two shoals," he points to a passage, with a small rock in the middle.

"And you can tell that by ear?"

He smirks, proud of himself. "The water flows different when it be shallow and deep… And the seals like the deep better."

I can now see that the dark shape which I took for a rock is the head of a seal, watching us as we enter the gateway at a snail's pace, in total silence, the sound of oars barely audible over the rippling of the waves. Muconius's instincts soon prove correct. The passage grows wider, and turns into an estuary, or a strait. To our left, the land rises into a ridge of low dunes, culminating in a broad, flat-topped hill at the southern end.

"There's your sunken city," I note. A line of lights marks what must be the edge of a wall, encircling the summit of the flat-topped hill. It's impossible for Haesta to have raised a construction like this on his own. More likely, it's another one of those ancient Briton hillforts, of the sort Aelle used as bases in his Andreda days. Indeed, I'm certain it must have been Aelle who discovered this fort and told Haesta about it. More proof, if more were needed, of how closely the two men cooperated.

Another pair of lights, bobbing on the waves, indicates the position of a ship moored at the pier. Only one ship, I note. This worries me, but I have no time to wonder now what happened to Haesta's other *ceol*.

"Get us around the southern end of that ridge," I order. "And hide that lamp before they spot us."

We can't reach the other side of the dunes. Between us and the western edge of the promontory is a chain of causeways, log roads and trackways, which runs across the marsh, connecting the fortress to the mainland. The route of this swamp highway is marked with another line of torches, but I can't see any patrols on it. Even with his local recruits, it seems, Haesta doesn't have enough men to guard the entirety of the road, the horses, *and* the ramparts of his fort. The only segment of the route that does appear to be guarded is a low timber bridge, thrown over a stretch of water, some thirty feet across. The causeway through the swamp reminds me of the way the Picts destroyed Odo's cavalry, back in the land of Ikens all those years ago… But I dismiss this idea instantly. Here, the horses are on the other side of the causeway, away from the marsh. By the time Haesta's warriors got to them, it would be too late. Still, it doesn't take a trained strategic mind like mine to see that we must make the best possible use of this choke point if we are to win. It's time to put all that study of ancient authors to good use…

"Thucydides," I whisper.

"What did you say?" asks Muconius.

"Nothing. We can go back. I think I have a plan… But I'm afraid you may not like it."

By the time I return to Meon from Clausent, the remains of the huts are barely smouldering. The village is no more; the fascine fence is torn down, all the houses are razed to the ground. The livestock lies slaughtered in the dirt, the carcasses broiled by the flame. It must have been a blazing inferno, while it lasted, until the morning rain washed the fire away. I notice that the pony enclosure is empty, but there are no pony corpses anywhere around the village.

[468]

To my relief, I find no human bodies among the rubble. As I investigate the ruin, I see Haegel and the others return from their hideout. Just as I advised them, they all fled deep into the marsh as soon as the sentries reported the enemy approaching.

The villagers enter the ruined village, rooting through the remains, lamenting the loss of everything they owned and vowing revenge on the spirits of the enemy — not being warriors themselves, they have little chance to exact their vengeance on the attackers while they still live.

They came just after dusk, from the sea. The other ship, that led us towards the island fort, was yet another ruse. Once again, I fell for Haesta's tricks. Not that my presence would have changed the outcome of the attack. There had to be another reason why Haesta decided to show us where his base was; like the assault on Meon, it was a clear challenge. He was ready to face me, and he couldn't wait any longer to resolve the conflict.

"They took the horses, I see," I say.

"I let them go," replies Haegel. "I could not bear to see them killed or taken. They're all out in the moor somewhere."

"We'll get them back. As soon as we defeat Haesta," I reassure him. "And we will rebuild all of this, as well," I add, pointing to the village. "Bigger and richer than before."

"And have you figured out *how* we defeat him?"

"I have a few ideas." I look south, towards Wecta. "The *wealas* will start bringing in warriors from the island tonight, after sunset."

[469]

"They agreed to help the pagans?"

"I told them they're a band of *foederati* Rome sent us from the Continent."

In truth, I could never have convinced Muconius if it wasn't for Betula. The Clausent fishermen were reluctant even to take me to the Briton village on Wecta. There were some ancient animosities there that I didn't even bother to explore; something about Wecta *villas* competing with Clausent in trade with Gaul, back when such things mattered, which must have been more than a century ago. The world of small town Britons, like everywhere else on the island, may have shrunk in physical distance, but it extends far back in time...

Betula welcomed us at the landing, alone. She wore her silver crucifix over her tunic, in plain view, and greeted Muconius with a blessing. This shook him visibly; he was clearly not used to the sight of a "barbarian" Christian.

After showing Muconius around Wecta, we took Betula back to Clausent, for a Sunday Mass at the tower chapel. There, she further impressed the Britons by serving to the Mass and praying in Imperial Latin, just like Fastidius taught her. Even all of this wasn't quite enough for Muconius; in the end, it took one of my golden solids, added to the town's treasury, to make his mind up.

"All that sailing around took time we could have spent fishing," Muconius explained. "It's not about myself, but the poor fishermen need some... compensation."

It took an effort not to laugh when he made his demand. There was nowhere he could possibly spend a coin like this;

there weren't enough pieces of bronze and copper in his entire domain to match its worth. This wasn't about any monetary reimbursement, it was all about his prestige as a *Comes*. Most likely, he would refashion it into a piece of jewellery — a brooch, or a pendant — and show it off during whatever feasts the two-man "Council" organised in the town, or on his official visits to the Wenta.

"I will need more than just your boatmen's time for this," I told him, twirling the coin in two fingers before his face. "I will need their boats."

"What need would you have for boats without the boatmen?"

"You'll see. Do you think your people can spare four of their largest vessels?"

"They will if I tell them to," he said, the gold gleaming in his eyes.

Haegel listens to my tale with pretend interest. He strokes his grey beard in thought.

"I would like to join you in this battle, *Hlaford*," he says.

"You? Why?"

"I may be old, but I am the only warrior this village has left. If I could take out at least one of those bastards, my people would have their revenge."

"You would die."

"To die in battle is my destiny," he replies, strengthening his back as much as his age allows. "I would be welcomed at Wodan's table."

"The Wecta folk already lost one leader. I was hoping you would take Eadgith's place when I return to Cantiaca."

"I am too old to rule that many people. And I don't want to die in bed."

I can see he's determined. "Do you even have a weapon?" I ask, looking at his ash staff.

"I have everything a warrior needs in battle."

"Then I cannot stop you from going. But I will treat you like I treat all my warriors."

"I wouldn't like it any other way."

When he reaches the field of muster, Haegel is transformed. He wears a beaten bronze helmet with a wild boar figure on the ridge and one round eye guard — the other one is missing; under his grey cloak jingles a coat of mail; and a sharp leaf-shaped blade is affixed to the end of his ash staff, which, I now realise, was a spear shaft all this time. A great battle axe is slung over his back. A thin band of silver adorns his right arm.

"I got this from Hengist himself," he says, with a proud twinkle in his eye. "When we fought our way out of Hnaef's mead hall…"

[472]

He insists that we must perform a sacrifice ritual before marching out to the battle. This annoys me; the fight would barely count as a skirmish in the wars I fought in the east. We have wasted enough time already. If the word of a pagan rite would get to our Christian allies, it might put the entire plan into jeopardy. Besides, after my experiences with the *Hellruna*, I'm loath to get involved with the Iute gods again.

I look around the gathered war band. The Briton boats, trying to stay out of sight of Haesta's patrols, brought twenty warriors from Wecta to a sandy, twisted stretch of coast between Port Adurn and Haesta's hidden fortress. My *Hiréd* are ready and eager to fight. I taught them not to rely on omens and auguries, but on the strength of their arms and the quickness of their wit. But the men from Wecta, even those who served in Eadgith's guard — and only about a half of them, the rest are just the ones strong, young and keen enough to hold their own in a fight — seem less certain of victory. There is no spark in their eyes, no spring in their step, no willingness in their grips on the shaft of the spears. They came because I ordered them to, and because they know they have to defend their homes, but few of them have ever fought before, fewer still have seen their blade extinguish life in another man.

I remember to what lengths Beormund had us go in Londin to obtain beasts for the *Yule blot*. I remind myself that I am supposed to be more than just their commander; I am their *leader*. A leader who knows when his men need more than uplifting speeches and precise orders.

"Fine, but make it quick," I say.

[473]

Haegel leads the men to the edge of a murky, reed-lined pool. He slides the silver band from his arm and, singing an ancient chant to Donar and Frige, casts it into the water.

"Take this silver, gods, and remember the blood that was spilled because of it," he chants. "Bring us glory in victory — or glory in death!"

The others raise a loud cheer, though I notice the mention of "glorious death" does little to quell the unease of some. I must hope that witnessing the simple ceremony was enough to lift their spirits. It did nothing for mine. I do not sense the presence of the gods; no shiver, no goose-bumps. I wonder if that means they haven't answered Haegel's prayers — or have I lost what little faith in them I still had?

I wave at Betula to come closer — she stayed away from the rite — and tell her it's time for her to take the band away on the long march towards the horse enclosure. It will take them the rest of the day of wading through swamp and heath to reach the tip of the marshy promontory. I will not be with them — not even during the fight itself; I must trust in Betula's skill as officer. After all, were I to become a *Drihten*, or return to the Britons in Londin, she is bound to be the next *Gesith*…

"Don't worry," she says. "I know what I'm doing."

"I'm glad someone does," I reply with a grin. "I know I don't have to tell you this, but do try to keep the losses to a minimum. This is not our only chance to defeat Haesta. Death is not worth it if it doesn't bring us closer to victory."

"I'm not in a hurry to die, or let others perish for my glory," she says. "I don't believe in Wodan's Mead Hall or the

[474]

waelcyrge. If God sees it fit for me to die today, so be it, but I'm not going to make it easy."

She smooths her hair and puts on a helmet. The eye-and-nose guard covers half of her face, leaving only mouth and dark pupils exposed, giving her a stern, martial look. She puts a hand on my chest.

"God speed, Aeric," she says.

"God speed, Betula."

Muconius crouches in the wet sand and watches the water receding from the beach with great intent. I have never seen him this serious. This is him doing what he does best: studying the sea, the waves and the wind; he is a far better sailor than he is a Councillor.

He stands up and nods. "Release the first one," he says.

The order is transferred along the beach to where ten small fishing boats are resting in the shallows, tied into pairs. One of Muconius's men lowers a flaming torch to the deck of the left boat in the first pair. The hull, filled with bundles of firewood, jars of cooking oil, covered with animal fat and soaked in still more oil, bursts into flames. We push the pair of boats into the sea. The helmsman on the right boat guides the pair as far as the rising heat allows, before cutting through the ropes and rowing hastily away. The same procedure is repeated, on Muconius's command, on the second pair, then the third.

Once all the flaming hulls are released into the current of a quickly ebbing tide, like slow-moving arrows, the only thing left to do is pray. Muconius and his fellow fishermen have mapped the currents and tides of the Seal Isles as meticulously as they could, but this is not a precise science; the sea is a random beast, full of hidden dangers, twists, whirlpools that are there one day, and gone the other. The fire ships failed the ancient Greeks in the battle described by Thucydides, because of this randomness, and I do not consider myself more clever or fortunate than the Syracusan captains. I can only hope at least one of our flaming vessels can reach its target as intended.

"We should be leaving, too," I tell the four *Hiréd* who joined me on the beach. We board the last boat and lie flat on the bottom, covering our heads with our cloaks, as the oarsman steers us towards our destination. Peering through a gap between the cloak and the edge of the boat, I observe three of the flaming vessels disappear beyond the bend. The last one is destined for a different route, and can still be seen burning in the distance, as the current draws it towards the island fortress.

With the ropes that bind us to the other boat cut, we too are now at the mercy of the tide. As we round the corner and catch up to the floating missiles, I see the line of torches marking the causeway approaching fast. I breathe out in relief. Two of the fire boats are heading straight for the timber bridge. The third one got entangled in some seaweed and struck a shoal, where it is now burning out harmlessly. The guards on the bridge have spotted the incoming flames, too, but they're not yet sure what they are, or how to react to them. One of them calls for water to extinguish the blaze; the other two hesitate, until it's too late. The two boats strike at the bridge supports. One overturns, spilling the flaming brushwood all around. The oil jars break, and the fire spreads over the surface of the water. The second boat gets stuck between the supports, with flames shooting straight through the boards. Now, finally, the guards snap out of their astonishment and make a futile attempt to extinguish the blaze, but pouring water on the burning oil only makes things worse.

Our own boat is heading straight for the inferno, so I whisper an order to my men, and we reveal ourselves from under the cloaks, paddles in hand, steering towards the northern end of the burning bridge. The guards are so preoccupied with the fire, they only notice us when we're already behind their backs.

We drag their dead bodies into the sea. My men draw hatchets and hack at the nearest bridge boards. Damaged by the fire, they give easily; soon, the current pulls them away, leaving a breach in the middle of the bridge, too wide to leap across. Satisfied, we go into hiding: just in time. A rider approaches from the north, in full gallop. That's the second time tonight that everything has gone as planned. The rider must be a messenger from the horse enclosure, with news that Betula's group launched their assault.

We had no time to spy out the enclosure enough to find out how many warriors man the low stockade and earthen wall that surrounds it. I'm hoping Haesta could spare no more than a dozen men to protect the distant outpost. I'm not counting on the Iutes being able to breach the enclosure's defences, no matter how bravely they fight — I just want them to sustain the assault long enough for Haesta to realise what's going on and send out reinforcements.

The rider reaches the burning bridge and halts in confusion. A band of warriors runs from the other side — a small sally from the fort, to investigate the fire. Separated by the raging flames, the rider and the men shout to each other across the channel. Eventually, the messenger manages to convey his meaning, and some of the warriors rush back to the fortress, leaving the rest to handle the blaze. By now, the flames are slowly dying; it was never possible for the fire boats to burn down the entire bridge, built of water-logged boards a few feet above the surface of the water. The tide current dragged the burning oil away; the waves lapping at the supports smother what remains of the fire. But, between the flames and our hatchets, the damage is done; the bridge is no longer passable.

I leap out of hiding and drag the rider off his horse. I cut his throat and jump onto the animal's back. My men throw their javelins across the breach, each missile striking one enemy down. The remaining handful flees back to the fort.

"Slow them down if they manage to get across, but pull back if you're being overrun. We'll be waiting for you on the other end," I tell my men, before riding off down the marsh highway towards the horse enclosure.

I arrive at the horse camp by the grey light of dawn. A thick haze rises from the marsh, shrouding everything in a pallid cloud. Betula and her warriors are still fighting at the stockade, but their numbers are severely depleted. Bodies lie strewn along the earthen bank and before the broken gate of a store house on the enclosure's eastern edge. There are fallen on both sides, though most of the dead are from Wecta. Betula's men managed to tear several of the stakes out of the ground, creating gaps in the palisade, but they failed to penetrate through. It looks like there are more than just a dozen defenders beyond the fortification, or perhaps they are just fighting so well that they seem to be everywhere at once…

Counting the slain, I'm struck by how insignificant this battle is compared to the ones I fought in the past. Nobody would bother writing a song about it. There are as few warriors fighting at the stockade as there were when Aelle's bandits fought Pascent and Catigern at the Medu River. A merchant quarrel on the Forum would cause more casualties than this brawl.

But the fallen do not care how many of them there are. To them, it is the most important battle they ever fought. The last and, for many, the first. Death is always significant — to the ones who die. Even I can be slain today if I'm not careful, by a stray sling stone or arrow, a random spear thrust or a cut of the axe. If I died today, which battle would feature more prominently in the song of my life — the Crei Ford, where I fought Wortimer for the first time, the Eobbasfleot, where I helped to stop the Britons and save the Iutes — or here, on this unnamed marsh, where I achieved nothing but getting myself killed in what amounted to a horse rustling raid?

Betula spots me and nods, before returning to the brawl. The axe whirls in her only hand, jabbing and biting at the enemy like a snake, leaving a bloody mark at every stroke, but her valour is not enough to make a dent in the enemy's defence. She glances to me again, but I cannot give her any more advice. I have no plan for breaching the stockade with the meagre force at my disposal. All I can do is watch the men from Wecta perish at the hands of Haesta's recruits, until I decide they've suffered enough and announce a retreat.

I don't know what more I could have done. Everything went according to the plan. The bridge has burned down. The causeway is in our hands. Have I miscalculated the prowess of Eadgith's household guard? Or the strength of the defenders of the horse camp? Or maybe I simply couldn't concede that we never had a chance of victory…

The sound of a single battle horn rings out in the mist. The muffled echo makes it difficult at first to determine its origin, but soon the horn is joined by a war cry, and it's now clear that the sound is coming from the north. Moments later, the haze is torn asunder by a charging Saxon war band.

I spur the horse and ride out to meet the Saxon chieftain.

"Hrodha!" I cry, as I dismount. "You came! Did Aelle agree to help us?"

He punches me welcomingly on the shoulder and scoffs. "A pox on Pefen's spawn! Haesta attacked *my* villages. I will not let a child tell me I cannot have my vengeance. And I will certainly not let a bunch of Iute peasants and *wealh* fishermen have all the glory."

"There would be no glory to share if you hadn't come."

"I just hope you know what you're doing!"

Hrodha's men leave no doubt who is the superior force on the battlefield. Conquering a poorly built stockade like this is a task barely worth their effort. The first line of young warriors leaps up the poles, climbs to the top and showers the defenders on the other side with javelins and darts. The second line of the attack launches arrows and slings stones over their heads, to pin down anyone who would think of

[480]

counterattacking. Soon the first of the younglings are inside. They overpower the guards and throw open the gate. The panicked horses spot the gap and rush towards it, trampling the fence that held them in and any men who stand in their way.

"Leave them!" I order my warriors, some of whom make feeble attempts to stab the galloping beasts with their spears, or capture them. "Let them run free. They're of no use to anyone like this."

I try to spot the chestnut mare with a white blaze among the fleeing animals — Haesta's mount. I cannot see it. Its absence makes me anxious. What else have I missed?

Within minutes of Hrodha's arrival, the battle at the enclosure is over. A few of Haesta's men live long enough to fight their way out of the stockade — Betula is quick to finish them off with her axe.

"The causeway," I tell Hrodha. "Shield wall."

He nods and orders his men to move out again, not even giving them a moment to catch their breaths. The end of the swamp highway, where a track of fallen logs meets dry land, is a mile to the south. I fear we might be too late to establish a defence there — we fought at the stockade for too long, and lost too many men; but Hrodha is eager. The brawl at the horse camp served only to whet his appetite for a real battle, not with green recruits, but with Haesta's best, seasoned mercenaries.

I tell Betula to gather whoever is still keen to fight and meet us at the swamp road.

"I'll see what I can do," she says. "But it might be just me and Haegel."

I look for the old man among the Iutes. I almost forgot about him being there, and I'm surprised to see he is one of the few who still stand straight and strong, a bloodied battle axe in his hands, two slain enemies at his feet. He's breathing hard. The left half of his face is covered in blood, spilling from his eye socket, but he doesn't appear to be bothered by the injury in the least.

"He fights like Donar himself," says Betula.

"Maybe he *is* Donar," I quip. She winces at the blasphemy. "Don't take too long," I say. "Glory will not wait."

Two men emerge from the mist, one stumbling, the other leaning on his shoulder, both bloodied, limping towards the two rows of locked Saxon shields stretching across the end of the swamp causeway. I tighten the grip on my sword, before seeing they are two of my *Hiréd*.

"They're coming," the stronger of the two reports, when the Saxons pull them back behind their line. The other one lies down on the ground, gasping for air. One of Hrodha's shieldmaidens tends to his wounds.

"We slew as many as we could as they waded across… Uffa and Deormod stayed behind to slow the rest of them down."

"How many are left?" I ask.

[482]

"Twenty, maybe more."

"Have you seen Haesta?"

He shakes his head. "I haven't noticed anyone like him."

"Any horses?"

"Only footmen."

A cry from Hrodha's line turns my attention back to the causeway. Dark shapes appear in the mist, like wraiths; the first few rush out straight onto the spears of the Saxons, and perish instantly. But those who come after them are more careful, gauging the enemy before them from a safe distance. The haze is too dense for archers and javelin throwers to have any chance of hitting anyone hidden within it.

Hrodha bellows a command, and the Saxons tighten their wall of shields. They perform the manoeuvre better than any of my *Hiréd* in training. With a shrill war cry, Haesta's mercenaries charge down the causeway in a three-abreast column which hits the Saxon wall like a spear, with a roaring thunderclap of steel and flesh against board. The mercenaries spill out along Hrodha's line, pushing the Saxons momentarily back. Hrodha cries another order and the men on his flanks stamp their feet into the mud.

The two sides are well matched. Haesta's men are clearly better fighters, one on one, than Hrodha's Saxons, experienced in the battles on the Continent and trained in the Frankish way, but they are tired from having to swim across the burnt-out bridge, drenched in cold sea water, and having to fight their way out of the swamp against a tight, focused defence.

I look for a spot where I could join the line to help the Saxons with my sword — not that one more *seax* would change things much — when I hear a sloshing tumult of horse hooves beating on mud. It's not coming from the direction of the causeway, or the horse enclosure — but from the east, where there should be nothing but a marsh plain descending into a brackish pool of reeds, impassable even by boat; east, where we have no defences.

Three Thuringian warhorses ride out of the mist. On their backs, three riders, Haesta in front, lances gripped tightly in their hands and raised above their heads. I turn my mount towards them, but I spin too fast for the horse's liking. The beast rears, throws me off and, finally free of my burden, bolts away into the mist, leaving me aching on the ground just as the three unstoppable bearers of death charge in a wedge straight at the rear of Hrodha's line.

I knew I should've brought Frige instead.

Seeing the destruction wrought upon Hrodha's ranks by a mere three riders, I can only imagine how soon the battle would have been over if we'd had to face Haesta's entire mounted force. Even in this chaos, Hrodha shows off his skill as commander. I'm glad he decided to stay out of the fight with the rebel Franks, back at the Anderitum beach — he would've made a formidable opponent. The Saxon left flank rolls up to shield the vulnerable centre, like a warrior protecting his wounded side. Haesta's men pour through the gap, but they can't quite break through the shields. They fight better on horseback than on foot, and it's beginning to show.

Haesta and his two riders drop their bloodied lances, their tips bent on the mail coats — and bones — of the Saxon warriors; they draw their swords and turn a tight circle for another charge. In the middle of the manoeuvre, Haesta spots me through the clouds of dust raised by his riders. He barks at the other two to continue their attack, but he himself turns towards me. It's his second chance to trample me under his mount's hooves, and he's not going to waste it this time.

I grab a shield from a dead Saxon and cover myself with it just as Haesta strikes a blow. His cavalry sword, of Gaulish design, is a slashing weapon rather than a stabbing one, and his strike doesn't penetrate the wood of the shield, just cracks it in two and throws me down to the ground with a numb arm.

He rides a wide turning arc. I notice his horse lists to one side as it runs — not through any injury of its own, but because Haesta's leg, wounded in the fight at the farm, is disturbing its pace. The injury doesn't stop Haesta from performing an astounding feat, one he must have learned from the horse archers in Meroweg's employ; as the horse turns, he leans in the saddle and swoops down until his hand reaches the ground. He grabs a javelin from the dirt and pulls back up. He lets out a yell, not a battle cry, but of pain — the strain on his leg must be overwhelming.

I throw away the shattered shield and search for a javelin around me, but I can't see any near enough. To my right spreads an empty grassland, shrouded in mist, rising quickly in the morning sun. To my left, a battlefield, where Hrodha's Saxons and Haesta's mercenaries are locked in a fight to the death. In desperation, I do the only thing that's left for me, and start running at Haesta with Eadgith's sword tight in my hand.

[485]

Our eyes meet for a moment. I see no hatred in them, only determination. Our rivalry is completely different to the one I had with Wortimer. I am just an obstacle in Haesta's way, and only because I chose to be. If only I stood aside, he would have left me alone. Maybe I should have... But it's too late for regrets.

A throwing axe flies through the air with a whirl; it passes several feet away from Haesta — not even Betula is that good a shot. But it distracts him from throwing the javelin for a few precious seconds. I dodge the charging horse and aim a sword thrust at the rider, but I miss clumsily and instead just throw myself at the beast's flank. My sword slices through the horse's hide, and across Haesta's shin. Following through with the thrust, I crush his leg between my body and the horse's. I hear a crack in my arm before I feel it — the impact is so powerful it throws my shoulder out of socket and launches me spinning into the air. Haesta howls in pain, lets go of the rein and nearly falls off his horse.

Betula comes running down the misty moor, with Haegel and a couple other Iutes in tow. But it's not their arrival that stops Haesta in his tracks. On the edge of the bank of mist, closing the field of battle from the north, stands Aelle's entire host, in a long line of shining spears, gleaming helmets, unfurled banners and blowing trumpets. Aelle himself is in front, riding a small ship pony, the black *ballista* slung over his back, his father's gold-trimmed helmet, slightly too big, sitting askew on his head.

Haesta, grey-faced and leaning heavily in his saddle, calls his men to him, once again choosing discretion over valour. He shares none of the other Iutes' willingness to join Wodan's feast by dying in a hopeless battle, no matter how glorious. The two horsemen join him in retreat, and the

surviving warriors break off of Hrodha's band, spilling out
eastwards onto the moor in an unruly mass. Hrodha's Saxons
have no strength left to pursue; all they can do is launch a few
stray missiles after the fleeing mercenaries. Haegel, his one
remaining healthy eye gleaming with fire, rushes towards
them on his own. He manages to reach one dawdling
mercenary and slice him across the back with his axe, but the
rest of Haesta's men are already too far to catch up to —
even if we did have enough rested men to fight them. The
only force in the field capable of stopping them belongs to
Aelle — but the line of gleaming spears stays in place.

I shuffle-limp up to Aelle, wincing with every step as my
shoulder flares up in pain.

"You're going to just let them get away?" I yell.

"Let who get away?" Aelle looks at the battlefield, then
turns to me with a mockingly confused expression.

"Don't screw with me, Aelle!" I point at the fleeing
mercenaries. "Your warriors can defeat them with ease! You
just have to say the word!"

"All I see are some Iutes fighting each other over a scrap
of moor," he replies. "I don't know why *you're* here — or how
you convinced Hrodha to join you, against my orders — but
I would appreciate it if you got your men out of my land."

The Saxon Might

[488]

EPILOGUE
THE LAY OF THE KING

Only once the last of Haesta's men have disappeared into the haze, does Aelle allow his host to assist Hrodha's men. He nods at one of the shieldmaidens to tend to my shoulder, and waits until I am bandaged before dismounting.

"Come with me," he says. "Let's take a walk."

We move towards the reed-grown shore. The mist has all but cleared now around us. The dune ridge looms on the horizon, with the abandoned hillfort rising tall over the marsh. Thin columns of smoke mark the smouldering remains of the fire boats. Some distance to the east, I spot a wine-red sail, filled with easterly wind.

"If you're not here to stop Haesta, why have you come?" I ask.

"I needed to make certain," he replies.

"Certain of what?"

"Of what I should tell my people about what happened here. What story are *you* going to tell when you return to Cantiaca?" he asks.

"A *story*? I don't need to tell a *story*, I'll just tell the truth."

"The truth?" He laughs. "So you will tell everyone that your *Drihten* is so unable to control his own family that he lets his cousin kill his own subjects and get away with it?"

"Everyone knows Haesta has always been troublesome."

"Sometimes it's convenient to have a troublesome relative."

"What do you mean?"

He scowls. "Come now, *Hlaford* Aeric, you're supposed to be the clever one." A host of a hundred spearmen behind us is the only thing that stops me from punching him in his smug grin. "Remember what happened at your *witan*? In the middle of a difficult vote that could decide the future of the tribe, a messenger arrives bearing news of a new conflict. A conflict that would justify Hengist's position, one that might sway the elders to his side… a conflict that, as it turned out, just happened to be instigated by his *cousin*."

"That's a preposterous lie," I say, wondering just how many spies Aelle has among the Iutes.

"You know that. *I* know that. But how easy would it be to convince others that it's true, I wonder?"

"So this is how you wage your wars now? With words, instead of spears?"

"It doesn't have to be like this. We don't have to be enemies."

"I will not be your puppet. Nor anyone else's."

"You will do what you want, of course. You always do."

I clench my fists. "If you hurt my people again, I *will* destroy you."

"Good!" He laughs again and pats me on the shoulder. "Spoken like a true *Drihten*. Hengist chose well. Don't worry. With you on the throne, Wecta is safe. I will find other ways to keep the Saxons on their toes."

"Are you saying you *will* attack Wecta if I don't agree to rule the Iutes?"

He shrugs. "I will do what I must for the good of my tribe."

"And what story are *you* going to tell them?" I ask.

He looks around. "I haven't decided yet. I don't think I should associate myself with a failure like Haesta. Maybe I'll blame the Britons at Clausent for the attacks. Or Hrodha for another rebellion… Whatever it will be, it's going to be a song of victory — *my* victory. A glorious battle in which I vanquished enemies and secured the borders of my kingdom. An auspicious beginning to my reign." He laughs. "You'll never guess who I learned it from."

"Wortimer."

"Oh. You guessed." His gaze falls on the hillfort. "This is a good spot for a town. You could control the entire shipping trade across the Narrow Sea from here. I should never have given it to Haesta. Maybe I'll make the Regens come here instead."

"What's wrong with Regentium?"

"It's too good for the *wealas*. They don't deserve it back." An odd shadow mars his face; something must have happened in Regentium, but I don't care about his troubles enough to prod further. "Funny how it turns out. We keep making plans, but we never ask the gods about *their* plans."

"Like when your father died," I say. "Just before his greatest triumph."

He smiles, mysteriously. "Yes. Just like when my father died." He kicks up a plume of dust with his foot. "We should go back. You've a long way ahead of you. I imagine you'll want to bring news of what happened here as soon as possible to the *witan*."

"You've become too much like Wortimer, Aelle. Remember what happened to him in the end. Whoever gets rid of you, will be doing the world a favour."

"If you really think so, what are you waiting for?"

He looks down at my hand clutching the grip of the sword at my waist. He's unarmed — he left his sword and *ballista* at the saddle. I could kill him right here and now. Even if a hundred javelins pierced my back a second after, would it not be worth it?

I remember my promise to Fastidius. *We must do all we can to make sure the war never returns.* If I killed Aelle now, the Saxons would want revenge, just as the Iutes demanded it after Rhedwyn's death, and Britons after Wortimer. To them, it would just be an escalation of the attacks on Hrodha's villages, further proof that the Iutes wanted war. Right now,

I'm the only one who knows of Aelle's and Haesta's involvement in the attacks. I'm the only one who can stop this conflict from escalating into a full-blown war.

The tense moment's gone. Who am I to judge Aelle's actions? To decide if he deserves to live or die? He's only doing what he believes is best for his tribe. Who's to tell I would not have done the same in his place? Gods know I've done worse in Londin — much worse. And in the end, he *is* one of us; a heathen warlord, leading a heathen army. An ally more often than an enemy. He's helped me against the Britons so many times before, what if one day I need his help again?

"You're playing a dangerous game," I say. "And I think the only outcome will be more death and suffering, until you realise how much you've lost, and how much you could have gained if you played differently."

"Maybe you're right." He shrugs and turns around to face his army. "I guess we'll have to wait and see about that."

The island slowly disappears on the horizon, and as the merchant ship takes us back east — first to Londin, then to Cantiaca — I wonder if I will ever have reason to see it again, even though I'm still, officially, their leader and representative to the *witan*.

As soon as the *witan* is over, the people of Wecta and Meon will have to choose someone else to lead their little clan — or maybe they will just revert to deciding things by vote... None of this concerns me anymore. Eadgith was the only reason I cared about the fate of the Wecta colony in the first place. I have since gained two more, but I have them both with me on the ship: Frige is tied safely in the hold, with a supply of fresh oat, and little Croha lies asleep in my cabin.

"How's your arm?" asks Betula.

"Better than yours," I reply with a grin. "But for a while, I may need you to teach me a few of your tricks."

She turns her gaze north. We are just passing the Seal's Isle promontory. It's peaceful and quiet; a fat seal rests on a sea-polished stone, watching the ship pass by with a lazy stare.

"I wish my aim had been better on that marsh," says Betula.

"You'll get another chance. I have a feeling this wasn't the last we've seen of Haesta."

"And what will you do when he comes back?"

I shrug. "Whatever I'm ordered to."

The seal decides it's bored with us and slides into the sea with barely a splash. Betula hangs her hand over her right shoulder, in a gesture which I know is the equivalent of her crossing her arms in annoyance.

"What is it?" I ask.

"I hope you appreciate how important it was that you came to Wecta. How much you've achieved."

"I haven't achieved anything. If Aelle hadn't come, Haesta would have slayed us all. I should have sent for the rest of the *Hiréd* as soon as I realised what was going on."

"You forced Aelle to make a move. You found allies among the *wealas* and the Saxons. You gave people hope. And in the end, we won the battle, just by ourselves, without Hengist's or Aelle's help. None of us would have ever accomplished anything like that."

"Where are you going with this, Betula?"

"All I'm saying is, you've proven yourself as a leader. You're much better at that than you ever were at… obeying others."

"You mean Beormund? I always tried my best to follow his orders. It's not my fault he could never decide what he wanted to do."

She turns around. "I mean your Master."

"Oh. So you did talk about me with Eadgith. That… was a long time ago."

"Some things never change."

"I have."

"Then prove it. Show that you care about something other than yourself."

"How would I —"

The door of the cabin creaks open. Little Croha staggers out into the sun, yawning and rubbing her eyes.

"Are we there yet?" she asks.

"Not yet, dear," says Betula. "Do you want to see the nice man who holds the steering oar? Come with me."

She casts me a meaningful glance before she and the girl depart towards the aft.

"Why won't you try to look at yourself the way everyone else looks at you?" she says. "You might be surprised at what you see."

I recognise the blank stare in the boy's bloodshot eyes, the stare of a broken heart. I cannot think of a way to console him, and I don't think he expects me to. I'm the wrong man to try to take him out of the darkness, teetering as I am on its edge myself. I'm too afraid it will bring back my own sorrow to the surface, just as I finally managed to keep it shackled.

"Why do you want to take me to Cantiaca?" the boy asks. "I'm happy here. At least, I was, until you came."

"You are the firstborn son of the *Gesith* of the Iutes," I tell him. "Your place is among your people."

"A *Gesith*? You mean… you?"

I can see it's all too much to take at once. The revelation disturbs him almost as much as the grim tidings of his mother's death. He reacted with indifference to the news that he was my son. It meant nothing to him — he was raised by Caeol, and he would always think of him as his real father. But now, I see a change in the way he looks at me. I wonder, is this what Betula meant on the ship?

"Who *are* you?" he asks. "I thought you were just some Iute warrior my mother knew."

"And you never wondered how a Iute warrior is a friend with the Bishop of Londin?" I say and smile. "I will tell you all about it on our way home."

"Home?" He scowls. "This place is my home. Why would I need any other?"

I know he's going to hate me for springing this unwanted destiny on him, just as much as I hated all those old men thinking they could decide my life for me. Pascent, Wortigern, Hengist... They all thought they knew better than I did what was good for me, but in reality, all they ever cared for was their own plans. And now I am just like them, another old man with my own designs for another young boy's future.

"There are things you will not be able to learn from books or from talking to Fastidius," I say. "You can only learn leadership by observing others."

"Why would I want to learn leadership? I told you I wanted to be a priest."

"Whatever you decide to do with your life one day, these lessons will be invaluable. Even a priest can one day become a Bishop — and what is a Bishop if not a *Dux* of the souls?"

"You are my father and my *Gesith*," he replies with a shrug. "You could have just ordered me to go with you."

He's almost the same age as I was when I tried to run away from Ariminum with his mother. If he's inherited any of my madness, any of my darkness, I need to be careful. If I push too hard, he might do something we both would later regret.

"I will never order you to do anything, Octa." I stand up. "If you really want to stay here, you're free to do so. But think about my offer. I'll come back after the *witan*. We'll talk again. There's no hurry."

"You will, I assume, vote against me at the *witan*," says Hengist, once I finish recounting the full tale of what happened on Wecta. I omitted no details, no matter how painful — I wouldn't give Aelle the satisfaction of hiding even the slightest of truths.

"You assume wrong."

"Oh?" He perks up. "What's changed?"

I'd been thinking of my conversation with Aelle for days, as the ship slowly sailed towards the Dubris harbour. Hengist was right, I concluded. The days of peace were gone forever. There was always going to be a war in Britannia, interrupted only by periods of ceasefire, like the one we had for the past three years. Without the Legions to keep the peace, the Iutes, Saxons, Briton factions, Angles, and gods knows who else, will always be at each other's throats, at least until one of us gathers enough strength to conquer everyone else on the island. The *witan* could never hope to deal with all those threats. With heavy heart, I have to admit that the Iutes need a strong leader to survive the coming conflicts.

And I realise that I'm not sure if Hengist is the right man for the job.

"But I have one condition," I say. Hengist's face darkens again. "You won't like it."

"I'm listening."

"This will be a new kind of war," I say. "I caught a glimpse of it in Londin, under Wortimer. Aelle's learned how to wage it, too, quite deftly, and soon the others will do the same. A war fought with rumour and gossip, with false chronicles and heralds spreading lies, with flattery and bribery, just as much as it is with swords and spears. And you, uncle... You may be a hero of the past wars, but I don't think you'll be able to handle this one."

He smooths his moustache. "I would hope to have you at my side to deal with that sort of thing."

"It won't be enough. Didn't you tell me yourself, just a few weeks ago, how you were getting too old for this new world?"

His eyes flash with sudden understanding. "You would usurp me, boy?"

"I would *ask* you to transfer the diadem to me. Legally, before the whole of the *witan*. In exchange for my vote, in exchange for agreeing to change the future of the tribe. Not for my sake, but for all the Iutes."

"I have led the Iutes for thirty years. I can deal with whatever Aelle or anyone else throws my way."

He grows angrier than I expected, but I've gone too far to retreat.

"Can you, really?" I stand up, with both my fists on the table. "I have been a Councillor in Londin for half a decade. I've dealt with trade negotiations, diplomacy, court intrigues the complexities of which you couldn't even begin to fathom. I've read all the Ancients. I speak Imperial Tongue like a native. And don't forget, *I* was the one who saved you from Wortimer and the *wealh* armies when all you had left was a few muddy huts on Thanet."

My outburst has shaken him. His face goes pale, as do the knuckles of his fingers on the edge of the table. I now see how tired he looks. He's almost sixty years old; half of his life he spent on a filthy, squalid island, struggling to take care of his tribe of refugees and beggars, at the mercy of the Britons. Yes, he'd been a great warlord — once. Now he is just a shadow of his own self. He must know my words are harsh, but true. Between Aelle and Haesta on one side, the Britons in Dorowern and Londin on the other, all plotting against him and each other, the amount of problems he'd face would soon overwhelm him. It is time for him to retire.

He orders me angrily out of the hall, but in his eyes, I can see the shadow of defeat.

The old Rutubi amphitheatre has not seen such crowds since the times of the Roman garrison. It's not just the Iute onlookers — even the Britons have come, by the dozens,

[500]

some from as far as Dorowern, curious to witness something none of them has ever had a chance to see before.

In the end, the vote was not even close. Once the other elders learned of Haesta's betrayal and of my decision to support Hengist, only a few remained determined enough in their conviction to oppose us. Hengist got what he wanted — and more. And now, here I am, standing in front of the *witan* and the gathered crowd, at Hengist's right hand, the warriors of the *Hiréd* — soon to be *my Hiréd* — surrounding us in a half-circle, swords raised over their heads in salute.

Hengist bows down and takes off his golden diadem. He gives it one last forlorn look and hands it over to Haegel. I brought the old man from Wecta to perform the ceremony, since I cannot bring myself to trust any of the elders in Cantiaca. Some of them, I now know, have to be Aelle's spies; others must still sympathise with Haesta's cause, even if they don't ally with Haesta himself — others still would prefer Hengist to remain on the throne. One day, I promise myself, I will need to clean this nest of vipers. But for now, I need to play the part of an obedient servant of the *witan*, just one of the elders elevated to the position for the time of war, a first among equals, like the Imperators of old.

Haegel whispers the words of a ritual, and the elders behind him chant it aloud. So far, everything proceeds as planned. I look around the crowd. Little Croha stands in the front, with a finger in her mouth, her eyes wise beyond her years. She has her hair tied in twin pig-tails, same as Betula used to, back when she called herself "Birch". Standing to the side of the main gathering are two small groups of official delegates witnessing the ceremony, one sent from Dorowern — the Britons watch the proceedings with some confusion — the other from New Port, the Saxons observing the rite with derisive expressions which remind me so much of Aelle's mocking smile. It doesn't matter. I will deal with them and their Master later.

I kneel. Haegel raises the diadem and puts it slowly on my head. With his one healthy eye, the other covered with an eye patch, his grey beard and grey cloak, he looks like Wodan himself — and suddenly, I remember. Coming from the mist of distant past, the vision I had all those decades ago, in Fulco's underground shrine. I have seen this moment before. It followed me all my life. This is how everything started. This is how it ends.

"This gathering of the elders entrusts you with the future of all of the Iutes," says Haegel, "for such a time as is necessary to achieve peace again."

"Forever, then," I murmur to myself.

What follows is a last-minute change to the ritual. One that only I and Haegel know about. I'm still not certain if it's the right thing to do, but I feel I have no choice. In the war of words, symbols and rituals count for more than armies. I can never hope to defeat Aelle in the field, now that he's united all the Saxons and Regins under him — but I can beat him to the title he's been struggling to win for so long. I glance at the Saxon delegates, and smile, knowing how much Haegel's next words will confuse and anger the man who sent them here.

"May all the gods and spirits of ancestors bear witness to this day," says Haegel. He steps back and kneels. I close my eyes and brace myself for the cries of shock and outrage. I'm prepared for it. Unlike Aelle, I don't have to contend with rival clan heads. My only rival, Haesta, is gone, in hiding somewhere, licking his wounds. The *Hiréd* is loyal to me alone. The Iutes are united under Hengist – and will now be united, and stronger, under me.

"Arise, *Rex* Aeric," cries Haegel. "Lead us all to glory!"

The Tamesa is the colour of fresh manure, and smells only a little better. The rushing spring tide rises all the way up to the boards of the pier. Octa and I sit on a gravel bank, waiting for the crew of a small Iutish *ceol* to tell us it's ready for boarding.

I'm as wary of coming back to Cantiaca as Octa. I used having to bring my only heir back from Londin as an excuse to escape the immediate, chaotic aftermath of the *witan* for a couple of days, leaving Betula in charge of the *Hiréd* — and of the tribe. I'm hoping things will begin to calm down by the time I return. In the meantime, I tell myself, my son needs me more than my people.

In the end, it turned out that the right man to talk to was, as usual, Fastidius. After several nights of confessions and conversations, lasting long into the dawn, the boy emerged from the dark bowels of the Cathedral into the sun, with dried-up tears gluing his swollen eyelids. For a moment, I feared he would refuse me again — but I underestimated Fastidius's powers of persuasion.

"I will come with you," he says. "But not because I want to learn how to be a leader. His Grace told me if I remained here, in mourning, the sorrow would close my heart to God. He said I needed to return to my own people, to not be alone with my grief."

"The Bishop knows well how hearts of men work," I replied. I knew that Fastidius wasn't talking about Octa. The boy was too young, too vigorous, too like his mother, to wallow in sorrow for long, with or without the company of others. Fastidius must have hoped that the true meaning of his words would reach me; one last piece of advice he could give to his little pagan brother, before our ways parted for good — a Bishop can no longer remain close friends with a *Rex* of heathens; it just happened to be the same advice Eadgith gave me on her deathbed.

The Captain of the boat waves at us from the deck. A sudden squall brings the muddy water lapping up to our feet. As the waves recede, Octa bows down to pick up something from the wet gravel.

"Look, un... father."

I take the find from his fingers and clean it from mud. It's an old cloak brooch, rusted almost beyond recognition, but with the spiral pattern rendered in enamel still clearly visible at the hinge end.

"It must be centuries old," I say, examining it in the sun. "Maybe even from before the Romans came."

"Can I keep it?" asks Octa.

"You know, I have a better idea." I unclasp my own cloak and give the pin to Octa.

"Why don't you bury these two together in this mud. That way, one day, hundreds of years from now, some other traveller might find them both, and think about us."

[504]

"Will they remember who we were?"

I smile. "Always."

THE SONG OF ASH ENDS HERE. BUT THE STORY WILL CONTINUE IN **THE SONG OF OCTA, BOOK ONE: THE BLOOD OF IUTES**